PRAISE FOR
ARNON GRUNBERG

"The wit and sardonic intelligence that shine through Arnon Grunberg's
prose make it a continual pleasure to read."
—J. M. Coetzee

"A gold mine."
—*New York Times Book Review*

"A self-deprecating, desperately funny, achingly longing voice."
—*Boston Globe*

"Absurdist humor, grotesque situations, and snappy rejoinders reminiscent of
Saul Bellow or, rather, Woody Allen. . . . Mr. Grunberg is without question
a talent to watch."
—*Economist*

"First rate. . . . Inspired."
—*Philadelphia Inquirer*

"Both hilarious and tragic, but always readable. . . . It is utterly unlike
anything written by British or American novelists."
—*Times* (London)

GOOD MEN

by Arnon Grunberg

Translated from the Dutch by Sam Garrett

OPEN LETTER
LITERARY TRANSLATIONS FROM THE UNIVERSITY OF ROCHESTER

Originally published in Dutch as *Goede mannen* by Nijgh & Van Ditmar
Copyright © 2018 by Arnon Grunberg
Translation copyright © 2023 by Sam Garrett

First edition, 2023

Library of Congress Cataloging-in-Publication Data: Available upon request.
PB ISBN: 978-1-948830-65-2 / eBook ISBN: 978-1-948830-95-9

Printed on acid-free paper in the United States of America.

This publication has been made possible with financial support from the Dutch Foundation for Literature

N ederlands
letterenfonds
dutch foundation
for literature

Cover design by Anna Jordan

Open Letter is the University of Rochester's nonprofit, literary translation press:
Dewey Hall 1-219, Box 278968, Rochester, NY 14627

www.openletterbooks.org

GOOD
MEN

I
The C Squad

II
He Refused to Call the Animal Manya

III
A Miracle

IV
French Comfort

A Letter—*Intermezzo*

V
Homecoming

VI
The Tenth Year

VII
You Should Have Been There

Acknowledgements

I

THE C SQUAD

1

The Polack did what he'd always wanted to do, all his life: he was a fireman. His name in fact was Geniek Janowski, but everyone called him "the Polack," and at a certain point he had resigned himself to that nickname, the way you might resign yourself to having bushy eyebrows. He started forgetting his real name. In his life, that name no longer played a role of any significance; it was only to government agencies, banks, insurance companies, and to his father that he was still Geniek Janowski. It was a tricky name, at least for non-Poles, and most of the world consisted of non-Poles. Had he simply lived in Poland there would never have been a problem, but now he had to keep explaining to everyone that it was Geniek and that the "g" was pronounced hard, like in the German "gut," and then "yek," Gen-yek. His colleagues had started calling him the Polack from the moment he joined the department, more than sixteen years ago. There he had received training as lineman backup and lineman backup first-class. They had tested him for fear of heights and fear of depths and for claustrophobia, they had tested to see if he was a team player. He had fear of neither heights nor depths nor was he claustrophobic. In addition, he was something of a team player, but the men of the C squad felt that the name Geniek was too tricky, and it was

Beckers who had said: "That name doesn't fit you anyway." If only for that reason, Geniek had come to regard "the Polack" as a badge of honor, the men felt that that name fit him. And after a couple of years on the squad he *was* the Polack, from head to toe, as though he had finally become who he had been all along.

Now, on this misty November morning, he was sitting around in the squad commander's office with his colleagues, waiting for Beckers to open his mouth. The Polack liked the mist; he liked all kinds of weather, but he had a weakness for mist. The landscape was already beautiful, and the mist made it even more so. The trees, the hills, the fields; the Polack enjoyed walking in the mist. The sooner he could get out of the city, the better.

The squad commander had called his men together because Beckers had something to say, and even though the C squad knew more or less what it was—the squad commander had briefed them: two sentences, that was all he'd needed—still they sat around the table in suspense. As though they were there to take a test, without knowing what for. All the men looked at the Polack. Were they expecting that he, and not Beckers, had something to say?

Neel from admin walked by and waved cheerfully. A couple of years ago a woman had joined the C squad, for the first time ever, but she hadn't stuck it out very long. Not because she was a woman, but because she didn't fit in with the group, because she was difficult, because she criticized the meals the firemen had prepared with such dedication. Then they had played a trick on her. They had stuffed the room she slept in full of old furniture and mattresses, so she couldn't get in the door anymore. Fire department humor. Beckers was the instigator. Pranks, Beckers was good at those. The way they had once looked at their female colleague, that's the way they were looking at the Polack now.

He felt that he knew exactly which words Beckers would use; they had joined the C squad at almost the exact same time. If there was anyone on the team he felt connected to, it was Beckers, despite all the differences between them. Beckers, for example, was a true carnivore. A good guy. They belonged together, they had worked together for so long.

12

The way they were sitting around this morning was different from the way they sat around the firehouse together around seven o'clock on other mornings. Different, too, from the evenings when they ate dinner at the same firehouse, hurriedly, because you never knew when a call would come in. And when they needed you, it often happened that you came back only hours later, barely remembering that there was a plate of cold food waiting for you there. Sometimes the meat was already starting to turn blue, because the quality wasn't always up to snuff, which was no big surprise in view of their budget.

There were always a few men who spoke little, preferably not at all. They did puzzles or watched a movie on their phone. Usually the same faces, the silent ones, but it was never as quiet as it was now. As though they were in church, even though they never went. Even their parents barely went to church anymore, except for the Polack's father; you could barely drag him out of church. He liked going to church more than going to the café. His God wasn't dead, his God was still alive and kicking.

The Polack ran a finger over a scab on his nose. He didn't know how it got there. Maybe from the cat he'd taken down from a tree three days ago. The animal hadn't seemed to want to be rescued, or at least not by the Polack.

At the far end of the table sat Beckers, who had been on family leave for a while already and who was here to say something to them now, but he didn't speak a word. He was holding a plastic cup of cappuccino from the machine and he stared at the cup, even though he was supposed to tell them something. The men felt it was inappropriate to egg him on, and even more inappropriate to start telling stories of their own, even though they were good at that—even the silent ones always had a story ready. Even young Nelemans, although they all agreed that Nelemans, who in his free time sang songs he'd written himself, had little to say, and they shut him up regularly but always teasingly, never in a mean way. They weren't mean, the men of C squad, if anything they were good, they thought of themselves as good men. The C squad was the best squad, and although every squad probably thought the same of themselves, they felt that they had more reasons to believe it, because they were decent men, each and every one of them, who wanted nothing but to be decent, with their hearts in the right place. Nelemans, though, was more ambitious than that, he was trying to break through as a sing-er-songwriter, with happy songs, songs that made you laugh, because there were enough sad songs already, there were already enough funeral dirges. He had sworn that he would always remain faithful to the C squad, even after his musical breakthrough. He didn't know of many other singing firemen, and he was determined to become the first of his kind. Yes, Nelemans wanted to be a singing fireman.

The Polack looked at Nelemans, the youngest of the group. The singing fireman hardly had a beard worth shaving, maybe he would never really have to shave, and he looked dejected, as though he was expecting a reprimand, as though someone was going to shut him up again. The Polack wished that Beckers would finally get around to telling them what they already knew, then it would be done with, then they could get back to work. Even though their work, of course, consisted largely of waiting, there was a difference between waiting for a fire or an accident and waiting for Beckers to say something. The Polack thought about his son, Jurek, who would turn twelve in ten days' time. They had named him Jurek because Wen thought that Geniek and Jurek sounded so good together, Geniek and Jurek, Jurek and Geniek, but no one called him Geniek anymore. These days, even his own son called him "the Polack." When Jurek came home from school, he would ask his mother, "Is the Polack home?" Even though the kid should have known that his father was at home, the Polack was on for twenty-four hours, then had two days off, then another twenty-four-hour shift, a rhythm he liked, a rhythm that not only he but the whole family had integrated into their lives. The father had the feeling that the boy only asked because he knew the father could hear him, so the father would know what they called him, even right here in his own home: the Polack.

He took it as a term of affection; it was adolescence, or pre-ado-lescence. When the son asked the mother: "Is the Polack kicking up a fuss again?" or "Aren't things going the way the Polack hoped they would?," the father let it slide. Adolescents were like that, boys that age were like that. Girls, apparently, were very different, but he had no experience with that.

"You could also just call me Dad, you know," the Polack had said once. "Just plain Dad, the way you used to." But pre-adolescence was tough and, according to some experts, indistinguishable from adolescence itself. The Polack couldn't remember ever having been a teenager like that. From the age of eight he *had* been alone with his father, a good, virtuous man who tolerated neither rudeness nor contradiction.

What he'd been like as an adolescent didn't matter, you shouldn't take yourself as the measure of all things, he'd read that in a book about raising teenagers and so he didn't do that, he didn't take himself as the measure of all things. Even without that book, it would never have occurred to him to do that.

Once, the Polack and his son had been inseparable, he had been like a god to Jurek. Jurek wanted to be a fireman too. Everything had to be extinguished. As a child, the Polack had felt drawn most of all to the flashing lights, the shiny trucks, and the he-men in their uniforms who came to save both man and animal. A he-man, that's what the Polack wanted to be, and he was that too, in his own fashion, unflinching, he wanted to save whatever could be saved. He wanted to offer the helping hand; when no one else dared to go inside, he wanted to go in.

Jurek had wanted to be like his father, he climbed on his father the way other children climbed in trees, but in the same way the weather can turn, Jurek turned. Pre-adolescence arrived, heavy weather in the midst of summer.

By now, Geniek Janowski had resigned himself fully to his son calling him "the Polack," as though even in his own living room he had to remain the foreigner he already was, merely by virtue of his name. The most important thing was that he loved Jurek, flesh of his flesh, his own son, and that Jurek loved him. He knew it was love, the teasing, the wheedling, the surliness—the love of a child, of a pre-adolescent who no longer knew how you did that, express love, show love. It was hard, after all, love.

Geniek had not been born in Poland and although he could understand Polish and speak it reasonably well, it wasn't his mother tongue. He never spoke much anyway, just like his father. His father had come to Dutch Limburg to work in the asparagus fields, and he had stayed because of a German girl who worked there in a pancake restaurant *à la ferme*, in the kitchen—Geniek's mother, who had died after a lingering illness at the age of thirty-three. The mourning card read: "Taken into God's gracious hands after great struggle and suffering, our loving wife and mother Ulrike Janowski-Zimmermann."

That was written in German and in Polish. As an eight-year-old, the bit about the gracious hands hadn't meant much to the Polack at all, only later did he start to understand what grace was about. Even though his father, after his wife's death, had spoken regularly of heaven.

Geniek's father, who had climbed the career ladder from asparagus picker to IT specialist, lived in Haarlem these days, with a new wife and two new children and with his God, who was alive and kicking. Geniek had a half-brother and a half-sister, not even in their teens yet, the same age as his own son. He saw his half-brother and half-sister no more than a few times a year. The Polack's father had let him know that he didn't need to see him all that often anymore. "You remind me of the dead, of the past that's dead," the father had said when Geniek was eighteen and about to leave home. "We both need to start a new life. Better for both of us."

The man had wanted to get back on his feet after the mourning, after the loss of his young German wife who had died too soon, people aren't supposed to die that young and that's why he had relegated his son to a sort of half-death too. To ease the pain, to not have to think about it all the time. That's how Geniek had become a sort of orphan. He didn't blame his father, he understood. The man had started a new life, a new family, a new house in a new town, he didn't want to be pursued by the old life that reeked of death. The Polack wasn't sure that he himself didn't smell of death, if only because of his profession. A fireman encountered death regularly; when someone jumped in front of a train, it was the fire department that scraped the body off the rails and off the locomotive because the ambulance paramedics thought they were too good for that, they were there for the living, and the police didn't feel like it either, they didn't like cleaning up, and when the police and the ambulance fell through, that's when the fire department came in. That's the way it was, that's just the way the world happened to be put together. There was no sense in complaining. Keeping your mouth shut and doing what was expected of you, that made sense. That's the way the Polack had brought up Jurek too.

The Polack loved his father, a real Pole who spoke proper Dutch with a heavy accent. And because he loved him, he accepted the man's silence and his absence, even though he found it hard for Jurek sometimes when the boy asked: "Why doesn't Grandpa want to have anything to do with us? Why is Grandpa so angry at us?"

That cut him to the quick, the boy's questions. Then the Polack would explain that Grandpa wasn't angry, and that under different circumstances he would have been a good, maybe even an excellent grandfather, but that Grandma had died young and that was why Grandpa had run away from the past, sort of the way people ran out of a burning house.

Other people called it uncaring, his wife for instance. "Your father's an emotional cripple," she said at times, but the Polack didn't use words like that. What good did words like that do? And so he explained it to his son in his own way, until Jurek stopped asking about it and after a certain point no longer wanted to go along to Haarlem on Christmas Day, that one day in the year when Grandpa was willing to admit his past into his living room. For a few hours, the past was allowed to sit on Grandpa's sofa and around Grandpa's table, but Grandpa got too wound-up soon enough and then the past had to go back where it came from, to South Limburg. It got to be too much for Grandpa, you could see it on him, he started turning blue, began sighing and groaning as though he was short of breath. His new wife and new children let it go. Well, they did ask: "Are you okay? Do you want a glass of water?" But more as a formality. They let him go on, they seemed a little afraid of him, of the big, old Pole turning blue there in Haarlem.

The younger Polack told himself that, sooner or later, everyone became an orphan, that was one's destiny and it didn't really matter much *when* it happened. An orphan is an orphan. Maybe it was good to have it happen early on, then you were done with it.

In the final account, he had joined the fire department because he was convinced that fires needed to be put out, that you shouldn't leave saving people to God or to other people, you should do it yourself. As a child, whenever people asked him what he wanted to be when he grew

17

up, he always said "a fireman." Without really imagining that it would ever happen. He had never felt particularly confident that his wishes would come true. But this wish had, and other wishes too; a wife, a child, a house. What more could a person want?

Beckers still wasn't talking, but tears were running down his cheeks, the man sat there crying in front of everyone. He turned aside discreetly, turned to one side in his chair, stared even more intensely at his cappuccino, you could only hear the sniffling. The Polack couldn't help but feel embarrassed, and at the same time he felt pity. Was this what was left of Beckers? This sniffling body that had once been the most competitive volleyball player on the C squad?

When they weren't out on calls, they played volleyball a couple of times a week, to stay in shape. Beckers had always played as though winning was the only option, and now he was sitting there, sniffling. There wasn't much left of his bravado now, of the man who played volleyball in order to smash his opponents.

The Polack had showered with Beckers from time to time, in the shower they had talked about their children, their families, they joked about women, shared their worries. Beckers had his daughters' names tattooed on his left bicep. Yes, he had shared many things with Beckers, but he had never seen him cry. Crying, he felt, was a private thing, he didn't want to see Beckers cry, and that was why he stared at his own mug of lukewarm coffee, an emerald-green mug, and thought about what he should give Jurek for his birthday. The boy wanted an iPhone, but the Polack thought that was too much, no, not too much, he was simply against it because he knew what would happen with that iPhone, it wouldn't be used to call anyone, people had stopped calling each other on the phone a long time ago, only when there was no getting around it was the phone sometimes put to its intended use. Adolescents watched porn on their phones, boys did, but the Polack had heard about girls who did too. His wife said you could adjust the settings so it was impossible to watch porn on it, and that most of the other boys in Jurek's class had a smartphone too, but the Polack didn't believe it, he said: "Our Jurek is smart, smarter than any phone." He understood, of course, that his battle against pornography was a losing one, but twelve, he felt, was too young. At twelve you weren't supposed to come home from school and crawl under the blankets to watch men and women fuck, or God knows what else you saw in porn movies these days. The Polack knew more or less what you saw, of course, and it was for that very reason that he waged his battle, because in addition to a good fireman it was also his ambition to be a good father.

Beckers sniffled loudly and the men listened to Beckers sniff and didn't look at him. They must all have been thinking what the Polack was thinking too, that you shouldn't watch other men cry and that you shouldn't let other men see you cry either, and in fact the Polack was hoping the fire alarm would go off, so that they would have to answer a call, go to a huge conflagration, that's what he hoped for, even though it was better, of course, if such conflagrations never took place. The Polack couldn't deal with this kind of pity. And finally, when all of them had reached their limit, Beckers said: "You all know that my wife's been ill for a while. It looked like things were going well, that her scans were clean . . ."

The man, this colleague who had already been on family leave for a while, to see to his wife and children, sniffed loudly again. When he seemed to have his emotions back under control, he said: "It came back, two weeks ago the tests showed that it had come back, and the doctors say there's nothing more they can do now, that it can only make her feel worse, that now it's a question of morphine and . . ."

Beckers had stopped looking to one side now, he looked down, at his cappuccino and then at his lap and the squad commander said: "Christ, Beckers, Christ." And the other men said nothing, they stared straight ahead or gazed at their coffee. The Polack had felt like saying something, but he realized that if ever there was a moment to be silent, this was it. Beckers ran his hands over his face and eyes, he set his cup down on the table and he said: "This weekend, in the hospital, I already had the feeling that something had gone wrong, she didn't want to eat, even though the nurses said: 'Let's wait and see.' There weren't that many doctors around, because it was Sunday. My wife doesn't want to go home anymore, she feels safer in the hospital."

The squad commander nodded. He said: "I can imagine that she feels safer there. She's the one who knows best, what she needs."

Beckers gulped, and when he spoke it sounded almost businesslike: "They say it's only a matter of days. It's going real fast now. I notice that with her, too. She's not struggling anymore. She's given up. The kids notice too, of course, but we haven't told them anything. I'll have to do that pretty soon now. I wanted to talk to my wife about it, about how we should do that. We thought about school, too . . . school just goes on."

Beckers sniffed again and the Polack recalled that his own mother had died in early summer. The teacher had told him: "Go to the hospital now, Geniek. It's better for you to be there, better than here." He had gathered his things and took the bus to the hospital, and she was lying there, dying. Summer vacation started right after that.

Maybe it was better for kids if their parents died during summer vacation, and then he thought that that actually wasn't better at all because then the whole vacation was ruined. And for a moment he felt that he should give his son, whose birthday was coming up soon, a smartphone after all.

"Fucked," the squad commander said. "That's really fucked, Beckers."

And the men nodded because that's what it was, fucked, there wasn't a whole lot more you could say about it. They left the talking to Beckers and to the squad commander, who was speaking on their behalf and who, after a brief pause, said: "If there's anything we can do for you, let us know."

And again, a silence fell. Beckers didn't know what to say, that much was clear, he didn't want to go either, not to the hospital and not to his children, he wanted to stay here with his colleagues, and the men stared into space, sometimes one of them mumbled something, words of endorsement, words of comfort. Fucked, that's real shit, we'll be thinking of you. Words like that. The Polack tried to summon up the face of Becker's wife, and then that of his own wife, and his mother's face. The memories of his mother had faded, what he remembered above all were the visits to the hospital, and a vague sorrow. The notion of danger. Fear. That, above all. Fear that he would be left alone with his father. Well, okay, he had been left alone with his father and it hadn't been all that bad, the fear had been worse than necessary.

After a bit, the squad commander rose to his feet to indicate that the meeting was over, that they needed to move on, no matter how fucked it all was.

Beckers said goodbye to the men. Some of them shook his hand, others gave him a hug, the Polack didn't know exactly what he needed to do, then he decided to give Beckers a hug too, and for a moment he felt the man's wet cheek against his. He smelled the sweat, the aftershave and, vaguely, the smell of the hospital. He hugged his friend, because not much else occurred to him in the way of comforting.

The squad commander said: "You've got our numbers, don't hesitate to call if there's anything we can do. Or come by."

Beckers nodded, first slowly and then more quickly, as though the squad commander's words had sunk in only gradually. From the way he nodded, the Polack could tell that he wouldn't call and that it might also be a while before he came by.

Once Beckers was gone, the squad commander said: "I know it's not something you should say, but still, I'm happy it's not me. Imagine having kids and then . . ."

The men nodded. They too were happy that it wasn't them, all of them, they knew you shouldn't say it but they were glad the squad commander had said it anyway.

Nelemans and the Polack, who was supposed to cook that evening, drove the water tender to the supermarket to do some shopping. That had never been necessary in the old days, you could just go to the supermarket on the bike, but all the cutbacks meant that the ones who did the shopping had to be on standby too, in case something went wrong, and so they took the water tender.

"Fucked for Beckers," Nelemans said. "He looks like he hasn't eaten in weeks. Did you see how skinny he is? And his skin all yellowish."

The Polack nodded. "When you're sad, you don't have any appetite," he said, "and when you're scared you forget to eat."

Then he started the truck. They were going to buy meat for kebabs; there were still French fries in the freezer.

2

The Polack's wife was in front of the mirror, a glass of water in her hand. She took a sip, put down the glass, and went on plucking her eyebrows. She was going to a party that evening, and on those kinds of special occasions she plucked her eyebrows first. One time she had asked her husband: "Do I need to do that?" And he had answered: "No, not for me anyway, I think your eyebrows are fine the way they are."

For parties she still did her eyebrows, for the partygoer who might just think differently about her eyebrows than her husband did.

With a curling iron she had worked a few nonchalant curls into her dark-blonde hair.

"You're early," she said.

He kissed her, first on the cheek, then on the lips, he took her in his arms, he kissed her deeply. It was important to kiss your wife deeply when you'd been at the station for twenty-four hours, when you'd had to free children and old people from flipped cars, save junkies from asphyxiating because they no longer smelled that everything on the stove was burning, then you had to kiss your wife when you came home. Otherwise, before you knew it, the deep kiss had disappeared from your life, it became something you only saw in movies or TV series.

His wife kissed him back, but after a couple of seconds she pushed away from his embrace. "Sweetheart," she said, "sweetheart," she caressed his cheek and then she went on plucking her eyebrows. One eyebrow was already done. She did it quickly, but carefully. After all the years he'd known her, she had hardly put on a pound. She had kept her girlish figure, she herself often said, laughing: "I just burn up my food fast, I can't help it."

He pushed her aside tenderly and washed his face, not using soap, only lukewarm water. The bathroom was neat and clean, they were both tidy people, they didn't like chaos.

The Polack ran through a set ritual whenever he came home from work. First he went to the bathroom, washed his face and hands, then drank a cup of green tea in the kitchen. If his wife and son weren't home, he crawled into bed for an hour, ninety minutes at most, depending on how the night had gone. That was luxury, that hour alone in bed, in a quiet house, although of course it had not always been that quiet, there had once been the sounds of a baby in the Polack's house, babbling, whimpering, crying. A toddler who jumped on the bed just when the Polack had crawled into it, the joyous reunion with Daddy.

"I always come home around this time," he said, his hand on the shoulder of his wife, whom he often spoke of as "my darling wife."

"Seven-thirty," she said, "it's seven-twenty now."

Wendela was her name, but no one ever called her that. It was "Wen," on rare occasions "Wentje"—half a dozen pet names had come and gone, including "my little broomstick," because she had always been spindly. She hadn't appreciated that "my little broomstick" business though, and the pet names had gradually disappeared from their lives, until she became "darling" and "my darling wife," and he became "sweetheart," and sometimes also "my husband," when other people were around. "You'll have to talk to my husband about that."

Jurek didn't call his mother "Mama" either, he wasn't allowed, he called her "Wen," she liked that more. Long ago she had told her son: "I'm afraid your father will start calling me 'Mama' too, someday. I hate that, men who call their wives 'Mama' or 'Mother.' My father did that. It just sort of creeps in. So call me 'Wen.'" She wanted to remain a wife to the Polack, and as far as he was concerned, that's what she had remained; she had not turned into a mother. Once he had said: "I really won't start calling you 'Mama,' so let the boy call you that." It hadn't helped, she wanted her son to call her Wen.

She was finished plucking her eyebrows and now she massaged her temples.

"Headache?" he asked.

"A little one," she said. "It'll go away soon enough. I just took two paracetamol." She pulled on a green dress that went well with her eyes, she'd had it dry-cleaned specially for this party.

"Looks sexy on you," said the Polack.

They went downstairs. In the kitchen, Jurek was eating a slice of bread with chocolate sprinkles and watching a movie on his mother's cell phone. "Turn that off," the Polack said, but nothing happened.

The Polack turned on the electric kettle, ran his hand over the scab on his nose.

"Turn that off," he said again. He tried to grab the cell phone, a little struggle ensued, the Polack succeeded in wresting the thing from his son's hands. He placed it on the counter while his wife poured yogurt into a bowl. She peeled a pear, cut it into little pieces and mixed the fruit into the yogurt. The Polack watched his wife's practiced movements. Lovely movements, precisely because they were so practiced. So natural. When someone was good at something, it was also lovely to watch.

"Can't you eat breakfast without a screen in front of you?" he asked his son once the pear had been mixed all through the yogurt. "Do you have trouble digesting your food if you're not staring at a screen? Do you think you'll get sick otherwise?"

"What else am I supposed to stare at?" the boy asked. "At you? Do you think you're that much fun to look at?"

The water began to boil. The Polack picked up the teabag, put it in a mug, waited a few seconds for the electric kettle to turn off, and said to his wife: "It's *your* phone, he doesn't have to use your phone. There is such a thing as privacy. Even within a family."

Wen was a teacher, a kindergarten teacher. The kindergartners, apparently, were wild about her, but in her own home she left the upbringing largely to her husband, or at least that's how the Polack saw it. She always had an excuse for the boy, he was even allowed to take her cell phone to the bathroom with him, where he would stay for an hour until the Polack couldn't wait any longer, until he knocked on the door and shouted: "What are you doing in there, Jurek? What's happening? Do you need some help?"

"I'm taking a dump," was the usual answer. To which the Polack shouted back: "That's ridiculous, no one needs that long to take a dump. No one takes a dump that lasts an hour, not even demented old people. Come out of there with that phone."

Raising the boy was a struggle, especially when he locked himself in the bathroom. What were you supposed to do, kick in the door? And then who was going to fix it? Did raising a child have to involve that kind of expense? If it was necessary, if it was for the boy's own good, then the door would have to be kicked in. A fireman kicked in doors sometimes, a father did too.

He sipped at his tea, it was still too hot and the Polack was a chronic tongue-burner. He was impatient. It was something he had to cure himself of, that impatience. While he was sipping at his tea, Wen handed her phone back to the boy, who started staring at the screen again. The volume was low, but you could still hear that it was a violent movie.

"I just took that thing away," the Polack hissed. "What do you think you're doing? Murder and mayhem for breakfast? Is that really necessary?"

"It's what they all watch," his wife said. "They learn from it too; do you think kids are really better off if you hide the world from them?" She hugged her husband, she came up to his chin. Gently, she pinched his haunches as though his body was dough that had to be kneaded. "Don't be so old-fashioned," she said. "Don't be such an old fuddy-duddy. We live in the here and now."

When the mug of tea was half-empty, he went over to his son, he put his mouth up close to the boy's ear. "Do your best at school," said the Polack. "Your future depends on it, your life depends on it, not doing your best right now means winding up in the poorhouse later on."

Sometimes, despite all the sarcasm, despite all the attempts to keep his distance, the boy would hug his father, as though he was little again, as though all was forgiven and forgotten, but this morning all he did was nod, never taking his eyes off the screen. The Polack placed a hand on the boy's head, hesitated about whether he should do something else, display affection, say something, he himself didn't know what, and finally he went upstairs. He brushed his teeth, washed his face again, which he never did twice otherwise, undressed, and lay down in bed. Downstairs, his son was getting ready for school. It was fifteen minutes by bike, and at the start of his secondary-school career he had sometimes complained about rain and cold, had asked whether he couldn't take the bus instead, whether they couldn't come with the car and pick him up. These days he hopped on the bike without a fuss, through rain and snow, hail and thunderstorms. That battle had been won.

The Polack lay in bed but didn't sleep, he stared at the wall and the ceiling and listened to the sounds in and around the house that were so familiar to him. Jurek slamming the door, Jurek getting his bike. That last bit he couldn't actually hear, but still, he could see it in his mind's eye.

His wife came in, sat down on the bed, she hadn't put on her shoes yet, otherwise she was ready for the day, for the party. A colleague of hers had been working at the school for twenty years, there was going to be a big celebration with a buffet. Twenty years was a lifetime. That made the expense of a buffet easy to justify.

"How's Jurek doing?" he asked. "Has he had any new reports?"

The first year of secondary school. Math was not going well, strange things happened during his math tests, as though during the test he forgot the most elementary principles of arithmetic. "Sloppy, he's sloppy," the math teacher had told them at a parent-teacherm-conference; the Polack was afraid that it was more than sloppiness. The Polack was afraid that the boy had no drive, that he didn't care about math at all, that he didn't care about the tests at all, that maybe he even hated math, and the Polack wondered what the boy *did* care about then, besides the movies he watched on his mother's smartphone.

Wen shook her head. "He's doing his best," she said. "He does what he can. Cut him a little slack."

The Polack rubbed his arm. He asked: "Isn't he getting too big for chocolate sprinkles? Chocolate sprinkles, all the time. Why doesn't he ever eat cheese on his bread?"

There was no reply. She looked at her nails and he looked along with her, she was sure to paint those nails at some point, sometime later in the day—if the eyebrows had been plucked, the nails were going to be painted too.

Then the Polack said: "Beckers's wife is dying."

Wen looked at him, he averted his eyes, scratched the stubble on his chin. She lay down on the bed and looked at the ceiling and he looked at his wife, the way she lay there. She looked good, in the pink of health actually, a pretty woman. He had fallen in love with her once, he no longer knew why, probably because she was who she was. The Polack never believed people when they claimed to know exactly why they had fallen in love: the sense of humor, the smile, the eyes. Lies they told because you had to say something when people asked you questions like that. Which, by the way, people did more and more, they wanted to know everything about you, they couldn't stand the silence. His wife couldn't stand the silence. "Say something, man," she'd shouted a few weeks ago, when they went out to dinner, just the two of them, for their anniversary. "Say something. I can't take it anymore."

He had said something then. If that was part of it, of love, that talking, then he was perfectly willing to talk. "I'm thinking," was what he'd said.

And she, she pushed back her chair and ran out the door, he'd gone after her, there was a lit candle on their table, old people in expensive-looking suits were in the restaurant, they watched him go, he cared about none of that; if his wife ran out of the restaurant, then he wasn't going to let her go alone. And then they were standing outside, it was snowing, wet snow, but still. She shivered and she said: "You're always saying: what can I do for you? What do you need? How can I please you? But what do *you* want, Geniek? What do *you* want, for god's sake?"

He could feel the wet snow. They were standing in the restaurant parking lot. Way too expensive for what it was. What did he want? To please his wife. "I have to think about it," he said, tasting the moisture on his lips. As he ran his tongue over his lips, he looked at the expensive cars parked in front of the excessively expensive restaurant and he realized that he had given the wrong answer. I want you, that's what he should have said, and that's what he said then: "I want you." And he took her in his arms and they had cried, kissed and cried, different from the way Beckers had cried, very different. Beckers had cried about death and they cried about life, and he went back inside and paid the bill, they had only eaten their appetizer, but he paid for the whole thing. "It's already on the stove, the main course, I'll just pay for it," he'd said, and they drove home, at top speed, as though trying to kill themselves, and back home they made love in the front hallway, they had no time to go anywhere else. And when they were done, they just lay there, on the welcome mat, like dogs. Until he stood up and said: "I'm going to make us some toasted cheese sandwiches, because we're hungry." The boy was staying over at a friend's house and the Polack made four toasted cheese sandwiches, which they ate in the living room, naked; normally she would have put on a bathrobe, or wrapped a towel around herself, his wife was prudish in a funny sort of way, but not this evening. She sat on the couch, naked as a jaybird, with two toasted cheese sandwiches in her hands. She seemed completely content, and when the sandwiches were finished she remarked: "Now you're not saying anything again." That was how they had celebrated their anniversary, about three weeks ago, and it had been a lovely celebration, a very lovely celebration, even though Wen maybe felt that he didn't talk enough, but he made up for that in other ways. At other moments.

"That's terrible," she said, after she had laid quietly beside him for a bit, her hands folded behind her head. "She's not even that old." She took a deep breath, as though she was in no hurry to get to school, this was how she breathed before falling asleep while they were watching a series in bed at night and sleep overtook her, even if the series was exciting, even if she really wanted to know who had done it, sleep overtook her, and then she sighed deeply. "Terrible for the kids, too," she said. "They're still pretty young, aren't they?"

"Adolescents, I think. Not that little anymore."

The Polack normally wasn't all that tired after working a shift, he slept well at the firehouse too. In fact, it was out of a sense of duty that he lay down for another hour when he got home. This morning he felt very tired, exhausted, as though he'd been up and about all night, though in fact he had slept the whole night through.

"Well," Wen said after a time, "then I guess Beckers will have to find a new mother for his kids." She sat up, put on her shoes, she sat with her back to her husband and he ran his fingers lightly over her shoulder, absentmindedly but at the same time concerned. He realized that, if they were to ask him "What does your wife do?," there wasn't much he could say: okay, "she teaches kindergarten," he'd could say that. "She's a kindergarten teacher. And a mother. She likes to keep the house tidy." After that a silence would fall. Maybe he would add: "She's my wife," although that was in fact superfluous information.

"I don't know exactly what time I'll be back," she said, her back still turned. "I promised to give Magda a ride home after the party. There's dinner in the fridge for you and Jurek. All you have to do is warm it up."

"I could have cooked something myself," the Polack said.

"I figured I'd do it. It's your day off."

She went downstairs but came back up a little later with her coat. The Polack opened and closed his eyes, he opened and closed them. "I'll go over there this afternoon," he said quietly. He had a catch in his voice. He was getting a cold; there was one going around. Or maybe he was just hoarse.

"Go over where?"

"To Beckers's wife. Feel like I ought to do that."

Wen was ready to go to school, she had her coat on, the car keys already in one hand, her bag slung over her left shoulder, the way she always did, the way she did five days a week. "No," she said, "you're not going over there."

The Polack kept opening his eyes and closing them again, and he could remember that as a child he had done that one time when he woke up early on his birthday, to see what would happen to the light, to see how he could make the light disappear. It never disappeared completely. His birthday was in the middle of the summer, and if there was one thing that had made him nervous when he was a kid, it was his birthday. It kept him awake.

"She's almost dead," he said. "What does it matter?"

It was a dreary day, there wasn't much light, you could make it disappear.

"We have an agreement, we agreed to something, Geniek, a long time ago. I stuck to my part of the bargain, the only thing you have to do is stick to yours too. That's all. There's nothing else you have to do.

"Well, an agreement. You forbid me to do something and I stick to it. I've stuck to it ever since."

"Not if you go over there now. Then you're not sticking to it anymore. So you shouldn't do that. You just shouldn't."

The Polack sat up in bed. "She's almost dead," he said. "What difference does it make to you? It's only common decency. Just to say goodbye. That's all."

She buttoned her coat. "Geniek," she said, "if you go see her today, then I don't want to be your wife anymore."

She went downstairs, and the Polack took a bathrobe from the closet and went after her.

In the front hallway he caught up with her, he blocked her path. This was different from that time at the restaurant.

"What is it?" she asked. "I have to get going."

He ran a hand over his scalp, as though there was still hair on it, he examined her face, he thought he saw something there, something like recognition, like a confirmation that she didn't mean what she'd said, that she was simply alarmed by death, by death's approach. He tried to kiss her, the way he had that evening in the restaurant parking lot when they had celebrated their anniversary. The wet snow, much too early for the season. The snazzy cars. The toasted cheese sandwiches. The rapprochement. This time she turned her head away.

"I have to go," he said. "It's common decency. To wish her well, because a miracle can always happen. No more than that. Because later it will probably be too late. I couldn't face myself if I didn't go. You should understand that."

"No," she said, very quiet and very calm, she looked at him and in her eyes he saw that she had actually already left, she looked at him as though he was some stranger, a handyman who'd done shoddy work and therefore needed to be spoken to firmly, "I don't understand that. You're not going. You have no reason to go. They're not looking forward to seeing you. She's Beckers's wife, not yours. I'm your wife. Leave those people alone."

She tried to barge past him, he blocked her path the way he blocked the path of people who tried to barge their way past him into a burning house, for their own best will, they wanted to get something out of the house, a pet rabbit or a coin collection. That wasn't good, their lives were more important than a rabbit or a coin collection. And he thought about his father, who had sworn off the past as though it were a bad habit, and finally he said: "I never explained anything, I always thought: the chance will come up, then I'll explain everything, but now I know that that chance isn't going to come if I don't go over there today," and he caressed his wife's cheek with the back of his hand. "Wen," he said, "you have to understand."

She shook her head. "For you, she's not going to die," she said. "For you she'll always be alive, and I don't want you to go over there, if only for that reason."

She slipped past him and he let her go, but he followed her, in his bathrobe, barefooted, through the puddles, until he got to her car, she was already sitting at the wheel, she rolled down the window. "You're going to catch a cold," she said. "And the neighbors can see you."

"Is there someone else?" he asked. "Is that what it is?" She sighed the way she sighed before falling asleep. Then she drove off and the Polack waited for a moment, because he thought maybe she would turn around at the end of the street and come back, but she didn't and finally he went back inside. The chocolate sprinkles were still on the kitchen table. He picked up the package, looked at it, then put it in the cupboard, and, in passing, dropped a stray fork into the dishwasher.

It wasn't enough. This, here, it all wasn't enough, that's why his son turned every morning, no, every minute of the day, to his mother's smartphone, because it wasn't enough.

In the bathroom he wiped his feet. How could Wen be so difficult about Beckers's wife? He didn't have much time to think about it, he wanted to catch a little sleep and go to the hospital that afternoon. In the end, she would understand, Wen would, he would explain it in a way that would soften her heart. He would speak in a way that left no room for misunderstandings.

3

The Polack was tall. Besides the fact that he was Polish, or seen as such, it was also his height that made him who he was. He was almost six foot three. And lean. He had put on a little weight through the years, but his body was well tended. How could you save someone else if your body let you down, just because you hadn't taken good care of it? In clothing stores they often said he had a "difficult size," even though there must have been plenty of people in Holland just like him. And he wasn't the tallest, not by far, six foot three wasn't that exceptional. He knew a few men who were even taller, and even though he towered over a lot of people, he was not taller than his former squad commander. They saw him coming from a long way off, it's true, he'd had that feeling ever since he was fifteen; no matter where he went, they saw him coming from a long way off.

He dawdled in front of the mirror, the same way Wen sometimes remained standing there for half an hour before she went out. A track suit didn't seem right to him, not if you were going to visit someone for the last time, but a real suit was so formal, as though the person you were visiting had already been buried, while they were only in the hospital. Half-dead, true, but still breathing, not completely dead yet. Besides, he didn't have that many suits, only his wedding suit. Finally, he chose a dark sweater and jeans.

He shaved attentively, carefully; he didn't want to nick himself. Not today.

Although he knew that he would probably run into Beckers there, and probably Beckers's children too, he arranged to arrive about ten minutes before visiting hours began; maybe they wouldn't be there yet. And otherwise, they would be sure to understand his coming by. A colleague, a good colleague, he had been to their home a couple of times and not even so very long ago, he had played with the children, he had lifted them high in the air, not all three of them, but one or two, at least that's how he remembered it. Beckers's children would know who the Polack was and what he was doing there.

On the way he stopped to buy a bunch of flowers. "Cheerful colors," he told the saleslady. Death may be knocking at the door, he wasn't going to show up empty-handed and not with a funeral corsage either.

At the hospital desk he said: "I'm here for Beckers, Mrs. Beckers."

The receptionist looked at her computer screen. "We have three Mrs. Beckers here at the moment, which one is it?" she asked. "What ward is she in?"

He had no idea which ward she was in. Oncology, is that what they called it? Or internal medicine? What ward had his mother been in, anyway? "Your mother's in a place where she's sure to be better off than she would be with us, and someday you'll see her again," his father had told him. After that, the Polack had felt guilty about missing his mother, because she was somewhere where she was better off than she had been among the living. That's why, at a certain point, he had stopped that missing.

"This Mrs. Beckers is going to die soon," he said, shifting the bouquet from his left to his right hand.

"That doesn't help me much," the lady replied. "There are a lot of people here who are going to die soon. Do you perhaps know her first name?"

"Frieda," he answered. "Frieda Beckers."

Then she found the information he needed, the receptionist did. She told him the floor and the room number and how he could get there, he thanked her kindly and then he walked to Mrs. Beckers's room, slowly, slower, and slower still. Was Wen right, maybe? Was she really waiting to see him? Who was he going there for? What was there left to explain?

This was the hospital where his mother had been, he had walked here at the age of eight too. In his memory it had looked different, the corridors had seemed endless, he had wandered the corridors for hours. He had made friends with some of the patients, stood at their bedsides like a member of the family, and every day his father had given him money for ice cream. Then he went downstairs to get an ice cream cone, because the old Polack, the real Polack, didn't want the child to witness the dying. No, his father didn't want to confront the child with death. It had been a lovely summer. A nurse had given him a present, a model plane he had to build himself, you needed glue to do that, except the glue wasn't in the box and ultimately the plane was never put together. First it ended up in the attic, then in the garbage.

Beckers's wife was in a room with two beds, the other bed was vacant. The hospital had draped clear plastic over the empty bed. Out the window you could see a bit of green. Beckers's wife had once said to him that Heerlen was the ugliest city in the Netherlands, but the Polack had learned to live with it, the way you learned to live with a wart on your cheek.

When the Polack got there, her husband and children were standing around the bed in silence. They looked up, they didn't even seem surprised. He greeted them with a wave of the hand, there was no reaction.

For a moment he remained standing in the doorway, not far from the sink, then he took a few steps forward. The room didn't smell of hospital, more of human, of sick and sweaty human flesh. The Polack couldn't see Beckers's wife clearly and he didn't want to push his way forward. The front row wasn't meant for him.

"Do you still remember me?" he asked the children, three girls. They had grown, the eldest was almost a woman. She didn't look like her mother. He tried to remember the girls' names, nothing came to mind. All he knew was that Beckers was afraid that one day his daughters would run off with an Arab or an African. Because the girls didn't answer, because they only looked at him, he said it himself: "I'm the Polack." They kept looking at him, but their faces remained blank. He couldn't tell from their expressions whether they still knew who the Polack was, or whether they had no idea what he was talking about.

To Beckers he said: "I just figured I'd come by."

Beckers turned to him, nodded, then turned back to his wife who lay dying in the hospital bed. The Polack wondered why they didn't sit down, Beckers and his three daughters. You could sit beside a dying person too, couldn't you?

He didn't know what to do with the flowers, the nightstand was already covered with cups and medicine bottles and cards, so he just stood there with the bouquet in his hands. After a couple of minutes, he put it down on the vacant bed.

"She's sleeping," Beckers said.

The children stared at their mother. And Beckers too stared at his sleeping wife.

He saw that all three girls had placed a hand on their mother's arm, as though trying to keep her from going away, as though they could stop the dying by physically hanging onto their mother. Beckers himself had his hands resting on the blankets.

At that moment a lady attendant came in with drinks. A relief, the Polack felt. A distraction. Death was, indeed, not for sissies.

"Would your wife like something to drink?" the lady asked. "I also have tomato soup."

"Only some apple juice," Beckers said, and the Polack saw that there were still two full cups of apple juice on the nightstand.

He stood there, in the second row, behind the family, you didn't come to the hospital just to turn and leave again. His bouquet was on the empty bed, the flowers already looked less than fresh. He looked around, but saw nothing that could serve as a vase. One of the nurses would see to the flowers, it was the gesture that counted. Cheerful colors. She had always liked cheerful colors.

The lady with the beverages left again, there were now three cups of apple juice on the nightstand, and then nothing happened, everyone just stood there, everyone waited. Until Beckers turned and went into the bathroom.

At last the Polack could get a good look at her. He had known what he could expect, he was prepared for the worst, but still he was shocked. Death began so much earlier than the actual dying. So much had already been eaten away from her face, he barely recognized her, her body lay under the covers and not much seemed to be left of that either, even though she'd always had something plump about her. The eldest daughter already had breasts, he could see that; they all looked at him again, all three of them, he wouldn't have recognized them if he'd met them out on the street. Finally, it was the youngest who said: "You're that colleague of my father's, aren't you?"

The eldest said: "Sssh."

And the Polack said: "That's right, that's who I am, I used to come over to your house sometimes."

Nothing more was said. The Polack could have used some apple juice, his mouth was dry as sand, but he could hardly take the apple juice that was meant for Beckers's wife, even if there were three cups of it that she probably wouldn't drink herself. And the girls kept staring at him, not hostilely, not friendly either, as though the Polack was part and parcel of their mother's approaching death, as though he were one of the apparitions of that death.

"It's warm in here," he said.

Beckers came back. The Polack had prepared everything he would say if he had the chance to be alone with Beckers's wife for a moment. Now, with death so close, the silence had to be broken. He had wanted to explain why he'd never been in touch again, back then, why he had blocked her. He'd been forced to choose, and he had chosen, the only choice a man who wants to be good could have made. That was the reason for his silence.

"Where are you?" she had asked, "why don't I hear from you?" It had been hard, the way men could be hard, he had acted like she was dead, as he had been told to. In the course of time he had come to believe it himself, Beckers's wife was dead to him, until her husband started saying that she was deathly ill. She was going to have to die twice.

It's a small town, Heerlen, but the first time he ran into her he had hid, with an agility that surprised even him, as though hiding was one of his talents. To keep it from starting again, that's why he'd made himself invisible now and then.

Finally, the Beckers had moved out to a nearby village, and he didn't have to hide anymore, because she stopped coming to town.

I chose for my boy, that's what he had hoped to say if Beckers and his children hadn't been there and if Beckers's wife hadn't been sleeping. Then he could have said that it had been the only possible choice and that's why he'd run away, not from the past the way his father had, but from passion, and he would do so again if necessary. Passion was not good for a person. A person couldn't live that way, with passion, it kept you from doing anything anymore.

The Polack was almost completely sure now that she wasn't going to open her eyes, not while he was there, not during these visiting hours, and probably not during the visiting hours to come, and once he had realized that he decided to go. He didn't regret having come, but there was no sense in waiting any longer.

"I'm going to get going," the Polack said.

"I'll see you around," Beckers said.

And then the Polack did it anyway, he wormed his way up past the girls, brought his lips up to the yellowish ear and whispered: "You comforted me." Then he stepped back right away.

At the door he stopped and said: "Something will come along to replace the sorrow. I know that from experience. Something will come along afterward."

He wasn't sure whether they had heard him, but it was still good that he had said it. You had to say something, more than just "that's fucked," even if that summed up the whole situation.

He paused for a moment, then went downstairs to the cafeteria where he had always bought ice cream as a child. He ordered a Fanta. Sitting at a table he looked at his phone and saw that his boy had sent him a text message, his boy who wanted a smartphone so badly. "Can I stay at Daan's? We're going to do homework too," the message said.

The Polack looked at his phone, he shook his head. They had an agreement after all, no playing at friends' houses on weekdays, not until the grades had improved. Then he called his son and, in fact, he had meant to say exactly that, you know what we agreed on, come home right now, you're not going to play at Daan's. Wherever Daan was, no homework was sure to be done; he had met Daan two or three times, he seemed like a boy who did no homework as a matter of principle, the kind who would rather die than start in on his homework, but because he had gone to see Beckers's wife, because that had softened him, the woman who looked like she'd been lynched, the dead past that now felt so alive and so fresh, and also because you had to be lenient in child raising, he told his boy that it was okay, as long as they really did do some homework, but that he had to be home by seven and they would eat dinner together then. Together they would heat up the food Wen had put in the fridge, together they would set the table and while they ate they would talk together. He emphasized all the things they would do together, but the boy didn't respond. After that the Polack finished his can of Fanta almost in one gulp. Then he burped, it slipped out, he was embarrassed by it, because there were people at the next table.

The lady from the hospital kiosk came over to wipe the table. "You're a fireman, aren't you?" she said. "My son wants to become a fireman."

"A great profession," the Polack replied. "The greatest profession there is." He rose to his feet. He meant it. Unlike when he was a child, when he had idealized it, he now knew what it really involved. Less exciting than he'd thought, but wonderful still.

He drove to the village where the Beckers lived, it was a good place to go for a walk. Beckers had felt the city was too hectic, too dangerous for his children. The Polack looked up the address on Google Street View and drove past the Beckers's house. He looked at it closely. It looked well kept. There was a big tree in front that blocked out a lot of light. Otherwise it was a village like so many others, with a church, a café, a main street which was also its main artery, and around it the hills where he liked to bike and walk.

At the edge of the village he parked his car, looked at his phone. No new messages from his son, not from Wen either. It was late afternoon, in late fall, not such a great time to go walking in the hills. It started hailing, but the Polack still felt the need to take a walk, to see the trees, to touch a tree trunk, to not see a soul. Not that he had anything against people, he wanted to save them after all, but sometimes he also wanted to forget they were there.

Today the forgetting didn't work, this afternoon the past had over-taken him. He would go for a good hike, almost up to the Belgian border, to put some more distance between himself and the past, to shake off the memories. Borys and Jurek. There had been two boys.

II

HE REFUSED TO CALL THE ANIMAL MANYA

1

There had been an eldest, a firstborn they'd named Borys. A quiet boy, tall and thin, a beanstalk. He probably would have grown to be as tall as his father, maybe even taller, but he was above all quiet. Silent. The sixth-grade teacher had told them: "Sometimes you forget that Borys is there, even though he stands head and shoulders above the rest, except when it comes to grades."

Borys was twelve and always sat at the back of the class, preferably slouched down in his chair. That's just the way he was. He didn't like to travel—on vacation he would ask: "When are we going home again?"—or friends; when a neighborhood boy would ring the bell on occasion and ask if Borys could come out and play, he would say: "Tell him I'm not here." What he liked most was being at home alone or with his younger brother, whom he called his baby brother. Because Wen felt that a life without friends was not a good thing, she insisted that Borys do something to make them. Being nice to your baby brother was fine, better than wanting to put your little brother out with the garbage, an urge she remembered well from her own childhood. But there was more than that to the world, especially for a child. He had to go outside, because that's how you made friends, by going out into the wide world.

Sometimes the Polack feared that his eldest son didn't want that, not now and not ever, but he didn't express that fear, he was afraid it would only irk his wife. Although her opinions concerning child raising were broadminded—"children know very well what's fair," she would say, "even toddlers know that"—still, she didn't like being contradicted. She knew what made their boys tick.

Borys didn't want to play basketball, even though his height lent itself to that. They had suggested it to him a few times, but it didn't interest him. "Other boys beg their parents to be allowed to play basketball," the Polack said. "So let them beg," was Borys's reply. He had a talent for athletics, but he didn't want to join any clubs at all. For a few months he had gone to a track and field club, where he'd become good at pole-vaulting and the hurdles, the trainer said he had real potential for that, but in the end Borys rejected the pole-vaulting and hurdles too. He didn't want to go anymore. "What I really like most is just staying at home," he told his parents. "I already go to school, so why do I have to go anywhere else?"

Wen said: "That's not normal and not healthy." She would know, she taught kindergarten, she had seen half a dozen children pass by who were abnormal and unhealthy. The Polack felt health and normality were important. He asked himself how his eldest son could achieve anything in this world without either of them.

There was another awkward thing about the quiet boy. Awkward, that was a word that fit his son, and it fit the Polack too. Sometimes Borys didn't make it to the toilet on time, like an old man or a two-year-old who isn't completely potty trained. It had started without them really noticing. Even though Borys had actually become potty-trained quite early. As a baby he had been quick to start talking, quick to walk, to sit on the potty, he was quick with everything. An intelligent child, people always said, even though his grandma, Wen's mother, had said a few times that Borys had an "old soul." Wen's mother took reincarnation seriously. Later, the lady at the well-baby clinic said: "He's definitely precocious." That was true, at the age of six the boy said things that made the Polack wonder where he got them from. Wen said: "He picks that up somewhere and repeats it, that's what smart children do. Learning is imitating. He himself doesn't know what it means."

After the Easter vacation, Borys had relapsed. That's when it started. He came home with poop in his pants. He didn't tell them about it, Wen discovered it when she found his dirty underpants in a corner of the bathroom. At first she thought: it was an accident, it could happen to anyone. Borys was embarrassed by it, which is why he hadn't said anything, that's why he had tucked away the dirty underpants. And it *was* embarrassing.

But then it happened again, and again. It happened regularly, pooping in his pants was no exception anymore. No one could have that many accidents, not even a twelve-year-old.

There were days, sometimes even a week and a half, when it didn't happen at all, when Wen told the Polack quietly after he came back from the firehouse in the morning: "I think we've fixed the leak."

And then, two days later, there was poop in his pants again. Often a number of times a day. At first Wen thought it only happened at school, but she soon discovered that it overcame Borys everywhere, at the supermarket for example, or during a family outing. But not at home, it never happened there. Wen got tired of doing laundry. She had to go out and buy new pants for the boy, because all the others were in the wash.

They talked to Borys. "When you feel the urge, go to the toilet right away," Wen said. And the Polack said: "Don't wait, not even if the teacher is talking, you just raise your hand and go to the toilet."

"But I don't feel it," the boy answered. "I don't feel anything, and by the time I do it's too late."

Wen took Borys to the family doctor. They felt that he should explain the problem to the doctor himself; he may be pooping in his pants, but he wasn't a little child anymore.

That night Wen told her husband how it had gone, how their son had said: "When I sit on the toilet nothing happens, and when I'm not on the toilet it suddenly comes out. I can't do anything about it." She added: "He was able to explain it perfectly, he wasn't shy."

The family doctor, a man with a beard and glasses who had been their doctor for years but whom they barely ever saw, for they were almost never sick—the Janowskis were sound as a bell—prescribed anti-diarrheals. That seemed to help for a bit, until one day the boy came home with poop in his pants again. "I can't take it anymore," Wen said, "it's driving me crazy. Do we have to make Borys start wearing diapers again, like his little brother?" She had tears in her eyes, and it was the tears that made the Polack see how serious the situation really was.

Then the teacher asked to talk to them. To make matters worse. She said the other children in the class didn't want to sit next to Borys anymore because he stank. She said that it was a real problem, she too had noticed that he often stank. She had spoken to him, he had answered evasively, that's why she'd asked to talk to the parents, because of the problem the stench was causing. "Sometimes the class is more involved with the stench in the room than with spelling," the teacher said. "That's not good for anyone, not for Borys either. Lately he's been having problems in the group."

The parents were dismayed, particularly the Polack. His son was causing a nuisance. The fire department was there to deal with nuisances, but within his own family he could do nothing about it. That his boy caused an odor nuisance was something the Polack took personally. As though it were he himself who stank, as though the boy was only spreading the father's stench.

"Can't you start opening a window whenever you smell it?" he'd asked the teacher.

"That's not a solution," she replied. "And besides, how many windows am I supposed to open? Do we all have to go sit outside because Borys can't go to the toilet in time?"

"It's not that he doesn't want to," Wen had said. "He really wants to, he just can't. We've been to the doctor, he says it's an intestinal problem."

"Intestinal problem or no, what are we going to do about this?" the teacher asked. "Maybe you should try taking him to a psychologist. This poop business is all in his head; I don't know anyone his age who makes it to the toilet too late on a structural basis."

She pronounced the word "structural" slowly and with emphasis.

The teacher must have seen the desperation on the Polack's face, for she added quickly: "Otherwise he's the same friendly, quiet boy he's always been. He gets passing grades, although he could do better. Have Borys talk to someone. Maybe something's bothering him."

And with those words, the parents went home.

They talked to their son again. They asked what was wrong, whether there was something he needed to tell them. Was there something making him sad? "Is something bothering you?"

But, as usual, there was nothing he needed to tell them, nothing was bothering him and nothing was making him sad, nothing at all. Not even pooping in his pants, he said. And, he added, he felt fine.

He had settled down in his usual corner with his little brother, the afterthought, an accident, actually, and said nothing. Wen told him they had been to talk to his teacher—Wen avoided the word "stench"—and that the teacher had advised them to see a psychologist.

The boy shrugged. "A psychologist is for crazy people," he said. "What's everyone so upset about? It's in *my* pants, isn't it?"

"They can smell it," said the Polack, who could no longer control himself, and he shook the boy hard, "they smell it, don't you understand that? You're not crazy, but people can smell what's in your pants because they're not crazy either. You do it to torture us. You do it because you hate us." The Polack, otherwise the very picture of calm, shook the boy harder and harder the whole time, until Wen pulled him away. The boy started crying, because he had never been shaken hard like that before. In the kitchen Wen said: "There's no use going after him like that, it only makes things worse."

"You can't take it anymore either, can you?" the Polack replied. He was breathing hard, more from emotion than from effort. He was not only tall, he was also in good shape. His body was an instrument that he maintained with care.

"We'll do what the teacher says," she answered. "We'll take him to a psychologist. It's not an intestinal problem, otherwise it would happen during the weekend too."

Then they went back into the living room. The boy was sitting with his back against the radiator, his baby brother beside him, and Wen told him that he didn't have to worry, that they were going to talk to someone and then everything would be all right.

The boy nodded. Wen went back into the kitchen and the Polack asked the boy if he wanted to play a game. The boy said: "Leave me be. It's okay." The Polack knew that it wasn't okay, and he grabbed his son, his big son, who shrank back for a moment, he squatted down quickly and picked the big boy up as though he were a feather, as though a fire was raging and he had to use the fireman's carry to get Borys out of the burning house, and he said: "It doesn't matter to me that you stink, other people smell that you stink, but I think you smell good. Believe me, Daddy thinks you smell wonderful."

The Polack didn't want to go along to the psychologist, it seemed to him something more for mother and son than for the entire family. The summer vacation was coming up, after that the boy would go to junior high school and then maybe everything would be different, things would go better at the new school.

A few weeks later, at dinner, Wen told him how the appointment had gone with the psychologist. The little brother sat babbling in his high chair, something intelligible came out on occasion (car, yum, cat, woof), you couldn't really call it talking, not yet. The rest of the family went on chewing their food imperturbably—silence brought a family closer, that's what the Polack's father used to claim, and the Polack himself felt he was right. Borys helped himself eagerly to the last piece of sausage that Wen had bought specially at the organic butcher shop, because she was against factory-farmed chickens and pig farms where the animals could barely breathe and almost never saw daylight. Pigs, too, had a right to daylight before being processed into sausage. That was Wen for you, a good woman, good for everyone, good for kindergartners and good for pigs.

"Let's hear it," the Polack said, once his mouth was empty.

She said that the psychologist was really quite nice and that he had asked their son whether he experienced a lot of stress. And about how it was going at school and at home, how things were there, whether he had friends and a hobby.

"And what did you tell him?" the Polack asked. Quietly, he added: "Aren't people allowed to have secrets anymore? Do they really have to know everything about us?"

The boy rinsed his mouth with a gulp of water and then said: "That I wasn't completely sure what he was talking about."

"Are you stressed?" the Polack asked. The boy shook his head. "I don't have stress," he said, and Wen told him that the psychologist had said it might be wise if the boy went and sat on the toilet at fixed times, after dinner for example, or before going to school in the morning, even when he felt no urge. And whether the boy felt like doing a yoga class. But the boy had told him resolutely that he didn't want to do yoga, not now and not later either.

"Do you guys have stress?" the boy asked. His plate was empty now. "Do I give you guys stress?"

"We have no stress," the Polack said. "We're a normal family. I have stress sometimes when I have to go into a burning house, but you don't think about that, you're trained to do everything without thinking about it, that's actually why you have no stress. There's no time for it. Because we get there with the six of us and we want to go back to the station with all six of us too. Safety first."

No one reacted to what the Polack had said. Maybe his family felt that he should leave his fire department stories at the station.

Wen took a sip of water, she rinsed her mouth too to get the grisly bits out of every nook and cranny. The social worker had ended the appointment by asking whether it wouldn't be a good idea for the whole family to come along next time.

Wen told him that she would have to talk to her husband about that. She put the youngest child on her lap, wiped his face with his bib. The Polack said: "Maybe you can promise not to do it in your pants anymore? And you know what? If you can do that for two weeks, you get a present from us. What would you like to have? What do you want us to give you if you haven't pooped in your pants for two weeks?"

Other boys played with Lego Technic, they played soccer or computer games, but their son didn't do any of that, on rare occasions he played computer games, but even that he didn't seem to particularly enjoy. Their son didn't have much passion in him, he viewed the world with a slightly bored gaze, as though he had already seen it all and nothing really appealed to him, and that worried his parents. How could someone so young already be so bored?

"Give me money," the boy said. "If I keep it up for two weeks, then give me some money."

The Polack thought about it for a moment, then said: "Keep it up for two weeks, you get ten euros from me. Does that sound reasonable?"

"Make it twenty," the boy said, and in the kitchen Wen told him quietly that this was silliness. What was the boy going to think? That he could make money by not pooping in his pants?

For a few days it went well, and the Polack said proudly to his wife: "You see?" At the fire station he still hadn't talked about it, he didn't talk much about his home life anyway, in the shower one time he had told Beckers that his son had intestinal problems, that was it. Beckers had replied that children always had something: intestinal problems, colds, acne, ingrown toenails. For a while, his second-youngest daughter had been deathly afraid of unfamiliar toilets. "And men with beards," he'd added. That had gone away by itself.

Borys didn't have to be paid; before the two weeks were over there had been something in his pants again, and Wen concluded then that it wasn't stress, just a lack of friends. Borys said he didn't need any friends and that what he liked most was playing with his little brother, but maybe he was just acting big, maybe he pooped in his pants because he couldn't take it any longer. Because he missed having friends, because he missed contact. The poop was a cry for help.

"No," the Polack said, "I don't think so. Poop is no cry for help."

2

Going to school was a catastrophe, those last weeks before the summer vacation. Borys hid, refused to get his bicycle, said that he would just walk, and then didn't. Then the Polack would have to go after him, while the boy clung to lampposts because he didn't want to go to school. He clung to trees as well. The Polack yanked him away from them, because not going to school was out of the question, you could get the Child Welfare Council or the truant officer after you. And the Polack's father had always said: "Be respectable and keep your head down, so the people here won't think badly of the Poles." And after the Polack had yanked Borys away from the tree or lamppost, he drove him out ahead of him, the way the sheepdog drives the reluctant sheep. For the boy's own good. Yes, that's the way it was. Borys was the sheep and the father was the sheepdog.

Something had to happen, so they pressed the point even further. Was there perhaps something else Borys wanted? Something he actually liked? Besides playing at home with his little brother? They came up with all kinds of things, from doing magic tricks to Boy Scouts, from a course in computer programming to music lessons. "Everybody has a hobby," the Polack said. "Please, why don't you take up one too?"

"What's *your* hobby then?" the boy asked.

In actual fact, the Polack was a man without hobbies, although you could of course say that he had made his hobby his profession. The firehouse was his hobby.

After a brief silence, the Polack finally said: "The garden, gardening is my hobby."

A week went by and then one morning Borys said: "Give me a pony. I'd like to have a pony."

Wen and the Polack were surprised. Never before had their son expressed any interest in animals in general or ponies in particular. He was actually a little afraid of dogs, even though he wasn't easily frightened otherwise. He was so quiet, you didn't know what was going on inside him, maybe he had been yearning for a pony all these years without having said anything to anyone.

The parents didn't really understand what their lanky son saw in a pony. It wasn't that he wouldn't fit on a pony, despite his height; animals like that came in all different sizes, after all, but still, a pony . . . where did he get that from? It made Wen suspicious. "Do other boys in your class have a pony?" she asked. "No, only girls," Borys answered. And he left it at that, and Wen didn't push things.

At first Wen was against it, she thought a pony was too much. "If we don't watch out, he'll have had enough of it after a week," she said. "Let's just rent one for him first." But in the end she succumbed to her husband's arguments. "If the animal really belongs to him," the Polack said, "then after a while maybe he'll develop a different kind of relationship with people, real relationships." To which, in vague desperation, he added: "If our boy wants a pony, then we'll buy one for him. After all, he never asks for anything else. Nothing at all."

That's the way the Polack was. If that was the solution, then action had to be taken. He was so pleased that there was finally something Borys wanted that he fanatically started searching for a pony. And he found one, on a farm close to where they lived: there was nothing you couldn't find on the Internet.

"I've found an animal that would be right for you," the Polack said, giving Borys a paternal thump on the shoulder. "Great," Borys said.

The Polack wanted to make an outing out of buying the pony. It was something that would create a bond, that's how he imagined it, when Borys was old he would still poignantly recall how one day he and his father had bought a pony together. Maybe he would tell his own children about the day he had gone with Grandpa to buy a pony.

They drove there on a Saturday. An old man was sitting at the window of the farmhouse, there was no one else in sight, only a cat wandering across the farmyard. The farm made a dilapidated and rather dreary impression, but all farms were probably like that. In any case, the Polack wanted to keep things upbeat, it was a red-letter day, even though the clouds were low and it had rained all morning. He said to his eldest boy: "Your pony must be around here somewhere." And he ran his hand over the boy's hair, patted him gently on the back, the way fathers do with their sons. At that moment the farmer knocked on the window and gestured to them to come inside. A crooked finger beckoned, a hand waved.

There was a checkered curtain in front of the little window in the farmhouse door. Through the kitchen, where a few days' dirty dishes stood piled on the counter, they arrived in a living room. The farmer was sitting in a wheelchair at the window. The living room was full of furniture that looked like it had been bought before the Second World War. The wood in one chest of drawers seemed half-rotted. The remains of a meal lay on the table. A sugar bowl. Bread on a napkin. The place smelled like a mixture of fireplace, manure, and stale food.

The farmer's hand, the one he'd gestured with, was now in his lap. A hand that had been in the soil often, or in animals. The farmer had probably assisted at a few births.

Borys must have felt that he was stepping into a different world, another world in another age, for he took his father's hand, which he otherwise rarely did. The father himself wanted to keep things relaxed, so that years from now his boy would think back with pleasure on this Saturday afternoon. It was that above all, the Polack feared, that was missing in the boy's life: pleasure. When he had said as much to Wen once, she had replied: "And you, what about you, do you set a good example? Do you radiate pleasure?"

Today of all days, the Polack wanted to radiate pleasure, it had to be a lovely afternoon, especially for his eldest boy, who finally wanted something. The Polack said: "We're here for the pony. I called, this is my son, Borys. It's for him."

He had developed a habit of emphasizing that he and the boy belonged together, because the boy sometimes acted as though his father was a total stranger, even at his own birthday party. First the boy refused to invite any friends, he said he didn't want to celebrate his birthday. He dreaded it like an execution, and when a list of ten classmates had finally been drawn up with the greatest of difficulty, and finally brought back by Borys himself to five or six children, he had sat there as though he had nothing to do with the celebration, as though his parents weren't his parents, his classmates weren't his classmates, and his birthday wasn't his birthday. And one time, when they were on vacation in Zeeland Province, when they were sitting in a restaurant and having an argument, the boy had said grimly to the waiter: "I don't know these people."

Upon which the Polack had boxed his ear, with the waiter still standing there, and the Polack had said, loud and clear: "We're your parents, Borys." The waiter looked baffled, but left it at that; he brought their orders and remained in the background for the rest of the evening.

That was the reason why the Polack spoke emphatically of "my boy" or "our boy," so that people would know how things stood, should there be any doubt. But now the boy held the father's hand and there was no reason for the Polack to stress that this boy was with him and that he was with this boy. It was clear that they were inextricably bound up with each other. Still, he did it all the same. Our boy. My boy.

The farmer in the wheelchair had a stubbly beard, there were bumps on his hands, he said: "Wheel me to the stable, the hired hand's out there."

The Polack took hold of the wheelchair and pushed it across the living room, past the dirty dishes, he couldn't quite see what was on them, it looked like porridge, or maybe soup, out the kitchen door and then down a sodden path. The farmer pointed to show where they had to go, he didn't say a word, only gestured. Occasionally he raised his right hand with the bumps on it and pointed the way to the right stable. There were a few stables.

The boy traipsed along behind them in the sweatsuit he liked to wear, the one with the hood, he liked hoods. Wen said: "He hides himself inside his hood." The Polack said: "His hood is his shield."

The wheelchair kept getting stuck in the mud. This was no path for invalids. The Polack would have much preferred to lift the farmer out of his wheelchair and carry him over his shoulder to the stable, but that would have been impolite. He hadn't come here as a fireman, he was here to buy a pony, and then you didn't lift the seller out of their wheelchair just like that, even if it probably would have been the best way. Occasionally the Polack turned and saw Borys picking his way down the wet path. It seemed as though the boy didn't really know where he was going, as though he could no longer remember wanting nothing except a pony.

At last they got to the stable. It was big enough for at least twelve horses or other animals, maybe even more, but inside there was only one pony. "I got rid of all the rest," the farmer said, "you can't care for animals when you're in a wheelchair. All I have left are a few sheep and cows, the hired hand takes care of those. My children aren't interested. They don't want to be farmers. They think it's dirty."

The farmer took the Polack's hand the way the boy had earlier, he squeezed it as though he was planning to pull himself up, and said: "No one's got respect for the farmers anymore. And you don't either. I can see that."

There was so much bitterness in the old man, so much anger at the world, which despite all the things that went wrong was still a fine world, and there was still so much strength in the hand with which he had grabbed hold of the Polack. The Polack didn't want to talk about farmers, and not about respect either, he wanted to buy a pony and he said to the boy: "There's your pony."

The pony was white, or gray, you couldn't tell very well in this light, there were spots on the animal and he didn't know whether the spots came from the mud or if they were part of the animal's hide, it didn't really matter anyway. He would buy the animal for the boy, after that they would go home. Maybe drink something together along the way and try, even though he knew better, to have a conversation.

"Everybody eats meat, but the farmers who provide them with that meat, who went to the trouble to fatten it up, they're dirty, those are the villains," the farmer said, and the Polack was afraid the quiet boy would get confused by the old farmer's words. The Polack gave the boy a little push in the right direction, and Borys walked over to the pony.

The farmer said: "Her name's Manya. She can be pretty mean. A nasty beast is what she is. She outlived all her brothers and sisters. That's the way nasty beasts are, they live the longest."

"Oh, I bet it's not all that bad," said the Polack loudly, so his boy would hear, "ponies are sweet animals."

"You folks don't know anything about animals," the farmer said, pulling on the Polack's hand in order to sit up straighter. Then, at last, he let go of his hand. "You city folks don't know anything about it. Everything's a crying shame these days, exact for the farmer himself."

"We live close to here, actually," the Polack said.

He saw his boy stick his hand through the bars of the fence.

"The city starts close to here," the farmer said. "You don't talk as though you come from around here."

"My father is Polish," the Polack said, "and my mother was from Germany. I grew up in Heerlen, lived in De Peel for a while, then in the west of the country until I ended up back in Heerlen."

"Oh, so you're a foreigner," the farmer said.

The pony seemed to be ignoring his boy. The Polack knew nothing about animals, he couldn't imagine that it was a mean pony, that there were really mean ponies in the world, otherwise the urban farms wouldn't be full of them, would they?

"How much do you want for it?" the Polack asked quietly.

"Eight hundred," the farmer said. "She's got plenty of years left in her still. Healthy as can be and strong as an ox. Mean, but you get used to that."

The Polack thought that was a lot of money. "Four hundred," he said.

"Seven hundred," the farmer said.

"Five hundred," said the Polack. "I'm a fireman," he added, "I'm not a rich man."

"Richer than I am," the farmer said. "I'll bet you every fireman's richer than I am. Six hundred and fifty, because it's for the boy. He didn't exactly win the sweepstakes, with you for a father. I can tell that much."

Maybe the farmer was a nasty character himself, but nasty or no, the Polack didn't want an argument, all he wanted was the pony.

"I'm offering you six hundred," the Polack whispered. He let the insult slide. Act like you didn't hear it. You could do your best work as a fireman, maybe any kind of work, if you regularly acted like you hadn't heard things. And the farmer said that six hundred was okay, as long as he paid in cash, on the barrelhead. He'd have to go looking for the pony's passport, the hired hand had put it somewhere, they would find it sure enough, he just had to pay in cash. That was important.

The pony had finally noticed the boy, it looked they were making contact, pony and boy. The Polack took four hundred-euro notes out of his wallet, two fifties, and five twenties. He counted the money twice, it was a load of money, but that animal was going to help Borys and so he gave it to the farmer. It was more than he'd counted on, a colleague had told him that three or four hundred was already a lot for an older pony, but Borys would be disappointed if they went home empty-handed.

"Manya used to belong to my granddaughter, she's not interested in it anymore. No interest and no time. Roll me back to the house. Then I'll look for that passport."

The Polack took hold of the wheelchair and they rolled back up the muddy path, through the kitchen with its piles of dirty dishes, and the living room where the remains of a meal were still on the table.

"Just put me down here," the farmer said. Right away, he took a bite of the porridge that maybe even wasn't porridge. Then he rolled himself, more energetically than the Polack had expected, over to a little, litter-covered desk that also looked fairly rotten, and after a few minutes the farmer had the pony's passport in his hand. He smacked it down on the table.

"All right," he said, "now she's yours. Are you going to take her with you right away?"

The boy was standing in the doorway between the living room and kitchen. More abashed than usual.

The Polack opened the passport. The animal's name was, indeed, Manya.

"I was actually hoping she could stay here. Until I've found something else." He stuck the passport in his wallet.

The farmer looked at him pensively and, in a funny way, slyly too, as though he had been counting on this all along. City folks who bought a pony without knowing what to do with it, the farmer seemed to know the type.

"A hundred for the box, a hundred and twenty for the feed. Per month. She eats you out of house and home, the nasty old bitch. And that's a steal."

"But the stable would be vacant anyway," the Polack said after a long silence. He felt he was being tested, not only by the farmer, also by his son. Things could still go wrong, and he feared that without the pony the boy would withdraw more and more, become even more silent, until silence was all that was left of him. "It's sort of weird that I have to pay rent for something that would be vacant anyway. I'm happy to pay for the animal's feed, but I'm . . . It's not that I'm . . ."

The farmer was back at the table again. He had maneuvered his way there handily, and he took a few bites. Then he said: "When you folks need an animal, you know right where to find us. But then it all has to be for free, right? We and our animals aren't supposed to cost a penny. Seventy-five for the rent, a hundred and twenty-five for the damn thing's feed. If you don't like it, you can take her with you right now."

The farmer spoke of the pony as though it were an ex he couldn't stand. Did the farmer even have a wife anymore?

"You can pay right now for the rest of the month," the farmer said, "then that's over and done with. And then on the first of the month, every month. Is the boy going to come and look at the animal once in a while, or will we never see him again, just like my granddaughter?"

"The boy will come here a couple of times a week, won't you, Borys? Maybe more often than that."

Borys nodded.

"He can bike from our place over here." The Polack looked at his boy, who nodded again.

"What's he going to do with the pony anyway?" the farmer asked. "Ride it?"

A silence fell.

"What are you going to do with it?" the Polack asked, just to be sure.

"I'm going to take care of her," Borys said.

The farmer shrugged. "Whatever he wants," he said. "You start off as a serious farmer and you end up a petting zoo."

A man wearing a black cap came into the house. He was even taller than the Polack, tall and skinny, and his mouth sagged a little to one side.

"That's the hired hand," the farmer said.

The hired hand nodded. He started to clear the table but the farmer said: "Leave it. I'm eating."

Then the hired hand went away again, the Polack heard him rummaging around in the kitchen, and from upstairs he heard the sound of creaking planks. Maybe the farmer actually did have himself a wife. One who couldn't get down the stairs anymore. The Polack had seen things like that before. If it got too bad, the fire department had to be called in.

"The boy will be back tomorrow or the next day, he'll have the money with him then," the Polack said.

"Fine," the farmer said. "Have him knock on the window." He took a few more bites and the Polack saw now that it was mushroom soup, what the farmer was eating, cold mushroom soup. Now he could even smell the mushrooms, faintly.

They shook the farmer's hand. First the Polack, then his boy, he'd had to give the boy a little shove first.

In the car the boy was silent, the way he always was, but when the Polack asked: "Are you happy with the pony?" the boy said: "Yeah, really happy."

They stopped at a McDonald's, where they ordered French fries and cola. The Polack asked whether the boy wanted something else, but he said: "No, Mom's waiting for us with dinner." He was, despite his incommunicativeness, a kind and thoughtful boy.

They drank their cola and ate their French fries and while the Polack was making attempts to keep the conversation going, his mind kept returning to the farmer in his wheelchair.

"It's not too far to bike, is it?" the Polack asked.

"No," said his boy.

"Why is it you wanted a pony, anyway?"

"Just did. Seemed nice."

The Polack put one last French fry in his mouth. "Do you want to be a fireman later on, like me?" he asked, for he felt that this was a special moment, he hadn't been this close to his boy in a long time.

"No," Borys said.

"So do you know what it is you do want to be?"

"No," Borys said. "Not yet."

"But you will go to the pony every now and then, right?" the Polack asked. "Don't leave that animal there all alone."

"No," Borys said, "I won't do that."

They got in the car, and in the car the Polack handed the pony's passport to his eldest son. "This is for you," he said, "it's your animal, you have to keep the passport." Then they drove home and only when they had parked the car did the boy say: "Thanks, Dad, thanks for buying the pony for me." He didn't look at his father as he said it, he looked straight ahead, as though the Polack wasn't in the car but standing right in front of it.

3

And that was how Borys got a pony named Manya, and from the start, just as the boy had promised, he went there twice a week, later even four or five times a week. At a certain point he went every day. Wen was relieved, she told her husband that it had been an excellent idea for them to buy their son a pony, much better than renting or borrowing a pony first. That the animal belonging to Borys and to Borys alone had helped him to get out of the house. She said he was really able to bond with the pony. Manya was, in fact, a person and a sport rolled into one. "Good that you forged ahead with this," she told her husband. "He seems to enjoy going there. I don't have to encourage him. He goes to the farmer completely of his own accord. He likes ponies, apparently."

That was true, there was no need to encourage him, and from the looks of it things were going better with him pooping his pants as well. Wen kept track of it on her phone. It went from happening an average of six times a week to only once a week. And the Polack barely had to yank him away from lampposts anymore. The last few weeks the boy had been going to school without too much reluctance.

The parents were no longer being summoned by the teacher, and the Polack said: "We've fixed the leak."

"Let's wait and see," Wen answered. "Let's not get ahead of our-selves." Like always, that fear of getting ahead of yourself. When you knew a lot about children, you knew that you should never get ahead of yourself.

"That teacher of his talked more about how Borys stank than about Borys himself," the Polack said.

Wen shrugged. As a kindergarten teacher, she showed solidarity with Borys's teacher. "She has so many children in the class," she said, "she can't spend all her time worrying about each one of them. Borys has to learn to stick up for himself. And he'll do that. He has your personality, he doesn't say much, he can be a little sullen, but he forges ahead."

The primary school year ended with a musical about a boat trip. Borys played one of the seven sailors. When it was over Wen told him she was proud of him, and the Polack said he'd been a good sailor and that the sailor's cap looked great on him. Borys beamed. The Polack had felt uncomfortable that evening, amid the other parents in the audience, as though he didn't belong there. He was afraid they could see that he wasn't really a father, that he was a fraud. Someone who pretended to be a father without actually being one, someone who pre-tended everything without really being anything, except perhaps for a fireman, he was that from head to toe.

Summer vacation began. With the exception of ten days on Crete, Borys spent almost the whole summer with the pony. When junior high school started, Manya remained his dearest comrade. His grades were decent, even excellent in biology. When his parents asked him how things were at school, he replied that a lot of children smoked and that some of the girls already wore makeup. One of the girls, the kids said, had been born in a powderpuff. That was all he'd say.

Sometimes the Polack broke the silence at the dinner table by ask-ing how things were with the pony, for he refused to call the animal "Manya." He would have forgotten her name long ago if his son hadn't occasionally referred to the pony as Manya. "And how's the farmer doing?" the Polack asked. Because he wanted to know that too. To be honest, the farmer interested him more than the pony.

"I never see him," Borys said.

"Never? You never see him?"

"No," the boy said, "only when I have money to give him. I see the hired hand sometimes."

The Polack listened to the clinking of their cutlery. Wen fed the youngest boy a spoonful, he said: "monka, monka, monka." His favorite stuffed animal was a monkey, and the animal's name was repeated again and again, especially during meals, like a prayer, until it drove the Polack crazy. Borys had never spoken that much, he had also never really had a favorite stuffed animal.

The next day—it was pouring down rain and their eldest son still hadn't come back from the farm—the Polack decided to go and pick Borys up. You couldn't let the boy bike home in weather like this, and besides, the Polack wanted to have a look for himself at how the animal was getting along, the animal for which he had, according to some of his colleagues, paid too much. He wasn't very good at bargaining. The farmer had beat him at that. Something in the man's eyes had made the Polack uneasy, he had felt unmasked. There, once again, he had been unmasked. Or was it the wheelchair? He might have expected anything from a farmer, but not a wheelchair.

Once, in the shower at the fire station, he had talked about the pony. People had joked about it, laughed. The men homed in unerringly on each other's weaknesses. That's the way they were. The C squad forgot a great deal, but never the other person's weak points, they called that "pulling a prank." Playing a joke.

In the shower they didn't just play jokes. They also talked about things that had happened during their shift, a child burned so badly it was doubtful whether it would pull through. They told each other that they wondered how the child was doing. They pulled people out of burning houses, they didn't hear how it went with them afterward. Usually that was all right, but sometimes they were curious. They told each other so in the shower, after they worked out. You had in stay in shape if you wanted to drag people out of burning houses. You couldn't go on doing this job until you were sixty-five or sixty-seven, and that was probably why lots of firemen had other jobs on the side, because they knew that life as a fireman could be over quickly. One of the Polack's colleagues imported wine, for example, and lots of firemen also worked as handymen. The Polack was the only one who didn't moonlight. He was exclusively a fireman, nothing else but that. In the past he had tried to pass himself off as a plumber or painter, but he hadn't liked it and his customers had not been impressed by his skill at unclogging toilets either.

Weeks went by sometimes without any burned children they could talk about. There were, in fact, relatively few fires in the life of a fireman. Most of it involved normal people who couldn't handle their own problems, that's where the fireman came in, and it usually had nothing to do with fires. Firemen dealt with things like cats in trees and with burst plumbing; only the misery of the soul, with that the fireman had no dealings.

And there were days when they washed the sweat and filth from their bodies in silence, and stood in the foam from each other's soap and looked at each other's hairy backs, each other's nascent baldness, each other's buttocks, each other's rolls of fat. Sometimes, laughingly, they would pinch each other's rolls of fat, because they had known each other for so long.

The rain had turned to drizzle, the Polack turned his windshield wipers down low and thought about the Saturday when he and his boy had driven out to the farm. That had been a fine day, he hadn't pretended to be a father, that day he had been one.

The Polack parked his car in the exact same spot he had the day they bought the pony. He walked straight to the stables, even though the farmer tapped on the window again.

The path was full of puddles. Under a tarp lay a dead cow, its hooves sticking out. The Polack stopped, wrinkled his nose. What was it about this place that appealed to the boy? What was he looking for here?

He saw his boy's bike in front of the stables. An expensive bike, tossed on the ground just like that. That's how boys were. Good thing he'd come to get him. Borys would be pleased that he didn't have to cycle home in the rain.

The Polack, who tried harder and harder as he got older to be a different kind of father than his own father had been, went into the stable. It struck him how dark it was there, how inhospitable, even for an animal it seemed like an unpleasant place to live, but then animals probably had other ideas about hospitability than people did.

He didn't see his boy anywhere. The door to one of the boxes was open, maybe Borys was in there. He walked toward it slowly. He felt a drop of moisture hanging from his nose. Was this any place for a twelve-year-old boy? Mightn't it have been better for him to stay home with his baby brother? What was so bad about that, anyway? Without friends, maybe, but safe in any case. And a little brother could be a friend too.

Then he saw his boy. In the darkest corner of the box, standing beside the pony. The child was murmuring. Yes, he was still really only a child, despite his height. The pony made no sound. The Polack stopped, they boy hadn't seen him, hadn't heard him, the father stood in the doorway of the box as though he didn't know whether to go in or go out, all he knew was that he didn't want to disturb his boy.

He couldn't make out what the boy was saying, and that didn't matter either. His boy didn't talk to people, his boy talked to animals. To an old pony for which the Polack had paid too much, but if it made his boy happy, then it had been a good investment. Only now he began to have doubts. They had wanted their boy to make friends, but they had really meant with people, not with an elderly pony.

He heard someone come into the stable, he turned and saw the hired hand. "The farmer wants to talk to you," said the man with that blank expression of his, he kept his distance as though he was afraid. He didn't look at the Polack either, he looked into the box, past the Polack.

Now the boy had seen the Polack too, he tore himself away from his murmuring, walked over to his father and said: "What are you doing here?" He didn't seem happy, more like angry, unpleasantly surprised.

"I came to get you," the Polack said. "It's pouring. Toss your bike in the back, we're going home." And then he thought that, as a father, as a good father, he should show some interest in his son's animal. He asked: "How's she doing?"

"She's got a limp," the boy said. "She fell."

"The farmer wants to talk to you," the hired hand said, louder this time, more forcefully. "Come with me." The hired hand was a man who took orders and passed them along.

"Wait here for me, okay?" the Polack said to Borys. "Or do you want to come with? It's so damp in here. How do you stand it?"

"I'll stay here," the boy said, and he looked at his father, not in an unfriendly way, more like questioningly.

The Polack followed the hired hand down the muddy path. Past the dead cow under its tarp, past a cat that was still alive. "Do you do everything by yourself around here?" he asked as they walked. Men together, that meant you struck up a conversation.

The hired hand shrugged. "Always have done," he mumbled, holding open the kitchen door. Just like on that Saturday, the Polack walked through a filthy kitchen to the living room, where the farmer was sitting in his wheelchair by the window, staring outside as though he was watching TV. The hired hand had not come into the house. Out the window, the Polack could see him crossing the yard. With a bit of a limp too, or so it seemed.

"You wanted to talk to me," the Polack said.

The farmer turned slowly in his wheelchair; the maneuver seemed more difficult for him this time. He coughed, a peeping sound came from his nose. With obvious difficulty, he rolled himself over to the table. The Polack didn't help him, he had learned that helping people without their permission could make them angry. The farmer put his elbows on the table, supported his chin with one hand, the man's face was covered in grooves, his skin looked like clay, and he assayed the Polack, unashamedly, unhurriedly. The peeping sound kept coming out of his nose.

Did the farmer still know why he'd asked him to come in? It seemed like he barely knew who the Polack was.

"Your boy," he said at last, "left the door to the box open. She got out and into the creek. The hired man got her out again, it wasn't easy, but he did it. Since then she's been lame, crippled as it gets. It's your animal, it's your decision, but you're no farmer, you don't know anything about animals. I'd have her put down, quick as possible. I know a horse butcher here close by, maybe you'd get something for her. Wouldn't be much. I know what you're going to say, that's cruel. But it isn't cruel, letting the beast live is cruel. When an animal's in that kind of shape, keeping it alive is cruel."

First the Polack had had to bargain with the farmer about the price of the pony, then about the price of her feed, now he had to bargain with him about her right to go on living.

"I just bought that pony," the Polack said, "so now I guess you want me to buy a new one? I can't afford that. My boy's happy with the animal. He comes here every day. He almost lives here. We barely see him anymore. He loves that animal."

Without meaning to, he had raised his voice. The admission that he didn't have that kind of money made him emotional. Not the lack of funds itself, but the need to admit it. And the boy they barely saw, that too was an unpleasant admission. What he should have said, in fact, was that the boy lived in the stall. Things were going better with him, it's true. He'd gotten better, there in the stall.

The farmer closed his eyes. "I don't have any more ponies." He opened his eyes again, blinked a few times, used his free hand to pluck at his eyebrows, as though making sure they were still there. "This was the last one. In a year or two this place is going to shut down, if I make it that long. Your boy left the door of the box open. He shouldn't have done that. He's not a little kid anymore. He has to live up to his mistakes."

The Polack placed his hands flat on the table, which was covered with a cloth that reminded him of a rug. "I'm not going to have her put down," the Polack said. "That pony means everything to my boy. Whether she limps or walks crippled, it doesn't matter. That animal wants to live, the way we all want to live."

"You know nothing about animals," the farmer said, louder now, still resting his chin on his right hand. "You don't know what animals want. You barely know what *you* want."

The Polack sniffed loudly. "The pony belongs to my boy, he has something to say about it too."

"So let him say something," the farmer said calmly. "He's never said anything to me yet. I can't force you to do anything. I'm just giving you my advice."

He rolled himself over to the window and looked outside again. The hired hand walked past, pushing a wheelbarrow. Was the farmer trying to say that the conversation was finished?

"I'd rather have it cold than hot," the farmer said after a while, in a different tone of voice. "I don't like the summer anymore. Dry. Hot. Then soaking wet again. Extreme summers, not for me." Maybe he was talking to himself.

The Polack remained standing there, because he had the feeling that he should say more. He stared at the farmer's back, at his shoulders, and he couldn't stop staring, couldn't get himself to go outside, to fetch his boy.

"My wife's lying upstairs," the farmer said in the same tone. "She can't get out of bed anymore. But she doesn't want to go anywhere else. She wants to die here, in her own bed. Can you blame her? No one's allowed to help her along with that. It's against her religion. Death has to come by itself. The hired hand feeds her like she's a suckling lamb, my wife. I can't do it. I can barely get up there anymore. Don't have the strength to. And what is there to see? I still see her once a month. Because the children want me to. They carry me upstairs and show me to my wife and they say to her: "Here's your husband." And my wife looks, she just looks. But she has nothing to say. She's not demented, she just doesn't have anything to say anymore. All right, that's the way the kids want it, they want us to still see each other once a month. Another pony will come along. What's a couple of hundred euros to a fireman? We farmers used to get subsidies. Not anymore. Not my kind of farmer. If I had money like the big farmers do, I'd give you your money back for the pony, but I don't have it. I can't afford it. An animal deserves not to have to walk around in pain either. A fireman ought to know that."

"The animal wants to live," the Polack said, "pain or no pain. Can't a vet come and look at her?"

All he could see of the farmer was part of his back, his shoulders, the back of his head. The farmer still had lots of hair growing on his head, it was gray and greasy hair, but it was still growing.

The farmer shook his head. "A vet like that costs more than two ponies put together. And what do you think he'd say, anyway? Have her put down. I say: take her to the butcher. He says: have her put down. And you pay a fortune for that."

The Polack remained standing there for a bit, he wanted to continue the conversation but he wasn't sure how. Finally, he went back to the stable.

The boy wasn't talking to the animal anymore, he was just standing beside it, and the Polack said: "Come on, we're going." Without waiting for the boy's reply, he went outside, picked up the bicycle, and dragged it like an unwilling animal to the car. Only when he was halfway there did he turn and see that the boy wasn't following him. He shouted his name, waited for a moment, then shouted "Borys" again. The boy appeared at last, dragging his feet despite the rain.

In the car the Polack told the boy: "The farmer says the pony needs to be put down. That that's better for her. That she's as crippled as it gets." The boy said nothing. He stared straight ahead, he acted like he hadn't heard, he acted as though the Polack didn't exist. The father waited for a while, you have to give a child time, but when they were almost home and there was still no reaction, he said: "I'm talking to you, do you think you could answer me? Could you stop acting as though I don't exist? Does that animal need to be put down, or doesn't it? Could you stop acting like I'm some kind of ghost? I exist. I'm your father."

"Don't kill her, please," the boy said.

4

At home the Polack repeated what the farmer had said, and Wen's reaction was not what he had expected. She was practical, to the point of being businesslike. When something was broken, it had to be replaced. The Polack, on the other hand, preferred to save things, because you never knew when they could come in handy, and maybe secretly because he'd also become attached, because throwing something away still felt as though you were dumping a living creature into the garbage. Wen had never been overanxious either. Not that he was overanxious, but as a fireman he knew that the first few minutes were what counted. If you wanted to save lives, you had to act fast. When Borys was still little and sometimes picked up food and other things off the ground and put them in his mouth, Wen's comment was usually: "It'll only make him stronger." The Polack pulled it all out of his boy's mouth, sometimes with difficulty, the boy refusing to open his mouth and the Polack having to jam his fingers in.

Wen's attitude toward life—her mother called it her savoir-vivre— must certainly apply not only to broken household items, but also to ponies. Levelheaded, unsentimental, which of course was not the same as unloving. That's why he had expected her to say: "Have her taken away. Listen to the farmer. We'll buy another one."

Having her taken away was, in the pony's case, synonymous with having her put down, although the Polack had to admit that having her taken away sounded better. It mattered, the way you put things. You could describe things in a way that made people feel okay about them. A kindergarten teacher had to be good at that, if only in a professional capacity, and Wen was good at that at home too.

But tonight, Wen had cast aside her purposiveness. When she finally opened her mouth to react to the farmer's verdict, she said: "I think that's a bad idea. Borys is attached to that animal, aren't you, Borys?"

The boy looked straight ahead, he said: "Manya is scared." The Polack had seen the way the boy stood there in the box, he had witnessed the moment of tenderness between his boy and the animal. Now that he had seen that, he couldn't forget it. He had heard the way his boy talked to the animal, not for just a moment, no, for minutes on end, and he probably did that every day, that was the main thing he did with that animal. Not ride it, not currycomb it the way girls did, but talk to it. Because their son didn't want to talk to people, or only barely, he talked to that animal, and because the Polack had witnessed that talking, he said: "Yeah, the animal means a lot to him. But she's not scared, Borys. She's lame. She's as lame as they get, that's what the farmer said." And he began stroking Borys. When you couldn't talk, you had to stroke.

The parents were in agreement, the animal had to be saved, saving the animal was saving Borys. It was as simple as that. Saving things was a typical task for a fireman, and if only for that reason the Polack regretted almost having lost his temper in the car. He didn't want to be that kind of person, a screaming, swearing father. "We won't let that animal be put down," he said with a resolve that took him by surprise, because he himself wasn't completely convinced that this was the best thing for the pony, a farmer like that knew what he was talking about. But he had no choice, pony and son were linked together, they mustn't be separated. At least not yet. Later, when the boy was stronger, maybe then.

And so he asked Borys: "Could you ask the farmer to have a vet come and look at her? Tell him your father will pay for it. That he doesn't need to worry about that. The Polack will pay the vet."

The boy nodded. There wasn't a lot of emotion to be seen there, but the father knew for a fact that Borys was happy.

It was going to cost him a bundle, a vet like that, he had never thought about taking out insurance on the pony, if such a thing was even possible. Was there actually something like health insurance for ponies? He had no idea, it didn't matter. It was too late, in any case, for insurance policies. If need be, they would skip going to Crete next summer. A bungalow in Germany was cheaper, and the weather could be nice there too.

Seeing as the pants-pooping had now come to a complete halt— Borys was depositing his waste, like all healthy people, in the toilet— and both the Polack and his wife were convinced that this was thanks to the pony, the Polack pressed ahead with saving the animal.

Each evening he asked if there was any news about the vet's arrival, and each evening the boy's reply was vague. In a few days' time, the farmer wasn't sure, the farmer had been asleep and the boy didn't dare to wake him up, the hired hand was working on it, until finally it began to dawn on the Polack: their boy didn't dare to talk to the farmer. The boy was afraid of the farmer, even when it came to saving his pony. That's the kind of son they had, a little timid, but he would grow out of it. Later on he would start talking to people. The fear would dissipate, the same way acne cleared up.

Two weeks after his last visit to the farmer, the Polack asked again about the pony's condition, just to be sure. You never knew, by the same token the animal might be lying under a tarp because the farmer had had no time to have it taken away, and the boy was afraid to tell his parents that the pony had been put out of its suffering. Borys didn't like to burden those around him with bad news.

"She has a limp," the boy said. To his parents' surprise, the quiet boy then stood up and imitated the way the crippled animal had to go through life. It was remarkable to see. Their eldest son, imitating his crippled pony. He limped around the living room. Father and mother watched him, then looked at each other.

"Too bad there are no wheelchairs for ponies," the Polack commented, for this evening too he wanted to keep it light. "But we're going to do something about it. We're going to help that animal. We won't leave her to her fate."

At the end of the afternoon, on his next day off, he drove to the farm. He was going to talk to the farmer, first he would ask him to summon a vet, then he would demand it, and if normal demands didn't lead to the desired result he would pound his fist on the table, and if the farmer still refused to help him he would get to work on it himself. There had to be someone in the C squad who knew a reliable veterinarian.

Like each time before, the farmer was sitting at the window, but this time he didn't wave to the Polack. The Polack had to admit that he was a bit afraid of the farmer too, the man made him feel uncomfortable, his monologues, his axioms, his attitude to life. His unkempt hair. The Polack had become a fireman in order to help people. There had been other reasons too, of course: the adventure, the dream entertained by the boy he had once been, the working hours, but something in him wanted to help normal folks. This man in his wheelchair didn't believe in help, he held no truck with it. The Polack was repelled by that skepticism, it made him uneasy. Even furious, after a certain fashion.

He walked to the stable, less hesitantly now than the last two times. The cow had been taken away. The tarp was still there, but there was nothing under it. The Polack stared at the tarp for a moment as he hitched up his trousers and wondered how many dead animals had lain there before.

He walked into the stable and called out: "Borys." No reaction came, but that didn't surprise him; the boy rarely reacted when they called him. He would come downstairs and sit at the table, but he never shouted back: "I'm coming!" Or: "I'm over here!" He was called and he appeared. And then he did what he had to do, he ate everything on his plate.

The box was open and at first the Polack only saw the animal. This afternoon there was no one holding a monologue. The animal had never made a sound before, and probably wouldn't start doing so this afternoon. The pony looked at him and then, in a corner all the way at the back of the box, he saw the boy squatting down. His pants down around his knees. And he looked, the boy looked back, not a word crossed his lips, he just kept his eyes fixed on his father.

The Polack couldn't go through with it now, his plan to embrace his boy, to press him to his bosom, to give him the warmth the boy longed for, the warmth every boy longed for. He came closer, the pony didn't move. In the same way the farmer remained seated in his wheelchair, so the pony remained standing. Too old and too stiff and probably too lame to move much anymore. There sat his boy, his tall, silent, skinny boy, not a Polack, a real Dutchman. He wanted so badly to be proud of his boy, the father did, but what he saw there gave him little reason for pride. "What are you doing back there?" the Polack asked.

"I'm pooping," the boy said, and now he was staring into space. Not as though he were in a trance, more like he was concentrating, as though he was trying to remember the key dates from a history lesson.

"But not in the stall, right?" the Polack said, and he came closer to his boy and placed his hand on his head. He could do that. Hugging would have been difficult in this situation, but a hand could be laid on the boy's head, a caring, protective hand. "You're not an animal, are you?" he said. "There must be toilets here you can use. And there's no toilet paper here in the box, what do you wipe yourself with, for god's sake?"

He looked around, as though he suspected that the boy had hidden rolls of toilet paper all around the box.

"With this," the boy said, and he took up a handful of straw and showed it to his father. He looked at him pityingly, as though he felt sorry for a man who didn't realize that you could wipe yourself with straw.

"This is where we go to the toilet," said the boy, and remained squatting because he was pooping and in his right hand he held the straw, probably straw the pony had stood on often, for the farmer was stingy with straw. It seemed as though the boy was trying to convince his father that he was a well-brought-up boy, that he wiped himself well, even under extreme conditions, even in this stall.

We. The Polack looked from the animal to his boy and back at the crippled pony again. "What does the hired hand say about this?" the Polack asked. "This isn't a people-toilet, is it? Is the hired hand supposed to clean up your poop? Not just the horse manure, but human feces too?"

His boy shrugged and the animal just stood there, immobile. The Polack couldn't tell whether it was in pain, but the immobility had him worried. "I'm going to see the farmer," he said. "Stay there. I'll be back in a minute."

He would talk to his wife about this later, first he had to arrange the vet. That had priority.

The Polack walked to the farmhouse, hurriedly, almost angrily, opened the kitchen door without knocking, and went into the living room. The farmer was asleep in his wheelchair by the window. The Polack remained standing on the far side of the table, and again he smelled that curious odor, this time mixed with that of sweat.

From upstairs he heard a knocking that went on and on. It kept getting louder. Someone up there was in trouble. It was as though a force outside the Polack was pulling him, someone or something was reminding him of his true mission: there, upstairs, a living creature had to be saved, probably the farmer's wife.

Cautiously, he opened the door to what he guessed were the stairs, then went up. The steps creaked, but he didn't feel like a burglar, he was used to forcing his way into homes. His self-confidence had returned. It was the fireman's sense of responsibility that led him up those stairs.

A boy who spoke of "we" in reference to himself and a pony. A boy who pooped beside his pony, in a cold, unheated stall. A father should worry about that. But first, someone here needed saving.

He was self-assured he was, but also tense. There was no fire, but he was prepared for anything, he had been trained to be prepared for anything.

The staircase smelled like raw sewage. Upstairs was a little hallway with three doors. He opened the first one, the smell of sewage grew stronger. A child's room, or at least what had once been a child's room, there was still a crib in it. He opened a cupboard. No clothing, only a few wooden toys. Blocks, no longer of this day and age. Empty drawers. A sink.

He opened the second door. There she lay, wide awake, eyes open, her face reminded him of an old queen, but then an unkempt version of that.

She had seen him, but she didn't make a sound. No scream, no cry for help, she looked as though she'd been expecting him.

He came a few steps closer. On a nightstand was a plate of gingerbread, or something that looked like it. The gingerbread had been spread with butter or margarine, the knife still lay beside it. The Polack had to fight back the urge to gag, even though he had absolutely nothing against gingerbread, but the way it lay there, so paltry, so old, so untouched, that was what made him nauseous. The plate had once been broken, someone had gone to the trouble of gluing together the two halves.

She looked better than her husband, her eyes were clearer. Her skin had suffered less from cold, sun and wind.

"Good evening." He had planned to introduce himself, and wondered for a moment about what he would do if the hired hand came in now. He would feel caught red-handed, even though there was really no reason for that. What was he supposed to say to the woman? Do you need help? Was that you knocking?

"Who are you?" she asked. Her voice sounded weak and hesitant, but at least she was speaking.

"I'm a fireman," the Polack said. He crossed his arms.

She looked at him and then shook her head. "No you're not," she said. She sounded convinced and maybe even a tad disappointed, as though she would have preferred him to be a fireman after all.

"I'm not in uniform," the Polack said, "I bought a pony from your husband. Now she's crippled."

She nodded. "Aha," she said quietly. Her concentration seemed to be slipping, she looked at the yellow blanket she was lying under. An old, faded blanket. There were spots on it that had never come out in the wash. Tomato soup, or blood. Or strawberry jam. She turned her gaze on him again. "You're tall," she said.

The Polack took a few more steps and now he was standing beside her. He could have caressed her, as though she was his own mother. It was probably inappropriate for him to be here. He was in search of a veterinarian, but a fireman is susceptible to cries for help. You were a fireman around the clock, twenty-four hours a day, even on your days off, even though some of his colleagues said things used to be different. Back then you used to *be* with the fire department, now you *worked* for it.

The Polack saw that the woman was strapped down, with old-fashioned leather straps that, like everything in this house, looked like they came from a previous century. Previous century or not, though, old people who were confused shouldn't be tied to their beds, and this woman wasn't even confused. He placed his left hand on the yellow blanket, making sure it didn't touch the old farmer's wife's body.

"They've tied you down," he said, because he wasn't sure whether she herself was aware of that, and he noticed that he was actually unsure again of exactly what his role was here. Was he his boy's father, the father who needed a vet, or was he in fact the man who wanted to help people in trouble? That there was someone in trouble here seemed clear enough to him. How was she supposed to get away if a fire broke out? If only in view of the measures people could and should take to protect themselves against the risk of fire, and in particular against possible smoke inhalation, he felt it was undesirable for the farmer to have strapped his wife to her bed.

"Did somebody maybe tie you down, ma'am?" he asked, just to be sure. The first time he had spoken it as a statement and there had been no reaction, so probably he should just ask. They had taught him that during his training. Not to go racing like an idiot into a burning building. To stop and think for a moment before doing something. If there's time to talk to the person who's called the emergency number, then talk to them. He or she may have vitally important information.

"Oh." She looked at him in a way that made him sense she had no desire to waste words on the matter. She was strapped down, that was just the way things went, she'd gotten used to it.

He wanted to go back downstairs now, he had no further business being here. You needed to know your place, helping people in distress was one thing, but when a person didn't want help then you had to turn and go, especially when you were off duty.

She examined him, with greater clarity than just a minute earlier, and it was this look that kept him standing there.

"I've been waiting for the fire department for so long, I've called them so often," she said. "Back then. But you people never came. So after a while I just gave up."

"You called the emergency number?" the Polack asked.

Should he offer to help her sit up a bit? She was lying there so awkwardly. He did it anyway. With a hand under each of her armpits, he moved her up higher onto the pillows. She was light as a feather. Despite the straps, it was no problem. She could escape if she felt like it, with a little effort, but apparently she didn't feel like it.

"I could tell you all kinds of nasty things about my husband," she said clearly. "But a wife always stands by her man. No matter what he does. She stands by him."

"True enough," the Polack said, "and I don't want to stick my nose into your business. If your husband wants to tie you to the bed and you have no real objection to that, then that's between you and your husband. But, as a fireman, I have to warn you. As a fireman, I feel that's irresponsible." He looked around. "Perhaps, with a bit of effort, you could wriggle your way out of those straps, but in the event of a fire, that would involve a loss of precious time. This place is something of a fire trap. It's an old house, it could burn down in no time."

Was Borys still squatting out there in the box? He needed to talk to the farmer. "My husband doesn't want me to come downstairs," she said, "it gets on his nerves, maybe because he can't get up here himself anymore. It's never nice when someone else can do what you can't. And the hired man brings me food. He strokes me too. I've got nothing to complain about. I'm fine right where I am. Sometimes I move around a little. In the morning I get washed, then I walk around the room a bit. As far as I'm still able. The hired hand helps me. If I need to, I can knock on the wall with my right hand, then they hear me downstairs. The world outside this room is way too big for me anyway, too scary. I'll be honest with you, mister fireman, it's too big and too scary."

The Polack nodded thoughtfully and started walking toward the door.

"You're tall," she said again.

At the door, he said: "I'll speak to your husband about fire prevention. Since I'm here anyway."

She waved her hand. Whether she was waving to him or signaling to him, he couldn't tell. "This is my nest," she said. "I'm fine right here. Sometimes I can hear the radio from downstairs. Or the TV. The news. My husband always turns the TV on loud, downstairs, so I can listen in too. Music's fine, but when the news comes on I crawl way down under the blankets. Even if you can't see the pictures . . . I wait until I hear them doing the weather report. And often enough it takes me an hour to recover. I don't want the world to get into this room. Do you understand that, Mister Fireman? I don't want to be chased out of my nest. So don't go talking to my husband about fire prevention. That would only mess things up."

Once again, he hesitated. Was he supposed to promise her now to act, when he saw her husband, as though he'd never been up here? As though he'd never seen her? Did she want to run the risk of burning to death, in exchange for a little peace and quiet?

"I have to go now," he said. "I came here for a veterinarian. I bought a pony from your husband for my son, and now she's sick. Crippled."

"Do we still have ponies? I thought we didn't have any animals anymore." She stretched out her hand to him, not to grab him, it was as though she was pointing at the stable, at where the animals had once been, where she herself had walked back before the world became too scary.

He approached her again, he had to bid her a polite farewell, maybe arrange the blanket for her. He meant to take her hand but he missed, he grabbed only her forefinger and so he shook that. Carefully, because she was brittle. Clearheaded but brittle.

Then he walked out quickly. He closed the door behind him, as he went out she shouted: "Careful, don't bump your head!"

He went straight to the farmer, who was still asleep in his wheelchair. He laid a hand on the man's shoulder. "Oh, it's you," the farmer said. His voice sounded wheezy again, it was hard for him to breathe.

"I'm here for the pony," the Polack said. "I want a vet to have a look at her. My boy's attached to that animal. He can't get along without her."

"That animal needs to be killed," the farmer said. "That boy of yours will find another one, ponies aplenty. Far too many, in fact."

"I bought that animal." The Polack didn't want to raise his voice, but he did want to show that he was serious, and so he pronounced each word with emphasis. "I want a vet to come and look at her. Even though the animal's staying in your stable, I paid for it."

"If you pay for the vet, I'll call him for you. You folks always think you know best. You folks think that death's such a tragedy." Then the farmer started whistling, or at least he made attempts to whistle, every now and again it actually sounded like something, and the Polack understood that the farmer must once have whistled a lot, and that their conversation was now over. He whistled to chase away the visitor, and the visitor let himself be chased away. Some other time he would start in about fire prevention and the peculiar practice of tying old people to their beds.

In the box the boy was still squatting, and the Polack, who had actually expected the boy to be finished by now, walked right over to him and squatted down beside him. The pony didn't move, she only turned her head and looked at father and son with eyes that made the Polack uneasy, because he saw melancholy in them, a silent sorrow. Only his imagination, probably, but still. Animals knew what melancholy was.

"Why are you still sitting there?" the Polack asked. "It's way too cold in here. Why are you still sitting like that?"

"Nothing's come out yet," the boy said, "it always takes a while. And I sit fine, right here."

The boy ran his hand through the straw beside him, and the father rested his left hand on the dirty straw. He resolved to ask the hired hand how often the box was actually cleaned out, the box he was paying for.

"We're going home," he said to his boy. "A vet's going to come and look at her."

The boy nodded. He stood up, grabbed some straw and wiped between his buttocks. "I always wipe, just to be sure," he said. "Even if nothing came out."

The boy pulled up his underpants and his trousers, he had three pairs of these same trousers, his mother had bought them in three different colors.

The Polack took Borys's bike and this time he didn't walk out in front, he walked beside the boy with one hand on the bike, and the boy said: "Manya loves those big carrots. She eats four or five of them in one afternoon."

5

"I'm also a hunter," the veterinarian said.

The Polack hadn't quite caught the man's name. Klepp. Or Klemp. It didn't matter. They were standing in the farmyard, this time the farmer was out of sight for a change, and the vet himself did indeed look more like a hunter than a veterinarian, like someone who liked shooting animals more than healing them. He was a good deal older than the Polack, with the mien of someone who thinks about his retirement every day, as though he were only a semi-veterinarian still, his spirit had raced ahead of him to the Costa del Sol, but despite that there was something vigorous about him. He wore a cap, with a few shiny gray hairs sticking out from under it.

Standing beside the Polack was his boy, it was an important day for him. The Polack was nervous, the animal's life hung in the balance now and with it, indirectly, that of his son. He zipped up his blue jacket. The jacket was a left-over from a skiing holiday. The holiday hadn't been much of a success, skiing was for a different sort of person. Wen enjoyed it, the Polack hadn't felt comfortable at the resort; he didn't like skiing either, he was too afraid of falling and too proud to admit it. At night the disco kept him awake, and when they got home a week later and the Polack was hanging up the jacket he'd bought specially for the trip, he said: "We're never doing that again. If our boys absolutely have to try out snowboarding, later on, let them go to SnowWorld, here around the corner." Throwing away a jacket like that would have been a waste, and besides, it was warm. This morning he had taken it out of the closet because he was going to meet the vet. He wanted to look decent for the veterinarian.

"Hunting and healing are not contradictory," Klep said. "The hunter heals by hunting. I also enjoy it, of course, but at the end of the day I do it for the animals. I help contribute to maintaining the natural balance. The hunter and the veterinarian co-exist, in perfect harmony. I became a vet because I loved hunting, and I started hunting because I always wanted to be a veterinarian, even as a child. Not everyone understands that, only those with ears to hear can understand."

The Polack wanted to be one of those with ears to hear. In the presence of the hunter who was also a veterinarian, he realized how much he wanted that, and if only for that reason he decided to understand the man. He had neither an affinity for nor anything against hunting, he just thought it was a puzzling hobby. As far as that went, it was easier for him to understand people who spent entire weekends out fishing.

Klep went on talking, but the Polack's mind was wandering, so he just went on nodding until he noticed that the veterinarian was looking at him in silence, undoubtedly waiting for a sign of assent, or at least something more than a nod. Feeling caught out, the Polack mumbled: "Sure, that's right."

"What's right?" the vet asked.

The Polack laid his left hand on Borys's head. "It's about his pony," he said then, quietly yet insistently still. "She ran into a creek and since then she's been crippled. We need something to be done about it. We don't want to say farewell to her."

"Yeah, sure," Klep said impatiently. Did the pony irritate him? The Polack noticed now for the first time that the vet spoke with a slight accent. "We don't want to say farewell," Klep went on. "No one wants that, but if it has to happen anyway then they blame the doctor. Then they act as though it's his fault that they had to say farewell. Farmers are different, they know how things go in nature. They haven't been ruined yet by the idea that everything is so pitiful. All right, let's take a look."

The vet hurried out ahead, left the Polack and his boy behind, he seemed to have only one goal: the stable. He ran along the path in his high rubber boots as though he sought out the puddles on purpose and stomped in them like a naughty child that has shaken off its parents. He didn't look around, he raced into the stable. The Polack and his boy followed him. The sun was shining weakly. Borys skirted the puddles. He was wearing sneakers. The Polack tried to take his boy's hand, but the boy pulled back right away. He seemed ashamed of the man in the ski jacket, the man who was his father.

In the stall, Klep walked around the pony, felt her, thumped her on the back, fiddled with her mane. "Ah," he said, "my girlie. The last of the lot. They used to have twenty ponies and horses here, until the farmer got ill. Always kids around, twenty ponies and horses. He didn't want to get rid of them. They understand nature, but they're pigheaded, farmers are. At first the hired hand carried him to the stable, but they realized soon enough that that was too much, and most hired hands don't feel like dragging the farmer around with them. Gradually the horses and ponies here died off, the rest were sold along with most of the cows. No one wanted to have this girlie."

Klep pronounced the words "died off" with peculiar satisfaction, as though that was simply the comeuppance for a farmer who refused to come to grips with his own illness.

"It's her back paws," the Polack said.

The vet waggled his index finger. "With horses, I speak of legs, not paws. To me horses don't have paws, they have legs. They're noble animals. And a pony is a noble animal as well."

The vet moved up close to the animal, examined its legs, took its flesh between his fingers, had the animal raise one paw—the Polack refused to speak of legs, only people had legs—and after he had spent a little time doing something like stretching exercises with the animal, came back over to the Polack and his boy. The vet wiped his hands on a handkerchief, which he then folded neatly and put back in his pocket. "She's an old girl," he said, taking off his hat. His well-groomed gray hair was now fully visible, it gleamed from the styling gel. "An old girl," he repeated, and there was something in his voice that could have been a sob, as though he was talking about his own wife, still a girl, but grown old. "I can give her medicine, then she can go on for a while. But do you have any idea how expensive that is?"

"So what's the alternative?" the Polack asked. He didn't want to know what it cost yet, not with the boy around.

"The knacker's yard," said the veterinarian, and he adopted an expression that said he could easily understand that no one found that an attractive prospect. "We don't live forever," Klep said, after licking his lips, "nature has to do its work, but nothing really perishes. The tiniest particles are indestructible. That's what I cling to. For me, death is nothing but a transition from one physical state to the next, and which of those states is the most attractive is hard to say. I don't dread death, not at all."

To the Polack, the indestructibility of the tiniest particles seemed like scant consolation for his son. And all that talk about the transition from one state to the next got on his nerves too. Had he become a fireman for that? If life and death were a matter of transition from one state to the next, the firemen could just as well stay in their bunks.

"How much is it going to cost?" he whispered.

"I also do acupuncture," the veterinarian said in a tone that sounded as though he had never before told this secret to a complete stranger. "In fact, only for racehorses, but in exceptional situations for older horses too, when the owner clings to the horse, can't let it go, can't imagine living without it. I once had a man," the vet's voice grew deeper and quieter all the time, "say to me: 'I don't want to sit on a horse, I want to sit on *my* horse. I could care less about horses in general.' He couldn't say farewell to his animal. He could to his wife, but not to his animal. Well, that's where I come into the picture pretty quick."

The Polack took his boy's hand and this time Borys didn't pull it back. "Is there any prospect of recovery?" The Polack felt himself sweating, as though he were taking an exam.

"Relief," the veterinarian said. "There's a prospect of relief. Listen, the owners of racehorses, and I'm talking here about the creme de la creme, know what they're doing when they ask me to come by for acupuncture. I'm no magician, but there are racehorse owners who've said to me: 'Klep, you've performed a miracle.' Medicines offer relief, acupuncture can cure the old girlie."

Having said that, the vet smoothed his hair, although it was completely unnecessary, and put his cap back on.

The Polack rubbed his right cheek with his free hand, he felt the stubble growing there, and he asked as casually as he could: "What does that cost, acupuncture for a pony?"

The veterinarian, who was no magician but only performed wonders from time to time, brought his mouth up close to the fireman's ear and for a moment the Polack thought the man was going to kiss him, but all he wanted was to whisper an amount to the fireman, an amount that came as a major shock to the Polack. Fair is fair, he was horribly shocked: the amount made him nauseous, he felt like gagging. His son must have sensed that, because he yanked himself free and the Polack said right away: "What must be, must be."

"Deal," said the vet with only mild enthusiasm. Had he taken the Polack for someone who would say: that's too expensive for me? Had he taken him for someone who didn't have enough money to save the animals around him from their demise? "I can't get started right this moment, I don't have my things with me, but I've got a slot tomorrow afternoon. I'll do what I can for the poor old girl." He slapped the pony on the back; the animal itself didn't make a sound.

"And where can I send the invoice?" the veterinarian asked as he picked up his bag from the straw.

He noted the Polack's address in his pocket diary, looked around at the big stable that could hold more than twenty horses but now housed only one sick pony, and walked out together with the Polack and his boy.

The vet talked and talked, he was obviously in a good mood now, he said that a good hunter was the best friend to animals that he could imagine, he told them about all the things he'd shot and added that he had hunted on every continent except for North and South America and Australia. "Otherwise, I've been everywhere," he said, "it's the only luxury I permit myself. And I enjoy hunting in Holland, but Africa, of course, is the real thing. Down there the hunt feels different, there you can still sense something of the old way of hunting, the real hunting, down there you shoot at other things besides just a pheasant or a deer, that's obvious. Pheasant's excellent eating, sure. A good hunter, and I count myself among the best hunters in this country of ours, doesn't kill his animals with a bullet, he tickles them to death, he kisses them to death."

By then the three of them had reached the farmhouse.

"How will I know if the treatment is working?" the Polack asked, and the veterinarian who kissed animals to death said that he should wait a while and then call him. "You've got my number, right? Here's my card."

"Klepp," the card read. "Veterinary surgeon." And then an address and a telephone number.

The Polack stuck it in his pocket. The vet climbed into his car and drove away slowly.

The Polack placed a hand on his skinny son's shoulder and said: "We have to wait and see, of course, but your pony won't have to go to the horse butcher. You can count on that. No horse butcher for that animal."

The boy nodded.

"Are you happy?" the Polack asked.

"Hmm," said the boy.

"Are you really happy?"

"Yeah, sure," the boy said. "Can't you tell? But Dad, do you believe in acupuncture? What is it, anyway?"

"Needles," the Polack said. "Needles that they stick into you. I think acupuncture is going to help, but we have to be realistic. Your pony's not exactly young anymore. And we all die sometime. The most important thing is that we're happy that you're doing better. Your problem with bowel movements was driving us to despair. It made us so sad."

"I couldn't stop the bowel movements, they came by themselves."

"That's right," the Polack said. "They came by themselves. Your mother and I, in any case, are very happy that they're not coming by themselves anymore. Even if you do poop in the stall, beside that animal. Later on you really need to try not to go to the toilet in the stall anymore, only in the toilet, for humans, that's what I do too. I don't go and squat down in a stall. I wouldn't dream of it."

"No," the boy said. "That's not something you'd do."

"And you talk to that animal too?"

"Yeah," said the boy.

"What do you tell it?"

The boy shrugged. "All kinds of things. Stories."

"What kinds of stories?" the Polack wanted to know. "Wouldn't you like to tell me those stories? Or your mother? We know so little about you. It's puberty. It starts early. Your mother says so. But you could tell us something too, sometime, couldn't you?"

"I don't have that much to say. It'll come sometime, when I've got time."

And the Polack pressed his hand down harder and more lovingly on his boy's shoulder and asked: "Shall I toss your bike in the back?"

The boy answered: "No, I think I'll stay here for a little while. I'll be home pretty quick."

Borys walked away, after a few steps he turned, came back. "Thanks, Dad," the boy said. "Thank you for the acupuncture." And he hugged his father, kissed him. The Polack was startled, because that almost never happened. He held the boy to his chest, very tight, and he said: "Of course. Of course, son. I know how important that old beast is to you."

At that, the boy pulled away. "It's not a beast. Her name is Manya."

"No, no, not a beast," said the Polack. He climbed in the car and drove home, and as he did he realized: that boy needs love, more love. But how do you give that? More caressing, the Polack supposed, more cuddling, more attention. There had to be more cuddling. He resolved to start with that right away, tomorrow.

When he got home he said nothing at first, his wife was busy in the kitchen and he helped her. He enjoyed cooking, he liked to cook for the men at the firehouse. Even if the means there were limited, he always tried to make something festive out of it.

Wen was fixing Thai curry and the Polack settled down to making the salad that went along with it. Only when his wife finally asked how things had gone with the vet did he say that they had probably found a solution. And after that he said nothing more for a while, and when the salad was more or less ready he told her that the animal was going to get acupuncture. Wen started laughing. "Seriously?" She laughed hard. On the floor in the kitchen, the youngest was playing with a colander, a wooden spoon, and some blocks. Again he said "monka, monka, monka," until his mother handed him his monkey.

"Seriously," the Polack said, and he told her that the veterinarian treated racehorses and achieved results with them that some people called "miracles," and then Wen wanted to know what it cost, a miracle like that, yes, she came up and stood right in front of her husband as though she was going to kiss him, as though they were lovebirds and had known each other only a few weeks, as though their desire had not yet been gnawed down by habituation and time. "What's a miracle like that cost?" she asked. "What are they asking these days for a miracle like that?" The Polack looked at the rice in the pan, he took one step aside, stirred the curry a bit while he pronounced the amount that the miracle was going to cost them. Per treatment. It wasn't a one-time miracle and then never again. A weekly miracle. At least that's how he'd understood it. His wife fell silent. He looked up. The color had left her face. That never happened otherwise, not when money was involved, not when other things were involved either. "Jesus," she said, "that animal's going to ruin us, Geniek."

Geniek, she almost never called him that. Wen walked to the other side of the kitchen. She had bought flowers, she liked having flowers around the house. The flowers were still in their paper wrapper, in a bucket. She took the wrapper off the bouquet and began cutting the stems and arranging the flowers. She took a long time doing it, and then she said again: "That animal's going to ruin us." She didn't look at her husband, she looked at the flowers and he replied: "Don't make such a production out of it, that's not like you."

The curry was finished, it only had to be served. Wen brought the vase to the living room and when she came back, she asked: "Where are we going to come up with that?"

"Well, we just won't go to Greece this year," the Polack said, slightly irritated. "We'll go to the Eifel instead. You can rent houses there for next to nothing. That's where my mother was born."

"What would I do in the Eifel?" Wen asked. "What am I supposed to do there? I could just as well stay at home. It rains in the Eifel. Even if your mother was born there. I don't want to go there."

"It doesn't rain all the time," the Polack said, "the sun shines too, even in the Eifel," and he threw an arm around Wen's waist and lifted her up onto the counter, beside the cutting board where he had just been slicing tomatoes for the salad, as though his desire had not yet been gnawed down by routine and a lack of time, by things that just happened to be part of a person's life. An adult without a lack of time is a useless person. "It's for our boy. I didn't have a choice. I told you already what he does there in the box, he talks to that animal, he tells her all kinds of things and he goes to the toilet in the box. He doesn't poop in his pants anymore because he poops in the box, he squats down there beside that animal. He uses straw for toilet paper, but you and I, we know that he's happy there, so what difference does that money make? I'll take it from my revolving credit."

He shouldn't have said that. His wife, who had been listening and nodding the whole time, slid down off the counter. She said: "I hate being in debt, you know that. No debts. I can't stand debts. They keep me awake at night. I can't think about anything else, only those debts. Even when we're having sex, all I can think about are our debts." The Polack said: "Okay, then I'll start taking on some odd jobs, on my days off. I'll ask the guys at the firehouse if they know of anything." And he added: "He needs more love. We have to cuddle him more."

Then Borys came home. They heard him come in, they heard the front door open and close, the boy didn't speak. They heard him walk into the living room and when they went and looked he was sitting at the table there, because it was dinnertime.

"Are you hungry?" Wen asked.

"Not really," the boy said.

"You're all sweaty."

"I biked fast."

"Could you help set the table?"

"Sure," he said, and the tall boy set the table in silence. He did it slowly, at last they could sit down. Wen dished up the curry and the Polack said it tasted good. Jurek went into his highchair and got a bowl of mashed food, the Polack chewed the salad he had made himself, until he said: "That animal's going to get acupuncture. I told your mother about it, and she's glad."

Wen nodded. "Yes," she said. "I'm glad that the pony can stay with you for a while, hopefully it can stay with you for a real long time. We're glad. For you, Borys."

A little smile appeared on the boy's face. And then he asked: "May I go upstairs now?"

"We've still got mango for dessert," Wen said.

The boy ate his mango hurriedly, uninterestedly in fact, it seemed impossible to the Polack that his boy could be enjoying it, even though mango was something special, they didn't have mango every day, and when the boy had knocked back his helping, he asked again if he could go upstairs. Wen nodded. "I love you," the Polack shouted as he boy climbed the stairs, and then they were sitting there alone at the table with their youngest son, they listened to Jurek's brabbling ("mango, mmm"), until Wen lifted him from his highchair to bring him to bed. "How do you think they do that?' she asked. "Acupuncture for a pony like that? Do they use knitting needles?"

"I don't have the slightest," the Polack said.

The Polack began clearing the table, and when he was done he said: "I'm on duty tomorrow. I'm going to go and lie down now."

He crawled into bed and later, when both boys were asleep, Wen crawled in beside him and his desire was not entirely dead, but he did nothing with it, because he was on duty tomorrow. His desire he saved for after work.

The next morning he greeted his colleagues at the firehouse, who were actually his second family. He leafed through the paper a bit, and the day passed the same way many others had, with sports and waiting, checking the vehicles, a drill. They were called out twice, both times it proved to be a false alarm, and at the end of the afternoon they got the message that they had to respond to a jumper, outside their deployment area. The other firehouse was too busy dealing with a fire in the kitchen of a retirement home.

They drove to the jumper. The police were already there. The platform was crowded. The express train to Amsterdam was standing still at the little station where it usually thundered past. Beckers said: "I always feel so sorry for those engineers."

The Polack looked at the people on the platform and at the train. Lots of kids, younger ones too. They were standing up at one end, they didn't want to go home, they probably knew the jumper. The Polack was already up close to the locomotive, where it was cordoned off, where curious passersby couldn't come anymore, only the emergency services.

In the distance he saw the squad commander talking to the police, and to the children who were wearing backpacks, carrying book bags and soft drinks, wearing headphones. Beckers stood waiting beside the Polack, his hands on his hips. Beckers didn't like these calls, no one did. "If only for that reason, I'd never want to be an engineer," Beckers said.

The Polack wanted to finally get out onto the rails to do the work that actually wasn't a job for the fire department, but the squad commander came up to him and he said: "You're staying here."

"Why?" the Polack asked.

"You're staying here," the squad commander repeated.

"Why?" the Polack asked again.

The squad commander ran his hand over his mouth and said: "It's your boy. It's Borys."

The Polack pushed the squad commander aside, he pushed Beckers aside, he pushed everyone aside and was the first one onto the tracks. He was going to scrape his boy off the rails.

Colleagues came up behind him and tried to stop him, but he beat them away.

He wanted to scrape his boy off the rails and off the locomotive, all by himself.

III

A MIRACLE

1

"We're going to pull you through this," the squad commander told him. "We're not going to let you folks down."

The Polack had been put on leave, of course, and his wife too. Now they stayed home and walked from one room to the other, from downstairs to upstairs and back again. They held their youngest boy in their arms, taking turns, sometimes they put him in his baby bed, because he needed to sleep, their arms got tired, they were afraid of dropping him. They looked at him and they knew without having to say so that they were both afraid of the same thing.

And the Polack asked his wife whether she thought their youngest boy missed his brother, whether he noticed that he wasn't at home, or if it seemed to him more like Borys must be on a field trip. Should they tell him about it, the Polack wanted to know, and if so, what should they tell him? What was he already aware of, and what not? Should they wait till he was older? The Polack thought it was better to wait till later, a moment would come for them to say it, when he was older, when they could show him a photo, but when exactly? And Wen said: "We'll see." She picked up her youngest boy and took him upstairs, laid him on the changing table there to give him a clean diaper. What did she see when she looked at the little boy, who was now the one remaining boy, the boy they may have neglected because all the attention had gone to the soiled pants and the pony and his older brother's silences? His uncommunicativeness that at times had felt like sullenness, his desire to be left alone, to not be hassled, but then Wen had always said: "That's the way boys are. Girls are very different."

They went back downstairs and he looked at their youngest son as he was carried around the house, but the Polack saw only the tracks. He had the feeling that from now on he would see Jurek on the tracks too, loose parts, never in one piece again. He wasn't afraid of it, he would love this boy too in that way, in pieces and all. The Polack would love Jurek's left foot, his right arm, and he would love an ear, an eye. Love each individual body part. It was up to God, or what passed for God, to make it whole again.

The men from the C squad came by, they sat on the couch in the living room and in the spare chairs that the Polack brought in from other rooms, even the garden chairs had to be brought in, and the squad commander said: "If there are too many of us, you folks just say so."

"There aren't too many of you," the Polack answered.

Wen's parents came, they didn't stay long because they were old and it was difficult for them. They summed up all the family members who had decided to take their own lives, and there were quite a few. A great-uncle, an aunt, a great-grandfather, a second-cousin, a nephew. When they couldn't come up with anyone else, they ran through the people in the village who had decided to end it all, and they went way back, to somewhere around 1950. Then Wen's mother mentioned the men who drank themselves to death, because those men had essentially taken their own lives too. At last they went home, because they didn't know where else to take their sorrow, they didn't want to burden their daughter with it.

Some of Wen's colleagues came to visit, looking grave, some of them had tears in their eyes. Those tears made the Polack uncomfortable, he didn't like that, it seemed to him that Wen's colleagues were claiming a sorrow that didn't belong to them. The C squad came by again. They talked so loudly that you couldn't hear Wen's colleagues anymore. Wen's visitors left at a certain point; the men of the C squad stayed. There was coffee, and someone had brought a pie. And the squad commander said again: "We're going to pull you through this." He wasn't much of a talker, he said only the bare minimum, but what he said was worthwhile. That was precisely what made the Polack respect him, and he had a sense of humor too, even if he didn't let it show very often. Quiet humor, hidden humor.

So the Polack sat silently, but proudly too, beside his men. Proud to have colleagues like this, proud that he had a wife and a son and a house and a job, he said nothing about how he saw his sons only as individual body parts now, a left foot, an ear, a nose. The men exchanged anecdotes, recalled colleagues now retired who were once fond of kidding and practical jokes, the kind of practical jokes that aren't pulled anymore, that wouldn't be tolerated anymore. Some of the men went out and came back with beer, but the reason for them being there was never broached, about the boy who vanished, who had stumbled, which is what the Polack said when asked. "He stumbled," the Polack said when pressed. Some deaths are a disgrace, others less so, and the Polack had no intention of living with any greater disgrace than he absolutely had to.

Beckers went to the toilet, he came back and said: "Your guys' paint job could use some fixing up. How about if we do that?" And Beckers and the other men went to buy paint to do the hallway, while the Polack and Wen sat in the living room with their youngest son on their lap. The Polack tried to join in the work, but Beckers said: "Stay where you are. We'll do it."

And Wen said: "Maybe we should go on vacation."

The Polack replied: "I can't even think about that."

Someone from the victims' assistance organization called to ask if they were interested in coming in for a talk, completely free of charge. "There's someone from victims' assistance on the line," the Polack said to his wife. "Whether we want to talk to someone, completely free of charge."

"We're not victims," Wen said. "And we don't want to talk to anyone."

The Polack passed that along to the lady on the phone, who said that if they changed their minds later on they could always call. Then Wen said: "Tell them to send someone over. Then we can check that one off the list." When no one was looking and no one was listening, she cried. Then the Polack would take her in his arms and say: "We had some bad luck, we were lucky for a long time."

"Sure," she said, "we were lucky for a long time. We have to go through this alone, we each have to get through this in our own way."

A lady from the victims' assistance organization came over and talked and asked questions and then Wen said: "We have to deal with this in our own way, we don't really need anyone. Especially not any professionals."

"We're not victims," the Polack explained. "We're the parents of a boy who had some bad luck. We have another son, too, and we assume that he's not going to have bad luck."

They sat on the couch, ramrod straight, and when the woman from victims' assistance stood up the Polack said: "Sorrow is a fire that breaks out, but we're going to put out that fire together. Still, nice of you to come by."

A few days later the C squad came to finish the hallway and Beckers said: "Your bedroom could stand repainting too. Is it okay with you if we do that? That sleeps a whole lot nicer, a freshly painted bedroom."

Wen and the Polack thought that was fine, if that's what they meant by "we're going to pull you through this," then let them by all means give the bedroom a touch-up. While they sat downstairs with their youngest son, the furniture above was dragged around and the room painted.

That's why the squad commander had become a fireman, that's why the men of C squad had become firemen, to pull people through things. Although it used to be better, back when there was more solidarity, the C squad still lived in a past that was better, the C squad wasn't your modern-day squad, this squad was different. And the wives of the men from C squad came by with food. They said: "You two probably don't feel much like cooking right now." Beckers's wife came and stood by the men. She took the Polack's hand and said: "I have three kids, I just wish I could give one of them to you."

"That's really nice of you," the Polack said. "But you don't have to do that."

And they ate, Wen and he, they ate reluctantly but they ate. The wives of C squad came by with even more food, and Wen and the Polack told each other that it tasted nice, even though they didn't taste much and the Polack had almost no appetite and Wen said: "I've had so many sweets already. I'm completely full." But she had eaten almost no sweets at all. They were just full. Chock-full.

The men wanted to go on painting, there were still some rooms they hadn't painted and those could use a dab of paint too, one of them even started talking about how they could unclog the toilets, but that wasn't necessary at all. The toilets were not in need of unclogging. The men wanted to have something to do. Just sitting around drove them crazy. The Polack understood that, but he said: "Okay, that's enough." Because all that painting and dragging furniture around was starting to get on Wen's nerves.

They all stood together there, in the freshly painted hallway, the men of C squad, they barely fit in the hallway, they were all squeezed in together, some of them had to hang over the backs of others. The squad commander took a picture and said to the Polack: "Get in there. You need to be in this too." And then he took another picture. All of them were looking at the screen, content, united, bound by solidarity, this was what comrades were about, this was what it meant to pull someone through. Again, they had pulled someone through.

After that, all the visitors left and they were home alone at last, Wen and the Polack. They stood at the foot of their bed like children in front of the lion cage at the zoo, and they smelled the paint in the bedroom. The men had done it neatly, and fast. They lay down on the bed with their youngest son between them.

The Polack asked: "Are the paint fumes okay for him?" But Wen said: "If we can take it, so can he."

The funeral had gone right past the Polack. He knew that he had been there, even if it didn't feel that way. He had been unable and unwilling to say a thing, he had gone up to the front when Wen insist- ed, and somehow was able to open his mouth: "I can't say anything." That was what he'd said. At Wen's urging, he had stood there like that. "That's the way you are normally anyway," Wen said. "You stand there and you don't say much." That was why he had stayed there like that, the way he normally was.

Wen had spoken, said something lovely, touching, he had forgot- ten exactly what it was she said, he hadn't been able to listen closely either, and the elementary school teacher had spoken and the junior high homeroom teacher, more a child than a man, with lots of acne, and two boys from Borys's class had read a poem that didn't rhyme but that touched everyone anyway, and the Polack's father, who wanted nothing to do with the past but in this case was willing to make an exception, came in from Haarlem. He sat there with his new family and looked the way he always looked, threatening and distracted at one and the same time. He looked like someone who knew that life was no laughing matter, but that's the way he looked, not only at cremations but also at weddings, and back when he went to the local fair as a kid, that's the way he'd looked too. He hugged the Polack and the Polack let it happen, the hug from the father who had sworn off the past in order to escape from suffering, and afterward the Polack's jaw felt like iron. The Polack thought that his mouth would never shut right anymore, as though it was stuck and would always remain open a crack. Fortunately, the Polack's father hadn't started in about mercy and heaven, because he was a man of the old school and men like that believed there could be no mercy for those who stumbled on purpose. And the men of C squad sat there, with their wives, some of them had brought their children along too. The older children, the ones who could take it, who you didn't feel you had to shelter, because this was a part of life. The ones for whom it was maybe a good thing to have experienced.

And then it was over. They went home.

The squad commander said: "Let us know when you're ready to come back. There's no hurry. These things take time."

The Polack took his time; his appetite hadn't come back, he ate reticently, sometimes he took a bite and felt like throwing up. Every three days he called the squad commander and said: "Things need a little more time."

"I understand that," the squad commander replied.

But the Polack didn't want to talk about it with Wen, he didn't want her to see that he was about to throw up whenever he had to eat.

The lady from victims' assistance came by again. "We can do this on our own," Wen told her. The lady left her business card, and Wen told her husband: "I have no desire to cry on some stranger's shoulder."

The Polack nodded. "Those people from victims' assistance won't take no for an answer."

And after about three weeks, it was Wen who said: "I'm going back to work. I called and told them I'll be coming in tomorrow."

"That's fine," the Polack said. "I think I'll go back soon too. We need to move on."

"We need to move on," Wen answered, "we have another child too."

And that evening when they were lying in bed, Wen tapped the dial on her wristwatch and said: "It's about time again."

"What?" the Polack asked.

She kept tapping the dial of her watch. "About time for what?" the Polack asked. "What are you talking about?"

Then she took off her watch and put it on the nightstand. "We haven't touched each other for so long," she said. "Just because our boy's gone doesn't mean we can't touch each other, does it?"

He wanted that too, to touch her, very much so, and for a little bit he did, with his big hands, but after that he said: "Let's go look in his room."

He was the first to get up, and she followed him to the door they hadn't opened this whole time. It wasn't that they'd talked about it, it was clear to both of them that they shouldn't go into that room. Only when Wen said that about it being time they touched each other again did the Polack think about the room, and he became curious. He really did want to see the room. He went there, wearing only his underpants, and Wen followed him in her nightshirt, which was really nothing more than a long T-shirt. He opened the door, turned on the light, breathed in the smell. It still smelled of the boy here, or was he imagining things?

They walked around his room barefooted. The bed was unmade, blue sheets, on the fitted sheet was a mark from a red felt-tip pen that had never come out in the wash. A pair of underpants lay on the floor, the Polack picked them up and sniffed at them. It was as though the boy could come home any moment. Computer games on the floor, some clothes, not even that many, *Donald Duck* comics, some other comic books too, soccer cards, a few old coins in a case the neighbor had given him, after which he had declared: "I think I'm going to start collecting old coins. Do you guys know how to do that?" After that time, they never heard him mention old coins again.

They went to his desk: pens, pencils, a dead mosquito, the pony's passport, an old pair of ski goggles, a couple of notebooks. The Polack opened one of them. Grammar exercises. Another notebook, more grammar exercises. A third notebook. A page had been torn from it and then stuck back in. Written on that page was: "I have no friends. I will never have friends. I never have had friends." Wen read it over his shoulder. The Polack closed the notebook, put it back in the exact spot where he'd found it, as though no one were to know that he had been in this room. Then they sat down on their boy's bed.

Under the pillow they found a pair of gym shorts and a chocolate bar, half eaten, turned white with age. "I told him so often," Wen said, "don't eat chocolate in bed. It makes nasty marks."

She sounded hoarse, as though she'd spent evenings on end in a bar with hard liquor and lots of cigarettes.

"Yeah," the Polack said. "You told him that all the time."

He stood up and Wen came after him, she took the chocolate with her. They closed the door of their boy's room behind them and both of them knew for sure—yes, that they both knew it, the Polack didn't doubt it for a moment—that they wouldn't be opening that door again for some time.

Their own room didn't smell of the boy, but it still smelled of paint. This time Wen didn't tap her watch, it was lying there on the nightstand. The Polack looked at it and realized that life went on, one's sex life too, that went on as well. On and on until it stopped. She laid her head against his arm and she said: "He didn't have any friends."

"Apparently not," the Polack said. He looked at his wife and didn't doubt that Wen was his woman, but for the moment he no longer knew how that went, intimacy. Being a man. Desire. Just like the desire for food, this desire too had been extinguished. There was only the memory of the desire. Vaguely he could recall what it was like to feel that.

Wen was busy setting up the alarm on her phone, because tomorrow she was going back to work. The kindergartners needed her.

"They came here to the door sometimes," Wen said, "friends of his. Back then. But he always said: tell them I'm not here. He really wanted to be alone."

"True enough," the Polack said. "He really wanted to be alone." And he tried to run his hand over Wen's hair, but it didn't go well. He couldn't summon up the tenderness. His hand was like sandpaper.

"Maybe we should have gone on asking more," Wen said, "but I did that so many times. So many times."

"He was a quiet kid," said the Polack. "Our Borys was." Fatigue overcame him, but still he knew he'd be unable to sleep.

"Should we have asked the teacher whether other kids were giving him a hard time?" Wen asked. "Or his homeroom teacher?"

"Why?" the Polack replied. "Did it seem like there was any reason to do that?"

"We still could."

"Too late for that now," said the Polack.

"We've still got Jurek," said Wen, messing with her phone, "if Jurek's quiet like that too, then we have to keep on asking. We'll never think that way again, like: oh, that's just the way he is."

"No," the Polack said. "We'll never think that way again."

He turned off the light and, as he lay there in the dark, he noticed that Wen wasn't sleeping either. But neither of them said a thing.

The next day, after Wen had gone to work—it had all taken long enough as it was and the Polack was home alone with his one remaining boy, he hadn't worked a shift yet, that would start tomorrow—a call came in the afternoon. The number wasn't in his contacts.

"She's better," he heard a man's voice say.

"Who's better?" the Polack asked.

The voice at the other end laughed. "Who do you think?"

"I really have no idea," said the Polack, with his one remaining boy on his arm.

"This is Klepp," the voice said, with more of an edge to it now and with that slight, unmistakable accent. "Klepp has performed yet another miracle. Klepp can't help it, he performs one miracle after the other. The old crippled girl is no longer crippled. She's still old, but there's nothing I can do about that."

"Oh, Christ," the Polack said, "the pony."

"Yes, the pony, who did you think I was talking about? Did you forget all about the poor beast? One moment life is but a vale of tears without the old girl, the next moment they don't even know who the old girl is. People, always the same song and dance. The bills haven't been paid either."

"The bills," the Polack said, walking to the kitchen where the unopened mail was lying on the counter.

"Yes, the bills," Klepp echoed. "Not that I'm only in it for the money, but if I tell someone beforehand what it costs to perform a miracle, then I really like to see that miracle paid for once it's been performed. I don't do it for the money, but I have to eat too. Even the vet isn't completely averse to money, much as he might have wished he was at times."

Among the unopened mail, the Polack found the bills. There were three letters from Klepp, two bills and a reminder.

"Haven't you heard what happened?" the Polack asked. "Didn't you read about it? It was in the paper, the obituary."

"What am I supposed to have read?" asked Klepp, and he sounded irritated, as though it annoyed him to hear that there were things in the paper that weren't about him and his miracles.

"Our boy is gone."

Klepp was silent for a moment. Then he said: "I'm sorry to hear that. My condolences. I'm really very sorry." And then he added: "I don't read the regional papers much, I actually only read the foreign press."

The Polack tore open the envelopes and, although the amounts were known to him, he was still shocked, maybe even more now that the boy was gone.

"Do you still want to see the miracle?" Klepp asked. "Shall I explain what I've done? Perhaps seeing the miracle will provide you with some comfort." And for the first time Klepp seemed hesitant, as though he too realized that his miracles were the kind of miracles that ultimately didn't comfort anyone.

"I'd like to see it," the Polack said. "When can we meet up?"

"I could come by this afternoon," Klepp said. "I have to be over close to the farm anyway."

The Polack said that he could be there in an hour. He stuffed the bills into his back pocket and bundled Jurek into his coat, mittens, and a wool cap, one Wen's mother had knitted for him.

"We're going to look at your brother's pony," he said to his one remaining boy. "We're going to see a miracle."

2

The hunter was pacing back and forth in front of his car, cap on his head and bag in hand, as though he were on guard duty. Apparently the ground was still too muddy for the bag, although it was an old bag that must have met with plenty of filth before.

After the Polack parked and lifted his remaining son from the car seat, the hunter stopped pacing and became the vet again. He stood still and, with the stern yet still-understanding look of a man in authority, watched as the Polack walked toward him with his child on his arm. Healing was his profession, hunting merely a hobby.

The farmer was sitting at the window again, chin in hand. The Polack couldn't see if the farmer was asleep or keeping an eye on things, but then he hadn't really bothered to take a good look. What the farmer was up to didn't matter now, now that his son didn't come here anymore. His attention was focused on the vet, on whom his hopes had been fixed while his boy was still alive, the vet who sent bills as though the pony were a racehorse for which money was no object. Now there was no longer any need to fix his hopes on the vet, the deal only had to be put to rest. And wasn't it his son who had been the racehorse for whom only the best was good enough? No, the boy had been no racehorse, more like a nag pulling something that had been too heavy for him.

"Again, my condolences," Klepp said. He spoke quietly, as though it were a secret the toddler was not supposed to hear. The secret of death, the secret of talking about death. Then he looked at the boy and asked: "Is this his little brother?"

"This is Jurek," the Polack said. "Our other son."

The vet tickled the other son under the chin, tickled his cheek and his nose and asked, in that same, solemn tone: "How did it happen? Was he ill?"

"He tripped," said the Polack. "At the train station. The express to Amsterdam was going by. He hadn't eaten much that day. He was dizzy."

"That's terrible," the vet said. "Did he have epilepsy? Some animals get that too, but different."

Without speaking further, he headed for the stable and the Polack followed, the other boy on his arm. Now that he was walking here, down this path, where he had only walked before with his son, the past became lively, livelier than during all those days when he and his wife had wandered aimlessly around their house. In those days the past had slowly faded, it had become shadowy, unreal, something that stood separate from the present and the future. The past seemed only to exist so that you could forget it, so that you could close the door on the past and then say: well, that was that. That door will never open again. Here in the farmer's yard, things felt different, and for a moment the Polack had the sensation of seeing his son's bike lying in front of the stable and the boy squatting beside the beast in its stall, with straw in his hand, looking at his father in surprise, in reproach too, not understanding why he had to be interrupted again.

The vet opened the stall door. The animal stood there the way it always had, still, unimpressed. The way the farmer sat in his wheelchair at the window, that's how the pony stood there in its stall.

"Yep," Klepp said, "the old girl doesn't have much of anyone to talk to anymore." And he tickled the old girl here and there, with the familiarity of someone who has been tickling young and old girls all his life.

With Jurek on his arm, the Polack moved a few steps closer. What the miracle looked like, that's what he wanted to see. That's what he had come for.

"Let's go for a little walk," Klepp said. "Outside you can see it better."

Then the vet led the old girl, easily, but also with a certain roughness, impatience actually, along the muddy path that ran to the pasture, for there, he'd said, was where he would demonstrate the miracle.

The old girl walked beside the vet, but since the Polack had never seen her walk before he couldn't tell the difference between the miracle and the lack of a miracle. He only wondered whether this was it, whether this was what he had come for.

"No longer lame," said the vet, "but old and lonely. She'll probably end up at the horse butcher's." And he let the animal parade a few times back and forth in front of the Polack. It was as though he wanted to prove that his steep bills were only correct, not a matter of greed, a reasonably modest reward for a miraculous rescue. Then he led the animal back to her stall, where the loneliness and the age were made bearable by roof and hay. The demonstration was sufficient, it hadn't taken long. The Polack would have to make do with this.

In fact, he didn't understand it one single bit. Not why he'd come and not why the vet had had him come. Had the man simply wanted to be sure that his invoices would be paid, even in this situation? He followed along behind the man and the animal, puzzled and also quite fatigued. This place was hard for him to bear, maybe even harder than his boy's room, the one that would not be opened again for a while. Everything here reminded him of his boy and the various and sundry pieces of the boy. Retroactively, it seemed as though the express train to Amsterdam thundered straight through these stables, straight through the farm, straight across the pasture. The Polack had simply never noticed it before. Now he thought about the horse butcher whom the vet had spoken of as offhandedly as he did about the hunt, but with less enthusiasm. The hunt was sublime; the horse butcher necessary at best.

Yet the Polack refused to believe that the veterinarian performed miracles solely for the benefit of the horse butcher. He had felt like reprimanding him for that. What a waste, he felt like saying, there's no need to slaughter the beast. She's been healed. But before he could do that, the vet said: "She won't be fit for human consumption anymore, but at the zoo they can always use an old girl like her."

"Does she have to go to the zoo?" the Polack asked, and he spoke of the old girl as though he had no say over her anymore. The word "zoo" rattled him. The animal belonged to his boy and now that the boy was no longer there, he was the one who should have taken care of the animal. To not do that was to betray Borys. It's was Klepp's autocratic bearing that put him on the defensive, that made him servile. The servility he had inherited from his father, and servility was something he'd always despised in his father. The Polack's father was a frightened man who bowed to anything that smacked of authority and wealth.

"The animals in the zoo have to eat too," the vet said, "but they're not picky about the quality of what they eat, not like we humans are. I've performed a miracle that will eventually become dinner for a lion or a tiger. Oh well, such is life." And having said that, the vet patted the Polack heartily on the shoulder. He did that in more or less the same way he had tickled the old girl. "Take your time and think about it," he said, "there's no hurry. Too bad it was all for nothing, but then again, nothing's every really for nothing. Meaning is everywhere, everything means something and most things mean way too much, a doctor sees that each and every day, and a hunter does too. I'll be getting back now, going to pay my respects to the farmer. He's also old and lonely."

The vet left the stall and the Polack remained behind with the old girl and his other son, who sat on his arm and babbled. ("Monka, car. Monka, car.") Till the Polack said: "That's not a monkey, that's a pony." He crossed the stall, it still felt strange without Borys, without him being here, he looked at the corner where he'd seen the boy squatting down but there was nothing there anymore. "Yeah, here," he said to the child on his arm, "this is where your brother lived. This is where he went after school." That's how it felt, too. In the stall his son had lived, everywhere else he'd merely existed.

The child on his arm seemed to be looking, seemed to be listening, the son who was still there, otherwise he didn't react. After the Polack had examined every corner of the stall, as though he expected to find traces of his eldest son, he went and stood in front of the pony, the old girl on whom miracles had been performed, miracles that had proven futile, but neither the vet nor the old girl could do anything about that.

He looked into the animal's eyes and in those eyes he saw nothing, and at the same time everything, you could see anything you wanted in them, but nothing was also okay. "What did he tell you about?" he asked quietly. "What did my boy say to you?"

He felt a stab of jealousy. Mourning was a word he'd avoided all these days, mourning was for others, for people who weren't strong. He was sad, but standing in front of the pony he realized that mourning was nothing compared to the jealousy he felt now. During his last weeks on earth, his boy had preferred the company of an old, lame animal to that of his parents. He had shared his secrets with this animal. All right, his parents had encouraged him to get out of the house, to make friends, to be less shy, but did that mean they had to be traded in for a pony? Was that what they deserved? Had he meant to punish them, their boy, was his death nothing but a punishment and had they been too stupid to understand why they were being punished?

The animal just stood there looking, and for a moment the Polack had the crazy idea that the old girl was going to speak back, that she would tell him everything he wanted to know if he simply asked.

"So what was it he told you?" he asked again, but there was no answer. The animal didn't react to his voice, it stood there stock-still. Would it stand stock-still before the horse butcher, too? Or would it finally speak? Would it finally open its damn mouth? Looking death in the eye, would it finally dare to tell the truth?

His remaining boy began to whimper. Was he hungry? Was the cap down too far over his eyes? "Easy," he said. "We'll go home in a little bit."

For a moment, the Polack was on the verge of cuddling the animal, the way he had cuddled with his son sometimes. Too rarely, but still. The Polack felt like pressing the beast against his chest, the old, lonely animal that the experts said would have to go to the horse butcher, but instead of caressing it he lashed out. He lashed out with his fist against the pony's muzzle. If you weren't going to speak of your own free will, then you had to learn to speak against your will. The animal began shaking, it kept looking at him. It accepted the blow the way it had accepted this stall and the miracle. "I'm sorry," said the Polack, and he ran his hand carefully over the animal's head. "I'm sorry," he said, "old girl."

Then he hurried out of the stall. No one must find out about this. What got into him? He'd hit his son's pony because it refused to speak. Fortunately, the one remaining boy had no idea what had happened. He had looked, but he saw nothing. The Polack closed the gate behind him with the haste of an intruder. His one remaining son was crying now, and from his pocket the Polack produced a cookie for the child to nibble on.

Klepp was waiting at his car. "The farmer wants to talk to you," he announced, sounding more businesslike than he had yet. The urge to perform miracles and to talk about them seemed to have faded. "I'm sorry that it was all for nothing," Klepp said. "I did my best, I came too late. If I'd come earlier, maybe I . . ."

"Earlier?" the Polack queried.

The vet shook his head, as though the question itself was untoward. "I know who you were trying to do all this for. Take ten percent off the lump sum. That's the least I can do."

The diligence was compassion. Ten percent was at least something.

"Thank you," the Polack said. If his wife had been here, she would have made it twenty percent, but he wasn't like that. This was difficult enough for him.

Jurek had stopped crying and Klepp climbed into his car. When he placed his bag on the backseat, he did so with a tenderness the Polack found surprising. It was as though Klepp served as chauffeur for his bag, the bag with which he performed miracles. Then he drove off.

There was the farmer, who wanted to talk to him. Deal with that first, then the Polack could go home.

This time the farmer heard his visitor coming in; he turned his wheelchair to face the Polack as soon as he entered and sized him up. From head to toe. The farmer's cheeks were flushed and his skin more yellowish than before. He opened his mouth, the Polack thought it was to say something, but he coughed. A hacking cough full of mucus that he didn't spit out but swallowed. Between his front teeth, obviously dentures, something green was caught, spinach or a bit of lettuce, but the Polack didn't say anything about it. The things that got caught between people's teeth were their own business.

"You wanted to talk to me," the Polack said.

The farmer coughed, two, three times again, this time without the phlegm. Then he said: "I guess you want to be free of it." He had a hard time talking, yet he still spoke with fire, the fire of the bitterness that the Polack had detected in him before.

"I haven't decided yet," the Polack said, shifting his young son from one arm to the other.

"It didn't help," the farmer went on, as though the Polack hadn't spoken. "I could have told you that beforehand. People don't stay alive for some old horse. They don't keep on living for an old person either, let alone an old horse."

"What do you mean?" the Polack asked, and his thoughts shifted to the farmer's wife, tied to her bed upstairs.

"That boy," said the farmer, wiping the back of his left hand over his reddened cheeks and the yellowish, unshaven skin around those cheeks. "I could have told you that the first time you came here. I've had lots of kids in here. Lots of ponies, lots of children. This farm used to be a kid's farm petting zoo. And I raised children of my own. People forget that, that the farmer is a father too. And then you get to know children the way you know your animals. You didn't want to hear it, and I don't talk to people who don't want to listen. But there was something wrong with that boy. I had him here in front of me a couple of times. The farmhand brought him to me. He wasn't right in the head."

"Not right?" The Polack shook his head. "There was nothing wrong with my boy. Maybe he was different from other boys. Quieter, sweeter. He wouldn't have hurt a fly, he talked to animals because he didn't trust people, that doesn't mean there was anything wrong with him. He tripped, he was dizzy, hadn't eaten much that day, too little."

On the table, beneath and around a plate, were some regional newspapers. The Polack's eyes scanned the papers, his boy had made the news. Not major news, but news still, a serious interruption of rail traffic.

"Tripped," said the farmer, and he started coughing again.

"It doesn't matter. I don't owe you any explanation. You wanted to talk to me. That's why I'm standing here. We don't have to talk about my boy, he's gone now."

"What are you going to do with the pony?" the farmer asked, gasping for breath. "I don't want her anymore. That animal has to go. I'm winding things down around here."

"No one's going to move her as long as I don't want them to." The Polack turned on his heel, he left the room. He didn't say goodbye to the old man, although he had toyed briefly with the idea of bringing up the farmer's wife, strapped to the bed upstairs. Talk about it from a fire-safety point of view. If people feel like tying their partner to the bed and that partner was okay with that, then it was none of the fire department's business, not the police's business either. People had been freed from the yoke of the church and the gentry. There were still quite a few of the gentry around trying to tell people what was good and what was bad, but they would eventually be free of them too. All that mattered these days were the fire-safety rules, beyond that freedom began.

Out in the yard, the Polack gave his one remaining son another cookie. The farmhand came by, pushing a wheelbarrow full of manure. The Polack called out to him: "Hey, hold on a minute." When that had no effect, he ran after him. Only then did the farmhand put down his wheelbarrow.

"Is the farmer giving up the place?"

The farmhand nodded. A beanstalk, never without that fairly filthy black cap of his. He seemed arrogant. It could also be shyness, though, they'd taught the Polack that at the firehouse.

"And what are you going to do?" he asked the beanstalk, because he couldn't believe that the farm would really cease to exist, that he wouldn't be able to come here anymore.

"Another farmer," said the farmhand. "Just across the border. German farmer. I work hard. Do everything. Don't ask much."

The farmhand made to walk away, but the Polack had one more question for him. "Did he ever talk with you? My boy? Did he ever say anything to you?"

"Your boy." The farmhand shook his head. "He was always in the stall with that animal. They were thick as thieves, the two of them. Not that he rode her. Maybe a good thing too. She probably would have broke in two if he had."

Then the farmhand took up his wheelbarrow and the Polack went to his car. He put the boy in the car seat, in the back. "Hor-sie," Jurek said enthusiastically. "Hor-sie, hor-sie."

As the Polack drove home, he thought about how to discuss the animal's fate with Wen, whether he should bring it up in bed or during dinner: "What are we going to do with the pony?" In bed would be the best thing, right before they had sex he would say: "Sweetheart, we need to talk about the pony."

3

When he got back to the house, there was a woman standing at the door. She wore a brightly colored raincoat and she had a shopping bag. At first he didn't recognize her, but when he got closer he saw that it was Beckers's wife. "I just can't stop thinking about all of you," she said, with no further greeting.

The Polack searched for his keys. She couldn't stop thinking about him and his wife, that's why she was here. He didn't understand completely, but then there were plenty of things he didn't understand. It was better not to dwell on that too much, otherwise you couldn't shake it.

"You want me to hold the baby?" she asked.

"No, that's okay," said the Polack. "I'm fine." He glanced at his one remaining son, sitting there quiet and content on his arm. He wanted to make his boy feel safe, give him a sense of security. Maybe he had overlooked Borys's needs, maybe he had failed as a father, although he couldn't quite imagine what he might have done otherwise. Had it been a lack of love? He had always lived with the conviction that he had loved his eldest son the way anyone would love a person, the way the boy himself had loved that animal.

"Come on in," the Polack said, once he'd finally opened the door. He put Jurek down on the floor, beside his wooden train, he smelled a dirty diaper but that could wait for a little bit, the visitor wouldn't be staying long. Then he hung his coat in the hall, where Beckers's wife was still standing with the shopping bag. She looked hesitant, shy. She seemed to think that coming in meant she had to stay in the hallway. "I kept thinking about both of you," she said again, "so then I thought, I'll bring them a treat." From her bag she produced something to show the Polack. "Tiramisu, do you guys like it?" The tiramisu slid back into the bag, as if she herself understood that a tray of tiramisu couldn't console, although she'd seen things differently earlier in the afternoon, in the supermarket she had entertained the hope that there was such a thing as edible consolation.

"Please, why don't you take off your coat?" he asked. She said there was no need for that, she had only come by to give them the food, to which the Polack replied: "Awfully kind of you." Kind, that's what it was. Thoughtful.

She sat down on the couch in the living room with her coat on. He was starting to understand; you scrape your son off the rails and then people come by to bring you tiramisu. You used to have heaven and the little clouds with angels sitting on them, he could still remember how they'd told him that his mother was now sitting beside a little angel on one of those clouds. A neighbor lady had told him that, if memory served. But times had changed, there were no clouds anymore, at least no clouds with angels on them, there were only rainclouds. And tiramisu, there was also that. People had been freed of the angels and their little clouds, and that was a good thing too.

Beckers's wife arranged the food she'd brought on the coffee table. "If there's something you don't eat, just say so, then I'll take it with me." She had a large bosom that moved up and down, as though she were out of breath. He was reminded of the farmer, he'd breathed so heavily too. "Can I get you something to drink?" he asked, while she Beckers's wife went on laying out food on the coffee table, as though she was planning to play shopkeeper with the Polack.

"I really have to get going," she said, "I have three kids at home. That's exactly why I kept thinking about you two. And I just kept thinking about it. About you, the way you stood there so quietly at the cremation. Without saying anything. And then I had this idea, I went to the supermarket and bought something nice for the two of you."

"What my wife said was nice," said the Polack.

The look on her face seemed to say that now, in hindsight, she thought her bright idea might have been a little weird, but there was no going back. There she sat, with her tiramisu and the other treats.

"Are you sure you don't want anything?" the Polack asked. "Tea? Coffee? Something else, perhaps?"

"A cup of tea would be nice," she said. "But I can only stay a minute." She toyed with her long, dark-brown hair.

In the kitchen he put some water in the electric kettle and checked the cupboard to see what flavors of tea they had. He put a few teabags on a saucer so she could choose for herself. He wondered whether he actually liked tiramisu. He couldn't remember for sure. His appetite hadn't come back yet. He ate largely out of a sense of duty.

Sitting across from Beckers's wife, he drank his tea in silence. Chamomile, she had taken something that was supposed to be for a good night's sleep, even though it was nowhere near bedtime, and they sat across from each other like that and he looked at the shopping she had laid out on the table. There were all kinds of things, pickled herring and tinned sardines, a wedge of camembert, aged cheese, and as though in a trance he stared back and forth between the shopping and Beckers's wife. Once upon a time, the Polack's father had been offered consolation with the angels and the inscrutability of the Almighty, these days they came by with camembert. At a certain point, the Polack realized that he needed to say something. They couldn't just go on sitting here like this. If he didn't say something, an hour from now they'd still be sitting here and Jurek would still have a dirty diaper.

"It's very nice," he said, picking up the tin of sardines and putting it back down again, "it's sweet of you, but we already have everything." He looked pensively at the sardines. He felt like gagging, even though he used to like sardines a lot. "My wife will be coming home soon," he said. "Would you like to wait for her?"

Beckers's wife shook her head. "I have to get going, the kids are at home alone. The youngest is just turning four. An afterthought. Just like with you two. The eldest is keeping an eye on them. My husband's off doing a job." She sipped at her tea, then took her coat off anyway. "It's so warm in here. When's your birthday, anyway?"

It took a bit for the Polack to reply. "The weather's changing. My birthday's in the summer." Then the Polack went upstairs for some baby wipes, salve, and a clean diaper, laid his one remaining son on the dining table so he could change him while talking to Beckers's wife, who seemed to have no intention of putting the things she'd brought back in her shopping bag.

He changed Jurek on the dining table quite often, even though Wen thought that wasn't good.

"Stop fighting, Jurek," he said, "help me out a little, buddy." And he wiped the boy's butt clean with five baby wipes, which was something his wife couldn't stand, she always said: "Three's enough, five's too many." He always used at least five, to be sure the boy's buttocks were nice and clean, he liked clean buttocks, and Beckers's wife had risen to her feet, she was approaching slowly, he saw when he glanced over.

"Everything okay?" she asked interestedly.

"He's covered in it."

The Polack had felt like saying all kinds of things to his remaining son, but he didn't, because Beckers's wife was there and all Jurek said was: "Hor-sie, hor-sie, hor-sie."

"How do you two do it?" Beckers's wife asked. "How do you go on living? I don't think I'd be able to."

He rubbed the boy's buttocks with salve, diaper rash was no joke. He rubbed it on thickly over the boy's buttocks and anus, a bit over the balls too, just to be sure, and he enjoyed the smell of the salve, those were little things he enjoyed. "It goes on," he said quietly. "Life does. He's here, my wife's here, I'm here. It wouldn't be like me to give up."

The Polack was finished with the diaper and he put Jurek in the playpen. The boy started crying, he let him cry.

Beckers's wife was standing there, a bit lost, her teacup in her hand. He saw that she was crying too, just like his one remaining son. It bothered him, frankly, they didn't need anyone making a fuss over their sorrow. Not Victims' Assistance, not Beckers's wife either. He wondered when his wife was coming home, she was used to a whole pack of crying toddlers. Surely she could handle a crying adult too.

Still, he felt sorry for Beckers's wife, with her three children, the way she struggled against the tears there in his living room. She was wearing a dress with big flowers on it, and a zipper down the front. Wen never wore dresses like that. With a zipper down the front.

He laid his hands gently on Beckers's wife's arms, not to usher her out of the house, but to comfort her, and he said: "You just flip a switch. That's something a fireman learns, to just flip a switch." And, after a brief silence: "It won't happen to you, it doesn't happen to almost anyone. He had bad luck."

She nodded a couple of times. She didn't seem completely convinced, as though she still thought it might happen to her, that bad luck was contagious.

He said: "I hope I'm not offending you, but take the things with you. We've really got everything we need."

Resignedly, she began putting the food back in the bag, the pickled herring and the sardines, the aged cheese and the wedge of camembert, it all went back into the bag. It was a defeat, from the looks of it, but he couldn't do anything about it, he didn't want those things. She had sat down again. When she got to the tiramisu she said, with a sob in her voice: "You'll keep this, won't you? It's so delicious." She was fighting back the sobs, she was trying to control herself and it wasn't working, the tears came, she was shaking a bit. He couldn't bring himself to turn down the tiramisu, and so he said that they would eat it that same evening. He took the tiramisu as though it were the Eucharist and, holding it, he squatted down beside Beckers's wife as she sat there in her chair. He looked her in the eye, he saw the runny mascara and he said: "He had a pony, it was the whole world to him. Now it has to go the horse butcher. But I'm not going to let that happen. I'll put a stop to that."

He kept staring into her eyes. He had never really looked straight at Beckers's wife before, you didn't have to look everyone in the eye, but what he saw there now scared him worse than death itself, and if only for that reason, he said: "It's time for you to go."

He stood up, led her to the hallway with her heavy shopping bag in her hand, and just as he was about to open the front door she said: "My coat." She went into the living room and came back with the coat over her arm, and she whispered: "I already had two girls, and then the afterthought came along and it was a girl too, I wouldn't have minded having a boy. I didn't know he had a pony, so sad for that animal." Fighting back the sobs had made her voice hoarse. Then the Polack hugged her to thank her for the things she was now taking along with her and he held her to him, with the tiramisu in his hand, as though she were his boy's pony in human guise, that's how he pressed her against himself, as though Beckers's wife too had to be rescued from the horse butcher.

"Did Borys resemble you?" Beckers's wife asked.

"Not really," the Polack said as he opened the door. He shouted after her: "Thanks for everything."

She paused in front of the house, the shopping bag in hand, the raincoat over her arm. She waved and shouted: "Call me if you need me. Let me know if I can do anything for you."

He closed the door, went to the living room, lifted the crying boy from his playpen, and walked around the house, patting the child on his back and singing in his ear, but the crying didn't stop. "Does it hurt somewhere?" the Polack asked. "Are you hungry?"

At last Wen came home, took the boy from him, and, when the boy was calm again, there was pasta with a mushroom sauce. The Polack said: "We've got tiramisu."

Wen didn't ask: "Where did that come from?" She said: "Then we'll have that for dessert."

When the tiramisu was on the table—they tried to enjoy it, with the magnanimous acting talent with which loved ones try to ease each other's pain—the Polack felt the time was ripe to remind his wife of the pony's existence. Not in bed, right now. Infatuation faded, it was replaced by something else, and sometimes the Polack feared that what took its place might fade as well, but now that he saw how conscientiously they both put on their acts he realized that the substitute for infatuation was what held them together, and so he dared to bring up the miracle. "Shall we talk about the pony?" he asked.

She looked at him with an expression that seemed to say she had no idea how she could have forgotten. They had been thinking about their boy so much, for some reason the pony had escaped their attention.

"Oh, the pony." She looked at the container of tiramisu. "Good thing you brought that up. What are we going to do with it? Sell it, I guess, don't you think?"

"I was there today. With the vet. He's performed a miracle." The Polack cleared his throat. The miracle preyed on his mind, but he had to talk about it.

Once again, he felt like gagging. The tiramisu was too sweet for him, but he forced himself to go on eating, not only because you had to flip a switch at some point but also out of respect for Beckers's wife, in her weird dress, who had bought groceries for the Polack and Wen because she'd wanted to help them to go on with their lives. Because she thought it could happen to her too.

Wen started laughing. "What miracle? Those bills he promised to send? Is that what you mean by a miracle? The crook . . ."

"He did send the bills," the Polack said, "and he's not a crook." He stared straight ahead. Their one remaining son was in his highchair. Wen was feeding him some tiramisu. She wiped his mouth. He was covered in cacao. "Don't blow in it," she said. "You nut. Stop blowing."

"The animal doesn't limp anymore," the Polack stated. "Of course I can't tell that much, they don't walk the way people do, but she seemed healthy to me." He raised his spoon, lowered it again, took a bite, and wondered to himself when swallowing would finally become less of a battle.

"We have to get rid of it as soon as we can," Wen said, eyes fixed on a fly circling above the table. "No one bothers with her anymore. That's not right. The pony doesn't deserve that."

But then what *had* she deserved, the pony? Did she deserve to be punished because she hadn't saved their son? Could you expect a pony to save someone? Could a pony do something people couldn't? Could their boy have been saved? All questions the Polack didn't want to think about, because it got him nowhere. He scratched his chin. "They started in about the horse butcher," he said quietly, "the vet and the farmer did. Borys would never have wanted that."

"But Borys isn't here anymore," Wen stated. She sounded angry. As though he'd neglected his schoolwork, played hooky, as though death were a malignant form of playing hooky and the dead themselves nothing but truants who needed a good thrumming to keep them from ever playing hooky again. "It doesn't matter what he wanted. We have to get rid of it. Go to the farmer tomorrow and tell him to do with her what he thinks best." She swatted at the fly.

"I don't want to leave that up to the farmer," the Polack said decidedly. "You've never seen him. That man is old and broken down. Not in complete possession of his senses. And yes, I think we do owe it to Borys."

Wen slammed her hand down on the table. She never did that. "He's not here anymore," she shouted, "we don't owe him anything, because he's not here anymore. If we owe anyone anything, it's this one here." And she stuffed another spoonful of tiramisu into Jurek's mouth, as though what she owed him now was mostly more tiramisu.

The child looked at the Polack with big, round eyes. He seemed to understand that they were talking about him, he understood a lot, in any case the Polack thought he did, that both his boys had always understood a lot.

"Well, I owe him something," he said, more quietly than usual. When his wife raised her voice, he lowered his, because he didn't like fights. "Even if he's not here anymore."

Wen lifted the boy from his highchair, pulled him into her lap, wiped his mouth with his bib, his lips were brown with cacao, ran her fingers through his light-blond, hair and finally, without raising her voice, she asked: "What do you want to do with that pony anyway, for god's sake? Were you planning to go out riding?" She laughed, not mockingly, more like a bit despairingly. "You've never had much of an affinity for animals. Not even for dogs."

"I don't feel much affinity for animals," the Polack said. "At most, I rescue them, if necessary."

"Don't start in with your heroics about kittens you've rescued from trees, please spare me that, just because you can't say goodbye to a dying pony. Because you let yourself be cheated by a vet, because you don't know what a miracle is, because you're gullible. If only you'd worried that much about Borys."

He stood up, began clearing the table. "We're not paying those bills," Wen shouted. "All I want is to go to Greece with you and Jurek.

You said that if the pony was too much money we could always go to the Eifel, right? I don't want to go to some dumpy house where we freeze to death for two weeks, just because you feel guilty. I want to go to Greece."

"I don't feel guilty, but I'm responsible for that animal," the Polack said, with the dirty dishes in his hand.

"But don't you feel responsible for us?" Wen asked. "Are the dead the only ones with a right to your attention?"

The Polack felt like admitting that the dead called to him, that their voices sounded sweet and sometimes threatening too, that their voices were often livelier than those of the living, but he didn't say that. He brought the plates to the kitchen and used his finger to lick clean the container of tiramisu. To prove that his gagging would not get the best of him, that he could overcome his constant nausea. The Polack didn't want to be the plaything of circumstance. He rose above the circumstances, and yet at the same time he wondered whether his wife was right, to say that he was gullible.

4

For days, he had no idea who to talk to about his resolution to save an old pony, and finally he was no longer sure whether he should save the animal at all, the same way people sometimes hesitate about their relationship or their calling. For years, they think that they should be working with flowers and plants, and suddenly they think, no, maybe I'm actually a barber.

The end of the month was approaching, and the farmer had said that if no decision was made by then he would have the pony taken to the horse butcher.

There were moments, after they'd been out on a call for example and come back to the firehouse again, that the Polack saw with a clarity that surprised him that it was foolishness to worry about the pony, that he shouldn't try to get between the animal and its fate. In between times he saw before him his son, in the stall, heard him whispering without being able to hear what he said and he had the feeling that he would go on hearing that whispering for the rest of his days, without ever making out a word of it. But he would go on doing his best to pick up something the boy said, even if it was only a conjunction or a definite article. If Wen had seen their boy like that, she would have spoken differently, she would have acted differently, but she had not seen him like that and that is why the horse butcher to her was a butcher like any other. That's why the pony was nothing to her but a rump steak on its last legs. And she had no problem with the lions and tigers in the zoo eating the old girl's flesh. Yes, there were moments when he thought their boy's whispering would drive him crazy, and then he felt like shouting: Stop whispering, speak up or shut your mouth!

One afternoon, after he had finally decided to go to the farmer and give the animal back, back to the farmer, back to his creator, he had a brainstorm. He hopped in the car, but he didn't go to the farmer. He went to Beckers's. He had been there once before, long ago, for a party. He rang the bell.

Beckers's wife opened the door.

"Is Beckers home?" he asked.

She shook her head.

"Do you want to come in?" She was wearing another weird dress, this one with flamingos on it, but this one had no zipper down the front. He had never realized that Beckers's wife was so extravagant. Beckers himself was just normal, the way all the men of C squad were in fact normal, although each of them special in his own way.

"I need to ask you something," he said, "but maybe I can do that right here."

"Come on in, the kids are upstairs." She took him by the sleeve and gently pulled him a few inches inside. He could remember one child from the time he'd been here for the party, one child who had danced friskily around the room before going upstairs, or maybe he was mistaken, maybe there had been other children there too. He couldn't remember much about that whole party. He and Wen had danced too. They drank, drank too much to drive home. They were planning to take a taxi and when they couldn't get one because everyone, for some reason, was trying to take a taxi that night, they walked home. That much he could remember, how they had walked home and how he, entirely out of character, had talked nonstop. He had talked a mile a minute, but halfway home he stopped and they had walked the rest of the way in silence. At first they held each other's hand, until the Polack started feeling warm, he pulled his hand away and they had walked on like that, down the empty streets, past the darkened houses. When they got home their son was asleep, the babysitter was sleeping too, on the couch. He'd had to wake her up, and when he succeeded in doing that, he paid her. Then he and Wen went to bed, they were too drunk and too tired to make love, even though the lust was there, he could clearly remember the lust, and Wen had said: "I can smell the alcohol. You're drunk." Beckers had thrown the party because it was his birthday, some nice, round number, and he wanted to make a bash out of it for once.

The Polack kept his coat on. Beckers's wife stood there holding a coat hanger, but he shook his head. He followed her meekly to the kitchen. Wen had said to him once: "You're so tall, but still, sometimes you look just like a little boy." That's how he felt now, like a little boy, but he knew what he was here for. He was on a mission.

"You've got three kids," he said, standing beside the stove. He looked around this kitchen that was not his own, and realized that this was a rather strange way to start a conversation. She knew all too well how many children she had. Still, she nodded as though it was completely normal for her husband's colleague to ring the bell and say: "You've got three kids." But then again, she had come to *his* door with tiramisu, camembert, and sardines.

She inquired politely, almost too politely, whether he would like something to drink, adding that there was also some apple pie left over from yesterday. Why an apple pie had been brought into the house yesterday she didn't say, and the Polack didn't ask. He didn't feel much like apple pie, but he would work back that piece of apple pie the same way he worked back everything these days, and he watched as she cut off a big slice. It was homemade apple pie from the looks of it, she put a big dollop of whipped cream on top, so he had to work back the whipped cream too, and then she asked whether he'd like to go to the living room or if he preferred to eat it here, standing up. "Here," he said. And she remarked: "Our eldest girl always eats in the kitchen, standing up." Men and their eating habits, children and their eating habits, there wasn't a whole lot she hadn't seen. She'd seen it all, been through it all. She watched him eat and he tried to hide the fact that he could barely keep it down, he hoped he could, that she wouldn't notice anything. And while she stood watching him, she said quietly that she still thought about him and his wife all the time, that they were never far from her thoughts. "My thoughts," she said, and shook her head the way you shake your head over a naughty child. Maybe her thoughts *were* naughty children. And he shook his head too, by which he meant to say that she didn't have to be concerned with him and Wen, that everyone should concern themselves with themselves. He took a big bite, chewed, he ground her homemade apple pie between his teeth and as he did he saw before him how she had kneaded the dough, in this kitchen, wearing her eccentric clothes.

"I told you about that pony," he said when his mouth was empty, "Borys's pony, that was miraculously healed, and when you're healed by a miracle it's a waste to take you to the horse butcher. That miracle cost me a pretty penny too, and now I thought that maybe the pony could be for one of your children. I don't need anything for it, I just find it such a waste to have to take her to the horse butcher."

"A waste," Beckers's wife said pensively, "a real waste. But my kids already have so many things going. Their hobbies and their girlfriends, they barely have time for school. And the youngest is way too little for an animal like that."

He felt how his hand shook, the one holding the plate with half a piece of apple pie still on it and some fairly soggy whipped cream.

"I was hoping I could help you," she said quietly, and it looked like she wanted to take his plate, as though she'd seen how he was shaking, but at the last moment she pulled her hand back.

Screams were coming from upstairs. "They have some classmates over to play," she explained.

The Polack took another bite, then placed the plate on the counter. He had done his utmost; no blame could be put on him. "Okay," he said. "Well, it's always worth a try."

"It's always worth a try," she said.

When he left the kitchen, she followed him. "Don't leave right away, I bet there are other children who'd love to have a pony. Only, my children . . . No."

In the hall, at the front door, she tugged on his sleeve again. "I really wish so much that I could console the two of you," she said, "so much. You do know that, don't you?"

For a moment he looked at her, he could still taste her apple pie, he ran a hand over his bristly hair, he liked to keep it short, his hair, if it were up to him he would have shaved it off completely. Wen preferred a little bit of hair, though.

"You're Beckers's wife," he said, "you should console your husband."

"That's right, I'm Beckers's wife and I always will be. My husband doesn't need consoling. And I remember the two of you from when you were here for that party, and then I saw you after the accident. So different. Understandable, sure. But I thought, I should do something for those people . . . I can't just leave them."

She threw her arms around him as though she wanted to say how literal, how physical this not wanting to leave them was, and it was only then it struck him how small she was. He let himself be hugged, he let it happen and with the voices of children playing coming from upstairs he pressed her to him and she was right, in the face of all expectations she was right, there was something comforting in this touch, something that pointed toward the future and not only to the past, something that liberated, that didn't hold him prisoner.

It was unclear who was hugging whom, but he didn't let go, that much was certain, and as he listened to the children screaming upstairs his emotions overtook him. Moved that an unknown person would see that they needed consolation, Wen and he. His colleagues had seen it too, of course, for them consolation consisted of scraping off the old wallpaper, of painting and renovating, yet that was still not the same as consolation. And the woman from Victims' Assistance, she came by only because people who remained without consolation could pose a danger to themselves or to society.

All this raced through his mind as he moved his mouth to the cheek of Beckers's wife and smelled her, her perfume, not like Wen's, he couldn't stand Wen's perfume, but he didn't dare tell her that it made him nauseous. You couldn't say that to your wife, especially not if she had been using that perfume for years. And his lips slid softly over the cheek of the woman who wanted to console him, they slid from her ear to her mouth, just before his lips could have touched hers they slid back toward her ear, more or less the same way a vacuum cleaner slides over the carpet, and when his mouth arrived at her ear he said: "My wife needs comforting too."

"I know that," said Beckers's wife, "I realize that all too well. But she's not here right now. First you, then your wife."

At that the Polack pulled free of the embrace. "What in the world are they doing up there, anyway?" he asked. "Your kids. Are they tearing down the house?"

"They're playing," Beckers's wife said. "They're only playing, you have to give them a little leeway."

The Polack said nothing more, he turned and walked to his car. In the glove compartment he found an old peppermint lozenge and stuck it in his mouth without thinking. Then, at last, he started the car and drove home. If Beckers's children and wife didn't want the pony, then he'd take care of the animal himself. On his off-duty days he would go to the farm and take care of the animal. The farmer had said that everything was going to shut down, that the animals would be taken away, but still, the farmer would keep living there, surely, along with his wife tied up in the upstairs bedroom. He didn't seem much like nursing-home material to the Polack. So his lonesome pony could stay there too. And he would come and clean the stall himself, if necessary.

At the house he heard his wife knocking about in the bathroom. She called to him. He went upstairs. She was giving Jurek a bath. She stood bent over the edge of the tub, and she said: "You weren't here, so I gave him a bath myself."

The Polack was cheerful, more cheerful than he had been for a long time. Even back when their son was still there and he had sat at the table without speaking a word, the Polack hadn't been this cheerful. That was something he blamed himself for, if only to himself, that he hadn't enjoyed their eldest boy more than he had. Wen must have seen something or smelled it, because she looked up from what she was doing, she looked at her husband, he saw disapproval in her eyes—or was it suspicion?—and she asked: "What is it?"

"Nothing," he said.

She scrubbed their one, remaining son. The boy laughed, he laughed more than his brother had, that was a good sign, the Polack couldn't help laughing along with him. Then he said: "I'm going to take care of the pony."

Wen had soaped the boy's belly and back, she was just about to rinse it off, and she stiffened. "What?" she asked, her hand motionless on the boy's back, "you're going to do what?"

"I'm going to rescue the pony. I'm going to save her."

"Take care of *him*, why don't you?" Wen said, and began rinsing the boy's back angrily. "Save *him*." That's what the Polack wanted to do, too, take care of Jurek, even save him if need be, but he felt there was enough time left over to save a pony too.

"In a few years' time, Jurek will have an animal to play with," the Polack said.

"The animal will be long dead by then, and maybe he'll feel more like playing soccer. Or hanging around outside. Has it ever occurred to you that Jurek may not have any desire for a pony at all?" She rinsed the rest of the soap away.

"Maybe," the Polack said. He didn't want to do anything to make Wen sad or angry, but he had already made up his mind.

Wen lifted the boy out of the water and began drying him briskly. "No," she said. "That animal has only brought us grief. Let's say good-bye to it. What more do you want from that pony?"

Jurek was dry now. She carried him to his room and put on his diaper. The Polack followed her. "You won't get him back," she said, "not even if you go out and buy twenty ponies. Borys is gone. Resign yourself to it. He's gone. Other people get a child with a metabolic disease. We got this. Now there's just the three of us. That's good too."

"That's good too," he said quietly. "That the three of us are together is fine. But the old girl doesn't deserve this. What can she do about it? Why does she have to die too?"

Wen went on dressing the boy. The child was still, he seemed to be listening. "We don't deserve this either," she said, "it's not about what people and animals deserve. Who gets what he deserves? Do I deserve you? Don't I actually deserve something better?"

The Polack left the bathroom and remained standing before the closed door, the door leading to their boy's room, the door they would not open again, not this year, maybe next year, that much was uncertain, probably not even next year, there was no hurry. Maybe they would only open the door to that room once they were old and their one remaining son had moved out. Or maybe they would die without ever having opened that door. That would probably be the best, to never open it again.

During dinner, Wen apologized and laid her hand on the Polack's arm. She said she couldn't think of a better husband, and that it wasn't nice of her to claim that she deserved something better. Not only unkind, but also untrue.

"Ah, well," the Polack's hands were folded on the table in front of him and he studied his knuckles, "ah, well, death causes stress and then we say things we don't really mean. But now the death is behind us, now we can start cutting back on the stress."

She kissed him, first on the cheek, his unshaven cheek, then she took his face in both hands, she pressed her mouth against his, she pushed her tongue inside, and, apparently, she didn't mind the fact that their one remaining son was at the table too. She obviously thought he was too young to remember this or that it was good for him to see this, and the Polack felt like gagging. He wondered whether she didn't feel like gagging too, whether she didn't feel nauseous, he felt like asking her: Doesn't your food start coming back up? But he kissed her back instead. He kissed the way he ate, with a sense of responsibility indiscernible from fanaticism. And in his chair sat their remaining son with his bib on and he said "Hor-sie, aminal, aminal," and so on. From the corner of his eye the Polack saw him sitting there, content in fact, and he said: "Come on, let's go upstairs."

He was nauseous, but he rose above the nausea. "It's been a long time," she whispered in his ear. And she kissed him as though they'd just met and were terribly in love, more in love than was good for either of them, but they were not terribly in love, they had lost their son and he felt like saying: Beckers's wife wants to console us. You and me.

He kissed Wen, about whom he had no reservations. His nausea was not a reservation, his nausea was a stroke of fate, the way the express train to Amsterdam had been a filthy stroke of fate and she said: "Let's go."

She stood up, pulled him out of his chair and he let himself be pulled, he followed her like an adolescent, and as they went he glanced at their boy, sitting there so peacefully in his highchair.

"I want you," she said on the stairs, and she turned to look at the Polack, who was fighting back the meal he'd just eaten. The bile rose to his mouth, he swallowed it down. "Do you want me?" she asked. "Finally I want you again, the way I wanted you then. The way I've really always wanted you, right?"

"Yes," he said, "yes." Without knowing exactly what he was saying yes to, at best that he was saying yes to this life, this house, this wife, his job, his retirement plan.

She sat down on the bed and unbuttoned his pants. He said: "What difference does the pony make, what trouble is it for you?"

She pulled down his underpants, she was the one who bought his underpants, she had for years, he trusted his wife about more things than only underpants, but he didn't want her to give him a blowjob now, he didn't have an erection, though he'd said "yes," true enough. It had been a general kind of "yes," a "yes" that could be taken a hundred different ways. She took his limp penis in her mouth and acted as though she hadn't heard the words about the pony. "I'll do it all by myself," he said, and gradually he got an erection, because everything still worked more or less the way it should. He decided to say nothing more about the pony, this wasn't the time for that.

He pulled his Wen to her feet, pushed her back gently onto the bed and struggled a bit to free her of her jeans, he pulled off her underpants, then began licking her legs. The insides of her thighs.

"It's been so long since you've been there," she said.

"It has," he said.

"Look at me," she said. "Look at me there like it's the first time."

The Polack grew impatient, because he didn't actually want to look at her, but he also didn't want to disappoint her, he wanted to please her, that's what he wanted more than anything else and so he looked as though this were the first time he had lain between her legs, and she said: "Tell me what you see."

"What do you mean, what I see?" he asked.

"What do you see? What do you see, Polack?"

She only addressed him as "Polack," in fact, when she was teasing him. Apparently, she wanted to tease him now that he was back between her legs again at long last. He loved her most when she teased him a little.

He looked at the inside of her thighs and what was in between them, her vagina, which she normally called her little pussy, insofar as she ever talked about her vagina. And he said that he saw her labia. "I see them," he said.

"Play with them," she answered, "touch them."

The Polack didn't know exactly how you were supposed to play with labia, but still he played with them—this too was among the obligations a good man needed to fulfill.

She had never used to give orders, but now the time for orders had arrived and that made him uncertain. He touched her labia carefully.

"With your lips," she said. "Not your tongue. Only with your lips."

He moved his lips over her labia and for a moment he thought of Beckers's wife and her cheek. Then he went back to concentrating on his wife's little pussy and on the fact that he and his wife needed no consoling, that she was right, some people got a child with a metabolic illness, they'd had this, except for the pony, he really did want to rescue it, because it was in his power to do so, on the sly if necessary.

He kissed her little pussy without describing what he saw, he wasn't sure how to describe the color of his wife's little pussy. He was no painter. Pink or red or brown or maybe more subtle than that. She said he could lick her now too. "But don't slobber too much," she said. "You always slobber so much when you lick me. Why is that, anyway?"

"I can't help it," he replied. "I have saliva in my mouth and sometimes it comes out." He thought about food again, and about the bile that still kept rising in his throat.

"Don't make it too wet, then I don't feel it anymore," she said. "Try licking me and fingering me at the same time. I like that."

He licked while trying to hold back his saliva, and he fingered her.

"This doesn't feel good," she said, "maybe you can't do two things at the same time. Stop fingering me. This isn't working."

"Oh."

He must have sounded a bit downcast, because she said: "It doesn't matter. You can do other things. This is where the boys came out. Our two boys."

"Yeah," he said. He had been there when Borys was born, and he hadn't thought of an express train to Amsterdam, he hadn't thought of that for a moment. To parents-to-be he would say, these days: The chances are slim, but think of the express train to Amsterdam when your baby comes, think of that just to be sure.

Wen grabbed his head and pressed it against her. It didn't feel as though the head had anything to do with him, as though this were only about his head, it could be anyone's head, his head just happened to be the head in question and that felt liberating. It had nothing more to do with him, it was down between her legs and it shouldn't produce too much saliva. The same way you need to put out a fire using the smallest possible amount of water.

She panted. She pressed him against her, she pulled his hair. If it was too wet she couldn't feel anything, but how can you keep from losing saliva when you're licking your wife's little pussy and that makes everything wet, your nose, your mouth, your cheek, your chin, the sheets? He did his best, but it seemed like there was saliva everywhere, as though the bed was made entirely out of saliva and his wife pressed his head against her even harder, as though she wanted to push his head inside her, as though it had to follow the route their boys had followed, but then in the opposite direction. Their boys, but he wasn't thinking about the boy downstairs, the remaining one. And then she came, she shook, she made noises, noises from another world, not the world of humans anymore, not the world of animals either, in as far as there was actually any difference between humans and animals, a very different world, a completely different universe, he had never heard his dear wife make noises like that and he concentrated on the saliva he had to keep back.

Her orgasm made him feel good, the way putting out a big fire did, a fire with casualties but also people who'd been rescued, who'd been carried or dragged out in time.

He moved up from between her legs. He tried to kiss her, to smooch with her, but she pushed him away. "I don't want to smell myself," she said, still panting, "I don't want to taste myself. You smell of me, I taste myself when I kiss you."

He realized then that the panting had turned to weeping, that maybe it had been weeping all along. "Go away," she shouted.

He didn't go away, he remained sitting beside her, and she wept as though another disaster had happened. Everything was fine now. The old disaster had happened a while back, if you made it through the first few weeks then you'd make it through the rest too. They had left the disaster behind, all that remained was the postscript in the form of a pony, and he was going to care for her.

"I disgust myself," she said.

He remaining sitting on the bed, next to his wife's head. The weeping went on. But was it actually weeping? Or was it some unintelligible indictment, a barrage of noises coming from his wife's mouth? He said there was no reason for it, that there was no reason to find herself disgusting, that she was a fantastic woman, that she was his Wen. He didn't say that Beckers's wife had offered to console them, although he'd been meaning to do that, but this wasn't the moment. The Polack fetched some toilet paper from the bathroom, dried her tears and then moistened a washcloth with lukewarm water and wiped the runny makeup from her face. Wen kept crying that she was disgusted by herself, that she didn't want to smell herself and that she didn't want to taste herself and that he should just piss off, because he had her smell on him. She didn't want to smell herself; she couldn't smell herself without being driven mad by the smell. He didn't piss off, he said that she should try to calm down, that the worst had already come and gone. The Polack sang a Polish song for her, one that his father had sung for him long ago, and that he had sung for both his boys. Gradually she calmed down.

The Polack helped her out of bed and the two of them went downstairs, naked. He was naked, she was naked. He heard it when they were only halfway down the stairs. He didn't understand why they hadn't heard it upstairs. Down below they saw their boy lying on the floor. He was crying too, he was wailing too, but differently. His high-chair had tipped over. Wen picked him up. "His head," she cried. "His little head. Do you think he has a concussion?"

She walked back and forth with him, the remains of their dinner were still on the table. She tried to calm the child, and because the Polack didn't know what else to do, he started clearing the table. He told her that if the boy wasn't vomiting then it probably wasn't all that bad, and that he didn't understand how he could have tipped over. Had he perhaps tried to climb out of his chair? They shouldn't have left him at the table like that, all alone, a child that young shouldn't stay alone at the table. First you put the boy to bed, then the pleasure. He didn't say that last bit though, and in the living room Wen was walking back and forth with Jurek. She asked if they needed to go to the hospital.

When the crying finally stopped, the Polack said there was no reason to go there. That everything had turned out okay, that their one remaining son would have a bump on the back of his head, but that was nothing serious. He was a sturdy kid.

They went upstairs, still naked, with Jurek in Wen's arms. She brought him to bed. The little boy was exhausted from all the crying, the wailing. He had screamed for so long that by the time they found him he was all red in the face. The Polack didn't want to think about it, not about what had happened upstairs and not about what happened at the same time downstairs. The one seemed to make the other only worse.

The boy fell asleep and the naked parents stood beside his bed, they looked at him with deep fondness. "It was nice, the way you licked me," Wen said. "That's not the problem."

She came closer and caressed his cheek.

"Yeah, did you like it?" he asked.

"Very nice," she said, "but maybe we shouldn't do that anymore." She went on petting him, first his cheek, then his chest, his hairy chest. "We'll just have sex, but licking, we won't do that anymore."

"If you say so," he replied.

"I love you, Polack," she said. "I love you very much. But that licking, I can't stand it anymore. I can't stand my own pleasure. Maybe I'll see things differently, in a year or so. A year and a half."

They stayed there like that, she still had her hand on his chest. They listened to their boy's breathing and then the Polack said: "Beckers's wife wants to comfort us."

He heard the boy breathing, he heard his wife breathing, it seemed as though his son's breathing segued into that of his wife, and finally she said: "We don't need that, we're strong."

"Yeah," he said.

"You were sure to thank her, though?" Wen asked. "Or should I do that?"

"No," he said. "I was sure to thank her."

Downstairs, they sat on the couch and Wen said: "I think there are a lot of people who want to comfort us. At work, they've offered me that a few times too. But they do it for their own good. They're like birds of prey, the comforters are. They're out to pick the meat off your bones."

The Polack turned on the TV, they watched the weather report. And, without touching him, without taking her eyes off of the weatherman, Wen said: "Nothing can drive us apart, we know that now for sure."

5

A deal with the farmer, that's what he tried to make, to give the pony a couple of months' respite. She was the last animal left on the farm. The cows had been taken away, the farmhand was gone, but by paying the farmer and giving him a little extra he hoped the pony would be able to stay longer.

He hoped fervently that the farmer possessed unseen compassion, that he could awaken some fellow feeling in the man, he didn't rule out the possibility that the farmer was in fact a sentimental person with a desire to show the world—or in any event the Polack—a little kindness. But things had gone differently, the farmer had come up with all kinds of reasons not to do it, reasons the Polack didn't understand but that sounded very decided, and finally the Polack brought up the fire-safety issue.

He told him that he had gone upstairs once on a whim and found the farmer's wife lying there, that it was none of his business but that he, as a fireman, was obliged to keep an eye out for possible safety threats. Tying someone to the bed ran counter to the basic rules of fire safety.

The farmer began moaning, but not at the thought of a possible fire; the idea that his wife might be allowed to move freely around the house apparently made him sick to death. He said: "You don't know what she gets up to, you don't know how she is, she acts all nice and polite when she talks to you, I've come to know her the way she really is. That I've let her go on living is a case of pure human charity, that alone is enough to earn me a place in heaven."

The Polack replied that, as far as he was concerned, there was no heaven, yet the possibility of there being a God was something he didn't completely dismiss. Fire safety, on the other hand, existed. He said: "I'm willing to forget what I saw up there if you'll put up with the pony for a few more months."

At first the farmer sniffed in contempt, but admitted quickly enough that the tradeoff seemed like a good one to him. Putting up with a pony was not a lot of work, and he would get paid for it too. In fact, the farmer demanded a hefty rental hike for the stall, even though the Polack himself would be the one cleaning it. The hired hand after all, the animal caretaker, was gone, a "hired people-hand" had come in his stead, someone who helped the farmer with the laundry, who brought food, did the grocery shopping, and who also took care of the farmer's wife.

"You'll come across the new hired fellow," the farmer said, "he's tall and blond. You can't tell it by looking at him, but he's a Jew. Not that I have anything against Jews, even though I've had some bad experiences with them. Sly and cynical is what they are. They call it irony, but it's pure slyness. Good people aren't cynical and they aren't ironical either. But when you go looking for a people caretaker, you can't afford to be too choosy."

"Oh," the Polack said.

"There was a cattle dealer around these parts once," the farmer said, "a long time ago. He was a Jew. He wasn't like the other cattle dealers. I knew he was out to cheat me, because that's what Jews do, they can't help it, it's in their blood. So I cheated him instead. At least that way I got there first. I didn't want to get there last. I didn't want them laughing at me, the other farmers."

The Polack understood that, and it dawned on him that everything in the farmer's life was aimed at not being laughed at, that the rest didn't matter all that much to him, as long as he wasn't laughed at.

Still, the Polack couldn't shake the feeling that the farmer was cheating him, even though he wasn't a Jew; he was just a normal, everyday Polack, formerly a Christian, now an atheist. Or did the farmer believe that the Polack had cheating in his blood too? The Polack didn't have the stamina to go on discussing things with the farmer; he knew it was a discussion he would lose. He was here for the pony.

It was for that same reason that he hadn't talked to his wife about his plan, because he knew she was stronger, stronger with words, stronger with the emotions that went along with the words or, better yet, the emotions that words summoned up. Words came out of her mouth and suddenly they were emotions and that made the Polack weak. That's why, for the first time in his life, he had started lying to his wife, because he was a savior, not a savior of men but a savior of animals. It wasn't really lying, it was more like withholding. He withheld information about where he was going and he took money from his savings account to give to the farmer so that he would let the pony live. The farmer prolonged the animal's life for cash, and the Polack's wife must not find about it, because they were not wealthy, not wealthy enough to go around playing savior.

Sometimes she asked where had been on his day off. Then he would say: "I was out with a few of the guys from C squad." One time she said: "You smell of horse." "One of the guys from C squad smells like a horse," he replied, "everyone who gets close to him ends up smelling like a horse." His wife accepted that as an answer.

But it wasn't that he got all that involved with the old, solitary pony, there in the stall. He didn't know much about horses and ponies, and in fact didn't feel the need to really find out much about them, so he barely dared to touch the animal. Sometimes, when he needed to clean the stall, he would lead her carefully outside. At first, he always hitched her to a fence, but she never went away and so he stopped doing that. He didn't want to impose on her. The Polack respected her age and her solitude. The latter he had no desire to take from her. Animals, too, had a right to their solitude. He simply spent a part of his days off in the stall, that's all. It would be too much to claim that they hit it off, they simply shared the same space without a problem. The Polack stood there and there were afternoons when he started talking to the pony because the silence was more than he could bear. Then he would say: 'My boy was crazy about you. You're old, and without the vet's help you'd be lame now, probably dead, but my son thought you were wonderful anyway. Except he's not here anymore. That's why I'm here. Instead of him."

He would stand there like that for a while. He didn't have much to say to the pony either. Sometimes he squatted in a corner the way his boy had squatted, but the squatting made his knees hurt, so he didn't do that very often.

Whenever he'd been to the farm he would sprinkle himself with aftershave, just to be safe, because he didn't want his wife to say again: "You smell of horse." And she didn't say that anymore, either. She didn't smell it anymore, or else she thought it was just normal: her husband had started smelling of horse and that was a smell she could live with.

One afternoon, as he was walking to his car, he ran into the hired people-hand. The man was just as lanky as the former farmhand, tall and skinny. He had white-blond hair and blue eyes. Indeed, there was nothing Jewish-looking about him. More like a Swede or a Norwegian. The Polack didn't have to go over to the people-hand, the people-hand came right over to him: "Allow me to introduce myself," he said. "I'm Ruud. I'm here to take care of the farmer and his wife, because neither of them wants to leave the farm."

"I know," the Polack said.

"And you're the man who's here for the pony?" the people man went on. "The farmer told me about you."

"I'm the man with the pony."

The people-hand smiled amiably. "I suppose he told you about me, too. He calls me the 'hired people-hand' because I take care of people, problem cases or people who live in isolation, way out of town, and who can barely get care through the regular channels anymore. They have to have means of their own to pay for me, of course, although I'm not expensive."

A silence fell.

The Polack pointed up at the second-story window. "That woman is upstairs, in bed," he said.

"That's where the bedroom is," the people-hand concurred.

"Tied up," the Polack said. "She's lying there, tied up."

The hired people-hand nodded. "I know," he said, "they tied her up, that was the tradition. The hired hand and the farmer did. She lived like that for years. She had completely reconciled herself to her fate. She couldn't stand the thought of not being tied up anymore. It seemed worse to her than death itself. I talked to her for a long time, and this week I finally untied her. As a caregiver, one has obligations, you take into account the wishes of the people you come to help, but sometimes you have to disregard them. Not everything people want is good for them. In fact, she doesn't want to leave the room, and then you have to respect that. You can't force people to go outside if they haven't been outside for such a long time, certainly not people that age. But I put an end to the tying-up."

"I'm a fireman," the Polack said, "and in cases like that I think about fire safety."

Once again, the people-hand nodded. "I understand that. Those two love each other, in their own way. She lives upstairs, he mostly stays downstairs, they communicate by pounding on the walls. They've developed a language all their own. Haven't you noticed?"

"No, never noticed a thing," the Polack said.

The people-hand looked pensive. He seemed unable to imagine that there were times when the farmer didn't pound on the walls at all. Then he said: "I'm sure we'll run into each other more often around here." He made to walk off, but there was something else the Polack wanted to know. "A strange question, perhaps," he said, "but do I smell of horse?"

The people-hand brought his nose a bit closer to the Polack's neck. "No," he said. "Not of horse. Maybe of farm. Everyone and everything here smells of farm. When I'm done working here I go home and hop in the shower right away. Sometimes my girlfriend calls me her 'little farmer.'"

Then the people-hand walked off in the direction of the farmhouse. The Polack went and sat in his car, sprinkled himself with aftershave from the little bottle he had carried with him ever since his wife claimed that he smelled of horse, and drove back to town. He drove past his own house, he didn't stop, he drove past the house as though it wasn't his, he looked at the front door and he had no trouble imagining that someone else entered and left through that door every day. His wife and son lived there, he no longer did. He had disappeared. The thought that he would not be missed caused him no pain, in fact it put his mind at ease. He drove past Heerlen's dismal train station, then arrived at the street where Beckers lived. Not the most cheerful street to live on either. The Polack parked and walked up to Beckers's house. He rang the bell.

A child opened the door. She looked at him grumpily and also a bit sleepily. " Is your mother or father home?" asked the Polack. "I'm a colleague of your father's."

The child looked him up and down. The Polack had the feeling that the little girl didn't believe him, that she thought: my father's colleagues don't look like this. "Mama's home," the child said, turning and walking away. The Polack remained standing in the doorway. He felt like he was there to sell something no one wanted. A set of encyclopedias, for instance. Who needed an encyclopedia these days? His father had owned one. A set of more than twenty volumes. He had never looked at it.

Beckers's wife opened the hallway door. She was wearing an apron. "You," she said.

From that word and the way she spoke it, the Polack couldn't tell whether she was pleased that he'd come or irritated. That was all she'd said. Only "you."

"Yeah," he said, "me."

"There's a café down the street," she said, "let's go there."

She shouted over her shoulder that she'd be right back, probably to her children. Or was it to her husband? Was Beckers at home, was he cutting work? The house remained silent. If the children were playing, they were doing it quietly this time.

She put on her bright raincoat, even though it wasn't raining, and walked with the Polack to the corner, where there was a cafeteria. They took a table close to the jukebox. The place smelled stuffy, but the Polack didn't mind. He ordered coffee, she asked for a beer. "It's muggy out," she said. "Or is it only me? I've been thirsty all day."

The Polack looked around, he'd never been here before.

"I'm doing it myself now," he said once he'd finished half the cup of coffee. Because Beckers's wife hadn't asked him a thing. Each time she sipped at her beer, he thought: now she's going to ask me something. Then she would look down at her glass or at him, and she asked no questions. And so he began telling her himself. "I couldn't find anyone for the pony, so now I'm doing it."

She frowned and tossed him a disapproving look. Apparently, she too thought he was doing something that he'd be better off not doing. Just like his own wife, even though she knew nothing about what he was doing. He had wondered a few times why she never asked about it anymore, he suspected that she simply didn't think the animal was all that important. She had forgotten about it.

"I suppose it's something of an adventure?" Beckers's wife asked.

An adventure.

The counterman was making a toasted cheese sandwich.

"No, it's not an adventure," the Polack said at last. It smelled like the toast was burning.

"Then why do you do it?" she asked. "Does it make things easier?"

He shook his head. "I talked to my wife about it, about you wanting to console us. But she said we had no need of that."

Beckers's wife sipped at her beer. "You two know best what you need and what you don't," she whispered, leaning over a little as though he couldn't hear her unless he brought her mouth a little closer to his ear. "You two know that I want only the best for you. I pray for the two of you. That doesn't get in your way, I don't need your permission to do that."

The Polack nodded. He hadn't expected that. That there would be prayers. To him, prayer was a hobby of people he used to know, back when there were no smartphones. They communicated with God because there were no games to play on their phones, no text messages to send.

She got up and went to the ladies' room, and he looked at the counterman, who apparently had been making the toasted cheese sandwich for himself, because now he was eating it as he read the newspaper. As soon as she came back from the restroom, the Polack would say goodbye to Beckers's wife and drive home. He no longer had any idea why he had come to see her in the first place. Was it really only to say that he was taking care of the pony now, and that it was working out well? That he stood beside her in the stall, sometimes for two hours at a stretch, and that they respected each other's solitude? Maybe he'd been hoping she would say: I can take care of the animal for a while too. If I can't comfort the two of you, then I'll just comfort the pony.

He wouldn't go to see her anymore, that first time had been a mistake, the second time even worse. Her vague promises had raised expectations in him that were unrealistic.

Beckers's wife still hadn't come back from the restroom, the counterman was wiping down the surfaces. He'd already finished his toasted-cheese sandwich. There was no one else in the cafeteria, where the odor of burnt bread now mingled with that of cleansing agent. The Polack stood up. He walked toward the restroom, he needed to be getting home, his one remaining boy would be waiting for him, he had chores to do. He knocked on the door of the ladies' room. "Everything okay?" he asked. "Listen, I have to get going."

At that the door opened and she dragged him inside, the way you might drag in a child you've been waiting for impatiently. Angry that the child has made you wait so long, but also relieved that it is still alive. She closed the door. She sat down on the toilet, even though she was still fully clothed. She wasn't taking a pee, she just sat there as though the toilet were a chair. "I'm praying for the two of you," she said, louder than before. "No one can keep me from doing that."

Then she stood up and began kissing the Polack, she kissed him on the cheek and, with a bit of effort, on the mouth, she had to pull him down toward her and he kissed her back. Cautiously at first, then less cautiously and after that he stopped and said: "I want you so badly, but you're Beckers's wife."

His own words startled him. Something inside him had spoken, against his will, he was not the kind of person who said: I want you so badly. He was a taciturn Pole, and although he knew that some people found that hard to take, in the course of time he had met enough people who actually enjoyed that taciturnity, because there was already so much talking going on in the world.

"Yes," she said, "that's who I am. Beckers's wife." And then she kissed him again, she held his head in her hands and kissed him carefully, but hungrily at the same time. Sometimes she pulled her face back, as though remembering at such moments that she was Beckers's wife, then quickly pressed her mouth to his again. She was the wife of his colleague, but she was also a different woman, a woman who stood kissing the Polack in the ladies' room of a rather seedy cafeteria.

He slid a hand down her body, over her back, down to her buttocks, and then back up. He didn't think about his wife, not about the first time he had kissed her, although he could very well have done so. For then too he'd felt like doing it, very much so in fact, but he hadn't said that, he had only done what people do when they feel like doing it. He didn't think about his son either, or about the stall, he thought only about her, Beckers's wife. Of her standing here in the ladies' room, still wearing her apron. Vaguely, he could smell the beer she'd had, above all he smelled her. He thought she smelled nice. He thought she smelled wonderful. With that thought in mind he clung to her, to the discovery that Beckers's wife smelled lovely, even here at this spot where the smell of the deep-frier, of cleaning agent, and sewerage were mixed. Was this what she meant by prayer and consolation? He didn't want to ask her, he didn't want answers, no conversations. He kissed her more wildly than she kissed him. Then she pulled back. She said: "I like it that you want me, I want you badly too, but I have to get home, the children are waiting for me. I was in the middle of cooking."

"Yeah," he said, swallowing down some excess saliva. "You were in the middle of cooking."

Again he kissed her, because she wanted him so badly too. She wanted the Polack, how could that be? He didn't get it: why him?

"I have to go," she said. "I've got beef bourguignon on the stove."

She arranged her clothes. Even though he'd kept his hands pretty much to himself, he hadn't put them under anything, she was Beckers's wife and he respected that. "You better wait here," she said.

She slipped out the door casually, he remained behind in the ladies' room. He counted to sixty, the counterman must have thought the Polack was constipated.

Then he walked out. She was sitting at the table, the beer in front of her. The glass was almost empty now, she raised it to her lips. Rhythmically, like the ticking of a clock. Even though it was almost empty already, she kept raising it to her lips.

"Well, there you are," she said.

The Polack sat down.

"That was pleasant," he replied.

"Yes," she said.

And he had no idea who they were putting on appearances for, the counterman was immersed in his newspaper.

They stood up at the same time. "My car's over there," he said.

She walked part of the way with him. "My marriage is loveless," she told him, in a tone that sounded in fact like it had nothing to do with her. And then, right away: "Oh, there's a pebble in my shoe." She felt around in her shoe, but there was nothing there. She started walking again. "Still, I love my husband very much, can you understand that?" she asked.

"Yes," the Polack said. "I understand things like that."

"You two are friends, aren't you?"

"We're colleagues. We're good colleagues, I don't think you could find better."

"When I saw you," she said, "when I saw the two of you, your loss, I wanted to forget that I was married. Sometimes I'm able to do that. Can you imagine that?"

The Polack shook his head. "But then I don't really have to, I guess," he mumbled.

She left him with a little nod, a hand that brushed his shoulder. Then she walked back home. She didn't turn around, the Polack watched her go the way he wished he had watched his son go that final morning, when he went to school. He had almost never watched his boy go. He had forced him to go to school when he didn't want to anymore, because he pooped in his pants. He had yanked him free of the lampposts and trees to which the boy clung. The Polack had never stood and watched the boy go, he had other things to do. And that day he couldn't have done it anyway, he was at the firehouse. Now, at times, he thought: if I'd watched him go, if I'd watched him go more often, then I would have seen something, then I would have understood a little better.

The Polack went home. His wife and Jurek were lying on the living room floor. She was on her back, with her head almost touching the feet of the boy, who was playing quietly with his blocks.

The Polack leaned down, kissed her. "What are you two playing?" he asked.

"I sort of fell asleep," she said.

He kissed the boy too, he patted him on the head and for a moment he no longer knew whether he was a father or simply playing the role of father rather convincingly.

"You smell like toast," she said.

"That's impossible," he said, startled.

"It's okay," she mumbled. "Nothing wrong with toast."

He sat down on the floor and played along with her and with the one remaining boy, and as they played he asked: "Are you sure we don't need comforting?"

"Very sure," she said, running a toy train over a set of wooden rails. "We've got each other, right? We've got him. We have Jurek. We have everything we need."

"That's true," he said. "We have everything we need." And as he said it he decided that he would tell her about it, about the pony, that same evening. That it couldn't go on like this. He would explain it to her. Surely, she'd understand. If he could find the right words, the right moment.

Together they took their remaining boy upstairs, together they bathed him, and together they dried him off. Wen preferred to do that before dinner, so he could sit at the table in his pajamas, and then all she had to do was read him a book and rock him to sleep.

When they were done, when Jurek had his pajamas on, when he smelled familiarly of baby shampoo and sat there babbling happily, the Polack said: "There's something I forgot to tell you."

"What?" Her voice sounded tense. Fearful, in fact. As though she'd known all along that there was something he'd forgotten to say and that she nevertheless had been hoping she was wrong. That he'd said everything, everything there was to say.

"Nothing world-shattering," he said.

Dinner that evening was from the microwave. Wen didn't like that, actually, but once a week, sometimes twice a week, she allowed herself the convenience and he went along with it. He followed her lead, not because he was submissive, but because he felt most conflicts weren't worth the trouble, so when she said: "Dinner tonight's a microwave meal," he didn't say: "Oh no, then I'll cook." He said: "Okay. Sounds good."

"There's someone else?" she asked.

"No," he said, holding Jurek in his arms. "Not someone else. But I didn't let them take the pony. She's still there. I go there a couple of times a week."

"No," she said, almost screaming, "No, Geniek. I'd stopped talking about it because I figured she was long dead. That she was already in a hamburger somewhere. That's why I never started in about it again."

"She's not in a hamburger. In fact, I don't think they ever put ponies in hamburgers."

She had called him Geniek. She never called him that anymore. With that name, she was holding him at arm's length.

"The idea of you going there . . . I don't want that," she said. "It feels unfair. You're shutting me out. You go there. To that place where he was. All these weeks, months, how long has it been anyway? I've never been there. Never. Never once did I go along to see that animal, to look at that animal, because I felt . . . because, in fact, I thought it was the wrong kind of thing for a boy. I thought: it'll pass. I didn't understand it. And now you go there. And you take him away from me. You take him away from me all over again. Not that you took him away from me the first time. But that he's not here anymore is something for both of us and if you go there, to that animal, then it's something for you. Only for you."

"Then go with me," he said. "Then it's for both of us. I don't do anything with her. I just stand there in the stall." Still holding their remaining boy, he caressed her arm, to show that he didn't mean to shut her out. That she could go if she wanted. That she belonged. That the emptiness was theirs, together.

"You stand in the stall?" she asked. "You stand in the stall the way cows stand in the stall?"

"Not like cows do. Our boy spent the last few weeks of his life there. We know that was his favorite place to go. And somehow it soothes me, to go there, to stand there. Where he stood."

"So that's what you were doing when you told me you were out with colleagues, you were standing in a stall. So I smelled right."

She ran downstairs, to the kitchen, as though he'd confessed to her that he'd had a mistress all those months, and he followed her and watched while she put a microwave meal in the oven. He held the boy on his arm and he didn't know what to say. All of a sudden, he didn't know how to explain it.

"My husband stands in a stall. Our son was hit by a train and so my husband stands in a stall all afternoon, beside a deathly sick pony that used to belong to our boy, because he had no friends. Because that's the truth, Geniek, he had no friends, no one wanted to be his friend and we didn't do anything about it, we just left it that way, we thought: it'll all work out in the end. As long as he doesn't go on pooping his pants. And when he stopped pooping his pants we were relieved, we were so incredibly pleased. And now you go and stand there beside that pony, and I'm supposed to think that's normal. Do you want to turn into your own son? Do you think it will help if you start looking like him? Are you going to start pooping in your pants too?"

"No," he said quietly, "of course not. And it's not about me wanting to become him, it's about me feeling that she shouldn't be killed, and I stand beside her because I like that. Maybe I should have told you before. Maybe I should have told you, but I knew what you'd say . . . That you wouldn't like it. That you're against it. That's why I thought: I won't start in about it. Then there's nothing for you to be against."

.He looked at the microwave. Chicken and rice. Then he picked up the plates, with the boy still on his arm, and began setting the table. She stayed in the kitchen the whole time, and when he came back for some silverware and when he'd done that, when the table was set, she said: "Maybe you think it's okay to stand around in a stall all afternoon, but that's because you never talk to anyone. If you told people about it, if you told your colleagues about it, they'd tell you it isn't normal. But you don't do that. There's no salad. I don't feel like making a salad. Do you mind?"

"No," he said.

She took the meal out of the microwave and divided it over two plates, then she heated up the mush for the remaining boy and at last they went together to the dining room. He put the boy in his high-chair; only when they were all seated did he say: "You once fell in love with a silent Polack. You knew who I was."

"I knew who you were and I thought your silence was mysterious and attractive, but now it drives me nuts." She mushed her rice with the back of her fork, although there was no reason to do so, she mashed the rice as though the grains were too big to swallow. "But still," she said when she was finished mashing, "it doesn't matter, it's not that I want to leave you, we grow toward each other like two trees, but sometimes your roots get in my way."

The Polack had to think about that. The roots, the trees, it sounded familiar. Slowly, he started eating. The chicken was a little sweet.

"I'll take you along," he said. "The next time I go, you go with me. I'll show you the farm, I know you didn't want to go there, after his death . . . Because . . . Because you thought it was unnecessary. The same way we didn't want to go into his room anymore. The way we thought: it's good, this way. We don't care what other people say, we'll do it the way we think is good. And, in fact, I talk quite a bit. Here at home, I haven't been the silent Polack for a long time already. I'm only the Polack."

She went on eating and now she was the one who said nothing, and when her plate was empty and his was still full of rice and chicken, she said: "Okay, I'll go along. If that's what you want. But I don't under-stand it. Nothing about the past can be changed anymore. Even if you stand around in that stall for the rest of your life. Why don't you just concentrate on the son you still have?"

The Polack did his best, even though he was pretty sure he wouldn't be able to finish all the chicken. And to prove that he was concentrat-ing on the son he still had, he lifted the boy out of his highchair and said to him: "I'm concentrating on you. The Polack is concentrating on you." And he walked around the dining room, above all as an excuse not to have to eat, but the boy laughed and then Wen couldn't help laughing either.

"We need to put it to a close," Wen said, "that's what I'm talking about. Of course, you can't really close it off, we just have to act that way, otherwise I'll go crazy around here. I can't stand the feeling that I'm talking to him too whenever I talk to you. From now on we need to tell each other: there used to be the four of us, now it's the three of us, and we accept that."

Walking around the room, the Polack said: "We can't put it to a close as long as the pony's still around. Don't you understand that?"

He took the boy upstairs. Luckily, his wife didn't mention the fact that he'd left half his microwave meal on his plate.

Only when they were in bed later on did she comment: "You're getting thinner."

"I was a little too heavy anyway," he replied.

"Come on," she said, "you were muscular. You are muscular. That wasn't fat, those are muscles. You're a good-looking man."

He hugged his darling wife but he didn't kiss her on the lips, he couldn't kiss her on the lips, in the same way that he had been unable to eat his chicken.

6

They were planning to go there that next Saturday, when they both had a day off. That morning he waited for her to say something, but finally he had to ask: "Did you want to go along?" It hurt him that she hadn't mentioned it on her own. As though she were doing it against her will, only for him, just to keep the peace. She asked: "Where?" Right after that she said: "Oh yeah, of course."

"I don't want Jurek to go with us," she added. "I'll take him to the people across the street."

When they had brought their one remaining boy to the neighbors across the street, she asked whether she needed to put on rubber boots. "Well," the Polack answered—he hadn't counted on a question like that—"we are going to a stable. But rubber boots . . . It hasn't been raining. No. You don't have to."

"I'll put on the boots anyway," she said. "Just to be sure." Apparently, she was afraid there would be a lot of filth lying around at the farm.

Wen went upstairs and came back with a pair of blue boots with red and yellow flowers on them. She had also put on an old pair of jeans that she usually wore only when she worked in the garden, which she rarely did these days. He couldn't recall that last time he'd seen her in those old jeans.

She put on her makeup at the mirror, worked concentratedly at the bags under her eyes. "Is it okay for me to go like this?"

"We're going to a farm," he replied.

"Don't I look okay, then?" she asked.

In the car she didn't say much. She listened to the radio and occasionally mumbled something about what she heard, about the crisis, the banks, she also mentioned the name of a female singer he didn't recognize and said she'd like to go dancing again.

When they got to the farm, she pointed at the farmer sitting at the window. "That man's staring at us."

"He always does that," the Polack said. "He stares. He's confined to a wheelchair. Didn't I tell you that?"

"I don't think so," she replied. "You almost never tell me things. And besides, there are people in wheelchairs who don't sit there staring out the window all day."

The walked to the stall and the Polack thought about the veterinarian, the miracle that had come too late, his eldest son. And he realized that there was nothing he'd rather do than stand in the stall with his wife, beside the animal. Just stand there and look at the empty stalls, the bars, the water trough. For hours and hours. Until they'd grown calm, until they loved each other again like before, until they understood that one could live this way too.

"There," he pointed at the only stable with a living animal still in it. The last living animal here, if you didn't count the cats, the mice, and the insects.

They went in, he turned on the light.

"So many empty stalls," the Polack's wife said. And she looked at her boots, they were the kind of boots toddlers love.

She walked toward Borys's pony, slowly. Wen put her feet down carefully. "It's not dirty here," the Polack said. "Just dark."

"So lonely," she said when they reached the stall. "Pitiful."

"But I take care of her." He didn't think the animal was pitiful. Just as, in the long run, he hadn't considered their boy pitiful either. Doomed, tragic, misunderstood, those were the words that came to mind, not pitiful. He didn't like that word. "I come here as often as I can."

"Exactly," she said, "and I wish you didn't."

He took her hand, but she pulled it away carefully.

The Polack opened the door to the stall and, as usual, the pony barely reacted, only a little movement of the head. He had the feeling he was introducing his wife to a long-lost member of the family.

"She's big," Wen said, "I thought ponies were smaller than that."

"You have big ponies and little ponies." He noticed that he was talking like an expert again, a man who feigned expertise he didn't possess. A man who had never been interested in animals and who now acted as though animals were his best friends.

"This place smells of you," Wen said.

"What do you mean?"

"It smells like you."

"I've been here a lot lately."

She looked at him. "Have you started smelling of the stall, or has the stall started smelling like you?"

He shrugged. He didn't much feel like it, but he kissed his dear wife and whispered in her ear, asking whether now she could smell the difference between the stall and her husband. She laughed.

"This is where I usually stand," the Polack said, and he went and stood beside the pony. Just to show how harmless it was, what he did here. For a moment, he placed his hand on the pony's head. He didn't pet her, she wasn't some cuddly toy.

They stood beside each other and both of them looked at his wife, the man and the animal. Wen's gaze shifted back and forth between her husband and the pony. "As though you're burying yourself alive," she murmured.

The Polack shook his head. "Not at all, this is where life is."

"Not with me? Not at home? Only here in this stall?"

He gave her the wrong answer, but he didn't want to lie, because she was his wife and she needed to keep on being that. There was no life outside of her, even if her tongue was as repulsive to him as chicken from the microwave. Now that he thought about it, her tongue reminded him of that chicken.

"Maybe the two of us could stand here together," the Polack said. "Then you'll see. How nice it is. Just standing. Beside her. Living, and at the same time lifeless."

"I don't feel like looking at the bars," his wife said, "just look, this old animal never sees sunlight anymore, only iron bars, she doesn't see any other animals, only you once in a while. Have her put down, if you really love her so much, have her taken away."

The Polack shook his head. This was going all wrong. "But come and stand beside me, then you'll see what I mean. Then you'll feel it. Sometimes I take her outside. If the weather allows. Then we walk around a little. Do you want to see that?"

"No!" she shouted.

The sound of her voice cut the Polack to the quick, because he enjoyed the silence and he had the feeling that shouting desecrated the silence of this place. What's more, he feared his wife's anger, not because he was afraid of her but because that anger made him feel that he had failed. Sometimes he knelt down here in this stall, because he was overpowered by emotions—the feeling of being nothing, except that continual falling short of the mark—with which he didn't know how to cope.

She walked around the stall while he remained standing, thinking about Borys and then about the C squad, his wife, Beckers's wife, keeping company with the animal that may not have even appreciated his company. He didn't want to take her loneliness away from her. He hadn't come here to provide solace, because he knew that was impossible. At most, you could say he stood here out of a sense of solidarity, though he himself would never have called it that. Every once in a while, he touched her respectfully, the lonely old lady, referred to consistently by the vet as the "girl," a hand on her back or head, when flies landed he shooed them away. By way of exception, he scratched her hide and said: "Our boy used to talk to you, but I don't have anything to say."

Behind him he could hear his wife shuffling through the straw, he didn't look around until she called him. "Come here, would you?" she said. "Did he walk around here? Did Borys stand here?"

He looked over his shoulder and said: "He squatted there."

The Polack walked to the back of the stall, to the darkened corner. "I told you about it, remember?" he said. "That he did number two back here?"

"I made myself forget," she said.

"I don't think he used the people-toilet anymore. I never dared to ask him about it."

"Animal-toilets?" she mumbled.

"He loved her," the Polack said. "At least, I think so. And that's why I love her now too."

She started pacing back and forth, faster and faster, as though she herself was a caged animal. "You call it love, but it's cruelty to animals. You talked about a miracle, that the vet performed, but I don't see any miracle. I see an old animal that needs to be put out of her misery and it's pure egoism of you not to do that. How can you call egoism 'love'? How can you neglect your family for this animal that's only waiting to die? A death you won't allow her to have, because you're too cowardly, because you think you can avoid the suffering, but you can't. Isn't that what our boy taught us? That you can't avoid it?"

She ran off and he went after her. In front of the stables, she stopped. "I don't want you to come here anymore," she said. "If you want to stay with me, if you want to stay with us, then you have to promise not to come here anymore. This is a disaster zone. I'm sure that none of it would have happened if he hadn't come here, if he hadn't gone to this place, like a possessed person, each and every day. This is where he got the idea. And if you keep on coming here, then you'll get those ideas too, that's why I'm being very clear about this. If you want to stay with us, then you'll take her away. And when you've done that you'll see that it was the best for her too. Sometimes love is putting a thing to sleep."

The Polack didn't know what to say to this, he closed the stall door the way he did three or four times a week, always with a sort of wistfulness, as though he was more at home here than he was at home, with his family. He didn't reply to all the things his dear wife had just said, he walked after her, back to the car, a few steps behind her. It felt as if he too had to be put gently to sleep.

"Have I made my point?" She spoke without turning, she spoke loudly. "Do you promise? Not to come back here again? That it's over, your visits? Do you understand?"

He said yes, but apparently that wasn't enough, for she stopped, turned to him and asked: "Do you promise me?"

The Polack promised, and then Wen said that if they buried themselves alive in the past, the two of them, if they went on wallowing in their memories, then Jurek might just as well not exist.

For a moment the Polack was about to say that he wasn't wallowing in anything, but he choked it back. He needed to choose for his wife, not for the pony, not for the past.

When they got to the car, they could hear the farmer tapping on the window. The Polack meant to ignore it, in fact, but the tapping went on and on, it sounded as though the farmer were knocking on the glass with a sharp object, a pair of scissors or a knife. It sounded to him as though the farmer meant to break the window.

"What does he want?" Wen asked.

The Polack shrugged. "No idea. He probably wants to talk to us. I don't feel like it." He started climbing into the car, but with a resolve that surprised him Wen answered: "Well, I *do* want to talk to him, I want to see him up close, I'll tell him a few home truths."

The farmer seemed to him like someone with an unshakeable belief in his own truths and little to no patience for those of others. But seeing as he had just promised to get rid of the pony, perhaps it didn't matter what kind of home truths she told the farmer. The worst that could happen had already happened. Although the Polack feared that now something else was about to happen. He couldn't imagine that the suffering they had coming was already done with. He wasn't the kind of person who asked himself: what did I do to deserve this? The disaster was not a punishment. The misfortune was meaningless, and that was precisely what made the misfortune so hard, so unbearable at times, when you least expected it.

Before he could think any more about misfortune, his wife had already walked to the house. As though she knew the way, as though she'd been here before. She pushed open the kitchen door. "What a mess," she said. "Decrepit inside and out."

The Polack shrugged. "It's to the right," he said quietly.

The farmer was sitting there, he maneuvered his wheelchair away from the window. The Polack was struck by how quickly the farmer had deteriorated, his cheeks were hollow, his lips were blue, he hadn't shaved for days, maybe weeks.

"Hello," the Polack said. "We've come to a decision." Because the farmer didn't say a word.

The old man raised his hand. He made movements with his jaw. It seemed like his teeth didn't fit in his mouth, and he was trying to move them back into place by moving his tongue and jaws.

"This is my wife," the Polack said.

The farmer waved his hand, probably to tell his visitors to be quiet, that it was not yet their turn to speak. Here one spoke only when asked.

At last the farmer succeeded in saying something. "I know who she is," he said, panting slightly. "I read about her in the paper." And he pointed at two clippings that were lying on the table, discreetly and yet not. Clippings dealing with the fatal accident.

"So now the lonesome girl is done for too," the farmer said, and it sounded as though he regretted that.

"What girl?" Wen asked.

"The pony," the farmer said, "the loneliest girl on this farm." He laughed with difficulty, as though laughing hurt him too.

"Do you live here all by yourself?" Wen asked once the farmer was done laughing. "Don't you have anyone to help you?"

The old tablecloth, in so far as you could call it that, had been replaced with a sort of carpet-like thing.

The farmer laughed again, the question seemed to amuse him. "Do I live here all by myself?" he asked. Then he raised his voice. "Don't I have anyone to help me?" he shouted with unexpected force.

The Polack was reminded of the woman lying upstairs in her bed-room, and how the people-hand had told him that the farmer and his wife communicated by knocking on the walls. The old man began coughing, and then went back to arranging his teeth with movements of tongue and jaw. The visitors remained silent, and the Polack realized that there was also an advantage to the death that equaled love—that he would not have to come here anymore. His wife took his hand and squeezed it. She had a hard time with decline, human decline too.

"I have children," the farmer said, "and they come here a couple of times a year to look at me. You lost a child." He tapped his fingers against the table where the clippings lay. "You wonder: why don't the children come more often to look at the old man? Because they detest him. People are strange creatures. I've always thought that cows are less strange than people. Sometimes a calf gets trampled, the cows don't get upset about that."

Wen squeezed his hand harder now and said: "People aren't cows. Our son is not a trampled calf. We're grateful to you that he could come here, that he found something here he apparently didn't find anywhere else. But we've closed the door on the past. We have to move on. We have another son too. Borys never talked about you, but still, I wanted to see who owned the farm that he biked to almost every day."

She was eloquent, that was because of the toddlers too. Screaming didn't get you very far. He noticed that she spoke to the farmer the way she was also able to speak to the toddlers' parents. It was her voice when she was annoyed. She didn't let go of the Polack's hand, she pressed it against her side. As though she wanted to show the farmer: look, this is my husband, not always easy, sometimes a burden, but I'll go on carrying that burden.

"Your son," said the farmer, and his hands rested on the table, on the clippings. For a moment the Polack thought the clippings had always been there on the table, and that made him feel uneasy. "I almost never saw your son, he went straight to the stall and from the stall back home. He came in here a couple of times. I offered him a piece of candy, but he didn't want any. Not a chocolate bar either. I said: take a bar of chocolate, kid, a nice candy bar. No. I saw it right away: he was miserable. I can see auras, animals and people. I used to be able to pick out the sick calves right away. I could see the color of his sickness. Bright yellow. So bright I had to look away. My father had that too. It drove him crazy. He took it personally. That people were sick. I don't. I can't help it that they're sick. I didn't make them sick. I wanted to tell you that. That it's better this way. With an aura like that, you can't stand up to life. I tried to help. I have healing hands. But it was too late. That's what I wanted to say. So you can be at peace."

Wen said: "I don't want you to talk about our child like that. The color of his sickness. His aura. He wasn't sick. You don't know anything about him."

The farmer laughed again. He hacked, spit something into a handkerchief. "He wasn't sick," he said. "That's what they always think.

They don't believe me. People don't want to know. I can see your colors too, and I'm telling you: do something about it, before it's too late."

The Polack heard a car pulling into the yard. His wife kept squeezing his hand. Out of love. The despair known as love.

"That's my people-hand," the farmer said. For the first time this afternoon, the farmer sounded scared. A silence fell. His aggressive cheerfulness, his need to confront others with truths and auras, it had all disappeared.

"Your ears still work well enough," the Polack said, and his wife scratched the back of his head lightly, the way you scratch a dog's fur.

"Yeah, my ears still work well enough," the farmer replied. "Something's got to work well still. And you want to know my secret? Never clean them. Ruins your ears. And never go to concerts. My kids wanted to take me along. I refused. The music in the house, from the radio, I thought that was enough. My eldest kid is deaf these days."

The Polack heard the people-hand coming through the kitchen. Then he entered the room, neater than the hired hand had been, but skinny as a bone too. He was carrying a plastic bag that he opened right away.

"*Babi pangang,*" those were the first words the people-hand spoke. "You like that, don't you?"

The helper took a tray of *babi pangang* and rice out of the plastic bag and put it down on top of the newspapers and the clippings about their boy and his fatal accident, because that's what they called it, that's what the Polack wanted to call it too.

"No," said the farmer.

Only then did the people-hand turn to the visitors, he asked: "You folks okay?" Then he looked at Wen: "I come and help out here every so often. In the morning. In the evening. Around dinner time. It's still early, the farmer eats dinner early. Usually I come by myself, sometimes it's a colleague."

"Yes," the farmer said. "I eat early. And with no appetite."

"Nonsense," the people-hand said. "You're eating better all the time."

The man sat down. He hung his coat over the back of his chair, pulled plastic gloves out of the bag, gloves that reminded the Polack of a hospital.

"The farmer calls me the people-hand," the people-hand said, "and that gave me the idea of calling myself that, too."

He pulled on the gloves and wormed two, three fingers into the farmer's mouth. "Just see if everything's in the right place," the people-hand said. "So he won't choke. You two might as well sit down. No reason why you can't stick around, it's quite an operation, feeding the farmer is, but that's no secret."

"No," said the Polack. 'We'll stand. We have to get going anyway."

The people-hand took some plastic cutlery out of the bag and began feeding the farmer, who sighed and groaned as he ate and occasionally waved his hand, as though trying to silence the others, even though no one spoke. "That's enough!" he shouted every once in a while. But the people-hand answered firmly: "No, we're going to go on eating." He still had a plastic glove on his left hand, as though he'd forgotten to take it off.

The Polack didn't understand why his wife made no move to leave. She stood watching in fascination, as though she'd never seen someone being fed before. "He can eat by himself," said the people-hand, shoving some rice into the farmer's mouth, "but he won't, that's why he hired me. Or rather, that's why his children hired me, because they have no time for it. And they don't live around here either."

It looked like the farmer wanted to say something, but the people-hand held one hand in front of the farmer's mouth. "Otherwise he'll spit it out, and that would be a waste."

Wen seemed unable to pull herself away from the scene, she stared at the people-hand as though she'd never seen a hired hand like him before.

He wiped the farmer's mouth with a paper napkin, which made the old man look even more helpless than he had while being fed and, retroactively, you almost couldn't help but forgive the man for talking about their son's aura.

"I work outside the regular home-care networks," the people-hand said. "I also visit people who are struggling with dementia and who want custom-tailored care. They have a hard time remembering my name. Martin. Laurens. David. Each time I'm someone else, but they can always remember 'the people-hand,' and so I've been the people-hand and nothing else ever since. I've even scratched out my own name, Ruud, on my business card." Still holding the plastic spoon in the farmer's mouth, he fished a business card out of his pocket and handed it, with difficulty, to Wen.

She looked at it. "People-hand," the card said. Underneath, the scratched-out name and then an email address and phone number.

"Assistance," said Ruud the people-hand as he stuffed a bit of meat into the farmer's mouth, "always comes top-down. People need assistance and there comes the caregiver, he gives something, and then you're lower in rank than the caregiver. A lot of people don't like that, they don't want to be looked down on by the caregiver, and that's the opportunity I seized upon. I stay small, the people-hand makes himself real small. Look down on me, says the people-hand. That's okay. You're allowed to do that. I'm here to provide care. And that's no fun for anyone. People want to take care of themselves. They're not babies. But that doesn't always work. And they're really not crazy about the idea."

He wiped the farmer's mouth. "Taste good?" he asked.

"No," said the farmer.

"There's not a whole lot he does like anymore," the people-hand said cheerfully, stuffing some rice in the old man's mouth. "But he isn't planning to give up, am I right, you're not giving up, are you?"

The people-hand waited until the old man finished what was in his mouth, and then the farmer said: "They'd like that, my children would, to have me give up. Never."

The people-hand nodded. "He thinks his children hate him, he lives to thwart his children because he thinks they'll throw a party when he's finally dead, and he begrudges them the celebration, he probably always begrudged them much in the way of celebrations. But they pay me a lot of money to keep him alive, they wouldn't do that if they didn't love their father. I'm not on the official list for the national health service, yet. The time will come, though. If you're poor, the people-hand won't be coming by, that's unfortunate but true. Not yet, anyway, I always emphasize that. In the future everyone will have their own people-hand. You're still alive because you begrudge your children the pleasure of having you die, right?"

The farmer nodded.

The Polack could contain himself no longer. "And later on, will you be going upstairs?" he asked.

"Of course," the people-hand said. "Then I'll feed the missus. Sometimes he knocks on the wall. One knock means: I love you. Knock twice means: I hate you. Sometimes you hate your wife, and sometimes you love her, right?" The people-hand leaned forward briefly and patted the farmer fondly on the back, as though the farmer were a man-sized baby who needed to be burped.

The farmer nodded. He swung his wheelchair around to face the wall and knocked twice, loudly.

"You're not finished eating yet," the people-hand said.

The old man turned his wheelchair back around to face the table where the people-hand was waiting with the spoon raised, but the farmer pushed the spoon away. A squeaking sound was coming out of his nose now.

"You do it all so professionally and lovingly," Wen said. "That's not always the way it goes, I know that."

"We have to get home," the Polack said. "The pony is going away, so you won't see us around here anymore."

He stepped away from his wife, walked around the table to the people-hand.

His wife followed him hesitantly. She was sweet, he was sure of that, his wife was sweet and always would be.

"You two have my number," said the people-hand. "If you know anyone who could use my services. I don't place myself above the needy, deep inside I'm needy myself, if you look closely you see that there are only the needy. That's why we need people-hands."

"Do you think," Wen asked, "that you could also help people to live?"

"What do you mean?"

"So that people can say: today the people-hand is living my life for me, I'm off for the day, I can't handle it today."

The people-hand shook his head. "What we do always involves caregiving; for the time being, people have to enjoy their lives all on their own."

While the departure ritual was taking place, the farmer turned his wheelchair around again and knocked loudly, twice, on the wall.

The people-hand interrupted the farewells. He looked at the farmer with endearment. "It's so lovely," he said, "when people that age communicate with so much passion."

7

The first butcher the Polack called told him that a pony was no problem, that he did horses too, he slaughtered everything really, except for poultry. The Polack could bring the animal by on a Friday or a Tuesday morning, preferably before 10. He could also come by the evening before, but then not too late. The butcher went to bed early. It cost 120 euros, not including sales tax, although that depended on whether the Polack wanted to take meat home with him.

The Polack said that he didn't want to take meat home with him.

"Then I think we can agree on 120 euros," answered the butcher, who said his name was Tim.

They made an appointment for Friday morning, and the butcher said the Polack would have to arrange his own transport. "I used to pick up animals sometimes," he explained, "but I don't do that anymore. I'm a butcher, not a trucking company."

The Polack hung up. All he had to do now was arrange one of those things they carried animals in. That wasn't easy. Most rental companies didn't have anything for transporting a pony, or at least not in their own fleet. At last he decided to check the Internet for horse transport. There was, as it turned out, a horse taxi, but it was nowhere close, and that made the horse taxi expensive. Besides, the term "horse taxi" bothered him. You didn't take a horse taxi to be killed. By way of the horse taxi he found a man who owned horses and who told the Polack that he had a panel truck he was quite pleased with, and also a trailer, and that he was willing to rent him either one of them. Especially when the Polack explained what it was for. "Yeah," the man said, "that's no life for a pony."

The panel truck didn't appeal to the Polack either, if only because it sounded wrong. He said: "I'll take the trailer." The trailer wasn't very expensive. And it was only for one day. Go out loaded in the morning, come back empty before noon, that's the way he imagined it; he tried to approach it in a businesslike fashion, because he feared he wouldn't be able to do it otherwise. Just to be sure, he rented the trailer for the whole day. He had taken the whole day off to do it anyway, he wasn't sure how long something like that took, you had to give yourself some leeway for problems along the way.

That morning he left early to pick up the trailer. He had bought a few extra fodder carrots and apples to take along. The man he rented it from helped him hitch the trailer to the Polack's car. "Don't drive too fast," he warned, "that thing might sway. Especially if the wind's blowing. And a horse never stands completely still either."

Before leaving, the Polack gave the man a firm handshake. He said: "You've got a nice place here." That was true, too. The man had a nice place. On top of a hill, with a lovely view. Especially by Dutch standards.

He hadn't told his wife that he'd be taking the pony away this Friday, that the notion of death as love would be put into practice today. He had no desire for her pity, if only because he felt that he didn't deserve her pity. He didn't want to talk about it anymore. He was making the sacrifice.

The Polack, careful as he was, drove slowly, not ignoring the warning the trailer-owner had issued. Although, then again, the slow driving might also have been him delaying things, delaying the moment when he would drive with the trailer into the farmyard, the moment when he would lead the animal out of the stall, fully realizing that it would never come back. The farmer would be sure to laugh triumphantly. What he had predicted was about to happen, and while the

Polack let a truck pass, he wondered how he was going to fill his days if he no longer went to stand beside the animal in the stall. What had he done before this? The days had raced by, even though he couldn't really remember how.

It was a little before 9:30 when he pulled into the yard. He was a little late for the butcher, but from here on it would go quickly. The farmer sat where he always sat. This time there was no tapping on the window.

Slowly and carefully, he walked to the stall, watched precisely where he stepped. He saddled up the pony as best he could, he didn't have much experience with that. "We're going to take a trip," he said, leading her outside. The saddle wasn't really necessary, he wasn't going to ride her, but somehow he felt that she needed to enter the slaughterhouse with her saddle on, with as much dignity as possible. Not as an old, lonely animal, but as a miracle, the miracle the vet had seen in her and made of her.

He led her into the yard, she walked beside him, the way she had often done on days that he had walked her around. Sometimes she would stop or try to walk on the other side of the Polack. She wasn't really what you'd call fractious.

Once she was in front of the trailer, though, she refused to budge. Acting on the advice from the man who had rented him the trailer, he had tossed some fresh hay in first. "Lure her in with an apple, or a carrot, if she gives you any trouble," he'd said, in the slightly condescending fashion of one who knows that he's dealing with an amateur.

She balked, she dug her hooves in, there was no way to move her, she did what she had never done before, at least not as long as the Polack had known her: she put up a fight. Now was the time to produce the carrot. The animal loved carrots.

From his car he fetched a big fodder carrot, he climbed up into the trailer and, waving the carrot, he called out: "Come on, come on, girl, come on."

But she did not come. No matter how hard he pulled on the rope. Not even the carrot could tempt her into it.

As he pulled with one hand and waved the carrot with the other, he realized that the farmer was watching him. He was being laughed at, he knew it. He was failing, he was a man who claimed to love an animal he couldn't even get into a trailer. He dropped the fodder carrot, pulled on the rope now with both hands, but the animal was stronger, it dug in, unexpected powers had arisen in the old pony. She tossed her forelegs in the air, she reared, and that for such an old animal. Was this the miracle expressing itself only now, at last? All this time the animal had stood dumb and silent in the stall and now it was bucking as though life started right here, so soon before dying. She refused to do what the Polack wanted. And because he had no doubt that the farmer was watching, because he thought he knew what the man was thinking, this was no longer merely between the pony and him. It was between him, the animal, and the farmer. The Polack had to prove something to the old, wheelchair-bound man. He stepped out of the trailer, rope in hand, went to the car, took out an apple.

He fed the old, lonely girl the fruit, which she ate greedily. "Later on I'll give you another one," he said quietly. "Once you're inside, I'll give you lots of apples."

He felt disgusted with himself for letting this happen. Because there was still no way to move her, she was stronger than the Polack. And because he feared hurting her if he pulled too hard, he went around behind her, he pushed against her backside with both hands, and the only result was that she kicked him. Not hard, but hard enough. There would be a bruise on his thigh. He moved up beside her, lowered his lips to her ear so the farmer couldn't see, and whispered: "You have to help me. The decision has already been made. There's no use resisting." And he stroked her carefully as he thought about their boy, and he couldn't shake the thought that it was their boy he was trying to push into the trailer.

Again he went to the car, again he tried to tempt the old, lonely girl, this time with a big fat carrot, but she would not be tempted, she stood stubborn and still and it seemed like she knew that she didn't have to move, like she knew that he would bring her that carrot anyway.

She was willing to go anywhere, but not into the trailer.

When she had eaten three apples and three fodder carrots, the tapping on the window began. With a sharp object this time, too. The farmer tapped on the window like mad, rhythmically, as though playing music, with the energy of a young but not particularly talent-ed musician, and although the Polack had meant to ignore it he soon could no longer concentrate on what he was doing, for all he could hear was the noise the farmer made.

He tied the pony to a tree and walked to the farmhouse. When he came closer, he saw that the farmer was tapping on the window with a pair of scissors.

There he was, back in that room where it seemed to him he had stood all too often before. The farmer said nothing, he wheeled himself over to a cupboard, yanked open a drawer and pulled out an old whip. Then he said: "Roll me outside."

The Polack pushed the old man outside, the farmer held the whip but said nothing. Only when they came close to the pony did the farm-er command: "Untie her. You pull. I'll give her a nudge from behind. The two of us will get her into that trailer."

The Polack began pulling on the rope again, although he had the feeling he was almost choking the big pony. The couple of hundred kilos of her would not be moved.

To the back of and beside her sat the farmer in his wheelchair, and now the Polack understood what the farmer meant by giving her a nudge. From his chair the farmer brought down the whip on the pony's back and flanks with a force and energy that amazed the Polack. For one last time, youth seemed to have taken possession of the farmer, a rage that seemed like life itself had taken control of the old man, all the resistance to his own death seemed to mean only that he was prepared to whip to death the old, lonely girl.

"Get," the farmer shouted. The harder he lashed out the more the animal resisted, and that resistance consisted of standing still, of not moving. The pony looked at the Polack, it looked right at him, and he couldn't help but feel that the animal was looking at him questioningly. Not imploringly, but questioningly, in amazement. Is this what your love means?

"Easy," the Polack shouted. "Take it easy. She doesn't have to die. Not yet."

He saw the blood beginning to well up from the animal's hide, and strangely enough that made the Polack weaker too.

"Get," the farmer went on shouting, "get, get in there, you." And he went on lashing, the way a boxer skips rope, no, the way a boxer throws punches. He wasn't training for the match, this was the match.

"Go on, pull," the farmer shouted, "pull, would you, we've almost got her broken."

A little later the Polack was able to pull the pony into the trailer. He hitched her to the bars, the way the man had showed him, and ran the back of his hand over her wounds. From his pocket he took out an apple. "Eat this," he said. "This is for you, girl."

He'd thought she would refuse, that she wouldn't eat this apple, but she ate this apple as well. She had no pride. Animals have no pride, and most people don't either. There were exceptions; the Polack didn't entertain the illusion that he was one of them.

He stepped out, closed the trailer, saw the pony look back at him.

The farmer was still sitting where he'd sat all this time. He was panting, the whip was in his hand. "Bring me inside."

The Polack pushed the farmer inside. They didn't speak a word. In the room where he ate and slept, where he lived and where he was sure to die too, the farmer put the whip back in the drawer carefully, almost solemnly, and the Polack had the feeling this was not the last time he would take that whip out of the drawer.

Beside the newspapers on the table lay the scissors the farmer had used to tap on the window. Apparently, he still cut out articles that interested him. But on the table, where everything the farmer seemed to need was strewn about, there were still only two clippings, the same clippings, about the boy and the express train.

The Polack left the farmer without saying anything, without asking any questions. He walked to his car, checked once more if the pony was fastened well in the trailer, then drove to the butcher's. Carefully, but hurriedly nonetheless.

He had never been to a slaughterhouse before. From the outside it looked like a normal farm. So far, nothing there spoke of death. There were animals in the stalls, all sorts of animals, with fences between them, to be sure. The Polack asked a fairly young farmhand where he could drop the pony. The farmhand only looked around, startled, then walked away.

And so the Polack went himself, in search of the man he'd spoken to on the phone. In an outbuilding that looked like a cross between a small office and kitchen, a man was sitting at a long table, smoking a cigarette. He had bright blue eyes, and although he had seen the Polack come in, he didn't greet him. He looked straight through the Polack. The distance seemed to interest him more than the man standing before him. That is why the Polack said: "We spoke on the phone."

"About what?" the man asked.

"About my pony."

The man took a drag on his cigarette, exhaled the smoke slowly and said: "True. You're late."

"We had some difficulties," said the Polack, and he wondered if it was all right for him to take a chair. He had already decided to say nothing about the nature of the difficulties, that was none of the butcher's business.

"Doesn't matter," the man said. "The meat's not for consumption anyway, if I remember correctly, so we can forget about the inspection. Where's the pony?"

"In the trailer," the Polack said, sitting down anyway.

The man reached across the table and shook his hand. "Tim."

The Polack introduced himself too.

"Coffee?" Tim asked.

The Polack nodded.

Tim got up, went to the coffee maker, poured a cup, and put it on the table. "It's been on the plate since early this morning, but it's still drinkable enough. Milk and sugar?"

The Polack shook his head. He took a sip.

"I've never done any butchering for you before, so I'd like to ask if you could make the payment now. Preferably cash."

"That's fine," the Polack said. He pulled out his wallet.

"The woman who does the books isn't here this morning. She'll draw up an invoice and mail it to you later."

"I don't need an invoice," the Polack said.

"I'll send you one anyway," and Tim tucked the money into his breast pocket. "These days, they watch every move you make.

Especially as a butcher. If you only knew the letters I get. They call me a Nazi henchman, apparently they've never paid much attention to history."

Tim ground out his cigarette. The Polack looked around. It was peaceful here, in this kitchen-cum-office. It reminded him vaguely of the fire station.

"Can you unload the animal yourself?" Tim asked. "There's a boy outside, he'll show you where to leave it."

"The young boy?" the Polack asked.

"He's not a young boy. He's a dwarf. Can't you tell the difference between young and little?"

"I didn't notice," said the Polack, and because he could be witty too, after his own fashion, he added: "I haven't had a lot of experience with dwarves."

Tim lit another cigarette. "Whenever there's an opening for that job, I always hire people who are at a disadvantage, persons with a disability, I see that as my social responsibility. He's a good guy. A bit skittish, but I mean, what do you expect from a dwarf? If he has problems with one of the big animals, the cows or horses, one of us comes to help him. For the pigs, a dwarf like him is perfect. They see the dwarf and I think they kind of figure: hey, that's one of us."

The Polack nodded.

"I don't rule out persons with disabilities," Tim went on, "they're welcome to work in my stalls. And you can get grant money for it, too. Not a lot, but still. What they give you with one hand they take back with the other."

The Polack was silent. He stared at his knuckles and without taking his eyes off his hands, he said: "I'd like to be there, I'd really like to stay with her for as long as possible."

"With the pony."

"During the butchering," said the Polack. "I'd like to be there when she leaves this world."

"Are you a butcher?"

The Polack shook his head.

"Have you ever slaughtered an animal?"

"No, I'm a fireman."

"Oh." Tim took the pack of cigarettes and stuffed it in his pants pocket. "Then I guess you've seen a thing or two. But I can't start doing that. This isn't reality TV."

"I'd really like to," the Polack said. "If need be, I'll pay a little extra."

"For what?"

"To be allowed to stay."

Tim sighed. He looked straight at the Polack with his bright blue eyes, it made the Polack uneasy. After all, his request wasn't all that strange. It wasn't that he'd said: I want to butcher her myself. He just wanted to stick around.

"This isn't some bullfight arena, we don't have grandstands you can sit on and watch, we're a business operation, I work for my keep. There's nothing to see here. Or are you from the animal protection agency or something?"

"I work for the fire department," the Polack repeated.

"Not even as a hobby? Protecting animals, while you're actually harming them, because that's what the animal protection agency does, they claim they're helping but they only make things worse. I love animals, otherwise I wouldn't slaughter them. You can slaughter, and then again you can slaughter. You can harm an animal, or you can help an animal to cross the threshold gently."

"It's not my hobby," the Polack said. "I don't have hobbies like that."

Tim shook his head slowly. "Sorry, but I'm not going to do it. Watch YouTube if you want to see it."

"That's not it," the Polack said, rubbing his hands over the table as though tried to wipe something clean, "I want to keep her company."

"Keep her company?" Tim's stare seemed even harsher now. "Are you one of those? Then they come here and then they still can't say goodbye. But once the animal is in my stall, it's a done deal, otherwise it's a possible source of infection. No matter how you look at it. Have you already taken it out of the trailer?"

"No, she's still in there."

"Theoretically then, you could still take her with you. Drive away before it's too late."

Tim pulled the money out of his breast pocket, but the Polack said: "You don't understand. I don't want to take her with me. She should . . .

But I'd really like to stick around. I'll stay in the background. I won't get in the way."

The butcher put the money back in his pocket. "You can wait up here. Then I'll tell you how it went. I don't want anyone looking over my shoulder."

Pale sunshine was coming through the window, you could see a few hills. A house in the distance, trees. The Polack realized that there was only one way he could convince the butcher, he had to tell him what he actually didn't want to tell him, he had to elicit compassion. Pity. He hated it.

"The pony belonged to our boy," the Polack said.

"And he didn't want it anymore?"

"No, not that."

The Polack rubbed his hands on the tabletop again. He massaged his knuckles. Had the butcher just said precisely what it was all about? Without knowing it? Borys hadn't wanted it anymore, this life.

"He went under a train," the Polack said. "Some people say jumped; I say he tripped. Sometimes, at first, I said: he was pushed. We never found a farewell note. But we didn't search through all his things, either. Soon enough we started saying: let's leave it at this. We know enough. In fact, we know too much."

The butcher nodded.

"So that's why . . ." the Polack said.

Tim inhaled and the Polack looked at the smoke. And when he'd had enough of that he stared back out the window and looked at the landscape he knew so well, because he had spent a large part of his youth in this landscape, without ever having identified with it. He wasn't sure what he had ever actually identified with. With the fire department, with his family, and, in the last few weeks, with the pony.

"Do whatever you have to do," said Tim. "I'll explain to the guys downstairs. Stay with the animal if you want. If that's what you need to do." He slid his chair back, went downstairs, and the Polack followed. He knew that he had to unload the pony now. He dreaded it, not only because of what was coming, but also because he feared another struggle, during the unloading. He saw the farmer again, with his whip.

The butcher disappeared into a room where they must do the slaughtering, and the Polack untied the pony. Taking her out of the trailer wasn't difficult. She came out by herself, he barely had to do a thing. He waved a carrot around, but even that seemed fairly unnecessary. He led her toward the group of buildings that still reminded him strongly of a farm.

There went the hired hand again—a young dwarf, then. The Polack wasn't blind, this dwarf was young. In one hand the Polack held the pony by her rope, in the other he had a plastic bag of fodder carrots and apples.

The dwarf said: "They're almost finished with the pigs. Give her to me."

"I want to stay around," the Polack replied. "Tim said that was all right."

The young dwarf shrugged, but that was all, he stood still and stared straight ahead. It may have seemed condescending, even though he didn't mean it that way, but the Polack laid his hand on the dwarf's head and squatted down a little. "Is there a place where we could be alone?"

"We?" the dwarf asked. "I have a girlfriend. What do you take me for?"

The Polack removed his hand from the dwarf's head—his head was warm, as though he were running a fever—and he squatted down the whole way. Now he was eye-to-eye with the young man, and now he was struck by his lovely eyes, clear eyes. The Polack felt sorry for him; little people have a hard time of it. He smiled, the way he did at times when the fireman went to the homes of people who were out of kilter, hysterical or neglected, a smile could do wonders. Once, he had told the younger firemen: "A smile costs nothing, and no one ever died of it." He himself had learned that from his squad commander. "I'm staying with the pony," the Polack said, "to honor our boy, on his behalf, you could say. I wasn't talking about you; I meant the pony."

"If Tim says it's okay," the dwarf said. "The horses come last." And then the Polack, still squatting down, explained all over again, just to be sure, that he wanted to wait along with the pony. He didn't say what he wanted to wait for, that was clear enough, because there was only thing you could wait for in this place.

The young dwarf seemed to understand at last, he took the Polack's hand and pulled him further into the stall, which was actually more of a waiting room than a stall, as though the Polack was just another one of the animals. The dwarf dragged the Polack and the pony behind him, but maybe he misunderstood the dragging, maybe the dwarf didn't mean anything nasty by it, maybe he simply saw the Polack as a friend, a man who could become a friend if he was able to stick around longer. A good person, one of his own kind.

There were pigs, piglets, lambs, cows, three goats, and all the way at the back was another horse. The horse was restless, and when the Polack saw that the dwarf meant to put him beside that other horse he said that he would rather stay with the pony in another spot, because he was afraid he would be kicked or smashed against a wall. Wasn't there some spot where they could be alone, without other animals, not private, just apart from the rest? At last the dwarf understood what he meant, he said: "Look, there." He pointed at square patch of floor between a few cows and sheep. Separate and vacant. The dwarf led the Polack, and the Polack led the pony, and while they were leading each other like that the dwarf, pointing at the cows, said: "Don't worry, those aren't bulls. Those are quiet cows." And then the dwarf pointed at the wounds on the pony's back, and asked: "What did you do to her?" But he didn't wait for a reply.

There they stood, he and the remnant of their boy, pinned in between all kinds of other animals, sloppily separated by partitions that could be moved, depending of course on the influx. That, at least, was how the Polack understood it. There were days with more goats or lambs. Every day was different, every day a new surprise.

He pulled a carrot out of the plastic bag and fed it to the pony. He ate one himself too, because he was getting hungry and had no other food with him. "Have another apple," he said to the pony, and he pulled an apple out of the plastic bag, watching as the young dwarf pushed a few pigs toward a sort of gate that must have led to the slaughterhouse. The Polack knew that it was weird to talk to animals here.

He hoped the pony was hungry. The bag was still full of apples and carrots, he wanted the animal to enjoy its final moments on earth.

What other enjoyment was there for lonely old girls like her? Food, perhaps, getting scratched, but he had never dared to scratch her very thoroughly.

The little hired hand came back. "Don't feed her," he said. "That's not good. She mustn't eat any more now." The dwarf took another look at the animal. And then he said: "Take off that saddle. Why did you saddle her?"

Now it was the Polack who was silent, he began taking off the saddle, and while he did he whispered: "We mustn't eat any more. Just like before an operation."

Still holding onto the plastic bag, he placed the saddle on the straw that was sprinkled around here and there on the ground. The Polack felt that it would be unsuitable to have an apple himself now, knowing that the pony was no longer allowed to eat. That was no good, you couldn't stand around eating when someone else had to fast. He looked at the animals being taken away, and occasionally he reached out and scratched the hide of the animal beside him, because there wasn't much more he could do now, this was all he could do to boost the animal's joy in life during its final hours on earth.

He was glad his wife wasn't there, that no one else was with him. "I'll stay with you till the end," he told the animal. "I'm a fireman. I should really read something aloud from the Bible, but I don't have a Bible with me."

The pigs and piglets had all disappeared. There was more and more space around them. The cows had become restless, the horse was still skittish, and the Polack had the feeling that he was finally performing his duties well, he was almost happy. Tomorrow he was working a shift, starting at seven.

The dwarf came over to him. "Tim says we can do the pony in between times. Follow me." He pulled aside the railings and the Polack, leading the pony, followed him to the gate. There was a cow in front of him. And between him and the cow was another sort of threshold, it reminded him of a checkout divider in a supermarket. He was the next customer in line.

He waited. Now that death was so near, he said nothing more to the animal, his hand rested on its back, to show that he was there for her.

Then there was a noise that sounded like they were pounding foundation piles into the ground on the far side, and the Polack looked around. The dwarf was nowhere in sight, and strangely enough he was reminded of the people he'd seen die during his years with the fire department. In his arms, on a few occasions, when it happened it was usually because they'd gotten there too late, because the smoke emission had gone too fast, the fire had spread in all directions.

"Okay," he heard someone shout, and now the dwarf reappeared and began pushing the pony from behind with a sort of rolling barrier. The Polack helped out. He pulled on the pony, trying not to hurt her. Now they were going through a plastic apron, strips of plastic marking the end of one space and the beginning of another. Unlike the stalls, the next space, the final space, was brightly lit. The Polack had to get accustomed to all the light. He saw the freshly slaughtered animals hanging from their hooks, the smell of the place reminded him vaguely of a labor ward. Sweetish. Otherwise, very warm.

Then he saw Tim in a pair of blue overalls. Just beyond the plastic apron was another barrier, painted a dark blue, that separated the animal from the butcher. They were standing in a sort of cage that was open at the top, he and the animal.

"What are you doing here?" Tim asked.

There were other men there too, and they all looked at him. They had stopped working. The radio was on, he recognized the song, he could have hummed along with it.

"But you said I could stay with her, right?" the Polack said, and for a moment he was embarrassed to be standing there, because it was shameful to die. It was shameful to be with the dying, to watch them go. The Polack's voice could hardly be heard above the music from the radio, that's how loud it was. He had come this far, and now would also share the final minutes with this animal.

They kept looking at him, the men, as though they'd never seen anything like it, even though he was a man among men, always had been. He'd never had to adapt, he had come into the world fully adapted.

"Not this far," Tim shouted. "Or do you want to be butchered too?"

A few of the men started laughing. They thought it was funny and he understood that. They had never butchered a person, and now he had ended up among the animals by accident. Despite the laughter, he was still sure that he would stick to his guns, even though he knew he couldn't explain it, he relied on the butcher's kind-heartedness, Tim would grant him these last few minutes too. It would make a good story in the evening, along with the coffee or a beer. The fireman who couldn't leave his pony. Not even at the very last moment. A stubborn customer.

"I'm staying," said the Polack, still holding the pony's rope. "That's the way our boy would have wanted it."

A lie. He had no idea what the boy would have wanted, the boy hadn't wanted to be there anymore, but even that he didn't know for sure.

Now Tim stepped over to him. He and the pony were standing a little higher than Tim, so the man had to look up a little, and that gave the Polack a sense of authority. He was standing now on the spot where the animals stood, in the seconds, the minutes before they were put out of their misery, but it was a spot not entirely devoid of authority. It was a sacred spot, because only death makes all things sacred; without death, nothing was sacred. Eternal life was the great desecration.

"We can't do everything your boy would have wanted, next thing you know your boy would have wanted you to fly around the world with the Easter Bunny, would you do that too?"

"I'm not hurting anyone," the Polack said decidedly.

Tim got angry now. "In a minute we're going to shoot something through her head, then she's dead as a doornail, then she falls on the ground, and if she falls on top of you we've got a problem."

"She won't fall on me," the Polack said. "I'll push her in the other direction."

"It's against the regulations," Tim said.

"Sometimes you have to ignore the regulations." The Polack saw that Tim was wavering.

"This is taking too much of my time," Tim said after a moment's pause. "Stay then. If you really have to. But if she falls on you, if she hurts you, then it's your problem. And afterward you're paying me a hundred euros extra."

"Fine," the Polack said. His wife, his dear wife, would curse him roundly if she found out, but that didn't matter. She'd never find out.

Someone pushed the pony all the way forward, until it could go no further. A man with sheer white hair climbed up onto a little platform, he was holding something that looked rather like a pistol, but not like other pistols, and he aimed it at the pony's head.

"When he shoots," Tim said, "you have to push her away from you immediately. The gate on the other side is going to open and she'll roll down there."

"All right," the Polack said, and his hand rested on the pony's back as he tensed his muscles. The pony was getting nervous now too, she moved, she pushed the Polack up against the wall. The Polack pushed back, and the white-haired man with the big pistol in his hand moved along with the pony, calmly and concentratedly, waiting for the right moment to shoot in the middle, a little above the eyes, for that was where he was aiming, the Polack had noticed that already. That much the Polack understood. That's where it happened, there between the eyes.

The pony had never been this skittish before. Could she smell it? Might she know something? A sort of premonition that animals maybe had, or was that the human imagination? Was she only nervous because she was in a space that was too small for her, and couldn't go anywhere? Was it the lack of room to move that made the old, lonely girl so nervous? Whatever the case, the Polack remained calm, with his hand on her back he tried to calm the animal, only he didn't dare to whisper anything, to say anything, no one spoke here and he thought about his boy, their boy, whom he'd caught talking to the animal in the stall. He was almost happy now, the irrevocability of the situation set his mind at rest, there was nothing more that could be done, they had come this far, the two of them, the rest would go automatically.

Then came the bang. At almost the same moment, the pony crumpled. With all his strength the Polack pushed the animal away from him—by pushing her away like that he had the momentary feeling that it was he who had killed her—the gate opened and the pony slid out of the confines and onto the floor.

From there she was rapidly hoisted up by her back legs. A young man cut her jugular and the blood gushed out while the Polack stood nailed to the spot, and a completely insane thought overpowered him: if there was no God, he didn't want to go on living in this world.

A few of the butcher's assistants were looking at him, pointing at him. The way he stood there, disoriented, not so much lost, but astray amid animals where he didn't belong. They laughed, the butchers did, maybe they weren't laughing at him, he wasn't sure about that, but they were laughing and they were saying something to him, but he couldn't hear them, the music was too loud, the machines made too much noise.

Then came the dwarf, he squeezed through the bars of the gate—now the Polack understood better why Tim had hired him—and took him by the hand and led him outside. From the corner of his eye, he saw two ponies being cut in half. He knew that he owed Tim a hundred euros, he concentrated on that, on the hundred euros he still had to pay. As though it were something you had to practice, because otherwise you wouldn't be able to do it.

There was still a plastic bag of apples and fodder carrots in the stalls-annex-waiting room, the saddle was there too. He left them. Finders keepers.

IV

FRENCH COMFORT

1

From the slaughterhouse, he drove to Beckers's. As though summoned. He could imagine only one person he would want to tell about what he had just seen, what he had been through. He didn't have to worry about Beckers being at home. On his days off, Beckers was usually out doing odd jobs. Money or, better said, the fear of no longer having it, played a major role in his life.

The Polack parked around the corner, on the street where he'd parked before. He walked to the house as though he were expected, as though he lived there.

Beckers's wife opened the door. "This is a bad time," she said after a brief silence, and she looked down, at his sneakers. "I've got a couple of girlfriends visiting."

The Polack tried to draw her in with his eyes, he wanted her to look at him and not at his shoes, and he replied: "It's reached that stage."

"What's reached that stage?" She looked frightened.

"I can be comforted. I'm ready for it."

She looked doubtful. Apparently, Beckers's wife had been expecting almost anything, but not this. "It doesn't work that way," she said quietly, "I offered it and you didn't want it. You can't order comforting."

Had the offer expired? Was he too late? Did comfort have a use-by date?

"Can you smell it?" he asked at last, and he moved his face closer to that of Beckers's wife, who was still standing in the doorway.

"What am I supposed to smell?"

"Blood."

"Whose blood?" She sounded startled. Did she take him for a murderer? A man who hadn't been comforted for a long time, and then drew his conclusions?—No comfort? Then there will be blood.

"The animal's. It's been slaughtered."

"I don't smell anything," she said. "I can see blood on your sneakers, but I'm visiting with to my girlfriends now. Can you come back tomorrow?"

He took a good look. There was indeed a big spot of blood on his sneakers, with straw sticking to it. "Tomorrow the C squad's on duty," he said.

"The day after, then?"

"All right," he mumbled.

He went to his car, he drove home and thrummed his fingers against the wheel as though he were listening to martial music.

His wife was at the kindergarten, the one remaining boy at the day-care center, and martial music was playing in the Polack's head. He made a pot of coffee. What he really wanted was a beer, but because he wouldn't allow himself that he settled for coffee instead.

Walking around the house, he drank his coffee, standing beside the toilet in the bathroom he jerked off. He concentrated on Beckers's wife, strangely enough in his fantasy she had Tim's face. Atop her rather voluptuous body was the head of the butcher, and no matter how he tried to separate that head from the body to which it didn't belong, it kept coming back.

Tomorrow morning, seven o'clock at the firehouse. Then the new, normal life would begin. New because he'd admitted that he needed comforting, he'd said it aloud, he was no victim, far from it, and yet still he needed comforting. He had started missing something he never used to miss.

He could still smell the blood on himself, Beckers's wife didn't have much of a nose. He sprinkled himself with some aftershave and went on walking around the house. On his phone, he looked for Beckers's number, but the only contact was for a cell. He didn't need that, he didn't want to call Beckers himself, he wanted to call Beckers's wife. Maybe they had a land line, but he didn't have the patience to look it up. He drank another half cup of coffee, cracked open the door of their boy's room. Off the cuff, just like that, something he hadn't done the whole time since that first evening. Now he acted as though it were the most normal thing in the world. Nothing had changed, he didn't go in, that would be taking things too far. He himself was shocked to see how hushed and yet how fresh everything was. The unmade bed, the books, the old stuffed toys, the clothes on the floor. As though he had just slept there, the boy. A bit dusty, but you could overlook that. Here, in this room, time stood still. At the back of his walk-in closet he found an old Bible he'd been given as a child. "For Geniek," his father had written in it, "to learn from, to guide your feet on the path of life." He flipped through it, read a few verses out loud: "But thou, O son of man, behold, they shall put bands upon thee, and shall bind thee with them, and thou shalt not go out among them. And I will make thy tongue cleave to the roof of thy mouth, that thou shalt be dumb, and shalt not be to them a reprover: for they are a rebellious house." Then he walked out to his car.

The Bible wasn't much use, that was clear enough to the Polack. Besides, he didn't want to reprove anyone, why would he? The tongue cleaving to the roof of your mouth didn't sound like much fun either, he was sure about that.

He had to get on with it, his wife had said so, what you can't change you just have to accept. He drove back to Beckers's place and rang the bell. He had to ring twice before she opened up. She seemed less surprised than she had been earlier, but was she pleased to see him? No. Even though this was he, the Polack who she wanted to comfort. "It's me," he felt like screaming, "it's me! Can't you see that?"

She could have been a little happier, she was the one who'd wanted to see to his needs, and now he was available. The Polack was a little light in the head, probably because he'd subsisted all morning on one carrot and a couple of cups of coffee.

"I told you I've got girlfriends over," she said.

"Yeah, you told me that."

He stepped into the front hall, she closed the door, he could hear the women talking but not what they were talking about, even though their voices were clearly audible. Cheerful, high-pitched, rather giggly voices. The Polack had to bend down a bit, but he was used to that, his size forced him to do that every day, he went through life bending down and now he bent to receive the comfort he longed for.

"I was doing a little reading in the Bible," he said, and then it all became too much for him, he took the head of Beckers's wife gently in his hands, pressed his mouth against hers, kissed her, played with her tongue, no, it wasn't playing, it was dueling. It was a duel between two tongues, a sword fight. He remembered how he and Borys had watched all the Star Wars films together.

"You," he said. "You."

She pushed him away, laughing as though it were some joke. His arrival, his kiss. "What are you doing?" she asked. "What are you up to, for god's sake?"

"What are *you* doing?"

"I had no choice in the matter, you overwhelmed me." She wiped her lips.

He laid his hand on her shoulder. She didn't pull back, there was no room to pull back. "You're comforting me," he said quietly.

"Lust isn't comfort," Beckers's wife replied. "This is lust, cheap lust."

"Forgive me." Cheap lust sounded bad. Worse than normal lust, and he wasn't sure he even knew where normal lust ended and cheap lust began, although he had an inkling. "I need to talk to you."

"Talk?"

"Talk."

"Today, after lunch. Maybe we can take a little walk, come and pick me up after lunch. I have to get back to my friends now." And he heard them laughing again. They were calling her name, he could hear that much, laughing, as though they were happy that she was coming back to them.

He took her hand. A cold hand. "Cold," he said.

"A female complaint," she said with a laugh. She pushed him out the door. He was a giant, the Polack was, but Beckers's wife knew how to push.

Then he drove back to his own house, he went and sat in the living room. At the neighbors', someone was playing the violin. He'd never heard a sound like that from the neighbors' before. Apparently, they'd taken up the violin recently. Or was it a cello? He wasn't sure. Sitting at the dining room table, the Polack started thinking about cheap lust and other lust, the less cheap variety. Might the difference between the two be something like the difference between the cello and the violin?

Later on, he'd have to tell Becker's wife why he needed comforting, why he didn't want to turn down her offer anymore, to the extent that it still applied. When he imagined himself explaining it to her, the only thing that came to mind was that he didn't become nauseous when he kissed her, that he didn't feel like gagging when he stuck his tongue in her mouth, even though he realized that Beckers's wife wasn't exactly waiting for such revelations. The real comfort was the forbidden comfort. That's something she'd understand.

He waited until noon, until he was allowed to go to her, the way the hungry wait for the soup kitchens to open. He didn't do much in the meantime. Before getting ready to go to Beckers's wife for the third time that day, he looked around in the shed for something he could use to wipe off his shoe, but all he could find was a bunch of carrots. He began chewing on one absentmindedly, he could always clean his sneaker later. What was left of the fodder carrots he put on the kitchen counter, Wen could run them through the juicer later. For a moment, he thought about the young dwarf who had kept the pony under control with all the strength he had in him.

This time Beckers's wife was actually expecting him. She was already waiting, with her coat on. "Let's take a little walk." She was about to close the door, then she asked: "Do you think we'll need an umbrella?"

"No," he said.

They walked side by side without a word, not the way a man and woman might walk, not the way people walk who need to talk about the difference between cheap lust and comfort, more like the way workers walk on their way to the factory. Hurriedly, but also with a touch of reticence.

As they walked, the Polack searched for words, but couldn't find them; again and again, he came back to that same announcement: that he didn't get nauseous when he kissed her, that he loved his dear wife more than anything, but that she made him sick, that he hated that but that's the way it was. Still, he didn't say this, and in the park they sat on a bench, even though it was too cold for that, and they remained silent.

Until Beckers's wife said: "When I was nineteen, my best girlfriend and I went to the south of France. I saved for that vacation for a long time. One of our first days there, we were sitting at a sidewalk café and this Frenchman came up to me, he pointed at me and said: "You're going to be my wife." Just like that, out of the blue. I didn't speak much French, but I understood that. He was older than me, but still we had something, a summer love affair, a first love, I don't know what you call those things, and at the end of the trip, when my girlfriend and I had to go back home, he said: "Pack your stuff in Holland and come back here the next day." All I said was: "I'll come as soon as I can." But when I got home, I didn't dare to go back. I called him to say I was coming, but that I needed some more time. And that's how the first days, and then the first weeks, went by. At a certain point he called me and said: "I know you're not coming anymore." But in my dreams I still see him. The weird thing is, in my dream I don't dare to go either. I never go back. I was scared, I barely spoke the language, I saw myself stuck there on the Côte d'Azur, I was so young. I was afraid of being betrayed, afraid of being naive. And at a certain point I went back to the boy I'd known ever since primary school. Beckers."

There was no one in the park. The Polack looked at the gravel scattered around the bench. Why was she telling him this? Was she trying to say that she was unhappy? That she had offered comfort because she was the one who needed comforting? Or did she mean that the Frenchman whose offer she had refused had something in common with his boy?

A bit hesitantly, he said: "I brought her to the slaughterhouse. That's what I really wanted to tell you." The Polack had never told anyone: "You're going to be my wife." He had proposed to his wife only when he was sure she would accept. From an early age he had learned that you need to avoid risks, because life was risky enough as it was. But he had made a sacrifice for his marriage, he had slaughtered a pony.

"It's better that way. Or should I be feeling sorry for you?" She stared straight ahead, he stubbed his feet around in the gravel. It sounded as though she, who had offered comfort, disliked pity. So that's the way she saw him now: as someone who demanded her pity. It sounded horrible. That wasn't the kind of person he wanted to be.

"Look," she lowered her head for him to see, "I'm already going gray."

"I don't see anything," he said truthfully. He went on staring at her head, at her hair, and with one finger, his right index finger, he moved slowly across her scalp as though he were mapping out a route, the route from South Limburg to the Côte d'Azur and back, and then she sat up straight again. She took his hand and she said that his was cold now too, and his hand played with hers, in the park, on the bench, even though it was too chilly to sit there on that bench and he ran his free hand over her back, beneath her blouse, to warm it—was that what he longed for? Warmth?—and for a moment he pressed his mouth against hers. She let him. Then she took his face in both hands and whispered: "It feels so familiar with you."

"Familiar?" he asked. "What do you mean?"

"Familiar, that's all. Like I know you. Like I know who you are."

"Everybody around here knows who I am."

She took his hand again, she looked thoughtful, and she spoke quietly in his ear: "You desire nothing more from this world than cheap lust, that's all you know of it, that's all you understand."

It felt like an accusation, a verdict he had to duck out from under. He shook his head, not daring to really deny what she'd said.

"So what is it you want from me then?" Beckers's wife asked. "What do you want from me?"

Now he had to say it. But he'd already said it. She had offered it to him, so was she waiting for him to expand on her offer? Was he supposed to repeat what she herself had said so many times?

"You offered me something," he said, "you wanted to give something to my wife and me. My wife didn't want it, she didn't need it, but

I thought about it a lot and I do want it, so give it to me." And now he was the one who took her head in both hands for another good look, and he said: "I really don't see any gray hairs."

She yanked away from him. "You're not looking carefully. For a long time, I thought he was going to come, because after having my third child I was ready for that. It sounds weird, maybe it sounds horrible, like I'm a bad mother, after that one was born I knew for sure: children or no children, I'm ready for the Frenchman. He'll come and get me. But he didn't come. He knows where I live because I send him a Christmas card every year. I was hoping that he would go on waiting for me, even if he had children of his own, even if he had a family of his own, he would go on waiting, but he didn't come and now I know for sure that he's not going to, and I'm already turning gray."

The Polack leaned his elbows on his thighs and took his head in his hands. "Sorry," he said, "but what does this have to do with me and my boy?"

"Nothing," she said. "And everything. When I think about you then I often think of him too, and at first I really believed that I could do something for the two of you, for your wife and you, but after our talk in that café I realized I can't. That I don't have anything to offer you. It's horrible, but you two have to do it yourselves, like I have to do it myself."

She seemed about to say more, some sounds came out of her mouth, unclear sounds, and the Polack was about to stand up and go to his wife but he said: "I've been thinking about it, and cheap lust and normal, everyday, civilized lust are related to each other the way the cello and the violin are related. They complement each other."

"Oh," she said. "Oh. I wouldn't have expected you to say something like that."

"You wouldn't?"

Then the Polack could no longer restrain himself, because he realized that the story about the Frenchman who'd said: "You're going to be my wife" was about missed opportunities, because he believed that she had told it to him for that reason, to teach him a lesson, and if he got up now without kissing her again that would be a missed opportunity. The missed opportunities were what hounded you, like how he'd missed the opportunity to ever wave goodbye to his boy, their boy, that he'd never yelled something to him as he was preparing to bike to school. Even if it had only been: "Careful on the bike!" Or: "Love you!" The only thing he had done was to yank him away from trees and lampposts. That he had done. He was violating his wife's trust by sitting here, by feeling what he felt, but she didn't know about it and all he could think about was the missed opportunity and that there was nothing he could do about his feelings. He was innocent. He took Beckers's wife's face in his hands again and he kissed her and she kissed him and so they sat there in the park like two teenagers. He knew only one thing, that he didn't want to let go of her. Until she said: "The kids will be home from school any minute now. A cello and a violin, what made you think of that? Were you thinking about playing with my feelings?"

The Polack shook his head. "No, it wasn't that. I don't know how I came up with it."

On the walk back, she said: "Don't go along all the way to the front door." He replied: "No, better not do that," while he thought about what she had said, that he felt so familiar and he hoped she would say it again, even though he didn't know exactly what she meant by it, but it comforted him, her saying that, her meaning that. Her feeling that, and that's why he wanted her to feel it one more time, to keep saying it, that it felt so familiar with him, with him, the terse Polack, familiar. But because they were walking down the sidewalk now with more people than there had been in the cold park, he didn't dare to grab her again and so he walked at an appropriate distance, as though he were the handyman and she the customer, until she said: "Here's where you need to turn off."

Before he'd had a chance to ask when they could see each other again, it was time to turn in the direction of his car. They needed to go on talking about the difference between lust and cheap lust, about the cello and the violin, he'd felt like saying, even though he knew nothing about violins or cellos and in fact didn't know much of anything at all to say, but for her he would do his best. He would tell her everything, the way his son had told the pony everything. The Polack looked around again, she was already far away.

At home he leafed through the Bible his father had given him as a child. "No," he mumbled, "there's no comfort here."

2

That afternoon, before it was time to pick up Jurek from the day-care center, he slammed his fists against the walls a few times, the way soccer players with no self-control pound on the walls of the locker room when they've lost a match. He thought about his wife, without whom he had no desire to live, and he was ashamed to know that he preferred kissing Beckers's wife to kissing his own. The shame was horrible, he felt unclean. Feeling that way, he picked up their remaining boy from day care and he cuddled with him, he played with his toy cars on the living room floor so his wife would see that he wasn't living in the past, but in the here and now. And lying on the floor with a miniature car in his hand, he said: "You're the sweetest little boy I know." And he took hold of the boy, who looked at him blankly, and held him to his breast. Jurek didn't know what his father was afraid of, there was no way he could know that.

When his wife came home, that's the way she found him, playing on the floor with Jurek. She said "hi" to her son and husband, and took off her coat. She didn't come and sit with them, she walked to the kitchen. He followed after a while, and saw that she was running carrots through the juicer. "Would you like some too?" she asked. "You brought home so many of them. I'm going to make carrot juice."

"No, not right now," he said.

And he realized that he mustn't wait any longer, that he had to do it right now. He put his arms around his wife, forced her to put down her glass of fresh carrot juice, and kissed her. In the same way, earlier in the day, he had pressed his lips against those of Beckers's wife, but now his wife pushed him away too. "What's gotten into you?"

"Nothing. I want you."

Did she believe him? Apparently not entirely, because she said: "Suddenly? Out of the blue? Not like I've noticed much of that lately."

"Wanting always comes out of the blue, doesn't it?"

"No, it doesn't. That's not the way it works." She picked up her glass of juice. "Go take a look at him, would you? He's so quiet."

The Polack went and looked, and came back right away. "He's just playing on the floor." He knew he had to do it now, after dinner he wouldn't have the energy for it, he would be too tired; lately, after dinner, he had been feeling a slight despair. His wife said that the despair was logical. "Our family has gotten smaller, we have to get used to that."

His dear wife was wearing a sweater, he tried to take it off as though she was a shopwindow dummy and he was a salesman-trainee who had never undressed a dummy before.

"What are you doing?" she asked as he tugged at her sweater. Carefully, because he didn't want to tear anything. He had to do it now. If he could feel desire for his wife, he could exorcise Beckers's wife. And the Polack needed to cast her out, the way he had cast out the pony, the way he had to cast out their boy, no, the thoughts of their boy. Her sweater was in his hand now. She stood there before him in her bra, a light pink bra. He closed his eyes and he kissed her and he started praying, not to any god, but to himself, to his desire. Come back, desire, he prayed, come back, delicious desire, take possession of me, overpower me the way you once, long ago, overpowered me. She is my wife. I must fulfill my manly duties.

And he'd kissed her convincingly, it seemed, for she took her bra off herself. She put her bra on the counter, beside the last of the fodder carrots, all that was left of the pony. And she said: "Take me here. Do it here. It'll be good for you."

Good for *him*? Was this good for him? Was she doing it for him? Sex like a shot against the flu. Do it because it's good for you, and don't put it off too long.

"It's good for us," she said, as though she'd guessed his thoughts. "It's been too long since we did this."

"I'll put him in the playpen, just to be sure," he said. In the living room he lifted the one remaining boy carefully and put him in the playpen. Jurek began crying. "I'll be back in a minute," the Polack said, "we'll be back in a minute, little buddy. Mommy and Daddy just need to do something."

In the kitchen, Wen stood topless, waiting for him. "Let him cry," she said. "We shouldn't spoil him too much. It's not good for him. We shouldn't overcompensate." The Polack unbuttoned his shirt, tossed it atop the washing machine, loosened his sneakers, took them off. In the background he heard his son crying and his wife, leaning back against the counter, waited for the Polack's desire.

He bent down in front of his wife to remove his socks, only then did he take off his jeans and underpants. Now he stood naked before his wife, he looked at the juicer and Wen said: "You're limp."

"I'll get hard in a minute," he answered.

"Do you want me to do it?"

"No. I'll do it myself."

In the living room, Jurek was crying. The Polack began jerking off, standing in front of his wife, his back a little bent, and he looked into her eyes. He stared into her eyes, those eyes he knew so well, that he'd seen for years upon waking and that he'd never thought about, because he wasn't like that. Long ago someone had asked him: what color are your wife's eyes?" And he'd had to admit that he wasn't exactly sure, somewhere in between gray and brown, maybe with a little green in there somewhere too. "I'll have to take a better look," he'd told them.

"It's not working," she said.

"Yes it is." He jerked even more fanatically—wasn't sex an activity par excellence for the fanatical? For the fanatic in you?—but, indeed, it wasn't working. She waited a bit, he saw that she was waiting, in her look he saw hopelessness, despondency. As though his limp penis was what had caused their son to end up under the express train to

Amsterdam. In utmost desperation, he thought about Beckers's wife, how she had sat beside him, how she'd said that it felt so familiar with him, but even that didn't help, until his wife gave him a little push, she shoved him away and said: "Leave it. This is no use."

"Give it a minute," the Polack said.

For a moment his wife seemed to pity him, the pity he detested because comfort was something different from pity, something completely different, and she asked: "Do you want me to rub my ass up against you?" She said it in a voice he'd heard her use before, that he hadn't heard for a long time, the voice of horniness, the voice of excitement or of feigned excitement, you never knew for sure. His wife using her naughty voice, or maybe she wasn't using it, it could also be that she'd actually been overcome by what Beckers's wife had called cheap lust.

She turned and, still wearing her jeans, pressed her buttocks against his limp penis, and he pressed against her buttocks, he pressed against her with all his might, against the ass-crack, he had to bend his knees a little not to press up against her lower back, that wasn't the agreement. They used to do this more often, making love with their clothes on, in the car, off in some corner of the firehouse when she came by to visit. Later, that was no longer necessary. They'd all the time and space they needed to make love without their clothes on. There was enough room for nakedness. Was it just a matter of time and space? Had that, perhaps, been the beginning of the end, when they started playing mommy and daddy? Had their son died because of a lack of love? Because the Polack hadn't loved his wife enough, and not their son either?

She held on to the counter and he felt like asking her if she didn't need comforting, whether she was sure about that, whether maybe she didn't want to reconsider. Hadn't they perhaps been too rigorous, arrogant almost, in their unapproachability? Wasn't it arrogant to think they could do what others couldn't, or at least could only do with so much more difficulty, that stepping over the loss of a child as though it were nothing more than some favorite parasol they'd lost? His wife had once told him that, as a child on vacation in Greece, she had lost her little parasol. For days on end, she'd refused to be consoled. Her parents gave her a new parasol, but it wasn't the same. Back when they had just met, that story made a great impression on him. He saw his wife, his randy, lovely wife, as a child, an inconsolable child, and he had bought her a little parasol. She laughed at him, kindly but still. "Nutcase," she'd said. Or was it some other word? A word like that in any event. "I got over that a long time ago."

As she was pressing her buttocks against his limp penis, he thought about the parasol. She'd gotten over that a long time ago, and that's how they should have gotten over their boy too. Inconsolability is the right of children, and, quickly enough, even they can't remember why they'd been inconsolable. That's how grieving should work too. Why was this different, this mourning? Reaching up, he tugged gently on his wife's hair.

"It's the jeans," he said hoarsely. He wasn't out of breath, but it was tiring, jerking off like this for such a long time. "Maybe you could take them off?"

She turned and looked at him lovingly. It wasn't pity, it was love. Not randiness, not arousal, he saw it in the way she looked. They belonged together.

Wen took another sip of carrot juice. Now the glass was empty and she took her jeans off and winked at him, as if to say that this should remain a secret between the two of them, that she was taking her pants off in the kitchen while she should actually have been fixing dinner, seeing to their one remaining son. This frivolity was not fitting for parents, this was not the hour for ruttishness.

She stood before him in her G-string. A pink one too, a different pink from her bra. She turned back around. "Do you like this?" he asked. "We can also do it later." Hesitation had struck him, maybe later on would be better anyway. Maybe this wasn't the right moment. Maybe she didn't actually like it.

"No," she said, "you're my man. It's important that we keep doing this. If we want to stay together."

"Yes," he said, "if we want to stay together. Then we should do this." And he bumped against her buttocks, he saw a bruise on her right buttock, she must have hurt herself.

"For god's sake, take me," she said. There was that voice of hers again, the voice of feigned arousal, he didn't doubt it for a moment, she was feigning horniness because she felt it was the right thing to do. She was too young never to be horny again, that's why she pretended.

And he tried to squish his limp dick into her cunt, there was no way around it. Squishing it in, why not? That's how human sexuality began, with squishing, it could end that way too, if this was the end. You never knew for sure, of course. But the squishing didn't work. She looked over her shoulder and asked what he was up to, if he himself had any idea what he was up to. He heard disappointment in her voice. Bitterness.

"I want you," he said. Saying that was the least he could do. If he couldn't do it, at least he could say it. He had always been a doer. A man was a doer, now he was becoming a talker because he couldn't do it. The talkers were those who couldn't do something and who therefore talked to hide the fact that they couldn't. The Polack cleared his throat. "I want to fuck you hard. I want to fuck you harder than you've ever been fucked before."

"Then do it!" Her voice told him that his words had aroused her, but nothing had changed about his penis. Again, he concentrated on Beckers's wife, even though he saw that as a transgression. It didn't help.

She turned around. "Knock it off," she said, "you don't really want me. So don't act like you do." She snatched her bra from the counter and put it back on, but before she could put on her sweater she burst into tears and he said, without giving up, still tugging at his sex organ: "Our one remaining son is crying, and now you're crying too. That's an awful lot. How can I get horny like this? I'm doing my best, goddamn it, I'm doing my best."

"Maybe you should take some kind of pill," she said, "or maybe we shouldn't have sex together anymore, maybe we should just raise our boy. And leave it at that." She was still crying and he went on jerking off, because he was a man of his word, a man who kept his promises, a man who could force the desire to be there, if need be.

"But that isn't enough, is it?" he said, still carrying on. "Raising a child together isn't enough, is it? We're not some day-care center, we're husband and wife, right?"

She shrugged, and for a moment he thought he detected progress, that some hardness was coming into it. She looked and he saw the way she looked and then, right away, he realized that it was an illusion. Nothing was getting hard, only his words, they were hard, his jaw muscles, his head.

"No," she said, "we're not a day-care center, but if you can't fuck me anymore then maybe we should stop these ridiculous attempts, because this is no good for either of us."

He caressed his wife with his free hand as he went on, and saw that it was starting to bleed a little, his dick was starting to bleed, he had rubbed the skin raw. "Just look," she said, "at yourself, standing there. Look at yourself. Is this what a husband is supposed to look like?"

The Polack knew he had to do something, but he didn't know what. He stopped and looked at his limp penis. The blood on his right hand he wiped off on a dishtowel.

"Oh, don't do that," she said. "Blood is so hard to get out. Just go get a piece of toilet paper."

"We can buy a new dishtowel."

He was no father, but then what *was* a father? Someone who fucked the mother of his children real hard? Someone who waved goodbye to his son as he cycled off to school? He had bought him a pony, he had seen to it that the boy no longer pooped in his pants, wasn't that what fathers were supposed to do too?

He turned his wife around. His penis may have been limp, but his arms weren't. The Polack picked up one of the fodder carrots from the counter, the smallest one he could find, pushed her G-string aside a little and shoved it inside her.

"What are you doing?" she asked. "What are you up to?"

He pulled the fodder carrot out and shoved it into her vagina again. Into the sex organ that he'd actually always left unnamed, because he didn't like dirty words.

"These were for the pony," he said, "but the pony can't eat them anymore, so now I'm fucking you with what the pony left over, because the pony's been butchered."

"When?" She was panting. Whether from pleasure or sorrow or anger, he wasn't sure, she panted.

He moved the carrot inside her, faster and faster. "Today." With his left hand he held onto the back of her neck, with his right he moved the big carrot inside his wife and from the living room he could hear the whimpering of their one remaining boy. "We need to see to our boy," he said. "Can't you hear how he needs us? We need to pay less attention to our lust and more to Jurek." He pulled the fodder carrot out of his wife's cunt and pushed it up her ass. She shrieked, differently from the way she shrieked otherwise, but then she didn't really shriek much anyway. "Oh, fuck," she said. Something she never said otherwise. The noise she made startled him. He loosened his grip on the back of her neck. She slipped away from him, grabbed the electric juicer with both hands and, before he realized what she was planning to do, hit him on the forehead with it.

He staggered and fell against the wall. He held onto the wall and the washing machine. He ran his hand over his forehead. There was new blood on his hand. In his other hand he was still holding the fodder carrot.

"Are you out of your mind?" he asked. "Are you trying to kill me?"

"You're the one suddenly shoving this big thing up my ass."

Wen still had the juicer in her hands, and she looked at him in a complete fury that might have been lust but was probably just plain fury. It occurred to him that she really wanted him dead. Because he wasn't a good husband, because he could talk about hard fucking but couldn't do it anymore, because the lust had left him. Because their son had jumped in front of a train. Because love and death could be the same.

"What were you thinking?" she asked, a bit calmer now. "What were you doing?" She put the juicer down on the counter, he saw tears in her eyes. New tears.

He grabbed the dishtowel and pressed it against his forehead. "I was doing what a man is supposed to do. I was fucking you." The dishtowel slipped from his hands onto the floor. Covered in blood. She was right, they should definitely throw this one away.

"With a carrot," she shouted. "Because you're too limp." And she tapped her index finger against his dick. It felt unpleasant.

"With what doesn't matter." The Polack went to the living room, calmed the boy, and came back to the kitchen. His wife was examining the electric juicer. She looked confused. If he had come into this house

201

as a fireman, he would have called in the fact that a confused woman was in the kitchen with a juicer. He understood. She felt rejected. His dick had rejected her, but he hadn't meant it that way. He couldn't do anything else, all he could do was love her. The fact that she'd hit him over the head with a juicer in no way detracted from that. Apparently, she didn't want to be fucked with a fodder carrot, although to him that had seemed better than nothing.

"You're bleeding." She put the juicer in the sink and pointed at the drops of blood on the floor. "Look at that," she said.

He went upstairs and examined the cut in the mirror. It didn't look like it needed stitches. He put a band-aid on it, that would stop the bleeding.

Then he went back downstairs.

There were still a few carrots on the counter. "I'll make some more carrot juice." When he tried to run them through the juicer, though, the machine no longer worked. "You broke it," he said.

She walked around the kitchen, still with no jeans on. And he was naked; he took his shirt off the washing machine.

"Wait." He straightened her G-string from behind. "You're pretty," he announced.

Looking at it objectively, she was pretty. Still pretty. Her hair, her nose, her eyes, her body. People always thought she was younger. She'd always retained something girlish. She still gave the impression of someone who might play hopscotch with her friends out on the sidewalk. Still, the lust had abandoned him. "I'm sorry," she said, "about the juicer."

"Doesn't matter, we'll buy a new one."

"It's still bleeding. It's leaking through the band-aid."

"I'll put a real bandage on it in a bit."

The Polack picked up the juicer and tossed it in the garbage pail. "These things aren't that expensive anyway." He stood by the garbage pail, still staring at the juicer. "We need to stay together," he said. "For our boys."

"Yes," she said, "for our boys."

3

First they played a game of volleyball, and only when they were in the shower did the squad commander ask the Polack if he'd been in a bar fight. "No," said the Polack, with a formality he himself found uncomfortable, "I bumped into something in the kitchen." He noticed that the bandage had half soaked away in the shower, and he yanked it irritatedly from his forehead, as though it was all the bandage's fault.

For the rest, no one said a thing, which saved the Polack having to explain anything, not how he had bumped into something, not whether his wife was there at the time. The men didn't joke about the cut on his forehead, because that day there were plenty of other things to joke about and above all because they felt they should spare him a bit. For the time being, the Polack was a man who needed to be spared. And although no one should think that firemen just sat around playing cards until a fire broke out somewhere—a preconception which the Polack, too, met with at times—their work did of course consist partly of waiting. That waiting the men filled with joking, because all that waiting around for other people's misery made them sorrowful and restless inside.

After lunch they did a blindfold drill. The Polack had done the drill countless times before. With a tank of compressed air on your back, you had to go searching by feel around the training location, a simulated home or office space, and leave it again by feel. Sometimes you also had to figure out if there were still people left in the space. The drill was routine, just like the games of volleyball, although you had to remain focused, which is what the drill was meant for, to keep you on your toes, to keep you from becoming overconfident, from thinking you were invulnerable. The men liked to think of themselves as invulnerable, until such time that their age caught up with them ineluctably; then they were usually given an administrative job or went into retirement.

The Polack was last in line for the drill, and when he put on the mask he noticed that he really had been hit hard with that juicer, she hadn't held back, his darling wife, the mask pressed painfully against the cut but it wasn't too bad, he didn't blame his wife for that. He would never blame her for anything. He couldn't imagine it. When people talked about unconditional love, this was what they meant, that they never blamed each other for anything.

Beckers was standing beside him, the air tank on his back. He couldn't see through the blindfold, but he knew it was Beckers, he could sense that. When you're around each other so often for so long, then you know almost everything about each other, then you're like husband and wife.

The drill area, this time, was a staircase. He had to climb two flights of stairs. He kept the back of his hand on the wall, always feel things with the back of your hand to keep from getting burned, otherwise you might grab something you shouldn't have. The fake apartment was on the third floor. He circled the apartment, then went back to the staircase, and down the stairs. He heard himself breathing the way you do when you're wearing a mask, like you're sucking air through a straw. The blindfold drill was his favorite, but he didn't know why. The walking around blind, the routine itself, soothed him in some strange way. Wasn't that why he'd become a fireman? To enter the dense smoke and see if any living creature was still in there, to see where nothing could be seen, to go where no one else went?

The Polack always remained calm, even though a fireman had to enter the very same buildings and factory halls that the normal citizens had evacuated. You didn't run away from the fire, you went into it. Even if the squad commander sometimes said: "The idea is that all of us get back to the firehouse in one piece."

Going down the stairs this time, feeling his way, cautiously, concentrating on the reference points he'd printed in his mind, a loose brick, a broken banister, he panicked. He had the feeling that the air supply was blocked, that he was suffocating. He had never been afraid of suffocating, never panicked, he cared too little about his own life, and now here he was overcome by the sensation. He knew that panic was a bad thing. When you panic, you use more oxygen, but he couldn't help it, the panic was stronger than the Polack. There was no doubt about, he was in the process of suffocating.

Maybe he was imagining it, but it was also possible that something was wrong with the air supply, that happened sometimes. Though not often, sometimes the technology did fail the firemen, which was why they checked things endlessly, again and again.

"Let's stop the drill," the Polack said as quietly and as calmly as he could. He tugged on his mask, but couldn't get it off. They must have heard him, even though no reaction came to his call. The tank on his back felt heavier than usual. It dizzied him. The Polack held on tight where he was, he was no longer able to move. "Let's stop the drill," he said again into the walkie-talkie, and he saw Beckers's wife before him, the way she was at eighteen, it was as if he had known her then, as if he had been there in that café on the Côte d'Azur when the Frenchman had pointed at her and said: "You're going to be my wife." It seemed to him that he was that Frenchman, that he had been a Frenchman in an earlier life. He heard disco music, he felt himself getting dizzier all the time. Why couldn't he take off his mask?

You weren't supposed to take off your mask in a burning building, but this was not a burning building, this wasn't life itself, this was practice.

"We're stopping the drill," he said and he heard his own, distorted voice. He was afraid he was going to say: I long for Beckers's wife, I can't help it. And there you go, he'd already said it. He had betrayed himself. Unbelievable, like some complete knucklehead. Like a schoolboy. That was also because he was in the process of suffocating, because he was dizzy, because he couldn't stay on his feet anymore. He had no more control over what came out of his mouth.

Where were they? Why didn't they come to him? They had to be close by. It wasn't mortal fear that overtook him, at least, he wasn't afraid of dying, but he thought about what a defeat this would be, dying during a drill, like slipping in the bathtub and breaking your neck. What a cowardly death.

Then they came. They helped him take off his mask.

"Where were you guys?" He noticed how hard he was panting, how constricted his voice sounded. They looked at him, the men, also a bit worriedly. As though they couldn't believe he had failed, the Polack never failed, the one who didn't say much but didn't fail either. Who did what he had to do. A hard worker. A team player. He'd been tested.

"I couldn't get any air," he said, "and the mask was stuck."

The squad commander took hold of his upper arm, almost tenderly. "We had a technical problem," he said, "we're going to try to find out what happened. Sit down for a minute."

The Polack sat down on the stairs. The announcement came, the drill was called off. A man they called Rabbit said: "I had that once too. Once the panic hits, there's not a lot you can do about it."

"It wasn't panic," the Polack said. "I couldn't get any air. And I couldn't get my mask off."

"That's panic," Rabbit said, in a calm tone that annoyed the Polack.

Then the Polack stood up, he took off his protective suit and Rabbit stayed with him, as though he felt sorry for him, as though he had been ordered to keep an eye on the Polack.

They walked to the living quarters of the firehouse. In the kitchen, the Polack washed his hands.

"You're cooking today, right?" Rabbit asked.

"Yeah," he said, "today I'm cooking." The Polack wanted to find out whether they'd heard what he said during that moment of panic, in those seconds when he'd thought he was dying. Had they decided to let him die, the men of the C squad, because they already knew before he'd said it out loud? That he lusted after what didn't belong to him, that he longed for what he mustn't, and that, therefore, the Polack had to die? Were they having a meeting about him right now?

Had they all come together to talk about what to do with him? The colleague who, on further consideration, turned out not to be a team player after all.

Then he saw a few of the men of C squad sitting at the table where they would soon be eating, and he realized that they weren't talking about him. They looked at him normally, as though nothing had happened. As though they hadn't heard a thing. As though he hadn't said a thing.

"You can start already, if you want," Rabbit said. And that's what the Polack did. He did so with pleasure and dedication, the way he used to fuck, that's the way he cooked at the firehouse. By the time he was done cooking, it would be time to eat. They ate dinner early, between five-thirty and six. Preferably at five-thirty on the dot. The men were fond of regularity.

For vegetables, they were having green beans. He tried not to think about Beckers's wife, but about the game of volleyball they'd played that morning. The Polack's team had won. He wasn't particularly fanatical about it, the other men were more fanatical, he only feigned fanaticism in order to be a good sport.

Beckers had offered to help with dinner. He stood beside him and fried potatoes. Between hamburgers, the Polack sliced tomatoes. That day, before the volleyball game, they had gone out on a call. False alarm at a shopping center.

While he was busy with the hamburgers and tomatoes, the Polack looked at Beckers and couldn't help thinking about Beckers's wife again. He thought about how he could say: your wife is waiting for a Frenchman. Ever since your third child was born, she's been waiting. He would never say something like that, but that was precisely why he was afraid of doing so anyway, afraid that from now on he would only say what he actually wasn't allowed to say.

It was as though Beckers sensed that he was being thought about, that he was being looked at, because he asked: "So how did things work out with that horse, anyway?" He had never started in about that horse again, and now suddenly, while he was frying potatoes, something must have reminded him of that horse.

"Pony," the Polack said.

"Pony, horse, what's the difference?" Beckers put a fry in his mouth. "How did things work out with the pony?"

The Polack drew his index finger across his throat, and Beckers said: "All the better."

Then Beckers went back to concentrating on the fries, and he shouted: "You can set the table now." The other men started setting the table, the Polack had felt like saying, casually: I long for your wife, Beckers. Ever since our boy's been gone, I haven't longed for anything, but now I long for your wife, Beckers. I can't keep my mind on anything else, I can't help it.

It seemed to him that it would be a relief to be able to say that, although he wasn't entirely sure that he couldn't help it, but he feared the reactions: once said, there was no taking it back. Then the Polack he had always been would be gone for good; the Polack who was known as a good colleague, a tall and reliable man, the team player, he wouldn't be there anymore. And it would be as though he'd never been there at all. They would talk about him like a rat, one who desired what he didn't have coming, who longed for what belonged to someone else. The men wouldn't take it lightly, they didn't like betrayal.

The plates came by and the Polack put hamburgers on the plates and then they sat down and the Polack did his best not to think about Beckers's wife, because it was the thinking that drove you mad. He was only able to do so when one of the men pointed at the newspaper lying on the table and said: "It's getting worse with those foreigners all the time."

The colleague they called Rabbit, because he had big ears, said: "Before you know it they'll have biological weapons. Then we can forget it. Then it's not twenty or thirty people killed anymore, it's thousands."

The Polack said: "We never should have let them in."

A brief silence lapsed, they looked at him, the men of C squad, and for a moment the Polack had the weird feeling that they knew. That they actually had heard what he said in a panic during the blindfold drill. He ate his green beans with a certain reluctance, until the squad commander said: "You did good again, Polack. You fry a mean hamburger. Yeah, the Polacks are good at that."

After dinner, they sat in their easy chairs around the TV. Two of the men did the dishes. The Polack had already helped clean the stove and now he sat down in front of the TV too, to watch a movie he couldn't concentrate on. Every now and then he dozed off, at other times his thoughts drifted away.

Halfway through he got up and went to his room, he lay down on his bed and called his wife to ask if everything was under control. She said that their son was sleeping, and that she was knitting something, that it was the first time in years that she'd felt like knitting.

"So what are you knitting?" he asked.

"I'm knitting a scarf for you."

"That's sweet." He didn't want to hang up, but he didn't know what else to say. Why had she started knitting? Knitting didn't seem right for his wife.

"Have a good shift," she said, "see you tomorrow morning."

"Sleep tight," he replied.

Then she hung up. And he stared at the ceiling, saw a cobweb, no spider, and remained lying there on the bed.

The squad commander knocked on the door, came in, and asked: "Everything okay?"

The Polack nodded.

"Are you feeling a bit better now?" He took a couple of steps toward the bed. Then he apparently caught sight of the spider web. "Well, looks like they could spend a little more time do a little more work cleaning the ceilings around here."

"Everything's going fine," the Polack said.

"Great. We're still checking to see what went wrong during your blindfold drill." The squad commander placed a hand on the Polack's shoulder and forbidden thoughts came up in the Polack's mind again, but all he said was: "Okay." The squad commander left the room and the Polack listened to his footsteps retreating down the hall, which somehow sounded reassuring.

Later in the evening they went out on a call. A disturbed man had tried to set a table in his living room on fire with a bunch of old newspapers. The police got there and came to the conclusion that the man shouldn't stay alone. The squad commander agreed. "Otherwise, we'll be right back here tomorrow morning," he said.

The rest of the night was quiet, but the Polack, who usually slept well at the firehouse, slept fitfully now. He kept waking with a start. In his dreams it seemed that everyone already knew all about it. In his dreams he was calling Beckers's wife from the firehouse and he said: "I have to hang up now, your husband's coming."

Early the next morning he picked up around his room, packed his bag, waited for his replacement, and then walked to the parking lot.

At home, his wife was busy getting the boy ready for the day-care center. She said: "I went out right away yesterday and bought a new juicer." And she proudly showed him the machine there on the counter. Bigger than the old one; a huge thing, in fact.

"This one looks big enough to kill me with," the Polack commented lightly.

She had to laugh. "It was on sale."

He went into the living room and sat beside Jurek, who was at the table in his highchair, to feed him his porridge. "Bee-bah-bee-bah," said Jurek, which meant fire department or fire engine. "Yeah," the Polack said, "that's where I just was." And then he whispered: "I'm not the kind of man who needs comforting. I was mistaken about that. All I need is you and your mother."

The one remaining boy laughed out loud, and then the Polack's wife came in and picked up her camera and took a picture. "Father and son," she said. "It's so nice, the way you two are sitting there."

The wife left with the boy and the Polack remained seated at the table, the way men sit who, after long hesitation, have finally come to the conclusion that they don't need any comforting. Then he went into the kitchen and looked at the new juicer. With this, in the next few years, they could juice thousands of apples and carrots. This was a solid machine. No, there would be no shortage of fresh juice around here.

4

After a brief nap, he jerked off in the kitchen to make sure everything was still working. Then he mopped the floor, which badly needed mopping anyway, and then he drove to Beckers's house. Halfway there he stopped at a florist.

"I'd like to buy a bouquet," he said.

"What kind of flowers?" the saleslady asked. "Is it for a special occasion?"

"I'm going to visit someone. Just normal flowers."

"What about roses? Roses are normal, but still special."

The Polack shook his head. He always bought roses for his wife's birthday.

"I have some lovely sunflowers," said the saleslady.

"Okay." Sunflowers seemed fine to him. And with the sunflowers he went to Beckers's house, where no one answered the door. He rang three times and hung around a while to see whether maybe she had gone shopping, but after five minutes he gave up. He went back home, put the sunflowers in a vase, and repaired a kitchen cupboard he'd been meaning to fix for a while.

After lunch—his appetite still hadn't returned, two slices of bread was all he could force down—he worked in the garden for the first time in months, which is probably why he didn't hear the bell. Only when he went to the kitchen for a glass of water did he hear it.

There she stood, umbrella in hand. "I've been standing here for a while," Beckers's wife said.

"I was out back, working in the garden."

She looked at him as though she didn't believe him. Did she think he considered himself too good to work in the garden?

"I'd rather you didn't come over anymore," she said. "It's not good."

He wiped his hands on his trousers, even though he hadn't put on old trousers this time to work in the garden. All his old trousers had been sent to the Salvation Army. His wife was trying to get rid of things they didn't need.

"Who's it not good for?"

"For you, not for me either."

"Come on in," he said. "I don't get it."

She laughed. "It remains a tempting offer," she said, "even if it's not good." She came in with the closed umbrella in her hand. He led her further into the house, and as he showed her to the dining room table he shoved Jurek's toys aside with his feet. She sat down, he came back with the sunflowers and put them down in front of her. "I kept the paper wrapper," he said. "For you."

"You shouldn't have," she said.

He sat down across from her. "I was in the garden," he repeated, "that's why my hands are dirty."

She looked at his hands, then at the garden. "Would you tell me a bit about him?" she asked. "About your eldest son? You always talk about that pony, never about your son."

She was still holding the umbrella, as though she didn't know what to do with it. "Give me that," he said. And he carried the umbrella to the umbrella stand in the hall. Then he sat down beside her. "I don't have that much to say about him. He's not around anymore." To that he added: "You're right. We need to stop this. I don't need comforting. I was reading something in the Bible and I realized that it was not good for me either. Kind words are no consolation. You have to keep on going. That's consolation. And you have your life, you have the

Frenchman. If we see each other again, if that ever happens, then it will be the way it was before, when we didn't know each other."

"Yes, it will be like that." She nodded a few times, as though she were imagining what it would be like if they saw each other again. Finally she asked: "Could I ask you for a beer? Or am I being presumptuous?"

"No, sure."

The Polack went to the kitchen and came back with beer, and because she was having one he had one too. He pointed to the garden: "I was doing some weeding."

"At our house, my husband always does the garden too."

He thought about Beckers. His colleague, his friend, Beckers was a team player just like him. Others had left or been let go, they were afraid of heights or they weren't team players. Beckers and he had remained.

She took a sip and said, more to herself than to the Polack: "I'm not the mother I'd like to be, but I deserve this beer. I believed that I could comfort you. A mistake. I'm sorry for burdening you with that mistake."

The Polack looked at his garden.

"What I wanted to ask you," Beckers's wife said, and she laid her hand on his, "even if we just become friends, don't use me to fill your emptiness, or to drive away your loneliness. Be gentle with me." These last four words she said in English.

"Be what?"

"Be gentle with me."

"What do you mean?"

"That I want you to be gentle with me."

"Oh," said the Polack, and he still didn't understand why she'd said it in English, which is why he'd asked.

"I'm waiting for the Frenchman," she explained, "even though I don't think he's coming anymore, I haven't stopped hoping. I haven't been able to stop hoping. And if he comes, I'll speak English with him, then I'll explain everything to him in English. I'll tell him: be gentle with me."

"But he speaks French, right?"

"Okay, but I don't," said Beckers's wife.

He put his beer glass down on the table and he didn't understand where the desire had come from. It was a daydream, no, an offense that a man his age, in his circumstances, shouldn't commit.

"So why are you telling me this now?"

Still sitting, she took off her raincoat and hung it over the chair beside her. "Oh, just because."

"You offered to comfort my wife and me, but actually you're the one who needs it." It sounded like an accusation. He hadn't meant it that way.

"Who needs it?" She shook her head. "No, all I was trying to say was: don't use me. Don't use me wrongly, use me the right way." She ran her hand through her long, brown hair.

People shouldn't use each other, that wasn't nice, and they shouldn't betray anyone either. Only their own desires, that's all they should betray, all they really ought to betray. He took her hand and led her upstairs and it was only when they got to the bedroom that he froze. She was the one who finally asked: "Is this your bedroom?"

"Yeah."

"Doesn't your wife ever make the beds?"

"Sometimes she does. Sometimes she doesn't."

"I make the beds every day." She took her shoes off and sat on the bed. "So this is where I could have comforted the two of you?" She sat on the side where his wife always slept, and she took off her blouse. "I'm sorry," she said, "I can't help it." To which she added: "This is the bra I'll wear when he comes to get me."

"Oh," the Polack said.

She stood up. "Show me his room. Where did your boy stay?" Before he could speak, she left the bedroom and headed for Borys's room. The Polack pushed her up against Borys's door and kissed her. He tasted the rather fusty taste of beer and saliva that wasn't completely fresh anymore, to him it was the most delicious flavor in the world and when he was finished kissing he said: "I want to fuck you."

She looked at him disapprovingly. "Is that all you can think of when it comes to comforting? You are such a vulgar man." She went back to the bedroom and, sitting on the conjugal bed, took off her bra as well. "Look," she said, "I'm turning gray, but my tits haven't started sagging.

That's also what I'll tell him when he gets here: "I'm getting gray hair, but just look at these tits."

The Polack sat down on the bed beside her, on the side where his wife always lay, his dear wife who made the beds only occasionally.

If Beckers's wife thought he was a vulgar man who didn't know the difference between fucking and comforting, then that was okay by him. "Put your bra back on," he said without looking at her. "Standing there in that stall beside that animal, the one we killed out of love, that was when I reconciled myself to everything, not just to dying, but my whole life."

He wanted to go on, but this was enough, and then he looked at her and she was still sitting there with her bare breasts and it wasn't the breasts, but the way she looked at him, she looked at him in a way that made him feel the need to say that he wasn't the Frenchman, just one of her husband's colleagues. The way she looked made him weak. The way she looked killed the team player in him.

"You came to me," she said. "It's no coincidence." Beckers's wife looked at her own breasts. "I'll show him the rest too, when he comes to get me. He always said he would come for me, and I don't think he's forgotten his promise."

Then she stood up and took off her skirt, then she took off her underwear, a pair of simple, black panties. The Polack didn't dare to look at all anymore, because his wife was the only woman he had ever seen naked. He had watched porn a few times, true, but it had always made him feel uncomfortable, embarrassed. Something in him had said that he would not escape punishment for such activities.

He was a man who had forgotten you could fall in love, he didn't want to look at her legs or at her crotch and so he didn't, he looked straight into her eyes and he said: "You look at me so lovingly."

"So you recognize it," she said.

"What do you mean?"

"You can see it."

"What?"

"You recognize love."

The Polack shook his head. "I don't know what I recognize."

She lay down on the bed, which is why the Polack thought she desired him, that she had come because she longed for his body, for his cheap lust, the cheap lust of a fireman, the vulgar desire of which he was ashamed, especially because it left him in the lurch, because so often there was nothing left of that desire except for a vague memory, an echo.

He had never thought about how he should live, because that had seemed obvious, because he knew intuitively how he should do that. In the presence of Beckers's wife he realized that there were other possible lives, with other opinions and other habits and that is why he undressed. His sweater, his shoes, his socks, his trousers on which he had wiped his hands, and finally his underpants, as though he were about to hit the showers with the men at the firehouse.

He stood there beside the bed, hesitantly, slightly aroused, and wondered what it was he expected from her, what he wanted from her, whether it was something truly different from what he'd wanted from the pony, beside which he had only stood in the stall, which he had smelled, which he hadn't touched to any particular extent. Her company had been enough.

She ran her hand over his thigh and then she wrapped her hand around his penis, his limp penis, and she played with it. There were all kinds of things the Polack wanted to say, he didn't dare to, he let her do it.

"You think you failed as a father," she said, "and that it's too late to do something about it." And she kept playing with his penis while he realized that his marriage consisted of a dead boy, that it was a dead boy that bound him to his wife, it was the dead boy who informed his life, his love, his desire.

When he was rigid at last, he went to lie down on top of Beckers's wife, but she said: "No, that's not allowed. Only the Frenchman and my husband are allowed to do that. You understand that, don't you?"

"No, I don't understand," he replied. "I want to fuck you. You wanted that too, right? Why would you play with my dick otherwise?"

She shook her head. "We can't do that. It's not allowed. Maybe later, but not now."

He sat down beside her and she ran her fingertips lightly over his back. He waited like that, for what would happen, and at a certain point he had the feeling that he'd been sitting beside her for so long that it was almost time for his wife to come home. For a moment he had the feeling that his bedroom had been changed into the stall, where he had sometimes lost track of time too, where he'd forgotten about his wife.

"I can fuck you," said Becker's wife. "Only, you can't fuck me, only the Frenchman can do that, but if it helps you, if it comforts you, I could . . ."

"What do you mean?" He shifted a little so he could see her face and then he understood again why he desired her. Because she looked at him so lovingly, so full of admiration, yes, that was the word for it, she looked at him as though she admired him, while there was nothing about him to admire. He was not exceptional, had never tried to be exceptional; for him, goodness was the inconspicuous.

"Like I said," she went on looking at him with all the love in the world, "I can fuck you. Do you have a dildo?"

"No."

"Doesn't your wife have a dildo?"

"No." He blushed, the word made him blush, he felt his face growing red. The Polack couldn't remember ever speaking that word out loud in front of his wife, or she in front of him. "And if she did have one, I'm not sure she would want you to fuck me with it." He said it so coldly, so dispassionately, to conceal the fact that he knew how flushed he had become.

"So what *would* your wife want, then?"

He had to think about that for a moment, and then he said: "I think she would want you to leave us alone."

"Oh." Beckers's wife sounded sincerely disappointed. "All she wants is for me to leave the two of you alone? That's all?"

"Yeah." He looked into her eyes, the eyes of Beckers's wife who was waiting for her Frenchman, and although there wasn't a lot he did know, he happened to know that the Frenchman was not going to come, in the same way the dead were not going to rise from their graves, not even if Jesus returned to earth, which he didn't believe anyway, but even then the dead were not going to rise from their graves.

"We still have some fodder carrots downstairs, for the pony," he said, more to himself than to her. "I bought a whole bunch of them, they haven't all gone through the juicer yet." And then he added: "But that's ridiculous. You're not going to fuck me with a carrot, are you? That's not love, is it?"

"No," she said, "that's not love, but what you wanted to do with me wasn't love either."

He paused to think about that, then said: "It was desire. And you started it, if you hadn't offered to comfort us, I would never have started desiring you."

He went downstairs, naked, and there they were, the fodder carrots he'd bought for the dead boy's pony, the animal that was dead itself now, the carrots his wife hadn't run through the juicer yet. They were there beside the potatoes. He picked out two of them, took them upstairs and he realized that they needed to hurry. "Here." The Polack handed her the carrots as though he were nothing more than a greengrocer.

He lay down on his stomach, beside Beckers's wife.

"I don't know whether you'll be able to handle both of these." She rubbed one of the fodder carrots over his back and his buttocks and he closed his eyes. Briefly, he thought about his boy, the dead boy was everywhere and, while she moved the carrot over his lower back, he asked whether she really believed that the Frenchman would still come. Beckers's wife said she hadn't given up hope, because she sent him a handmade Christmas card each year and then she began carefully pressing the big carrot against his anus. She said she needed to moisten it, and that she would have to put the carrot in her mouth, and whether the Polack minded that and he said, without looking at her, that it was fine by him, that he was in her hands, in her loving hands and that he was sure she knew what was best. Best for him, best for her, best for the comforting. And then he felt her fingers moving over his crack and he saw his boy in front of him, while she was still murmuring. You had to be careful, she murmured, but if you were too careful nothing ever happened, one could be too careful, you might damage something inside, but you couldn't go through life without damaging things inside. The Frenchman had damaged all kinds of things inside, because he loved her so much, she whispered, so much, with such abandon, and the Polack lay on his conjugal bed and waited and she said that she was going to moisten the carrot now. She licked the fodder carrot and then he felt how she drove it up his anus and he had to struggle not to scream, because this was not pleasure, this was not consolation, this was pain and he couldn't imagine that consolation could be pain.

"No," Beckers's wife said, "I never gave up hope, I tried but I don't know how to do it. Do you know how?"

Slowly she pulled the carrot out of his anus and he remembered how a few years ago he'd had recurring stomachaches and so had undergone a sort of biopsy. The pain needed to go away by itself, the doctor said, maybe he should eat less quickly, and the pain did indeed go away. He had stopped scarfing his food so quickly, because the Polack was not a man who distrusted authorities, he was a man who followed the advice of the authorities with instinctive obedience.

He lay on his stomach, waiting for what was coming, and he heard Beckers's wife breathing. He closed his eyes and said: "I love you, and I know that's unfitting, that it's not allowed, but I can't help it, I have to quit it."

"No," she said, "you're not allowed to love me. And you can't, anyway. Who do you think you are, loving me? You think you're a Frenchman? Do you know how to give up hope, is that something maybe you *do* know?" And again she drove the carrot into his anus, even more forcefully than before, and he felt he was being torn open, torn apart inside. He wondered if this was what having a baby was like.

The Polack clenched his teeth, bit down hard. The fear that his wife would come home overtook him, and he asked what time it was. Beckers's wife didn't answer, she only pulled the carrot out of his anus and waited a few seconds. All he could do was repeat that he needed to know the time, and one more time she drove the carrot into his anus, she drove in the fodder carrot the way she'd drive a nail into a wall, if she ever did that. The chores around the house she left to Beckers himself, of course.

"Are you comforted enough?" she asked.

"Yeah," he said. "Enough, that's enough for today. If that was comforting, then that's enough for today."

She pulled the carrot out of him and tossed it casually on the floor, then she got dressed and he dressed quickly too, and Beckers's wife said that she didn't do this for the fun of it, but that she felt sorry for him. And she also said that the Frenchman had a university education, what kind of degree exactly she didn't know. If she was ever with him again, she would talk about other things than the ones she discussed with her husband, and until such time she would comfort the Polack. Because he hadn't deserved the fate he'd been handed. Saying that, she smiled as though she knew exactly what fate he did deserve. And then she asked: "Have you got any body lotion?"

"What?"

"Body lotion, or something to remove makeup, I'm afraid mine ran a little."

The Polack led her to the bathroom and handed her his wife's body lotion, and in the bathroom she removed her makeup, which had indeed run a bit, on her face, as though she'd been crying while she jammed the carrot into the Polack.

They said goodbye in the downstairs hallway. She kissed him on the cheek and said: "We're getting to know each other better all the time, and I hope you don't go jumping to any conclusions about me. I'm not the kind of woman who deserts her children. I'm the kind of woman who hopes. Who can't help but hope."

He nodded and wanted to tell her that he understood that she was hoping for the Frenchman to come to her, but that now, now that they had shared such intimacy, now that she had shoved a fodder carrot up his anus, something no one had ever done before, as far as he was concerned she was the only one who did that and, to be completely frank, he wasn't sure it was an experience worth repeating, but now that they had that behind them he wanted to ask her if she didn't perhaps hope for him a little too, even if only as second best, for him, the tall, quiet Polack, Plan B.

But she slipped out the door, gave him a quick wave, and then he straightened the bedroom and examined a few spots there, trusting that his wife wouldn't notice them because she wasn't such a stickler for housekeeping. He found one of the fodder carrots on the floor, the other lay beside the big pillow.

Just to be sure, he wiped both of them off on a towel and put them back among the rest, in the kitchen beside the potatoes, then he threw away the beer bottles and washed the glass that Beckers's wife had drunk from. Finally, he went back to work in the garden. While he was working on the weeds again, he noticed that something was running from his anus. The Polack went to the bathroom, examined his underpants, put on a clean pair and, to prevent any accidents, went looking for his wife's tampons in the medicine cabinet. He hesitated for a moment, because there were larger and smaller tampons there, in the end he pushed one of the larger tampons into his anus. He felt relieved.

He went back to work in the garden, but could no longer concentrate on weeding, and so before long he started pacing restlessly around the house, feeling the whole time how the tampon was stuck in his anus, to keep any accidents from happening. Sometimes you had to break something to keep accidents from happening. He went and sat cross-legged outside the door of his dead boy's bedroom, and he sang a song he remembered from childhood. While he was doing that, he heard his wife come home and he stopped singing right away and hurried downstairs. She asked if he could pick up the boy from the day-care center, because she had to call one of the kindergartner's mothers right away. That was no problem, of course. He picked up the boy from the day-care center, with the tampon in his anus, and he wondered whether he needed to put in a fresh one, or whether the risk of having something run out had already been avoided. Holding the one remaining boy in his arms, he walked home.

When he got there, his wife asked: "Have you been using my body lotion?"

"Yes," he said, "you don't mind, do you?"

"What did you need my body lotion for?"

"I had to grease something. My skin. It was dry. I'd been working in the garden. After that, I moisturized my skin."

"Oh," she said, "but there's other stuff that's better for that, if it's really dry, I'll rub some of that on you later."

They went downstairs and in the kitchen she told him that she had bought fresh ginger and she ran apples, fodder carrots and ginger through the juicer with a passion, as though this were her life itself. He stood beside her with the boy on his arm and she put a glass of gin-ger-apple-carrot juice down in front of him. "We need to stay healthy. That's the most important thing."

He drank the juice his wife had made, the sweetest wife in all the world, the only one he was allowed to love, the only one he really wanted to love, when it came right down to it. And he echoed what she'd said, he drank the fresh juice down to the very last drop and he said that staying healthy was the most important thing, that was the long and the short of it. The rest was all details.

5

It was in the seventh month after the express train to Amsterdam had taken the boy that the Polack realized he was leading a double life, that there was no longer any denying it. Even though he had never penetrated Beckers's wife—she declared on numerous occasions that she was monogamous and would remain that way until the Frenchman came to get her—she had penetrated him, not only with fodder carrots but with all kinds of objects, she was inventive, and her claim was: "The bigger the object, the greater the comfort." To which she had once added: "I actually wanted to become an artist, but my parents wouldn't let me. They were respectable people, and they insisted that I become a respectable person too."

For the Polack, it seemed only natural that people should be respectable and want to stay that way. What alternative was there? It amazed him that artists, apparently, could distance themselves from that fundamental need. He had been to a museum a few times, a couple of times during their vacations, and he had found the museum to be a respectable place, perhaps the most respectable place he'd been to since he'd stopped going to church. But because he was afraid of displaying his ignorance, or rather, of underscoring that ignorance, he asked no further. He lay on the bed without a word while she worked on him. Sometimes it made him think of acupuncture, lying there he also thought now and again that God had manifested himself in the form of Beckers's wife. That was how he was worked on, yes, that's the way it felt, that he was being worked on, and it seemed plausible enough to him that God himself was also waiting for a Frenchman who lived somewhere outside Nice. God resided in everyone, in some people more than in others, and it seemed to the Polack that God lived most in Beckers's wife. His love for God was a forbidden love.

Through Beckers's wife, he had come to realize that people, like the soil, need to be worked on.

She had shown him everything, the dress, the coat, the shoes she would wear when the Frenchman came and got her. She was prepared.

Most of the time he didn't want to know what Beckers's wife was shoving up inside him, he accepted it because he longed for her company, for her presence, and because deep inside he believed what she said, that this was consolation, that this was the only comfort people could offer each other. And when it hurt, he thought: compared to being dragged along by the express train to Amsterdam, this is nothing, or not much, in any case. One time he hadn't been able to resist, he had looked over his shoulder while lying on his conjugal bed and he had seen how she took one of the shoes she wanted to wear when traveling with the Frenchman to the Côte d'Azur and shoved the heel into his anus, and after that he felt a bit nauseous. She had slipped a condom over the heel and when he asked her what that was all about, she'd said: "Well, we have to do it safely and carefully, otherwise it's not love."

She always rubbed him in with his wife's night cream, between his buttocks, because safety and caution were the prelude to consolation and love.

The Polack considered her words and finally he said, with the heel of her favorite shoe halfway inside him: "But this isn't love, is it? This is cheap lust."

"No," she said, "I was wrong about that; if it's consolation, then it's love. All consolation is love."

That, the Polack thought, was exactly the kind of thing God would say, and he noticed that he really only felt the pain in full when he saw what she was sticking in him. Briefly, he wondered what else she might stick in him, whether there wasn't a limit to what might disappear inside him. If this was consolation, then consolation was dangerous. Or was this the art she'd hope to create, the art her parents had obstructed? But then again, dangerous; it wouldn't kill him, even if everything inside was damaged it was always something he could recover from. The comforting would not have to last forever. One day the Frenchman might come to get Beckers's wife, or she would go there on her own and wind up with some other Frenchman and then the whole thing would be over anyway. Then she would be somewhere along the Mediterranean, then she would have forgotten all about him and his pitiful need for comfort. Yes, pitiful, that's what his need for comfort was.

It was not long after being penetrated with Beckers's wife's favorite shoe—an expensive, French brand of shoe, even though she'd bought them on sale—that the Polack's wife asked what in the world he was doing with her tampons. Because he had no ready answer to that, because he was unable to find one, because the lies of convenience that came from his lips confused even him, he realized that this double life could no longer be denied. And once he'd realized that, he wanted to end it right away. To end that double life. One life was enough, too much in fact, but two was truly way over the top. The longer it lasted the greater the chance that Wen would find out, and he didn't want to burden her any more than he had already.

The Polack told her that he'd been having diarrhea for a while, and to keep from complicating things during their drills he had occasionally stuffed a tampon up his rear, and his dear wife seriously believed him—she was not only sweet, she was also literal-minded, on their first date she had told him: "I have no sense of humor," to which the Polack replied: "I don't either, in fact, not at all . . ."—and she took his face in her hands and said, "But darling, where is the diarrhea from?"

Sounding almost alarmed, his wife said that a tampon couldn't help cure intestinal problems, to which he replied, truthfully as a matter of fact, that there was blood sometimes, too. "Then you need to see a doctor," she said with what sounded like a catch in her voice. "Blood isn't a good sign. Are you sure it's really blood, not that you ate beets or something?"

He said he was very sure that it was blood, because they rarely ate beets, at home, and at the firehouse they never ate them at all because the men didn't like beets, and his wife caressed him, Wen, the sweetest, the only, and yet not quite, said: "Have them do a complete exam, a tampon is no solution. A check-up, that's what you need. If you want, I'll go along with you."

It was still spring, but the midday temperatures were already summery, the heat weighed down on the whole country, and in the south of Limburg province the heat congealed, it was there that the highest temperatures were noted, it came with thundershowers that barely provided any relief. The evenings were long, the one remaining boy had been asleep for a while already and yet still it was light outside, as though the day would never end, as though night had ceased to exist, as though night were disappearing, and that evening, that hot evening filled with thundershowers, that evening when Wen asked what he was doing with her tampons, she said: "I bought a DVD."

"Oh," the Polack replied.

"A sensual DVD."

"Oh," said the Polack, and he hurried to the toilet to pull the tampon out of his anus, because he had a premonition.

"I think it's something we can learn from." The Polack's wife put the DVD in the player and they sat down on the couch.

A young lady appeared on the screen, she spoke English.

"She's a sexologist," Wen said.

"It's not subtitled," the Polack remarked.

"No," his darling wife said. "That doesn't matter. You can follow it, can't you?" He listened for a moment, then shook his head. "I miss about half of it. Her English is complicated."

"There's a film coming up," the Polack's wife said. "You don't have to interpret that. Shall I get you a beer?"

He nodded.

The Polack's wife fetched a beer for him and poured herself a rosé. Outside there was thunder and lightning, and in his living room the Polack was looking at a sexologist he could only partly understand.

"She says we should be 'quirky,'" he said. "Do you know what she means by that?"

"No," said Wen, "not exactly, but we can look it up."

"Quirky," he echoed, "quirky, quirky, quirky, like some bird chirping in a tree."

"Quiet," she said. "We need to listen." The Polack still didn't know what quirky meant.

They drank their beer and their rosé, when a vagina came on the screen the Polack thought about Beckers's wife. "Look," Wen said. "Tender, gentle, that's how we need to do it."

"We never have sex anymore," he whispered. He didn't know whether he could say that out loud. If you didn't say it out loud, maybe it would seem as though his desire hadn't died and he counted the seconds between the flashes of lightning and the thunder. "That was real close," he said, still at a whisper.

"We'll have sex again," his dear wife said. "We'll have a whole lot of sex. Because we're husband and wife. You still want me, don't you?"

Saying that, she looked at him with such sorrow in her eyes, as though the death of his desire was just as terrible as the death of their boy, as though the death of their boy and that of his desire had flowed together. Boy, desire, and death had become one thing in this family, one amorphous mass, and the sadness in her eyes was too much for him, it bowled him over, it reminded him of the pony, which is why he said: "Oh yeah."

"I just knew," she said exasperatedly, "and from now on we're going to do it real sweetly and tenderly. She can help us with that." She pointed at the sexologist who reminded the Polack of his high-school geography teacher, who was a nice lady too. After his mother died, she used to have him stay after class and talked to him in a way that had made him uneasy, but that he still liked.

"We brought two children into this world," he said, "without watching a DVD, and now suddenly we have to watch a DVD. Fine by me, you know, but do we really have to do this?" A vagina, manipulated by a pair of fingers, filled the screen.

"Look," Wen said, "that's how you do that."

"My fingers are big," said the Polack, "and those are little fingers."

"People with big fingers can be tender too." And she asked: "Does seeing that vagina excite you?"

He looked back at the screen. "Not really, it's a bit overexposed, the vagina's being filmed under fluorescent lighting, you can see everything, you can see too much, I'm no gynecologist." He drank his beer, the thunderstorm receded, the living room was still filled with the heat of the day and the Polack asked: "Didn't we do it tenderly?"

"You did it a little roughly, to be honest. You ignored my legs, you forget that I have legs. You went right for my pussy. For a long time I didn't say anything about it, because I counted on the tenderness coming back, then our boy died and then I knew that the tenderness . . . Well, that the tenderness wouldn't come back all by itself, and suddenly I wondered if it had ever really been there. Whether I hadn't imagined the tenderness. And it's not about bringing children into the world. We're not going to bring any more children into the world. That's over. We have sex these days because we're husband and wife, because we need to enjoy each other."

He sipped at his beer, he looked at the screen, he thought about Beckers's wife and he said: "Yeah, we need to enjoy each other. But we could also still bring a child into the world, couldn't we? To replace our boy?"

She set her wineglass on the coffee table. "No, our boy is not replaceable. Children aren't replaceable."

He wiped his mouth with the back of his hand. "We can always pretend, can't we?"

Wen shook her head resolutely. "There aren't going to be any more children. We're not going to replace anything. There is nothing to replace. I'm too old, and even if I wasn't . . ."

That was clear. He leaned back on the couch. This subject had been dealt with. People were not replaceable.

"So now we're going to start enjoying each other?"

"Yeah," she said.

"But we already do that, don't we?" he commented dubiously, as though he were in doubt, as though, without knowing it, he had fucked his dear wife's brains out in the last few weeks.

"No, we don't. First you ignored my legs, you forget that I have legs, and finally you forgot that I have a cunt."

"Did I really forget that?" That seemed steep to him. He went to the kitchen, got another beer, and the vagina on the DVD was now being manipulated by a tongue. The Polack wondered whether it was the sexologist's vagina, or a model's.

"You want some more rosé?"

"I'll get it myself." When her glass was filled, she sat back down beside him and whispered in his ear that people forget things sometimes, the most obvious things, to lock the door for example, that it was okay to remind people about that, about those obvious things, and she whispered: "I want to remind you that I have a cunt." Then she licked his ear. "Other women get a divorce when their husbands forget things like that, but I remind you about it." She pointed at the TV. "Look, the tongue is making figure-eights."

"Have you already watched the DVD then?"

She nodded. "I have to know what I'm going to show you, don't I?"

He counted the seconds between the flash and the thunderclap and said: "The lightning's coming back this way."

She took a big gulp of wine. It looked as though she was rinsing her mouth with rosé, like it was mouthwash, and the Polack realized that his double life had to end, it couldn't go on like this. He had to tell his beloved wife everything, she would understand. A woman prepared to remind her husband of the fact that she had a vagina would also understand that he had confused consolation with cheap lust.

"Look," she said, "you're not supposed to press too hard with your tongue, you have to make gentle, little, circular motions, but every once in a while, you can gently nibble a little on a labium."

"Is that what she's saying?" he asked.

"Yes, that's what she's saying."

"That I should gently nibble on a labium?"

"Shush now," said his beloved wife, "she's has more interesting things to say too."

He listened, but he didn't understand a word of it.

"Did I press too hard with my tongue?" he asked after a bit.

"A little. It's not supposed to be like using a meat tenderizer on a steak or something. And anyway, you just happen to have a very big tongue."

She tickled him on the side of the neck.

"It's been a long time since we . . . since I used my tongue. Not like that, anyway. You didn't want me to do that anymore."

"No, I didn't want that anymore," and she sighed a big exaggeratedly, as though she felt a sigh was needed. "That went with a different life."

"A life before the death."

"Yeah, before death, our sex life was before death, now we have to breathe new life into our sex life. Now we have to start on a sex life after death."

He drank his beer, listened to the rain, and he was determined not to love Beckers's wife anymore and not to desire her anymore. It had to stop, it was going to stop. The Polack felt so certain, so strong that it almost seemed as though he had never loved Beckers's wife at all, that he had never longed for her and that he had never recognized God in her.

"Are you ready?" his beloved wife asked.

"For what?"

"To try it out? Let's give it another try." She took another slug of rosé. Outside, he saw someone running down the street with an umbrella. It was raining much too hard for an umbrella. The man was getting soaked.

"With my tongue?" he asked.

She nodded, she stood up in front of him, she lifted her skirt.

"You're not wearing any panties," he said.

"I wanted to be ready. But I don't want you to start with my cunt. Start with my knee, start with my thigh."

The Polack took another sip of beer and then he started licking his wife's knee. The sexologist was still talking in the background, and again he realized how little he understood of her English. Besides, she talked awfully fast, as though she had too much to say for just one DVD. "Does she speak Scottish English, maybe?" he asked.

"Try to lose yourself in your arousal," his wife said, and he promised he would do that, that he would stop wondering what the woman was speaking, whether it was Irish English, Scottish English, Australian English, or maybe not even English at all.

He licked his wife's knee, moved up slowly, and then she showed him what they were doing on the DVD, she pushed his head gently between her legs so he could see the screen. "Just look." She murmured: "You can use your tongue and your fingers at the same time, see that?"

It was not a comfortable position from which to look at a screen on which, close-up, a vagina was being manipulated by a lovely tongue, you had to admit it was a lovely tongue, it looked healthy, the tongue did, with no coating on it.

"Shall I wash my hands first?" the Polack asked; he didn't think it was good to put his dirty fingers up his darling wife's vagina, he felt so dirty but she said that wasn't necessary, that he was clean, clean enough for her, and he ran his tongue over her thighs and when he had almost reached her vagina, he said: "I really thought you didn't want this anymore."

"That was then."

He went on licking, without touching her vagina, and then he said: "There's something I have to tell you."

"Not now," she said, "run two fingers over it, gently, as though your fingers are paintbrushes."

"Yeah." And he ran his fingers over her vagina as though they were paintbrushes, and she said: "You kept getting rougher and wilder. Now we're going back to who you were."

The woman on the DVD was still talking, and now he heard another woman's voice as well, it sounded like the sexologist was interviewing someone.

"You remember us talking about being comforted?" he asked.

"Let's not talk about that now. Can you feel how wet you're making me? You're making me soaking wet, but I still have a tight little cunt. Even after having two children."

"Tight," he echoed. She had never talked to him like this before. It must be because of the DVD or because of something else, because of death. She had started naming things. The pussy had become a cunt.

"And now use your tongue again," she said, "make figure eights with your tongue, like you're skating with your tongue and you don't want to hurt the ice too much with your blades."

And he pretended his tongue was a skate with which he didn't want to cause his wife too much pain, because she was the ice and he was the skater, and when he had to pause to catch his breath he said: "Lately, I've had a lot of contact with Beckers's wife."

"Okay," she said, pushing him up against herself again. "That's good, you've always been such a loner, always so closed. You remember how you had a pony as your best friend for a while there?"

He stopped licking. "Not *a* pony, *his* pony. And it wasn't that the pony was my best friend, it was that I felt calm there."

She nodded and he picked up the remote and stopped the DVD. "I can't concentrate like this."

"We'll watch it together again, another time, okay?" she asked.

"Sure." And he flicked his tongue around in circles, the way he'd seen on the DVD. Everything about him was so large, so unrefined, but this was who he was.

"Are you doing it the way they did it on the DVD?"

"I'm making figure eights." And he grabbed her buttocks and pushed his face with great devotion against her crotch. He pushed his tongue into her. He tried to do it in a way that didn't seem as though he were tenderizing a steak with a meat hammer. His wife said: "This is good, this is nice, you're making me horny, but when was the last time *you* got horny?"

"Now."

"I mean really horny, like you can't stop yourself. This isn't homework, you know."

"Aren't I horny enough? I've got an erection."

It was true, he had an erection and he recalled the years before their boy had been taken by the express train to Amsterdam. It wasn't that his desire had slowly guttered out after that. The desire had been dwindling before that, and maybe that wasn't even so bad. There were more things than desire alone. Except his darling wife felt that where the desire had disappeared, the dying had already begun, but that's not how things worked. And while he was making figure eights with his tongue, he decided that he needed to say it now, that this was the moment, that putting it off would only make it worse. If he didn't want to become a complete stranger to his wife, she had to know who he was and who he had been, and this was who he had been: a man who had loved Beckers's wife but had stopped doing so, with difficulty to be sure, because he realized that those feelings were mistakes. Improprieties.

He pulled his head out of his wife's crotch and said: "You taste so good." And he meant it, she tasted familiar, she tasted of the earth, of his boyhood when he played outside and rooted about in the earth.

"I loved Beckers's wife," he said.

At first she seemed not to understand him, because she only pushed his face in closer to her crotch and said: "This is nice, what you're doing. This is lovely."

She was breathing heavily. It was pleasant to see, no, to hear his darling wife enjoying herself. If she hadn't picked up on it, that was okay too. Then he had said it. That was the most important thing.

But then she pushed his head away and asked: "You loved *who?*"

"Beckers's wife."

"What's with that? Where did that come from all of a sudden?" And she pushed his head against herself again and he licked the way he'd seen on the DVD, he had the feeling that he was really doing it well. For the first time since boyhood, since his mother's death, he prayed to God. Licking the way they'd demonstrated on the DVD, even though licking was not the same as praying.

God grant me horniness, he prayed silently, give me horniness, not an erection, I've already got that, horniness so that I can't control myself anymore. Give me that, God, for otherwise I am a dead man among the living.

And then, right away, he wondered whether you could actually ask God for horniness. Wasn't that an affront to God? Did he actually pass out horniness? But if he passed out death and healing, couldn't he also involve himself with human arousal, with unbecoming human arousal?

"Why?" she pushed his head away again, "why did you love that woman?"

"I couldn't help it," he said. "It happened."

"It happened? Things like that don't just happen. You let things like that happen. And she thinks she's something special. With her little dresses and shoes and her combed, curly hair, but she's nothing but the wife of a fireman. No more than that."

His sweetheart didn't like Beckers's wife, that much was clear, she saw through her and he hadn't told her a thing yet.

"Yes," he said, "that's what she is."

And then his darling wife pushed his head back again, into her crotch, into her carefully tonsured pubic hair. And he licked and he prayed, he prayed and he licked. The Polack did what he had seen the tongue and fingers on the DVD do—had that actually been a man's tongue, or a woman's?—until at last he was overtaken by something that could be called horniness. Lust welled up inside him. He clamped his lips down on one of her labia and straight through the loud pounding of the rain he heard his darling wife breathing heavily, she never really panted, she just breathed heavily, and while he listened to her, he realized that the lust was hatred. The lust that had overpowered him was loathing. Bloodlust.

And he thanked God for hearing the pitiful prayers of the pitiful Polack and for granting him horniness, even if that horniness happened to be bloodlust.

He could have murdered her for not wanting to give him a new child, for not wanting to replace their boy, while life was about replacement, after all, replacing everything, replacing everything all the time. And dying was stopping with replacement.

"Stay tender now, honey," she said, and he was still sitting on the couch and she was squatting down now, his dear little wife. She squatted down in front of him so he couldn't lick her anymore, but still he went on thanking God for the horniness sent to him at the last moment, just in the nick of time.

"What happened with Beckers's wife?"

He wiped his mouth and she did too, they wiped his mouth, she picked a hair from his lips. "One of mine," she said.

"Nothing," he said.

"Nothing?"

"Not much."

"That's what happened?"

"Yeah," he said.

"You loved her."

"I loved her. Nothing else happened. But I'm horny now. Let's enjoy each other. Like you said."

"No. Later. How many people do you love, anyway?"

"I love you, I love our boys."

"Why did you love her? She's so affected. So pretentious. So fake."

"Why did I love her? That's a hard question to answer." He felt the lust starting to desert him. "Maybe because she's so affected." So warm and so cold at one and the same time in her affectation, he felt like adding.

"Can you just explain why you loved her? Can you? Can you tell me that?"

She wanted to know because she wanted to punish him. She wanted to punish him for his love, the Polack's love was love you had to be punished for, and that's why he would stop doing it too, once and for all.

"Because she comforted me?"

She frowned. "Is that a question?"

"Yeah."

"How did she comfort you?"

He looked his wife straight in the eye and he thought: these are the eyes of a stranger. I don't know this woman. This is not the mother of my children. "With objects."

"With objects?"

"Yeah"

"Objects?" She was screaming now. She didn't like that word. It made her furious, that much was clear. Even though it was such a normal, such a neutral word. "What kind of objects?"

"Her shoes, for instance."

"Her shoes? Are you sick? Are you hallucinating?" The Polack's wife took her husband by the shoulders and shook him, but without hurting him.

"No, I'm not hallucinating. And I'm still horny. Let's do something. That's what you wanted, isn't it? You wanted to do something with my horniness. I want to do something with it. I'll lick you."

She grabbed his cheek and squeezed it. "What did she do with her shoes?"

He wasn't sure whether he should say it, but complete openness was probably best, then she didn't have to fret about it, then she didn't have to wonder precisely what had happened with those shoes.

"She stuck the heel of her shoe up my butt. What difference does it make? It didn't last that long."

The Polack's dear wife sat down beside him on the couch and began to weep, quietly, inaudibly, but still he could see it, still he felt it and he put an arm around her but she pushed his arm away. They sat there until the Polack asked: "Shall I turn on the DVD again?"

She stood up, he thought she was going to turn the DVD back on, even though they had a remote for the player, but maybe she didn't know where she'd put it. His wife took the DVD out of the player, and standing before the TV she crushed the DVD with her hands, she tried to pulverize the DVD as though it were all the disc's fault, as though the sexologist were to blame, as though their boy had been taken by the express train to Amsterdam because the sexologist had failed. "Forget it," she said once the DVD was lying in pieces on the floor. "Forget it." And the Polack, who had begged God for horniness, for the fire he longed for so, realized that he had to do something. That he couldn't let this pass by, could not react with words like "take it easy" or "don't make such a big deal out of it."

He stood up and said: "It's over."

"Between us?" Wen asked.

"No, between me and Beckers's wife. There never was anything between us, so 'over' maybe isn't the right word. She'll never stick anything in me again."

"Jesus," she said, "is that what you wanted? Is that what you were longing for? And you were afraid to talk about it? You didn't dare tell me? All these years we've been together. You disgust me. I can't imagine ever letting you touch me again. She had to stick things into you, and you call that comforting? Don't desecrate our boy's memory. Your consolation is . . . Your consolation is no consolation at all. Your comforting is a curse. Your way of mourning is a curse."

He wanted to reach out and hold her, but he didn't dare, he couldn't.

"I'm not mourning. I mean, mourning is something different and comforting may be too." He tried to look at his wife with all the love he felt for her. He hoped she could see it, that she could see it in his eyes, in his hands, in his tongue, in the way he moved his tongue over his lips.

The Polack took a few steps toward the DVD that was lying in pieces on the floor. He picked up the pieces and it felt as though he was gathering up his beloved wife, as though she were nothing more than the DVD she had crushed in her hands.

"It wasn't that I wanted that," he said. "It was her idea."

"She wanted it? Coward. Is that why you needed tampons, too? Is that the reason why you've been filching my tampons for weeks?"

He looked at the broken DVD. Did the details have to be mentioned? Wasn't there anything that could just be left unmentioned? He had told her a few things, did he have to tell her everything now, absolutely everything? Did he have to tell her that she'd said: "We have to do it safely and carefully, otherwise it's not love"? And at the moment it struck him that this was the big lie, the big lie for grownups, that you could only call it love if it was done safely and carefully, while he believed that if love was anything at all then it was certainly something unsafe and not at all careful.

"Yeah," he said after a while, "if you really want to know, yeah. That's what the tampons were for. She shoved in all kinds of things that didn't fit, because if it fit it wasn't consolation. That why all kinds of thing came out again too. But that's not going to happen anymore. She's not going to stick anything in me anymore. I won't be needing your tampons anymore."

She looked at him with big, cold eyes, and he knew that look, she felt like hitting him. She thought he'd meant to hurt her, but it had happened because he'd been offered consolation and, in desperation, he had accepted it.

"You disgust me," she said levelly, "I regret ever having had children with you."

In her eyes he no longer saw aggression, only sorrow, and he realized that he could only comfort her by fucking her, right here, without hesitation, like someone who couldn't help himself, like a madman, a man who had no desire to be a good man, a man who had only one desire, to take his beloved wife, and so he begged God once again for horniness.

He tried to take her hands but she batted them away as thought they were a pair of giant flies. "I want to clarify things," he said, looking at his big hands. "I was confused, I didn't know the difference between consolation and cheap lust. That confusion is over now, now I know the difference again. Now I've understood the difference."

"What is it you know again?"

"The difference."

And once again he thought of God, who had sent him bloodlust, he would not give in to it. Never. He was a good man, a caring man, they could put him to the test, people could, God could, he would remain who he was, a good and caring man. Even if he had to break away from everyone and everything, even if he had to bury himself alive, he was going to remain a good man.

"I don't want you anymore," she said, "I don't know why I ever wanted you. I don't think I ever did want you. I was scared, I thought it was love but I was just scared, I thought: this one wants me, so let me take him. Now you know everything. I never cheated on you. I never really wanted you either. Never. Sometimes I fooled myself, sometimes I actually believed it."

She ran out of the room, he heard her footsteps on the stairs, and with the pieces of DVD in his hand he ran after her. She had thrown open the door to the bedroom of the vanished boy, she was lying on his bed, on his undersized boys' bed, her face buried in the pillow.

And he squatted down beside her, beside the bed. He had squatted exactly like this before, when their boy hadn't wanted to go to school, when he had refused to get up, when he threatened to go and hide or when he really did hide, under the bed, in the closet. As quietly and as calmly as he could, he said: "We weren't going to do this, we weren't going to open this room. This isn't your bed, this is his bed."

"Leave me alone," she said.

He stroked her back, she curled up against the wall in the corner, she took one of the stuffed animals that belonged to the boy who had vanished and held it tight. She used the stuffed animal to shield her body from the hands of the Polack who was trying to comfort her.

"This isn't your bed, this is our boy's bed. Get up. We have our own bed." He tried to wrap his arms around her but she wouldn't let him, she hit him with the stuffed animal and the more she hit him the more he could smell their boy and finally he lay down beside her on their boy's bed. He was still holding a few pieces of the DVD and he said it was really better if they got up, if they went to their own bed. But she didn't move, and she didn't say anything either. She just lay there and he remembered that she wasn't wearing undies and that he could console her if, overpowered by lust, he threw himself on her. That, he was sure of it, would comfort her. There was only one thing that could convince her of his love, that could silence her rage. He wasn't overpowered by horniness just then, perhaps he could pretend. Maybe it might still overpower him, in the face of all expectations, God might send him horniness again and he began to pray once more, so quietly that she couldn't hear him.

He stroked her leg the way she had told him too early in the evening, when it had rained so hard and he had listened to the thunder, and she let him. She didn't hit him anymore, not with her hands, not with their boy's stuffed animal, she let him stroke her leg and his hand went higher and higher, while in the other hand he still held the broken DVD and he prayed inaudibly to God for horniness, even if it seemed like bloodlust.

"You disgust me so much," she said with her face in the pillow, but still quite audibly. "Because you never said anything about it. Because you never said a thing about your desires. Never. In all those years."

He grabbed her by the back of the neck, pushed her face further into their boy's pillow. "You still don't get it, do you," he hissed in her ear, "I have no desires. My only desire is to be a good man, That's my desire. I have no desires."

And then he went right back to stroking her leg with his right hand, while holding the pieces of the DVD in his left, as if he would be lost if he let go of them. He manipulated his wife's genitals with the tenderness that the sexologist had described to him, as translated by his wife, and he prayed to God for tenderness and horniness.

"I'd been hoping so much . . ." said his beloved wife, with her face in the pillow.

"What?" he asked, without stopping the caressing, the fingering.

For a moment she was silent, then she lifted her head a little and said: "That if we watched the DVD together, everything would be all right, I was hoping so much, but nothing's going to be all right. You don't want me. You want someone else."

"No," he said, continuing his silent prayers, "I want you, only you, only sometimes there are distractions, nuisances. Deranged people who offer you comfort while they're the ones who need it. That's why you have to watch out for people who offer you comfort, because they need it just as badly, but I didn't know that."

What he was saying was a prayer. What he was thinking was a prayer.

And she sighed, she let him go on, in their boy's bed he fingered his wife as though his fingers were paintbrushes and her vagina were a delicate canvas that required painting with extreme prudence.

"Nothing's going to be all right," she repeated.

"We still have a boy," he responded, stroking and thinking about the sexologist, "everything will be okay, just because he's around."

"Stop it," she shouted into the pillow, "just stop talking about our boy all the time. Do you want me, or don't you? That's what I want to know."

"I want you," he said, and he laid the five pieces of DVD on the bed, the little bed that was too little for two adults of whom one was even a sort of giant. He stood up, took off his socks and trousers in their boy's room, and he saw their boy's notebooks, the homework he had worked on, here lay his secrets, and then the Polack was naked.

He rolled his wife over carefully and unbuttoned her blouse, attentively and carefully. "We'll buy a new DVD, we'll watch it together. I'm going to learn things I never knew I'd be able to learn."

"Forget it, maybe it wasn't such a good idea."

"Don't give up, don't give up." He helped her out of her blouse as though they were in the hospital and he tried to take her bra off too but she did that herself. He put the bra on their eldest boy's nightstand, carefully, because he didn't want to mess up anything, everything had to stay the way it was.

She rolled back onto her stomach and the Polack carefully slid his dear wife's skirt up around her waist and maneuvered his way in between her legs. The Polack had an erection and he felt the bloodlust welling up again, the bloodlust called horniness. God had heard his prayers. He moved his stiff sex over hers, in deep concentration. "I don't mind stuffing a shoe up inside you," she said in a loud, even shrill voice. "If that's what you want, just say so. Plenty of shoes around."

"No," he said, "that's really not necessary."

She squeezed the pillow and he moved his sex over hers until he thought he could put it in her.

"What else did she stick in you, anyway? A carrot? A beer bottle? A remote? What kind of objects do people stick into other people these days?"

"I don't know, I really don't know. Objects, that's all I know. I didn't look. I was lying there the way you are right now. I had my eyes closed, I was being comforted, that was enough."

"But we have objects around the house here too. I don't mind. If that's what you want, I don't mind. I'm prepared to stick every object we have around here up your butt. Really, I'll do it. If that's the way you want to mourn, if that makes you stronger. I'll do it." She was talking loudly, it sounded almost like screaming.

"No need," and he fucked his dear wife with the blind desire of bloodlust. Her breathing became heavier. "We're lying on his bed," he said. "That's what matters. We're on his bed. That's what you wanted, right? You wanted to do it on his bed. You wanted to do it in this room. You wanted to show that you . . ."

"Yeah, I wanted to do it in here," she said. "And now shut up. Take me." And he went on fucking her, every stroke brought him closer to God.

He concentrated on his orgasm, he tried to forget about the boy and his room and his notebooks, he tried to forget everything, he wanted there to be only this, this attempt at pleasure, this pathetic carnality. It was a word he couldn't get out of his head ever since he had led the pony to the slaughter. Pathetic he was, pathetic the desire he didn't have, and while he fucked he grabbed her buttocks the way he used to, the way he would go on doing, because they were man and wife.

And then she came, he could tell from her breathing, from the sounds she made, sounds that no longer had anything to do with him or with her, sounds from the stall is what they were, sounds of the animal, and after that he thought about pretending that he was coming too, but he knew she would check because she wasn't gullible, she would check whether there was sperm dripping from her vagina.

And so he went on fucking, thinking about his wife with someone else and only then, once he had lost her in his fantasy, did he come.

He lay down beside her on the cramped bed of the vanished boy, with his head on the stuffed animal, and now everything seemed good. He had proven that he loved his wife, that Beckers's wife had been nothing more than a wrong exit taken, even if something about that exit still glowed deep inside him.

"I don't want you to ever see her again," she said, facing him now, "Becker's wife. You're not allowed to see her anymore. As far as you're concerned, she's dead. And you don't know where they buried her."

"She's dead," he echoed. And the words startled him.

Everything in this family had to die, and everything died, because around here death was love.

"And you don't know where she's buried."

"I don't know where she's buried."

"As dead as the pony," his wife said.

"I had to have her slaughtered for love."

"Yes," his beloved wife said. "You had to have her slaughtered for love."

An awful lot of things had to be slaughtered for love.

"You promise?" she asked.

He looked at her, he made the credibility gush from his eyes, and he meant it, he was no liar. "Yes."

"Otherwise I'm leaving. If you keep seeing her. Because if you keep seeing her, then she'll keep consoling you and I can't live with her consolation. I don't want to live with it."

"I understand." He looked at the ceiling.

She stroked his hair, she brushed a flake of skin from his forehead and she said: "If I need to stick objects into you, just say so. If that's part of our love for each other, I'll do it. I'll be happy to. But I'm the one who does it, not that bitch Mrs. Beckers." She stopped stroking him. "Is that clear? I have to set my own boundaries, because otherwise you'll go crossing them all."

"Yes," he said, "that's very clear. People have boundaries, just like animals. But I don't need to have any objects stuffed into me. I took the wrong turnoff somewhere."

So it was this ceiling their boy had looked at when he lay in bed and couldn't sleep. There wasn't a whole lot to see, it was a normal ceiling. At most, you could say it could use some painting.

"The wrong turnoff," she said, and her voice sounded so sweet, so tender, "is that why you walk around with tampons up your butt? It was consolation, right? Can consolation be a wrong turnoff? But if it was a turnoff you shouldn't have taken, then that's okay by me too. So go see a doctor. A tampon isn't going to help."

"No, darling," he answered her, "I'm going to let it all heal now and then I won't be needing any tampons anymore. Then it's over."

She nodded, she said nothing more. Maybe she was thinking about her high-heeled shoes, shoes she wore only on special occasions, and maybe she regretted not being able to stuff them up inside him. "Shall we stay in here?" she asked when he was almost overpowered by sleep, when his eyes had fallen shut, and he was startled by her words, which he hadn't expected.

"We haven't brushed our teeth."

"That doesn't matter, we can skip brushing our teeth sometimes."

That was true, and so he got up and turned off the light in the vanished boy's room. He asked whether he should close the curtains too, she said that wasn't necessary. He lay down beside her again. Unbrushed and unwashed, unprepared for the night. He was afraid he wouldn't be able to sleep, but he fell asleep anyway, in their missing boy's bed. The Polack slept fitfully, every time he rolled over he felt he was kicking his wife or squashing her against the wall. And his own feet stuck out of the foot end. The Polack had always believed he could sleep anywhere, and that was true, he slept but not soundly.

Early in the morning, before his wife woke up, even before the one remaining boy was awake, he went downstairs to the dining room table and wrote a letter. The first letter he'd written in years.

"To Beckers's wife," he wrote. "I made a mistake. I never loved you. You were right. What I thought was consolation was actually cheap lust. I can't see you anymore, otherwise I'll backslide. In spite of everything. To me, you are dead. Excuse me for that. Nevertheless, thanks for everything. I will never forget it. The Frenchman will come to get you and you're waiting for the Frenchman, not for me. I'll pray that the

Frenchman comes to pick you up. I'm not a religious man, but recently I have started praying. Because if we keep seeing each other it will just go on and it needs to stop. I won't forget you. But you have Beckers and three daughters, I have one son and a dear wife. And what's more, you have the Frenchman. He will come and get you. Kind regards."

Then he paused, because he didn't know exactly how to sign the letter, finally he decided to close with simply "the Polack." That would be the best. That was who he was.

He went looking for an envelope, couldn't find one, and decided to buy one later, because he couldn't just put a letter like this through the mail slot. That wouldn't work.

But first he took the one remaining boy out of bed and carried him to his brother's room, where the Polack's beloved wife was still asleep in a bed that was too small for her too.

"There's Mama," he told the boy. "Today she's lying in a different bed."

And with the boy on his arm, he gentled tickled his wife's neck to wake her up. The boy laughed, he looked interested. And when the boy's mother opened her eyes the Polack said loving words to her, more or less all the loving words he knew.

It was early, he had to get to the firehouse, and together they dressed their son. The Polack asked whether she minded being awakened so early, but she said it was okay, that she would play with the boy for a bit, that it was fine, that she'd had enough sleep anyway. And the Polack said: "We shouldn't go in there anymore."

"We'll close the door again," his wife said, and as she went downstairs he heard her humming.

He went into the bedroom of the vanished boy, picked up the pieces of the DVD, and threw them in the kitchen trash. And in the living room his wife sang songs about love.

6

During the volleyball match that morning, Beckers collided hard with the Polack. Beckers jumped at the net while trying to block a ball and smacked his head against the Polack's. A headbutt is what it was, as if Beckers meant to block his colleague's head instead of the ball. Or had it been a fist that hit him just above the eye, that made him gasp for breath and made him feel as though his body consisted only of those few square inches above his right eye? Beckers's fist or Beckers's head, the effect was the same. The Polack remained lying on the floor beside the net. He was dizzy.

"Christ, I'm sorry," Beckers said, and he tried to help him to his feet, the way you try to help a friend to his feet who you've just accidentally knocked for a loop. In his black gym shorts, Beckers stood bent over the Polack. Was Beckers a friend? Yes, the men of the C squad were his friends. Whatever had taken place between Beckers's wife and the Polack stood apart from their friendship, it had happened in a different world, a parallel universe.

"Sorry, I thought it was my ball. You okay?" Beckers asked, and his shock at what he'd done seemed to grow by the moment.

"Leave me for a minute," the Polack said, "I'll be okay." He crawled off the court on all fours, like a dog, because he couldn't stand upright, not yet. He felt himself getting dizzier and dizzier, and defeated, that too. Never had he felt so defeated. That he had made love to his dear wife in the vanished boy's bed, that had confused him. The comfort Beckers's wife had given was confusing comfort. But maybe all real comfort was confusing. He had never really felt defeated before, not when his father dealt with the loss of his wife by withdrawing from his former life and starting an entirely new one. Not when he had scraped his eldest son from the rails. Even then, as he'd stood on the rails, he had thought about the one remaining boy and resolved not to let himself be defeated, because that resolve was what life was all about. Now he felt defeated. The headbutt had defeated him. The punch. Beckers himself had defeated him.

He wiped his forehead gingerly, then wiped his hand on his pants. It wasn't sweat on his forehead, it was blood.

The squad commander came over to him. The Polack was lying on the floor at one side of the gym. "You look pale," the commander said. "He whacked you good." A smile appeared on the commander's face, the commander didn't smile much otherwise.

"I think he hit me with his head," the Polack said with difficulty. "I think he headbutted me by accident."

"With his hand," said the squad commander. "It wasn't your ball either. What were you doing? You should have let him go. Oh well. That can happen."

The men brought him a bag of ice and pressed it against the Polack's forehead. He had his eyes closed, so he couldn't see which of the men were helping him, he only heard the squad commander say that he needed to take calm, deep breaths, and that is what he did. He breathed calmly and he wondered if this was what it was like to be defeated, if this was what it looked like. So ordinary, so normal. During a volleyball match, just to keep yourself in shape.

"You've got a good bump there, just above your eye," the squad commander said. "How are you feeling? You want us to get a doctor?"

The Polack shook his head and opened his eyes. He struggled to his feet and made it to the lavatory, where he threw up. Then he staggered to the sleeping quarters and lay down on his bed. Throwing up was a relief, the feeling of defeat had not gone away. For years he had gone through life with the idea that, whatever happened, a person would be able to handle it; despite everything, the Polack had contained a little drop of invincibility. Now that was gone. Vanished. So late in the game. He had persevered longer than his father.

The men came after him with the bag of ice. They pressed it against his forehead again, and said he should lie there with it like that.

"But what if we get a call?" the Polack asked, mumbling more than actually speaking. As though he was dreaming. As though they were standing around his bed in a dream and taking care of him in that dream.

"Don't worry about it," the squad commander replied. "If it's a major alarm, I'll ask some guys from another firehouse to help out." With these words, the men left the Polack alone in his room. And he lay there, sometimes with his eyes open, sometimes sleeping, busy arranging his memories. Arranging his new life, the life of the defeated man. But he would keep it a secret. No one would find out.

By lunchtime he was feeling a bit better, although he had no appetite, but that was nothing new, and when they went for groceries, the Polack was with them. If they had to answer a call, he would be there too. He was not only a good man, he was also a strong man. Defeated yet still strong. The squad commander asked again whether he really felt all right, whether everything was okay. "I don't need to have it looked at," the Polack replied. "It's bearable. A bump on the head at most. I have a pretty hard head."

Later he went to the corner supermarket and bought a pack of envelopes. And by dinnertime he was feeling much better. He still had a headache and there was, indeed, a bump on his forehead. The bleeding had stopped, there was no need for stitches. While the Polack was running a finger gingerly over his forehead, the men talked about refugees and about all the things being taken away from hardworking citizens of good will, especially by hordes of Muslims. Too much was being taken from them, while the politicians, those profiteers, did everything for the refugees and nothing for their own citizens, the men said, but they were the ones who had to put out fires and saw open cars and rescue the occasional cat from a tree, so they didn't have much time to fret about it. While doing the dishes,

Beckers remarked: "Before you know it, we'll be foreigners in our own country."

The Polack nodded. Secretly they already were that, foreigners in their own country, at least that's how the Polack felt. There was a time when that had been different. When the world lay at their feet, but those days were gone, even though they could still clearly remember when it had been different, better. And then the men spoke again of foreigners and refugees, Arabs and Africans, while they did the dishes. "They come here for our women and our money," Beckers said. "They don't give a hoot about our culture."

The squad commander chimed in: "Zero interest in our culture, but the politicians couldn't care less." And the Polack saw his colleagues' wives in his mind's eye, the women the Arabs and Africans had come for, especially for Beckers's wife, of course. For the moment he couldn't concentrate on culture, his head hurt too much for that.

And so they brought the evening to a close with recollections of the days when they had called the shots, without foreigners lusting after their women, without horrific visions of the future, and before they went to their bunks Beckers said he was afraid for his daughters. When he looked at them, he feared the future, feared what would happen to his girls.

And then he said: "Maybe it's weird to say that to you, after losing a kid and all."

"No," the Polack replied, "nothing is weird." He needed no horrific visions of the future, he let everything roll over him, although some would say that he himself had ended up in the midst of a horrific vision of the future, even if he didn't see it that way. It was painful, but you could live with the future. And while they were standing at the bathroom sinks before turning in, Beckers said: "Are you okay? I was hellbent on winning that game."

"It doesn't matter," the Polack said. He reached out and clapped Beckers on the back. The way friends do, colleagues who have become friends. Bosom friends. "I'm just glad I've still got all my teeth."

Beckers nodded and then went on about his daughters again; as they stood there at the sinks, staring into the mirrors under the hellish light, the Polack couldn't help but notice that Beckers's hairline was receding steadily, his wrinkles were growing more numerous, and while Beckers was still talking about the horrific future that awaited his daughters if nothing was done to stop it, the Polack went on brushing his teeth. "In my mind's eye, I can see what those Arabs are going to do with my daughters later. I see it almost every day, down to the worst details, and then you can't shake it anymore," Beckers said.

The Polack took the toothbrush out of his mouth and said: "Yeah, that's horrible. All those details. Good thing they aren't here yet."

"Then you're not looking straight," Beckers said, "right here in downtown Heerlen, they're here already, the Arabs are. That's why we're going to move, we want to go to a village. Cause they're not in the villages yet."

"Are you guys going to move?" the Polack asked.

"We're working on it," Beckers said, "for safety's sake, for the family."

And all the Polack could think was: they're going to move. As though Beckers's wife knows that she's already dead and that he was not to know the place where she would be buried.

The next day, the Polack threw away the letter he'd written to Beckers's wife. "Mrs. Beckers," was what he had written on the envelope, that had seemed sufficient, now the letter seemed awkward to him. He had to write a new one, a better one, one that did justice to the insane feelings he'd experienced for a brief while, and before that evening arrived she called him but he didn't answer. On his voicemail, she left a message: "I want to see you."

He deleted the message. In the days that followed she went on calling and went on leaving messages, and four days later she even showed up at his door but he didn't open it. He saw her standing there and he hid. First in the kitchen and then, when she kept ringing the bell, he ran upstairs and lay down on his bed with his fingers in his ears and he prayed.

"Is this what I deserve?" she spoke later on his voicemail. "For opening myself up to you?" That message he deleted too. If he didn't, he feared, he would go on listening to it. Then he would weaken, and that mustn't be allowed to happen.

One time he answered because she wouldn't stop, because she refused to accept his silence. What she said, literally, was: "You won't get rid of me this easily."

Was that how it went, the expulsion from paradise? You're seduced into eating of the forbidden fruit, then you're punished by expulsion, and still you can't leave it behind you, not the one who seduced you, not the fruit you ate either.

Did this call for more radical measures? To keep the seductress from further seduction? Their boy had taken radical measures. That's why the Polack answered the phone, to make it clear that they really needed to put each other behind them. Quickly, before she could say anything, he said: "You're dead and I don't know where you're buried, that's love too." Then he hung up. He would write another letter, a good one.

Only later did he come up with the idea of blocking her number. If you wanted to rescue love, you had to be hard, clear and hard and without a grain of mercy.

She was inventive, Beckers's wife was, she called from other phones, always a different number. At first she begged and coaxed. The coaxing had gradually become an attack. "You're worse than the Frenchman," she said in a voicemail message, "the Frenchman at least had style. You're a measly little Polack. Without any style. You're nothing. I was mistaken about you."

He deleted all the messages, and the more stalwart he became the more he prayed, and the more he prayed the more he saw Beckers's wife. He saw her everywhere. In the car that had belonged to a ghost driver, one dead, one badly injured. In the proprietress of a clothing store, after a fire, no one injured, only property damage. In a restaurant kitchen, one minor injury. And everywhere she berated him for his pettiness. Everywhere she said to him: You have nothing to offer. And you are nothing. Unkind and bad is what you are. But she said it so lovingly. With such incredible love in her voice. She said it to save him, that much was clear.

On one single occasion all she did was look at him, but in her eyes he saw what she meant to say. She took on the most varied guises. One moment she was walking around the supermarket, squeezing avocados, the next moment she was back outside, cycling down the street with a big blue shopping bag on the handlebars. She sat in a wheelchair in a city bus, she was of every age, from her early twenties to her late sixties. The more he saw her, the less he was able to concentrate. He was not so much a foreigner in his own country as a stranger in his own home, for he saw things his wife and child didn't see, he heard voices his wife and child didn't hear, even if only because he knew what had been on his voicemail and they did not.

He went to a sex shop and told the man at the counter, an older guy with no hair—but still, for a brief moment he had taken him for Beckers's wife: "I'm looking for an educational DVD."

The man cleared his throat, ran one hand over his bald head and said: "You mean sex in the classroom?"

"No, not that," the Polack said. "I mean something about how you can learn, how you can get better at it."

"Better at what?"

The Polack had the feeling his leg was being pulled, but the man went on looking at him amiably and from that he concluded that no legs were being pulled here. "At sex. How the sex can get better. Tender. More tenderness. More exciting. The techniques. You know." The Polack took his left hand in his right and cracked his knuckles.

"Who's it for?" the bald man asked.

"For me and for my wife."

"Oh, the techniques," the old man mumbled, "the techniques."

He went to the back of the store, was there for a few minutes, and came back with a DVD that he tossed on the counter as though the Polack had insulted him. "I never expected," the man said, "that I'd ever sell this one. But my wife always says: don't get rid of that stock, there's always someone who'll want it. You've always got collectors. No matter how weird, there's always a collector who wants to have it. Well, she was right."

The Polack looked at the DVD.

"Technique," the man said. "This is about technique."

The Polack wondered whether his wife would be satisfied with this, but when he read what was on the cover—that your sex life could become a celebration again—he decided that this did indeed come close to what he and his wife were waiting for. "Can you wrap it for me?"

The man shook his head. "We don't have any wrapping paper. I can put it in a plastic bag for you."

The plastic bag in one hand, the Polack cycled to a department store where he bought wrapping paper—nondescript wrapping paper, blue with a few gold stars—and at home, at the kitchen table, he gift-wrapped the DVD that promised that your sex life could become a celebration again. No one need despair. There was no ridding yourself of people, not without taking some awfully drastic measures, but there was always the salvation of technique.

"She's dead and buried," he said to his wife that evening, "I've kept my promise. No idea where. A burial at sea." Then his wife reached up and tickled the side of his neck, out of gratitude, un-doubtedly out of gratitude.

They were both still there, the sorrow and the Polack were. He couldn't shake the feeling that he, the Polack, was that sorrow, and in fact he didn't want to be that, but the DVD promised that no one need despair.

He went and fetched the DVD and said: "I got a present for you."

She took the present, smiled, asked: "Did you wrap this yourself? I can tell that you wrapped it yourself."

She tore open the wrapping paper on the DVD. The smile faded; she turned the cover around, began reading. About that celebration that was waiting for one and all, even for those who had been living in despair for years. With a new smile, a smile that was a little sad, she said: "That's not necessary. We can get along without it."

"Because you broke that other one, you know . . ."

"That's sweet," she said. "So sweet. You're really sweet. But maybe it wasn't such a great idea of mine."

She put the DVD on the table, then went to the kitchen. She ran carrots, apples, and ginger through the new juicer, which played an important role in this household. And then they went to bed. Tenderly but still with a certain melancholy, they lay beside each other, the one remaining boy slept in his room. They went in and looked at him, he was breathing calmly.

It took about three weeks before the messages from Beckers's wife stopped coming. The little digs, the entreaties, stories about the pain he had caused her, there were those too, the businesslike messages in which she said that she respected his decision but that she wanted to end things in the right way. He had responded to none of them, each and every message had been deleted. For a while he had thought that he would write another letter, until he realized that that letter would never happen. That the silence was perhaps better. More honest, above all else.

And when she stopped bothering him, when he had made clear that he could and would avoid her, only then did Beckers's wife truly come alive. She wandered through his house and through his dreams, she followed him to the firehouse, she took part in the drills, she lit fires and helped put them out. She stood in his living room, she lay in his bed, fixed meals in his kitchen, and ate with them when he and his wife and child sat at the table.

He prayed to God to make Beckers's wife disappear, the woman he had pronounced dead at his wife's behest—and it was better that way, people were actually quite bearable when dead. This time God didn't heed his prayers. Instead of deader, Beckers's wife became more and more alive, perhaps because God lived in her more than in others.

The headache he'd had ever since the run-in with Beckers went away at last, the bump did not, and she didn't either; she kept saying the same thing to him, over and over: You have nothing to offer. And you are nothing.

And one afternoon, before his wife came home, he decided to go for a walk. He left a note for her on the dinner table. "Welcome home, love," he wrote, "she's dead and buried, that Beckers bitch, and I don't know where. Still, I run into her all the time. I'm going walking in the hills, to clear my head. Don't count on me for dinner. See you later, the Polack."

Then he went out.

He walked down the street, out of the town, into the hills. The sun was shining, it had been a warm day, one of last really warm days of the year, probably, but the air in the woods, among the trees, was pleasantly cool. Way back, long ago, he used to go running here. When his knees started bothering him, he'd stopped running. Now that he walked here again, he realized what he had been missing, the beauty of the hills. So livable and yet so empty, so void of people. He should do this more often, go walking. Two hours later, he realized that he should have brought some water along, but he was trained for emergency situations, he would make it through. Besides, he had an objective.

The Polack walked on, came past horses, for a moment he thought he saw the pony or at least an animal that looked a lot like their boy's pony. He stopped to look at it, tried to lure it over with sounds and sweet talk, but it would not approach. Then the Polack walked farther, disappointed in some strange way, until he reached his destination at last. Dusk was already settling in, but the heat had not yet lifted. The Polack was sweating.

There was an old-fashioned bell beside the gate. He had to ring twice. At last the gate opened. He saw himself standing shyly before this big, old wooden entryway, but his shyness, his insignificance were no mystery to him. They were there. They went along with the defeated man he at the core. If he had anything like a double life, if anything of his former double life remained in him, then it was this, that he was a secretly defeated man. The words of Beckers's wife echoed inside him.

The man who opened the door and stood before him had a face like so many others in this part of the country. His eyes were brown, his hair flaxen, to the right of his nose was a large birthmark and he wore sandals. He must have been around fifty, maybe a little older.

When the Polack, who was looking at the ground shyly, got a better look at the man's feet, he noticed that the toes were covered in strange lumps. It looked quite gruesome. The man's toes were misshapen, almost all of them. The big toes in particular.

"How can I help you?" the man asked.

"I want to stay here." It was hard for the Polack to talk, he was so dehydrated. It felt as though there was a spiderweb in his mouth and the web was stronger than his jaws.

"The guest rooms are all occupied," the man said calmly and routinely, as though he had said the same thing twenty times today already. "We'll have vacancies starting next week. I could make a reservation for you."

"I'm not here for the guest rooms. I want to join the order."

A silence fell. The Polack heard the sound of birds. He cleared his throat. Should he have put that differently? Used other words? Better words?

"That's a big decision," the man said guardedly, "one no one should take offhand. Not just like that. On an evening like this. Such a lovely evening." The man glanced up at the sky, pointed to the trees, the grass. Everything was still in bloom. It was indeed a lovely evening.

"I've been thinking about it for a long time," the Polack said. "I didn't come here unprepared. I'm a simple man, but I . . ." He didn't finish the sentence, he looked at the man, he looked him straight in the eye as though he hoped this man would do the talking for him. That he would pronounce the words the Polack was unable to find. Praying hadn't helped. God had granted him horniness, not words.

The man just looked back at him, expectantly it seemed, and at last he said: "It's late, in fact for us it's already very late. The day begins early here and the night does too, but come in. We never turn anyone away. I'm sure you want to talk. Even though you probably get closer to Him when you're silent. Did you know that? We don't ask anyone to speak, but if people can't help themselves, then we listen."

"I like being silent, being silent is my specialty." The Polack followed the man through the gate, then turned to the left and entered a small, dusky room with a wooden desk. There was a cupboard with two document files and a few books. The Polack couldn't see what kind of books they were.

They sat down across from each other. The Polack was thirsty, but he didn't dare to ask for water. The thirst was a part of him, he had come here to conquer the thirst as well.

"Oh yes," the man said, "the silent ones, I've seen them here often enough before. People come here for so many different reasons. They come to us from every walk of life. Not all of their reasons are good reasons, let me make that clear right away. Some people want," here he lowered his voice, "to play monk. They feel drawn to the uniform, the habit. But that's not the reason why they should come here. And when it is, they don't stay for very long. It's the uniform that draws them." He smiled wistfully, as though he understood the uniform's attraction but didn't let himself be drawn into it.

"I'm a fireman," the Polack said. "I already have a uniform."

"We've never had a fire in all the years that I've been here. During the war there were Germans here, and British planes were shot down.

But fires, no. I doubt whether the fire department would be admitted everywhere. Part of the complex is closed to the general public, we call that "the Fortress." The abbot is a practical man too. He shows us the way. Someone has to show us the way, someone has to tell us where to go. Like if there happens to be a fire, for example"

The Polack nodded, then said: "I want to call Him to accounts, that's why I came, and what better place to do that? I can't hold people to accounts, people are . . . I issue a challenge to your God; if He loves people, if He loves me then He should show that, for once, then He should . . ." The Polack didn't finish his sentence, he placed his hands flat on the wooden table. The Polack's father was very fond of heavy timbers.

"It was only here, after a while," the man said contemplatively, as though he'd never said it before, which couldn't have been the case, dozens of people like the Polack must have shown up here before, and all those people would have sat at this same table, they surely had the same desires, had posed the same questions, exhibited the same pathos. "It was only here that I found out what love is. That takes a while. It took me years. God loves us, you can't challenge Him and His love. That's absurd. You can only submit to it."

The Polack remained silent, because he didn't know what to say to this. It might also have been because he was seeing Beckers's wife again, as a nun this time. Strangely enough, she was still waiting for the Frenchman. She wore shoes that she'd bought on sale, especially for him. She was ravishing.

"Your body," the man went on, "my body is no longer my own, it's His. He decides what happens with it. That's a process. It takes a while too. Surrendering takes time. Surrender also requires a sacrifice, but after a while it stops feeling like a sacrifice. People still ask: is it a sacrifice? No, I say, no. A liberation. Where you see sacrifice, I see liberation. There's someone walking around here, a monk, all you have to do is look at him to see what love is. The look in the man's eyes is something unbelievable. So gentle. His eyes. His words. When he talks. He doesn't talk much, though. His lips, so tender."

Another silence fell and the man sitting across from the Polack wiped something off the table, but the Polack couldn't see what.

"My body has never been my own," the Polack said. "I have no idea whose it is. It must be society's; as a fireman, your body belongs to society. The idea, of course, is to leave the burning building alive, you go in alive, you should come out alive too. We all go back to the firehouse in one piece. That's how it's supposed to be. We do all we can to make that happen. That's the most important thing, the squad commander always says. I don't have that certainty anymore. I no longer know what the most important thing is."

The man nodded. His kindly eyes scanned the room, coming back to the Polack each time, but not for long, never for long.

"I wanted to be a good man," the Polack said at last. Because somebody had to do the talking here, didn't they? Then he would do it. It wasn't his specialty, but if necessary he could. "That's not a desire. It's something different. I've come to the conclusion that I'm not a good man. Not a good father. Beckers's wife, you don't know who that is, but that doesn't matter, Beckers's wife is enough for now, she saw through me. She told me, Beckers's wife did: you're nothing and you have nothing to offer. That's the main thing you need to know about me. That, and that I have no more desires. Or maybe, still . . ."

You could hear the birds. What a racket they made, those birds.

"You said something about issuing a challenge," the man said. "Maybe you need to think about thankfulness. What would that challenge look like, anyway? Our mortality is a detail. Mortality gets in people's way so much. But it's just a detail. People look at existence through the drinking straw of mortality, no wonder they get confused."

"A detail?" the Polack asked.

"Our mortality. What we take to be mortality. Our body. The mortal body. We fixate on it, we're fixated on this life."

"Death is a detail?" the Polack inquired, fearing he had misunderstood. If so, they would never allow him to enter here.

"Not death. Our mortality. Those are two different things."

"I don't understand the difference between mortality and death. Where there's mortality there's death, and where there's death there's mortality."

The man nodded. "We do a lot of reading here, but we always read the same thing. Once we've finished the book, we start all over again.

And gradually things become clear. What I wanted to say to you was: everyone can think about thankfulness. Anyone can do it. Love begins with thankfulness. Without thankfulness, love will always be foreign to us."

"I didn't come here for thankfulness."

"People come here for thankfulness. Sometimes they call it something different, you know. They apply different names to it, the strangest names, but those of us who live here, those of us who belong here, we know that, we see it, we feel it, they come for the love that is thankfulness."

"No thank you."

"Not everyone who comes here knows what he's coming for. Visitors have to find that out for themselves. Or else they already know, our guests, the newcomers, they just don't dare to say it out loud yet."

"I'm not here for love. I've had love. Maybe even too much."

The man shrugged. "Maybe you don't like the word. Maybe you don't like my beliefs. But you came. We didn't summon you. You rang the bell. We don't ask much of our guests. That they respect the silence that begins here at ten. That they attend one service a day."

"I don't want to be a guest. That's not why I came. I've already explained my situation." The Polack looked down at the table, he wondered whether they had made it themselves, and finally the man said: "I advise you to go home, and if you feel the same way two weeks from now, come back. Then there will probably be room in the guest quarters too. Redemption exists. Your assumption is correct, if that is your assumption, but when you've been here for a long time you discover that redemption is such a small thing. It's so easy to overlook the redemption." He used his fingers to show just how small it was, as small as a wee little spider.

The Polack stood up slowly and for a moment he actually be-lieved that he was about to go home. It was probably too late to walk on, darkness would overtake him. There was sure to be a bus stop somewhere close by.

But as he stood there, before taking a single step, he already realized that it was impossible, that it was physically impossible for him to go back home, that it was unwise, perhaps even dangerous. There was no home anymore, to the extent that there had ever been one, and he walked around the table, not toward the door, but toward the man. The man who was sitting there. He stood beside him and placed his hands, his big hands, around the man's throat and the man did nothing to resist, he sat there as though nothing in him wanted to defend itself against the Polack's big hands, as though the Polack was allowed to squeeze the life out of his fragile body. As though that might even be a good thing. The Polack said quietly: "You don't understand. I can't answer for my own actions, that's why I came here. I prayed for horniness and I was given bloodlust."

He released his hold on the man, took a few steps back, leaned against the wall, the cold stone wall. Now he had blown it. They weren't going to admit him. He had shown himself to be just another dirty rat.

The man rubbed his neck. He didn't seem surprised. Perhaps any number of people had tried to strangle him before. He turned to look at the Polack, shifted in his chair, and said: "Horniness? That's not something you should ask for. It doesn't matter to me what people ask for, they can ask for whatever they like, but He's not some distribution center. He doesn't distribute anything. If you ask me personally, I'd say: He has nothing to distribute. And why ask for horniness? What are you going to do with that? If you have to ask for it, then you don't believe in it yourself. Perhaps you're better off without it."

For a moment the Polack thought he saw a twinkle in the man's eyes, but he might have been imagining it. The Polack was still leaning against the wall. He was, more than usual, conscious of his size and of his timidity. He could have crushed the man's life out of him, he could have done it. It wouldn't have been hard. "I've escaped from love," the Polack said with a calmness that surprised him, with an ease he didn't recognize in himself, "and others have escaped my love. My son, for example, our boy. What I'm looking for now is love from which you can't escape."

The man leaned on the table, supporting his head in one hand. The Polack had the feeling that he'd been forgotten, that the man no longer knew that he, the Polack, was in the room as well, but finally the man said: "I wouldn't send a dog out on a night like this."

A LETTER

INTERMEZZO

Dear Reverend Father,

I am writing you at wits' end, because you refuse to speak to me, even on the phone. Even though I know that you have a phone. And you could see me, you must have seen me, because I have often been to see you. At least once a week I stand in front of your door. I see you, but you don't see me, I gesture to you but you pretend not to see my gestures, which is why I am resorting to this letter. Reluctantly. Because I would have preferred, would so dearly have liked, to say this straight to your face.

A friend is helping me to write this letter, because I am not much of a writer, I am more of a talker, but you did not want to talk to me. Now I have to write and that is why I asked for help via a good acquaintance. Because I want to be sure that you understand me, because I can't allow myself to make any mistakes.

Please read this carefully. I can explain everything further, if need be. My hope is that you will invite me for a talk once you have read this letter.

My husband has been with you now for more than six months, my husband who is not only my husband but also the father of Jurek, my only son. My one remaining son. At least once a week I have attended the services along with my boy, with our boy, to let him see his father, so that he won't forget him. But my husband also acts as though he doesn't see us. Just like you. He sings, but he doesn't sing for us and we hear him talking but he doesn't talk to us. He sometimes looks in our direction, but then he looks right through us. And afterward I say to my boy: "That was Papa. Did you see Papa?"

Then our boy looks sad, intensely sad. In his baby talk he says that he doesn't understand why Papa didn't say anything. "Where's Papa?" he asks.

That is what I too would like to ask: where is he?

He is back there behind the wing you call the Fortress, where normal people like us aren't allowed to come. We laymen. We civilians. He is back there in the Fortress, invisible to us.

Lately we don't see him at all anymore, not even during services. We sit in the pew and wait, but we don't see him.

The brother who is responsible for guests and who has always been friendly toward me says that people have a free will. That this is God's grace, that the free will is not absolute, it's a gift.

A gift. What a hideous gift God has given us.

They are allowed to come and go, says the brother who is allowed to speak to guests. No one has to stay, certainly not in the beginning. But I'm telling you, my husband, the father of my boy, has no free will anymore, because if he did he would not be with you, without telling us anything, without acknowledging my boy, who is his son. He has turned his back on us and you can't imagine how painful that is.

I thought I could handle anything after what happened to us, but this is too much.

If you could feel my pain, the pain my son feels, then you would no longer tolerate my husband in your community. Then you would show him the door. Then you would say to him: God doesn't want your love.

Because according to the brother who talks to me, it's all about love. Love, love, and more love. I can't stand to hear that word anymore. Because doesn't my son need a father? Isn't that love too?

The brother who speaks to me, who listens to me, he never says "now it is time for you to leave," he told me that my husband now answers to the name of Malachi—but his name isn't Malachi, I refuse to acknowledge his new name, I will never call him Malachi. And this Malachi has become a hermit and has moved his quarters to a chicken coop. That is the reason we no longer see him at the services, these last few weeks, because he no longer attends services. He only comes to the kitchen, the brother says, to fetch his food in a pan, then he eats his food in the chicken coop. The next day he washes the dirty pan and fetches his food in it again and eats it in that chicken coop where there are no chickens anymore, only my husband. And the brother, who has gradually become a friend to me, says that my husband no longer speaks to anyone, that even the chickens would obstruct him in his search for solitude. God is in fact the only one he can bear anymore, my husband. So we shouldn't take it personally. He says.

That that is why he became a hermit, to be closer to love and hence the chicken coop.

"He wasn't running from anything," that brother says, "because then the Reverend Father wouldn't tolerate it, we're not a Zen community, silence is not a goal in itself. Speaking can also bring us closer to Him, as long as it isn't just to fill the silence. But in silence you can sometimes hear God say 'yes, and in silence your husband hears a deafening 'yes' from God."

I can't get those sentences out of my mind. I fret. I have nightmares. Why doesn't he belong with us, my husband?

The brother says that it happens on occasion, that a monk distances himself from his fellow monks, that a few years ago there was a monk who moved into an abandoned laundry room, and he never spoke another word either, never attended another service, he was love through and through, he lived among the old washing machines. And the brother said: "God is everywhere, but sometimes people find Him at a specific spot."

"In the abandoned laundry room?" I asked.

"Yes," the brother said. "Even there."

If it had been a woman, I could have accepted it. It would have made me sad, but I would have moved on. We would have moved on. But a chicken coop I cannot accept. I can't do it. Can you understand that?

That is why we keep coming to the services, to catch a glimpse of him. Because we haven't given up hope. Because I tell my boy: "Maybe Papa will come out of the chicken coop today. He knows that we keep coming, he knows that we're sitting there, right? In the church, to look at him, to listen to him, to see how he wastes his love? Maybe he'll come out of the chicken coop for us today." That's what I say to my boy.

I'm sorry to have to write this down, but he is wasting his love. It a huge waste, what's happening there, if it's even love at all.

You may find this insulting. I'm not religious, but I don't mean to insult anyone. The brother says that love is never wasted. I can only try to convince you that I am not lying. The brother also says: "The Reverend Father, the abbot, can't talk to you." Even though I begged him: "Let me talk to the abbot, my husband needs me, he's confused."

I told him: "We humans aren't made to live in chicken coops, are we? And he's so big, my husband, how can he fit in a chicken coop? He must have to lie there all folded up. That's not a life, is it?"

At night, in bed, in our empty bed, I try to imagine how my husband lives in that chicken coop. It's horrible. I never missed him before, now I miss him. Who was it, lying there beside me all those years? Who was that? Was he already in the chicken coop in his thoughts while he lay beside me?

My husband never troubled himself about your God, never mentioned your God's name, never worried over things like that, not even when our eldest son died. There was no God involved. Just so you know.

Reverend Father, I've heard that you can remove people from your monastery, that you can expel them. Please expel my husband. I beg you. I hate to beg, but now there's no way around it. There's nothing I won't do anymore.

If you would go to the trouble to come by and ring our doorbell, you would see how we are slowly being destroyed.

My husband and I were not destroyed back then, we stayed strong, we stayed together, after the death of Borys, our eldest, but now that my man has decided to forswear us, God knows why, we are being destroyed because I don't understand it. And I don't want to understand it. I can't come to terms with it.

If it had been a woman, I could have gone to that woman and I could have said: "So you're the one." And I could have said to myself: She's prettier. She smells nicer. She has no sorrow. I understand. Or: What an ugly witch, what an insult, leaving me for her.

But the chicken coop, that I do not understand.

The brother says that he walks with a slight stoop now, not like before, as though he carries the chicken coop around wherever he goes. That celibacy is a precondition for union with God. Is that love? That a person lives as though he's trapped inside a chicken coop?

The brother says: "Celibacy is a highway to God, but sometimes accidents happen on that highway, like on any highway."

What kind of accidents should I be thinking of? And if someone per se has to go to God, then why take the highway, if so many accidents can happen on it?

Of course, I ask myself whether I gave him enough love, whether I chased him away without meaning to. I ask myself that, it gnaws at me, but how much love can you give another person? Exactly how much love do you have to give another person to make sure he won't turn his back on you? And what if he doesn't want that love, if the love only annoys him, gets in his way?

Send him away, my husband. The brother who answers my questions says: "There are secrets, I can't tell you everything. This is a place of love."

My girlfriends say: there are so many other men. True, there are. There are so many men.

But I can't get over it. I don't want to get over it, and that's why I don't want some other husband.

No one deserves to spend the rest of his life in a chicken coop, no one deserves to believe that that coop is a coop of love. I beg you.

Respectfully,

Wen, the wife of the man in the chicken coop, the mother of his son, Jurek

V

HOMECOMING

1

She opened the door, and he could tell she was startled. It wasn't happiness in her look, more like disgust, and he hadn't been expecting that. She said nothing, only stared at him.

How was he supposed to behave? Was she still his wife? Was this his house? Should he kiss her? Shake her hand? He wasn't sure, although he had a notion. She took his hand and held onto it, as though the hand was a fledgling that had fallen from the nest. "Did you walk all the way here?" she asked.

"Yes," he said.

"Your hand's so dry. So rough." She rubbed his hand gently. Then she looked at his bare feet. She still hadn't told him to come in, which gave him the feeling there was someone else. Another man sitting in his chair. Another man sleeping in his bed. If that was it, he would turn and go. Not back to the monastery, that was closed to him now. He would rent a little apartment or move temporarily into a holiday bungalow. He knew divorced men who had moved into a holiday bungalow and never left.

"Have you got a glass of water for me?" he asked.

Amiably, but sternly too, she pulled him inside, the way you pull a child inside who has been playing outside too long. She let go of his hand and closed the door. Then she walked away, leaving him standing in the entranceway, and he heard her shouting: "Papa's here. Papa's back." Her voice betrayed more excitement than her face had.

She came back with the boy on her arm. The child turned away from him. The Polack must have changed, his already-sparse hair had become even sparser, the look in his eyes was different, he had seen that himself, as though he'd come back from a war, that's how he came back from God's love. Everything about him had changed. When he had decided once and for all to leave God to himself and return to his wife, he had taken a good look in the mirror.

Wen tried to hand the boy to him, the child began crying, kicking at the air. She put the boy down and he went trundling off. The Polack watched him go, he realized that he loved his one remaining boy. It was not a joyful sensation. For the Polack, love was bound up inextricably with failing, where love was you failed, and where you failed there was also sometimes love, only the painful solicitude of the Eternal towered above the failure.

"It's your beard," she said apologetically. "He's not used to it."

He ran his hand over his beard. "I'll shave." He realized that he missed the poignancy. He had been looking forward to it so much, and now that things had reached that point, he felt too little. Again, too little.

"So are you going to stay?" she asked. "Are you staying?" She still hadn't told him to come further. Hadn't hugged him either. They just stood there in the entryway and she hadn't brought him a glass of water yet either.

"Yeah," he said a bit hesitantly, as though he didn't know whether that was okay: to stay, to resume his duties, to act as though nothing had happened. "Yes, I'm staying. I'm back again." He thought: if I have to, I can also leave. I've forfeited my spot. She had traded him in for another. That suspicion caused him pain, although there was also relief, his love for God had done her no harm, she had found a replacement for the Polack. Now he knew what was expected of him, and he'd almost come out and said it: a good man steps aside when necessary.

"You stink," she said.

"I can't smell it."

"When was the last time you took a shower?"

"I washed whenever it was necessary."

"Didn't you ever see me? I went to you so often, I sat there so often, with Jurek, our boy, your boy, you never even nodded at us. Not even that. For you, we didn't exist. Didn't you want to see us?"

"I was afraid."

"Afraid? Of what?"

He leaned one hand against the wall. "That I would harm the two of you somehow."

"Harm us?" She ran a hand through her hair, she seemed to be growing angry. "Why would you hurt us any more than you already did? You hurt us badly enough when you left us."

"Could I get a glass of water?"

She led him to the kitchen. The boy was sitting on the floor, playing with a firetruck, and his mother said: "He's back. Papa's back, sweetheart. That's Papa." She had a catch in her voice, but the boy didn't look at him, he went on playing with his truck, stubbornly, almost proudly.

"He can already walk," she said. "Did you see that? He was so proud when he started walking. When he took his first steps. Look." She showed him a photo, attached to the door of the fridge with a magnet.

"Nice," the Polack replied. "Proud, yeah, you can see that." He felt like picking up the boy, touching him, cuddling him, telling him that he too was proud that Jurek could already walk, but he didn't dare. He didn't want to force himself on him. The father had left, he would wait until the boy accepted him again. He needed to be patient.

The Polack looked around. Not much had changed in the kitchen, yet it was only with difficulty that he could recall having lived here, as though it had been someone else playing father back then. A different man had been hit on the head with the juicer in this place.

"Is this a convenient time for you?" he asked.

"Of course," she said. "Of course it's convenient. It's always convenient when you come. You're my husband, right? We belong together, don't we?"

Yes, he was that, her husband, they weren't divorced. Still, he wasn't completely sure.

He leaned against the counter. "Did you wait for me? Isn't there someone else? I'd understand if there were, you know. I'm the one who left you two in the lurch."

"There is no one else," she said resolutely, "what do you think I've been doing all this time, what we've been doing? We waited for you. What else were we supposed to do? What other choice did you leave us? Were we supposed to forget about you? Were we supposed to act as though you'd never existed?"

At last, she hugged him. It felt good and, at the same time, suspect. Compared with his fantasies about the embrace, the embrace itself could only be a letdown. He asked himself why he felt no remorse. Where was the remorse? Where was it? He had come back to make good on a debt, the debt had proven stronger than the love of God. Before he could think any further about love and guilt, his wife stopped hugging him. "You stink really badly, you need to take a bath. It's unbearable. Didn't anyone there ever say anything about the stench?"

He shook his head.

"And the way you look. So scruffy. So . . ." She turned to the boy and said: "Come on, we're going to give Papa a wash." As though the father were only another child, a lost son.

His wife took his hand and led him upstairs. "I'd actually given up hope. You'd moved into a chicken coop, that's what they told me at the monastery."

He nodded and, sunk in thought, barely noticed that the boy had clambered up the stairs behind them.

In the bathroom she began tugging at his habit. "My god, couldn't you have put on your own clothes before you came here?"

"I didn't have anything anymore."

"Not anything?"

"No, nothing."

"And your house keys?"

"I don't have them anymore either."

"I've got spares. This is your house, isn't it?" It sounded as though she wasn't sure about that anymore herself. Whose house was this? Whose man was this, more prodigal son than husband? She asked her son: "Are you glad that Papa's back?"

The boy was standing in the bathroom doorway. His happiness looked more like fear, like a fearful, fateful suspicion.

She finally succeeded in pulling off his habit and the woolen vest he wore underneath it. Then he was standing before her in his underwear. He wasn't embarrassed, only ill at ease. As though he were standing naked before her for the first time, as though her eyes were examining him for the first time.

"I don't recognize these underpants," she said. And then: "What happened to your chest? All those wounds . . . even some pus."

"Oh, well, a little pus. It'll go away." He reached up and ran his hand over her hair. She was wearing it a little shorter these days.

"How long did it take you?" she asked. "You really came on foot?"

"I rested along the way. I went on foot to . . . I went there on foot, so I wanted to leave Him on foot too."

She combed his beard with her fingers, as though trying to get the snarls out, and once again he said: "I'll shave."

Then she turned him around gently. "Christ, what did they do to you?" She ran her fingers carefully over his back. "What did they use on you? Hot pokers?" The boy was standing in the doorway and saw everything.

The father sat down on the edge of the tub and said calmly: "There is love that is not of this world." Then he stood up right away, went to the sink, drank some water, his thirst was unbearable. And she stood behind him and felt his back. "Have you had a doctor look at it?" she mumbled. "What did they do to you, for god's sake?" She ran the back of her hand tenderly over his body, his shoulders, his lower back, and he drank more water. He was so thirsty.

"Your neck," she said, "your neck looks all bent. Is that from the chicken coop too?" It sounded like she was angry at the chicken coop.

He shook his head and sat back down on the edge of the tub. "You didn't open his door again, did you?" he asked. "Our boy's room, you never went back in there, right?"

"No." She filled the bath. "We never went in there. There was no reason for us to go in there."

He saw how she looked at Jurek, who remained standing in the doorway like an inquisitive and also frightened little animal. "It really is your beard," she said, "he doesn't recognize you with that beard." She tested the bathwater with her hand, added some liquid soap and bath salts, and said: "Take off your underpants, we'll give you a wash. Then I'll fix you some food. I bet you're hungry." Once again, she seemed prey to uncertainty: "You are staying, aren't you?"

He nodded. "I'm not all that terribly hungry." He stood up, took off his underpants, and stepped into the bath.

"Jesus, your butt, what did they do to it? Did you sit in barbed wire or something?"

Slowly he lowered himself into the water, the hot water hurt his skin, and once again he mumbled: "There is love that is not of this world."

"No, that's not love, that's a beating." She took a washcloth and carefully began washing the Polack; despite her care, there were moments when he couldn't hide the fact that the washcloth caused him pain. "All those cuts," she said. "What is that, anyway? Is it eczema? Did you scratch at it?"

He closed his eyes. "I scratched myself," he said, "it itched so badly, they scratched me too, did a job on me . . . What we understand by love, our caresses . . . our tenderness . . . that's not love, that's . . . commerce. A way to pass the time. Kidding around. Frivolity. God loves us by the sword, by fire, the whip, and barbed wire. His representatives on earth, they know how to go about it . . ." the Polack opened his eyes and saw Wen frowning.

"Well, okay," she reacted, "I don't follow completely. I guess you're tired. It must be confusing for you too. Explain it to me later. Once you've calmed down." She scratched at a scab on his arm. "When we were sitting there in the chapel, we hoped so badly for a sign, for one little sign, but you never saw us."

He tried to relax in the water and she ran a washcloth over his arms, as though she no longer knew how to wash him without hurting him. She washed his feet too. That took an especially long time. "Look at these calluses. You need to scrape that off. That business about barbed wire and the sword is too much for me. I'm sorry. I can't take that."

"No, people aren't ready for that." He took a deep breath, he felt his ribs, his stomach muscles. "Have you been in contact with the fire department?" he asked.

"At first, yeah. The Beckers have moved." She washed his armpits and his face, and tried again to remove the dirt from between his toes. "You're so incredibly dirty. I've never seen anyone so dirty. The way you smelled when you came in. It wasn't easy, not financially. I had to do some fast talking. If he's sick, then why isn't he at home, that's what the welfare people said. Because you weren't at home. You were in the monastery."

"I wasn't sick either."

"Well, I did my utmost to convince everyone that you were, so I wouldn't go denying that, and when I look at your body now, I think you look pretty sick."

Jurek came a little closer. "This is Papa," Wen said, "you remember Papa? Say something to Papa."

Eyes half shut, because of the water running down his face, the Polack smiled at the boy, he even stuck out his hand, but the boy ducked out of the way.

"He was so used to being alone with me." She went out, the boy followed, and she came back with a big, blue towel. A towel he didn't recognize.

"New?" he asked.

"Yeah, I bought new towels. Step on the mat. You were gone for a while, it wasn't a week or so. There are a lot of new things here."

He did as he was told. "A year," he said. "Almost."

She dried him off as though she was his mother. "Do you have any idea how we got along here? How we had to live? While you . . . were busy with that love of yours?"

"No," he replied, and that was the truth. He didn't know; his thoughts, his prayers, his body had been elsewhere.

She went on drying him, rougher all the time, as though she wanted to hurt him, as though she wanted to show him that she could cause him pain too, that he really wouldn't have needed to go to the monastery for that. He wanted to tell her that the pain he had received there was no ordinary pain, that the kind of love that racks you is something radically different. He didn't dare to say it. Better to explain as little as possible.

"You don't have to be afraid," she said to Jurek, "this isn't a stranger. This is Papa."

He looked in the mirror while she dried him off. "I'd better report to the firehouse again, I need to get to work."

To that she said nothing, she only fetched a pair of underpants for him, one of his old ones, blue, and he stepped into them like a little boy. "There you go," she said, "I'll rub your back and your butt with ointment, I still think it would be a good idea to have a doctor take a look at it."

She rubbed the ointment on him and he couldn't help feeling that he was a stranger to her, that he had always been a stranger, even though she rubbed him lovingly with the ointment, even though she treated his wounds. Nurses did that too. They stood before the mirror and then she turned him around, picked up a pair of scissors, and said: "Once that beard's gone, he'll recognize you again."

"I bet he's angry," the Polack said. "I can understand that. It'll take some time. I neglected him. I neglected a lot of people."

"You're back now, that's the important thing."

He sat down on the edge of the tub and she used the scissors to trim his beard. "That a beard like that can get so long," she said, seemingly deep in thought. "Lots of people asked about you at first. Colleagues came by, but when it got around that you were living in a chicken coop, well, people started getting leery. I called in sick for you. All kinds of people were here, medical officers from the fire department, city workers, they wanted to know the whole story and when I told them you were living in a chicken coop—they'd known about it for a long time already, even if they pretended not to, everyone did, things like that don't remain a secret—I had to move heaven and earth, I talked about Borys and then they said: okay, we'll just report that he's sick, temporarily unfit for work. They weren't allowed in at the monastery either. The abbot kept everyone away from you, even the company doctors."

She went on clipping at his beard.

"The Reverend Father is a wise man." He sighed. Had he come back here to explain himself? To tell stories about events he himself didn't understand? He looked at the hair that had fallen to the floor. "Are you glad I'm back?" he asked.

"We looked forward to having you back so much. What do *you* think?" He looked at the boy who was now standing in the bathroom doorway with a big firetruck. "It's going to take some getting used to," she went on. "I don't know who it is I got back."

"I look like the old Polack."

"You'll have to shave off the rest yourself." She put away the scissors and stood in front of him with her arms crossed. "I mulled over it so often that I was afraid I'd go crazy. What's he looking for there, I kept asking myself. Is he punishing us? Is he punishing me? You don't have to tell me now, sometime I'd like to know, so I can come to peace with it."

He went and stood before the mirror, she handed him a razor. "It sounds weird," he said, "but I couldn't stay here anymore, I went there to come alive again. God is nothing other than life, and I was no longer alive."

"Alive?" She bent down and said to the boy: "Papa came back because he loves you so much." The two of them, his wife and his son, stood looking at him as he lathered up his face, and he thought he saw what they were seeing, that he had grown old. It's love that makes one old, he mused, the love that is not of this world. And once his face was covered with lather he began shaving, slowly and thoroughly. It had been such a long time since he'd shaved that he had to change razors, apply a new coat of lather, and repeated the process. "These are tough hairs."

Wen said: "I guess I need to know anyway. What were you doing there? Did you come alive again? Weren't you alive enough when you were with me? Did it help?"

He looked over at her. She sounded so angry, so full of accusations. Always a failure, no matter what you did, you failed everywhere. He said it again: "I was afraid of harming the two of you. There was that too. I didn't want to be among people anymore."

"You would never harm us." She used a towel to wipe the shaving cream from his face and then she picked up the boy and hugged him. The boy still hadn't made a sound, his expression was blank.

"I'll fix some food for you." She put down the child, he followed her to the bedroom, and there she took some clothes from the closet, clothes that were hanging there in the exact same spot where they had hung one year ago. When he had pulled on his jeans, she said: "You're skinnier. I'll make sure you put on some weight."

"I don't eat meat."

She stopped in her tracks. "Since when?"

He shrugged, tightened his belt to keep the jeans from sagging.

They went downstairs, the child, his wife and he, and in the kitchen she asked: "What shall I make for you? You always used to love meat." She caressed his cheek. "Soft," she said, "that beard was worthless. It didn't look good on you either, it made you look so old. So sad, you're not a sad man. You never have been. You're a quiet man. What do you want me to make for you?"

"Whatever's not too much trouble. I don't eat fish either."

"Then I'll make you some pasta." He looked out at the garden. "Did you miss us?" she asked. "Were we on your mind? What did you feel when you thought about us?"

Without turning, he answered: "You two were on my mind, yes. That's what I felt." She started cooking and the child sat silently on the floor with the firetruck. "The garden" he said, "looks good." She nodded, she chopped mushrooms and commented: "Well, yeah, everything's starting to blossom. I'll make spaghetti with creamy mushroom sauce." Looking at the garden, he replied: "I love both of you, I wasn't made for love, but I don't give up."

She cooked the spaghetti, made the creamy mushroom sauce in a pan and said she would fix what she called "a simple salad," while the boy sat so sweetly on the floor, playing with his firetruck. So quiet, so well-behaved.

After a while, when she had drained the spaghetti in a colander in the sink, she turned around abruptly and said: "Hold me tight."

He held her tight.

"You smell much better now." And she asked: "Are you still fond of my meat?"

The chicken coop flashed through his mind, then he whispered in her ear: "Yes, now at least I'm able to appreciate your meat."

"It's yours again now," she whispered, as though the boy must not hear this, as though he could hear anything else, but not this. "You've left that chicken coop behind, am I right?"

He said nothing.

"I want you so much," she said, still at a whisper, "we're not going to bury ourselves alive. You're not in that chicken coop anymore, dearest. You're here, with me. With my meat."

"The chicken coop," he mumbled. "No, that's done with."

"You're finished with that god of yours. That's done with."

"I tore myself away," the Polack said.

She divided the spaghetti into portions on their plates. A little plate for the boy. A child's plate, with monkeys on it. The plate was new too.

"Do you want some mushroom sauce with it? Or just butter and cheese?" she asked the boy.

"Butter cheese," said the boy, "yum, cheese." He still hadn't spoken a word to the Polack.

His wife put some butter and grated cheese on the boy's spaghetti, and it struck the Polack that his return had happened just as intuitively as his departure, but he would follow his intuition in the same way he had then.

They ate without talking. Only when she was finished, when her plate was completely empty, did she say: "I'd really like to know how you got those cuts. I mean, you're my husband. The father of my child. Of my children."

He looked at his food. "The greater the love, the greater the wound."

"Oh," she looked at his plate, "aren't you hungry?"

"I'm not used to eating so much anymore."

She started stacking the plates. "Wasn't our love enough for you? Did I inflict too few wounds on you?"

He hesitated, wiped his mouth with the paper napkin. "Our love was of this world."

He carried the salad bowl into the kitchen. "I'll bring him to bed," she said, "brush his teeth, and read him a book. Wait here. He still has to get used to you, it's a big change for such a little guy." And he waited in the kitchen while Jurek was read to, his Jurek. He didn't sit down, he remained standing, leafed through a newspaper that was a couple of days old. The husband heard his wife reading aloud upstairs, then finally she came down. She stood beside him. "He's asleep," she said. "I'm so happy you're here. Are you happy too? I've become insecure. I don't know what I'm seeing. Am I seeing happiness, or not at all?"

He nodded. "I've never been much good at happiness. But I've come back, that's the important thing. Don't you think?"

She tossed the remains of the salad into the garbage pail. "But why? Did you miss us? Did you miss us the way we missed you?"

He thought about it. "I heard your voices. During prayer, and while I was working. And work is prayer, prayer is work."

"Oh," she said again. Whenever he tried to explain something of what he had experienced there, she mostly said: "Oh."

"I heard your voice, that above all, and then I knew that I belonged with the two of you, after a while I no longer doubted that at all. That I need to leave that place, that it wasn't the right place for me. That I needed to tear myself away."

"And what did you hear when you heard that?"

"You were talking."

"And what did I say?"

He ran his hand over his scalp. "That it was my fault."

"What?"

"The state you were in."

"And that's why you came back?"

"Yeah. You said that I was tormenting you." He was silent for a moment, searching for words. "Our abbot said that we can't take God's place, but that we should also not be too modest, and at a certain point I realized that I had been too modest, there in that chicken coop. And that's when I started hearing your voice." He wavered. "There's no difference between the heavenly and the earthly, the soul and the body, those are false assumptions."

"Assumptions?"

"Yes. When the soul suffers, the body suffers."

"Oh," she said, "I can't stand that abbot of yours, do you know that? I spit on him. "And she kissed him, as though by kissing her husband she was spitting on the abbot. At last she kissed him. He wasn't very pleased about her spitting on everything he loved, the pony, Beckers's wife, the abbot. Maybe that was love too, spitting on the things your husband loved because you wanted his love all for yourself. While he himself had doubts about that love. She led him upstairs. "I wasn't expecting you, otherwise I would have dressed up nice for you. I didn't shave my legs, but you don't mind, do you? Actually, I'm always ready for you. I made sure our boy didn't notice . . . He never noticed how desperate I was. I thought about you so often while I masturbated. About the way you took me." She kissed him again. He kissed back. He wasn't used to kissing like that anymore, he had come to know the sword and the barbed wire, but he had torn himself away. He was the man who tore himself away.

"You never used to do that, never used to miss me."

"No," she said, "but back then you were here. I thought: if I masturbate enough and think of you, you'll come back, you'll sense that I need you. I called out to you while I masturbated." She ran her hands over his belly, his chest.

"I'd given my body to the Lord. At first, all I could hear was God's voice. That's why I moved into that chicken coop. What was it you called out to me, then?"

She lay down on the bed with her clothes and shoes on. "I lay here like this," she said. "And then I shouted: 'Come back, Polack. Polack, come back, please, come back.'" She stayed on the bed for a moment, looked at him, the way he stood there, in clothes that no longer completely fit him. He wondered what it was she saw. Could she tell what he had been through, just by looking at him? That he had come to know something he couldn't talk about? Not now, at least, maybe never.

She got up, pushed him against the closet door. "I figured," she said, "that if I masturbated often enough, then we'd be able to cast him out, that god of yours, I even thought about the fodder carrot. I knew I'd been ungrateful; I should have been pleased with the carrot you stuck in me."

"The carrot," he murmured, "that was a long time ago."

She caressed his smooth cheek, he felt the way the skin still tingled. "What's to become of us?" she asked. "What's to become of us now, my sweet Polack?"

He let her caress him, he felt like pressing her against him, he didn't dare to yet, he couldn't do it yet.

"I don't know. We're strong."

"This," she said, "this is what's to become of us." She started taking her clothes off. "I think, I know it may sound weird, that I cast him out, your god, by masturbating here every day. I never missed a day, not even when I wasn't in the mood, so I called out to you and that's why our boy has a father again. I exorcised him, that god of yours."

He stood there, hesitating, in his stocking feet, he hadn't put on shoes yet and he didn't know what to do. After all those months he had to get used to, all over again, love that *was* of this world, the day-to-day love that went along with the brushing of teeth and the ring of an alarm clock instead of the pealing of the bells, the day-to-day love that went along with his dear wife.

"The monk who talked to us said that there are various roads that lead to God, that celibacy is only a fast road and that accidents sometimes happen out on the fast road. Did accidents happen? Did you have an accident out on that fast road, my sweet Polack?"

She was wearing only her panties and a bra now, and her shoes. She squatted down and unbuttoned his trousers, as though she wanted to examine that accident he'd had out on the fast road. She wanted to look at it, she wanted to inspect it.

"I don't remember anything about accidents," he replied, "but God did touch me, if that's what you mean. There was that. You might call that an accident."

"Oh," she giggled uneasily, playing with his balls. "I think God's silly."

"Maybe He is." He felt himself getting an erection, felt the urge to take his wife, hard and ruthless, the way God could be.

Then she took his cock in her mouth. She blew him with an abandon and a vigor that almost caused him pain. For just a moment he thought about that other love, about visions, psalms, about the gentle abbot who had let him drink the blood and eat the flesh. She took his penis out of her mouth and asked if God had ever done this to him too, if he had pleased him like this, that god of his with his love that was not of this world, and he said he never had, that he had never done that. "Then I bet this will make him jealous," she said, "seeing me lick your balls and cock right now. That god of yours must be pretty cross right now, he must feel left out in the cold. Humiliated."

"It's up to us to pleasure God," he mumbled, leaning against the closet door. "God wants to be pleasured." She went on licking and he wondered if maybe his wife was right, if this would make God jealous. Might God be jealous? In pain, divine ecstasy could reveal itself, he had been taught that much, but he had learned little concerning jealousy.

Then she stood up. There was spittle around her lips, and a little hair, he saw, probably his own. "You taste different," she said. "It doesn't matter." She wiped away the hair.

She turned around and pulled down her panties. "You remember?" she asked. "The fodder carrot? You remember that?"

"Yes. I remember."

"Take me there."

He hesitated, she must have seen him hesitate. "Take me in my unfruitful place."

"Your unfruitful place?"

"I want you to savage my unfruitful place."

"Your fruitful place is okay by me too. I never had any problems with that."

She took his head in her hands. "I want you to fuck the shit out of me. That way we'll show him that around here we do everything with each other, everything, whatever we feel like, and that he didn't do a thing to you, nothing, and that he's not going to do anything either. I've won, I beat that god of yours, he'll never get a hold of you again. I cut him down to size. Other people are allergic to dogs or cats, I've got a God allergy. And believe me, as from today he's allergic to me."

Was she saying this to arouse him? Or did she mean it? "You don't have to show me that we do whatever we want with each other here, that you've won. It's over, I'm back now."

She leaned against the closet, the closet where they kept their clothes, where his were still hanging, the clothes of a dead man who had come back to life, the closet where her only cocktail dress still hung, the one she'd bought for a party that had ultimately been a letdown. "Do it," she insisted.

"I don't want to hurt you." He stood there in what had once been his bedroom, his pants down around his knees. If this was a part of his homecoming, if this was what he had to do to be received again into the bosom of the family, then he was prepared to do it. Even though it took a lot of getting used to. He had the vague feeling that he had missed a service somewhere, the prayers, the kneeling, it was still in him, like a reflex.

"Show that we've beat that dopey god of yours," she said. "Rub your cock over my ass and then stick it in me real fast. I can take a little pain. I'm no baby, really."

He felt like saying that God, whatever else you might think of him, was not someone you could beat, and definitely not by sticking your cock up your wife's ass, even if that was completely normal these days, except he had never stuffed much more than a fodder carrot up hers but that was because the Polack was a timid man who had for years been perfectly satisfied with her vagina and her mouth, until their eldest son had his fatal accident. Satisfied, that was the word for it. Maybe that satisfaction was superficial, sinful in some strange way; if so, then so be it. He hadn't missed anything all those years, and so he had not gone looking for anything either. The searching had taken him by surprise, as had the end of the search.

He went and stood behind his lawful wedded wife and did what was expected of him, with passion, with an arousal for which he did not have to beg. "Do you like it?" she asked him halfway through. "Do you like this as much as I do? I can feel how horny you are. Now that you're in me, now that you're taking me in that hole that belongs only to you, that's yours and yours alone, now there's nothing left of that year that you were gone, it's as if you'd never left."

"This is mine," he said, and he fucked her as though intercourse were the better class of religious ecstasy.

"I want your cum dripping out of my ass." He did his utmost. Just as he had in the chicken coop, here too his did his best.

2

He walked to the firehouse this time, he didn't feel like driving, he wanted to approach the firehouse slowly. He looked forward to seeing his friends, to the rituals, the voices, this too would be a sort of home-coming. They would ask him lots of questions, his friends would, they would think he was strange, he knew how they thought about things, in the end happiness would rule the day. That was the way he walked through the town, which seemed less ugly to him than it had before, if you've lived in a chicken coop it changes your opinions about pretty and ugly, what was pretty became ugly, what was ugly became pretty, love became kitsch, pain became tenderness.

At last they were all sitting in the squad commander's office. The C squad was complete again. The squad commander had been the first to say so when the Polack walked in, and they had all come to welcome him. Not as a prodigal son, but then not as a pariah either. And that was exactly the way it felt to the Polack, they were complete again. The men looked just the same as they had on the day he'd left them— yes, he had left them too—they slapped him on the shoulders just like they used to, they smelled the same, mumbled the same words of greeting. And now they were all sitting around the squad commander's office, the way they often did when there was something that needed discussing. Still, he had the feeling that something had changed, something you could barely name but that he noticed anyway. There was something in the air.

They drank their coffee and looked at him without a word. Maybe that was what had changed, they looked at him as though they'd never seen him before.

"Of course, you're welcome back," the squad commander said once they'd finished their coffee. "We took someone on temporarily, because we always told each other: the Polack will be back."

The men nodded.

That was good to hear. They hadn't forgotten him, they hadn't written him off. Here too they had waited for the tall, silent Polack. It was heartwarming. These men, these members of the family, had waited for him as well, had missed him, he could not disappear unawares.

"Even though, at a certain point, it felt like an awfully long time," the squad commander said. The men nodded again. "An eternity," Beckers added.

Someone made the rounds with the pot and they all had a second cup of coffee, the rare individual took tea, and they looked at him as though they expected him to say something now. Something about the eternity, his disappearance that was now no longer a disappearance, about happiness maybe, being happy to find himself back with them.

An eternity, had it really lasted an eternity? There in the monastery, all sense of time had slipped away. The days all looked alike and at a certain point he had the idea that all the days had in fact always looked alike. The seasons, the weeks. Summer. Winter. The weekends. What difference was there?

His wife had told him: "We need to enjoy ourselves a lot, and when you weren't around, when we were slowly falling apart, I still tried to enjoy myself in between times."

One pleasure made way for the next, in the meantime you fell apart and from there, from that other point it had seemed as though one pleasure could no longer be distinguished from another. Everything was pleasure, even suffering was a pleasure when you looked at it in a certain way. The right way.

"Of course, we understand that there was something that came before all that," the squad commander said. "You didn't just disappear out of the blue. You had a whole lot of troubles come your way."

The Polack toyed with his empty coffee cup and said: "I'm back now, that's all that matters. I'm ready to give everything I've got for the squad, just like before. I'm ready to give even more."

The squad commander nodded. "We heard that, at a certain point, you were living . . ." he coughed, licked his lips, "in a chicken coop."

They all looked at him. So that's what this was about. This was the reason for their get-together. They were suspicious. A colleague moving into a chicken coop was not the way things were supposed to go. Could you still count on someone like that, if you all had to enter a burning house together? Is someone who's lived in a chicken coop still a team player? He had to prove that he was still a team player, and that's exactly what he was going to do.

"Yeah," said the Polack, after a brief silence, "but there were no chickens living in it anymore. No one lived there at all. Just me. It was actually a kind of vacant house."

"A house?" Beckers responded. "Yeah, for Africans maybe, but not for you."

"We were wondering . . ." The squad commander picked up something from the floor, a pen, and when he had placed the pen on the table with something almost like solemnity, he went on: "We wondered what you were looking for there. In that vacant house, so to speak."

Beckers took over: "We're all just beating around the bush here, so I'll come out and say it: we thought it was weird. Look, you go to a monastery looking for peace and quiet, we can understand that, but that chicken coop business, that was too much. We thought that was strange, extremist stuff really."

The squad commander tapped a finger quietly and rhythmically on the tabletop and said: "It's good to get this business out of the way, so we don't have to talk about it again later. We're a team, and we have to stay a team, so maybe you could tell us what you were trying to find there, what you were up to. In that chicken coop. Then we're up to speed on that. Then we can say: oh, was that all? And then we can get back to business as usual."

They all looked at the Polack as though they were now going to hear the secret they'd been waiting to hear all their lives.

"Boy," said the Polack, "there's not a whole lot I can tell you about it. It was that I had a hard time . . . tolerating people."

"Tolerating them?" Beckers asked.

"I wanted to be alone and then . . . how can I put it, there was an opening in the chicken coop."

"An opening . . ." echoed the man they called Rabbit.

The Polack recalled the days, the weeks he had spent in the chicken coop, his memories of it were foggy. He no longer saw the coop so sharply in his mind's eye, and could barely recall what had prompted him to move into it. Becoming a hermit had seemed like a solution to him. He had gone looking for the love from which there is no escape and he had found it, he had never known how much pain that love could cause until he felt it burning on his body, then he knew. One thing led to another, love had lured him to the chicken coop, the love that made you want to embrace every wound, to approach each pain with a song on your lips, accept all death as a gift, even if that wasn't something he would talk about. Fransen, who would be retiring soon, said: "We said to each other: he was never an extreme kind of person, was he? The Polack is a Polack, but extreme? That's what we said to each other. That wasn't the you we'd come to know. Today a chicken coop, tomorrow a . . . We told each other: it's like he's some Muslim fundamentalist or something."

"A Muslim fundamentalist?" the Polack asked.

Beckers stepped in: "Yeah, extremist, Islamist, fundamentalist, whatever you want to call it. We were afraid of you and your chicken coop, and at the same time it seemed like some kind of April Fool's joke. Until we talked to your wife. Then we realized it was no joke. Then we said: Jesus Christ. Holy shit. He's gone off the deep end. Our Polack."

The squad commander interrupted Beckers. "How did you live there, anyway? Can you tell us that? So we can kind of form an idea. How about if we start there? Just to give us an idea. Is a coop like that fit for human habitation? Did you put down a mattress or something?"

Upon which the Polack wiped his hands on his trousers and thought about his wife, who had urged him to see a doctor. He realized that they too would see his wounds here, in the shower, they would comment on them. That wasn't anything terrible. Not even if they made jokes about it, he could take it. They would be well-meaning jokes, no doubt. A little teasing, a little pestering. Just a bunch of guys together. Boys. Only kidding.

"They'd got rid of the chickens already," the Polack said, "they've got animals there, they didn't want the chickens anymore and then it came to me in a flash. I said to the abbot . . . I talked to the abbot. I had these thoughts . . . I heard what they said to me. I said: I'll go live there. I'll move in. It's vacant anyway. People are too much for me. I say to the abbot. The world is too much for me. But a mattress, no, not that. I just lay down where the chickens had their nest. On a bunch of straw."

"We're having a hard time following this," Beckers cut in, "but maybe we shouldn't try to understand. Were you trying to do penance? Was that what it was? Did you feel guilty about something?"

The Polack kept rubbing his hands on his trouser legs. "The chicken coop made me feel calm, I felt at home there, a person doesn't need all that much. People . . ." He saw the way the men were staring at him, as though he were a giant chicken, a sideshow attraction that had ended up at the firehouse. Tomorrow he would be on display somewhere else. This couldn't be fixed. He could tell from the way they looked. The squad commander shook his head slowly and the Polack felt his colleagues silently declaring him unfit, almost in spite of themselves. They had no choice.

"It's over," the Polack said quickly then. "I was mixed up. I would never do that again." It was best to say that. People could get mixed up, of course, as long as it didn't last too long. And if they apologized when it was over, then it was okay. He was mixed up, the confusion was over now. He should keep it at that.

"Had you been drinking?" Beckers asked.

"When I was mixed up? No," the Polack answered.

"Drugs?" Fransen wanted to know.

The Polack shook his head. He crushed his empty throwaway coffee cup, until it was nothing but a flat, circular object.

"Did you get it on with men there?" Fransen asked. "Was that chicken coop a place where you did it with men? You can tell us. I mean, it's not my kind of thing, going for men, but I've got nothing against it either. Everyone has to figure out for himself how he gets his kicks, as long as you keep your hands off of children."

"Want some more coffee?" asked the squad commander, who apparently wanted to avoid homosexuality and pedophilia as subjects.

"Did you break out the Vaseline?" Beckers asked anyway. "Is that how it went?"

The Polack nodded thankfully. "A little more coffee, yeah, thanks," he said. "If you please, and no, I didn't get it on with men. I got to know love . . ."

That last bit was something he shouldn't have said, fortunately they hadn't heard him or else they pretended they hadn't. The commander handed him a new cup and Fransen wanted to know whether the Polack really hadn't come to the Lord over there.

"No, definitely not," said the Polack, "and I never did either. The Lord came to me, I didn't come to Him."

"Good thing too," said Fransen, who had barely given the Polack time to finish. "I've got an uncle who's born again. You can't even talk to the guy, the way he spouts nonsense all the time. This here is the fire department, we save bodies, not souls. And that's that."

The squad commander tapped his hand on the table. "We've known each other so long," he said, "that's what matters to me. Starting next week I'm putting you on a shift again, and we'll see how it goes. Forget about the chicken coop. Over and out. You were mixed up. Happens to the best of us. Now you're back with the C squad. Now you're one of us again."

"Thanks," said the Polack quietly, and he noticed how the man's words moved him, it almost made him cry. To hide that, he acted like he was coughing.

The squad commander rose to his feet and, one by one, the other men did too. Fransen was the last; he stroked his mustache, the way he'd done for years, ever since he'd decided to grow one, and one by one the men shook the Polack's hand. To Beckers, he said: "I heard you guys have moved."

"That's right," Beckers said, "we live in Wahlwiller now. More room, which is especially nice for the girls. No Arabs hanging around. That helps. There isn't a single Arab in all of Wahlwiller, and no Negroes either."

The Polack nodded, then went and shook Fransen's hand. They all smiled at him amiably, yet he couldn't shake the feeling that he was no longer their colleague, that he had become an enemy, someone they had to get rid of somehow.

"I'll let you know as soon as I schedule your shifts," the squad commander shouted to him. The Polack walked outside, the cup of coffee in his hand. He had to get used to people again, to their day-to-day worries, to the real world which had, in some peculiar way, become more fleeting since he had lay in the chicken coop. It wasn't living that he'd done there, he had lain there. He had lived lying down.

The Polack wandered through the city. The ugliest city in Holland, his wife always said, but the ugliness felt comforting to him. He was at home here, in this ugliness you could feel at home, in this glorified strip mall, and if you walked on at a good pace for half an hour or so you were out in the hills and then the ugliness was behind you, then you were alone with natural surroundings as pretty as any in the world. He did his best to smile at people and, without planning to do so, he found himself headed for the house where the Beckers had once lived. There was no need to fear running in Beckers's wife, these days she lived in a village where the Arabs hadn't shown up yet. He wanted to see the house. Something in him drew him to that house, the way pilgrims are drawn to sacred spots.

The drapes were different now, curtains with a childish print, the sign beside the door now said: "Fam. Schwabe." For a moment he toyed with the idea of ringing the bell, then he decided to walk on, for what was he supposed to say to the Schwabes?

A neighbor lady, standing in the front yard next door with a shopping bag in her hand, called out: "They've moved, the Beckers. They don't live here anymore."

She was staring at him, she seemed to recognize him. "It's you," she said.

"What do you mean?" the Polack said.

"You're the man who went into the convent, aren't you?"

"Yes," said the Polack.

"They went on about you all the time. You were the talk of the town, you were. Horrible, the way that all went." She took another step in his direction, she was standing at the ornamental hedge now, she could come no closer. "Is it true, what they say?"

"No, I don't think so." He gave her a friendly nod and walked on.

So people had gone on about him. That's how it went. Hopefully, now that he was back at work and about to resume his paternal duties, they would start talking about other people. They would forget about him, and that was good. The unassuming existence was his existence.

A new lady was working at the daycare center; she greeted him with the kind of suspicion that goes with the world of the child and the daycare center.

"I'm here for Jurek," he told her. "I wanted to pick him up a bit earlier. It's my day off." He pointed at the boy.

"Are you his uncle?" the new lady asked.

"I'm his father," the Polack said proudly.

The lady turned to Jurek: "Is this your daddy?"

The boy only looked at him. He didn't make a sound. There was no look of recognition. Then the lady asked if the Polack had any ID he could show her. He said he was perfectly willing to show her his ID, but that perhaps she should ask her colleague first. "Zetta knows who I am."

"Zetta's on maternity leave," the new lady answered.

"Oh," said the Polack, "oh, I guess I missed that one. Sorry." Then he knelt down and said to his son: "Don't you recognize me anymore? I'm your daddy. Go on, you little nut. I'm your father. I'm Papa. I love you so much."

It was warm in the daycare center, a heat that reminded him of some evenings in the chicken coop when the sun had been shining on the roof all day. He had laid there, life and death had become indistinguishable, eternity had knocked at the door of the chicken coop, life and death mixed together into one big, hallucinatory cocktail.

The Polack rose to his feet and looked at the new lady, a girl really, who was eyeing him carefully. More a female prison guard than a daycare worker. "I was abroad for a while," said the Polack, and he stood up in order to get a better look at her, to speak with greater conviction. "The boy had to do without his father for a while."

Once again he knelt down and held out his hands to Jurek, who was playing with blocks, but the child didn't come to him. He examined him the way the men at the firehouse had examined him, as though the child too could not get used to the thought that his father had moved into a chicken coop. Only temporarily, but still, it was a blot the Polack apparently could not wipe out.

Then, from one of the rooms at the back, Tess appeared; she recognized him, although she kept her distance a bit. "Yes, this is Jurek's father," Tess said. And to the Polack, she added: "Nice to see you again. He's grown so much, hasn't he?"

He could tell from her voice that she had been informed about the whole situation too. He picked Jurek up. Fortunately, the little boy didn't start crying. Tess handed him Jurek's coat and a little backpack. "Let me help him with his coat." She took the boy from him. He smiled at her but, now even more than before, it felt like he was only pretending to be a father.

While Tess was helping Jurek, the new lady said: "We can't be too careful. I apologize."

"Right," the Polack said. "We can't be too careful."

Jurek had his coat on now. "Bye, Jurek," said Tess. "Are you leaving with your papa now? Are you going home, is that it? Will be you be back tomorrow?"

"He's leaving with his papa," the Polack said. He picked up Jurek, who didn't resist. "See you tomorrow, Jurek," Tess called out. Jurek waved to Tess rather weakly and the Polack walked out of the daycare center with his son. Still, he couldn't shake the feeling that he was in the midst of committing a kidnapping.

Outside, the wind had picked up. He held the boy to his chest, firmly. "I know you can already walk," he said quietly, "but let's go home fast. Before it starts raining." And, for the first time since his return, he saw warmth in the eyes of the one remaining son. Recognition. Maybe something like love, he wasn't sure. It was an awfully big word, anyway, too big for one little, remaining boy.

He was about to cross the street, but he noticed a man staring at him. Obviously, someone who had talked about him. His picture hadn't been in the paper, had it? How would they recognize him otherwise? Had people shown each other his picture? Look, this is the guy. This guy lives in a chicken coop now. Had they laughed? Or, like his colleagues, merely shook their heads in dismay? He suspected that his colleagues had laughed too, they had laughed about the Polack, the liberating laughter of disdain. It didn't matter. There had been a time when he would have laughed at himself too.

"Don't you remember me?" the man asked.

The Polack shook his head.

"I'm the hired people-hand," the man said. "We met at the farmer's."

"Oh yeah."

The man looked different these days. Urbane, almost chic. "I have bad news for you," he said.

"Oh." The Polack held Jurek even tighter.

"The farmer passed away."

"My condolences." The Polack made as if to walk on, but the hired people-hand had more to say.

"His wife too. All within ten days of each other. She refused to eat. And the children said: 'Let her be. Don't force her.' She said: 'I never liked him anyway. Not from the very first day. But without him, there's no reason to go on either.' Lovely, isn't it? How strong love can be. Invincible. Yeah, it gave me a lot of hope and courage."

"Well," said the Polack, "lovely." He started to cross the street again, but the man stopped him.

"Wait. Allow me to give you my new business card. We've grown. We have almost twenty employees these days. I'm no longer called the hired people-hand, lots of clients felt uncomfortable with the hired hand stuff. Thought it was a little outdated. These days I call myself 'the human extension.' Assistance is an extra arm, an extra leg, an extra hand: an extension, in other words. I'm an extension of the other. We are the extension of the other, because we've grown."

He pulled out his business card and handed it to the Polack, who accepted it for courtesy's sake. He glanced at it. It said: THE HUMAN EXTENSION, INC. RESPECTFUL CARE TAILORED TO FIT,

FOR EVERYONE, YOUNG AND OLD." And in fine print, at the bottom: "Care available with credit plan."

The Polack put the card in his pocket, then ran his hand over Jurek's hair.

"We still aren't on the insurers' list," the man said, "the powers that be are still trying blackball us, but it's only a matter of time. That's why we offer a credit plan. Ideal for the working man. After all, old-fashion caregiving is passe. People don't want an authority to care for them, they want an extension. We look up to our clients. The care we offer is a fantasy come true. Of course, you've got people who say: yeah, I'd rather not have had any care at all. I would rather have been able to go to the toilet on my own. Those days are over. The days when we were able to do everything on our own. We can't do anything on our own anymore. Not even go to the toilet. That day has come. And that's what you have to capitalize on. I've got a young Afghani guy working for me. He understands it. He's young, twenty-one, but he senses what the client needs. He kneels before the client. Not to degrade himself, but to put the needy person at ease. When you have to wipe someone's butt for them, that person needs to trust you, otherwise you could just as well have a robot do it. The needy person has to sense that someone is there, someone who wipes his butt with as much love as a father and mother used to. We are all in need of care, some just a little more than others. That's the motto of The Human Extension, Inc. The end of days is at hand, and then you have to adapt your health care to cope with that. In the future, people won't go on vacation anymore, they won't go skiing or skydiving. They'll buy care, because they need it and because they like it. They'll start buying care younger, and our clientele is getting younger all the time. In the end there won't be any difference anymore between care and love. I'm not just saying this to promote our company."

"I really have to be getting home," the Polack interrupted. "People are waiting for me."

"I'm saying this," the man went on, "because I see a potential extension in you. You understand. Open your eyes, I tell our people, the world is a hospital. In the future, we'll all wipe each other's butt. That's what paradise is all about. If something like paradise is even possible."

"Someone's waiting for me," the Polack said, more emphatically this time, "if I need a job, I'll give you a call. I'm a fireman, and I plan to keep doing that for a while still."

The human extension laid a hand on the Polack's shoulder and it really did feel like a caring hand, coercive yet caring. "I'm running this idea up the flagpole over in Aachen. See how it goes there. I think they're open to my ideas over there. They can't get by on their own anymore, people can't, they're lost. And the human extension says: that doesn't matter. We're going to assume the practical care for you now. That's not the whole world, but it's an awful lot. If you can't eat anymore, or don't want to, if you can't lift a fork to your own lips, then it's nice to have someone come and feed you lovingly, instead of just stuffing the food in your mouth. If you can't make it out the door anymore, we'll come and take you out for a walk. We're not cheap, I'll admit. But what's more important? Good care in the future, or going out to dinner today at restaurants you will have forgotten all about the next day? What do you think? Is Germany ready for my ideas too?"

"I think so. See you around." The Polack's farewell was very resolute this time, and he went on his way home. Once he was far enough away from the man, he started talking to Jurek. "I'm going to open my mouth," he spoke quietly in the boy's ear, "I'm known as the tight-lipped Polack, but it's time for me to start speaking up a little. I'm your father. You don't have to act as though you don't know me. You're allowed to recognize me. You're the one remaining boy. We'll keep each other company. That sounds weird, but isn't that what fatherhood boils down to? That you keep your child company. And your child keeps you company. Bringing up a child, I'm not so sure. We raised your brother. Your sweet, big brother. Apparently, it didn't agree with him much, our way of parenting."

The boy didn't reply. He looked at his father, though, and in that look the Polack saw everything he needed, everything he had expected from the boy.

When his wife came home, he was playing with Jurek. He asked how her day had been. She didn't say much. Back when they had first met, he had known the names of all her kindergarten pupils by heart. He knew all their foibles. New kindergartners came along, and gradually he stopped learning the names of all the children. It wasn't a conscious decision, it was just the way it went. She told him less and less about her work, and he asked less and less. You couldn't keep track of everything the other person did. There was too much information. You didn't need to know everything.

She sat down beside him, cross-legged, without taking off her coat. "What was that like," she asked, "when you were in that chicken coop? That you suddenly decided to come back? How did that go? I'm trying to picture it. I can't get it off my mind."

At first he said nothing, because he had resolved to stop talking about the chicken coop. He was no longer sure whether the coop was a vision or whether visions had driven him into the coop. There he had discovered the formidable and violent power of love. But because she kept looking at him questioningly, he said: "Yeah, how did that go? First God called me, then you two called me. That's what life is, isn't it," he said, trying to kiss his wife, "that there's always someone calling you?"

VI

THE TENTH YEAR

1

He had gone to Beckers's wife as she lay dying in order to say goodbye, to really say goodbye, because the letter had never been sent, because he had never explained his silence, because he had thought and hoped that silence would be enough. There had been comforting, it been done long ago, clumsily, and perhaps in a way that shouldn't be used to comfort people, but the comforting had never been terminated. No one had ever said straight out: we're done with the comforting now, it's no longer necessary.

When he got home, his wife was waiting for him. She was standing in the hallway with her coat on.

"What are you doing here?" he asked. "I thought you were going to that party."

"I decided not to."

"I thought it was important."

"It was."

"So why did you decide not to?"

"So I could talk to you."

She knew, he could tell by the look on her face. She must have smelled it, the hospital odor, the odor of death, more pungent than that of the forest. She looked at him, she stood facing him like a customs official about to check a passenger. She had countless wrinkles around her eyes, she was so different from back when the four of them were still together. His wife was surer of herself, she had become an authority. He noticed that from her stories about the kindergartners' parents, who were becoming more demanding all the time, there had been a time when she let parents intimidate her, now she made short work of them. The demanding parent, when faced with Wen, didn't have a whole lot to say. She tolerated backchat, but only because that was the courteous thing to do.

That's how she stood before him now, still wearing her coat, she looked him up and down and he said: "I went for a long, long walk. All the way to Epen, almost to the border, then back again."

"You went out for a breath of fresh air."

"Well, more than that, really."

She shook her head pityingly.

"I also went by the hospital," he said quietly, almost the way a child would. "I went just to say goodbye."

"To say goodbye?" she asked. "I warned you. We talked about it at length this morning. We've been through enough already. I've had it. I've had it, completely." She turned on her heel, strode off, and he followed her through the house.

Jurek was on the couch in the living room , a pair of earphones plugged into his mother's cell phone. He didn't look up. The Polack couldn't imagine that his wife, after all these years, would actually leave. It was like the way some couples wait to have a child. At a certain point, they know it's never going to come. To leave now was madness. She'd had the chance before, she'd let it pass, and he had too, in so far as he had really wanted to do that, to leave.

She climbed the stairs, very calmly in fact, and he went after her, without speaking. In the upstairs bedroom she took a suitcase from the closet, one of the ones they'd taken to Italy with them last summer. It was a new one, bought specially for the trip to Italy. Pink. She had wanted a pink suitcase. "You can see it a mile away," she'd said. "And besides, it was on sale." It had been a fine vacation, relaxed, more relaxed than ever before, in fact. A little house close to Lake Como, they stayed there for two weeks. At first the location felt like a disappointment, it was further from Lake Como than they'd thought, but they got used to the drive and the surrounding mountains were lovely. Maybe she had known even then. Maybe she'd thought: once autumn has really set in, somewhere in late November, I'll leave. Just a few more months. Why had she waited till late November? Had she been expecting a sign? A flash of inspiration?

She opened the suitcase. The suitcase, the Polack thought, smelled of Italy, of the summer. Jurek had lazed around in a hammock as though his life depended on it, the Polack had tried to do some reading. His wife had recommended a book for him, but he kept falling asleep. Finally, he gave up and concentrated on his sudoku booklet instead.

"I don't want to be hysterical about it," she said, "but this is the last straw. We had an agreement. I don't want any more ghosts from the past, and you keep dragging them in, and it's precisely Beckers's wife, of all people, who I don't want to have haunting me. She was already dead. She had already passed away. Over and out. I'm tired. I'm exhausted."

He looked at her in surprise. " Are you maybe starting to have a migraine attack?" he suggested.

"No, this is not the start of a migraine attack. This is no migraine. And no normal headache either. This is about you."

He couldn't imagine it ending this way, after all that had happened. After a certain point you no longer walk out, the same way that after a certain point you no longer learn to deep-sea dive. She was pretending, maybe she wanted to feel that he cared about her. That had to be it. A test. Things had become too harmonious, she was longing for some excitement, but deep down inside he knew that his own rationalizations weren't correct.

"You're a ghost from the past yourself." She took hold of his upper arm and said: "Admit it. Admit it, finally. We don't love each other anymore, maybe we never did. That's possible. We went through something together, but that's not the same as loving each other."

"We lost a child," the Polack said, "lost him in an unusual way. You're not supposed to lose a child that way. That was ten years ago. And we still have a son, he's downstairs on the couch."

"Yes, he's downstairs on the couch." She picked up a little stack of underwear. "It's not that I dislike you, it's not that we'll never see each other again. And you're right, we have a child. But I don't want this anymore." She put a pair of jeans in the suitcase, and a skirt he hadn't seen her wear for years, a skirt he had forgotten even existed.

"Where are you going to go?" he asked. "And what is it exactly that you don't want anymore?"

"I'm going to a girlfriend's house."

"Which girlfriend, if you don't mind my asking?"

"Magda."

"Magda, I didn't know you two were so close. Magda. And what about the boy?"

"The boy," she said. "Jurek. That's what I mean, is that the only thing we share? The boy. Nothing more besides that? The boy, the boy. What am I, some vestigial growth on Jurek's back?"

She picked up a sweater, looked at it, and put it back in the closet. "I'm not gone, it's not like I'm suddenly going to disappear. I'm leaving this house. I'm leaving you, but we'll still be connected, we've still got Jurek, that's right. He can live half the time with me, the other half with you, we'll figure it out." She sounded relaxed, it sounded like she'd been practicing for a while to be able to say this. It was no spur of the moment thing, no spontaneous move. Maybe she had talked to Magda and Magda had said: "So leave him, you deserve better."

He felt no urge to put up a fight, and that was the thing that surprised him most. No urge to shout: What difference does it make if I take a flower to a dying woman? Wen would come back, this was only an impulse, something she would regret tomorrow. "Do you think I've gotten old?" he asked.

"No," she said as she packed one of her summer dresses, "you still look good. I want you to know one thing: I've always been monogamous, all those years. I'm a monogamous woman. You are looking at a monogamous woman."

He looked at her suitcase, it was filled halfway. "That's nice. Monogamous. No cheating." For a moment he saw Beckers's wife before him, in the hospital, more dead than alive. It seemed better to him to say nothing more about monogamy.

"A pity," he said, pointing at the green dress she wore beneath her coat, "you had that dry-cleaned specially for the party and now no one has seen you in it. It looks so good on you."

She nodded. "I am in love, though," she said. "Just so you know. With another man."

"Oh." The Polack sat down on the bed. In love, he hadn't been expecting that. Wen came and sat beside him, her eyes were moist, she put an arm around her husband, the father of her child. "I wanted so badly to fall in love again," she said, "do you understand that? I wanted it so badly. Someday, I thought, I'll die without ever having been in love again. And then it happened. It bowled me over. But I've remained monogamous. I want you to know that. A kiss at the train station. Nothing more."

The Polack nodded. "Which station?"

"Heerlen."

She kept her arm around him. "Do you understand that? I mean, the two of us are . . . we're kind of dead. We have nothing more to say to each other. We go on living our separate lives. We share a house, a bathroom."

"You could have fallen back in love with me all over again," the Polack said, "or would that be asking too much?"

"Fall back in love with you again? Do you think that can really happen? Have you ever fallen back in love with the same person? What kind of world do you live in? Can you imagine falling back in love with that god of yours?"

"No, but I was never in love with Him."

"I did my best," she went on. "I worked at it, I worked really hard, they always say that relationships are hard work, that love is hard work, well, I put my back into it. That little bit of sex, that can't be all there is."

"Little bit?"

She was leaving. Compared to Borys, this wasn't so bad. As long as people didn't jump in front of a train, nothing was all that bad.

"I'll go on loving you," she said, "I just don't want to go on dying slowly. What I'm saying may sound harsh, but everything around you has a way of dying."

He felt the urge to defend himself, he didn't know how, anything he might say seemed futile to him. She was in love, monogamous and in love. What could he say to counter that? He had just said farewell to Beckers's wife.

"Who is this you're in love with, anyway?" he asked.

"What difference does it make? Do you want to fight with him?" She laughed, but it didn't sound very cheerful.

"No, on the contrary, I want to do all I can to be sure you have a good life."

"What else should I take with me?" she asked and she stood up. As though he should help her pack, as though she were going on a trip for a couple of days.

"No idea. Nice that you stayed monogamous all this time, but then what did you do with that man . . . the man you're in love with? What do you do exactly, when you're in love but still monogamous? Maybe that's a stupid question."

She sighed, as though she thought it was indeed a stupid question. "We write letters to each other. Didn't you ever notice that?"

He shook his head. "No, never noticed. What did the two of you talk about?"

"About astrology, he's into astrology in his free time."

"But you don't believe in astrology."

"No, but I'm in love. Everything's wonderful then. Everything. You remember, don't you? I'm not some teeny-bopper, I stop and think about things. It's lovely to think that everything's wonderful, even astrology."

"Yeah," the Polack said, "that's lovely. Astrology is pretty fascinating." He could have grown angry, but if there was one thing he didn't want, it was rage. He had been angry when he entered the chicken coop, his desire had been rage. That rage had been conquered. No more rage, never, that was his motto.

"I didn't touch him. I thought: if I touch him, I'm lost. I wanted to give us a chance."

"How sweet. So I missed out on a chance somewhere?" The Polack felt a momentary, deep sorrow, the way it must feel when you're dying. So this was it. Relief and sorrow, bits and pieces of anecdotes, a little shopping list of missed chances, a sort of litany. Sorrow over lives not led.

She closed the suitcase. "You know, when you said this morning that you wanted to go to Beckers's wife, that you wanted to say goodbye to her at the hospital, I knew that the past would never be over. That you drag it along behind you, and I can't take that anymore. It's not that we didn't try things, marriage counseling, weekend trips, swimming together, you name it. And I also thought: shouldn't we empty out that room? Maybe we should just throw away everything that belonged to him without looking at it." She took his hand, then let go of it again. "I have no regrets," she went on, "you'll always be the father of my children. If I stay here, it feels like I'm watching life from the sidelines. Waiting until Jurek leaves home, waiting for a retirement home with nursing care. Grandkids, maybe? Not that." She tilted the suitcase upright.

"Don't you want grandkids?"

"That's not what I mean."

"What are we going to tell Jurek?"

She shrugged. "I'm going downstairs in a minute, I'll talk to him." The Polack remained sitting on the bed. He was being left, his wife, the mother of his children, was going away. For the same reason, actually, that his father had once severed all contact with him; he smelled of death, he dragged behind him a past people didn't want to be reminded of. And he didn't do it on purpose.

"I've lost track of myself," she said. "I've misplaced myself, that's what I mean. All I have are functions. Teacher. Mother. Of a living boy. Mother of a dead boy. Wife of a fireman. Who am I, really? I no longer have any idea who I am. It seems like we attract misfortune, as if that's the only thing we are anymore, magnets for bad luck."

"Magnets for bad luck? Is that all we've ever had, bad luck? Is that all this family is, a collection of people who are down on their luck?"

First she shook her head, then she nodded. "It was something else I wanted."

"Something else?" He was reminded again of Beckers's wife and the Frenchman. Had she gone on hoping until the end? Had she ever called him? Had he come anyway, at last, only to have her tell him: No, no need to bother anymore. Too late. Too bad?

"I really don't know who I am anymore," Wen said. He saw that she was crying.

He was the Polack and he was a fireman. That was enough. What more did you have to know about yourself? These days, everyone had to do important things, take long trips, push their limits. The modest life didn't count anymore, there was no space for a life like that these days. The modest, the ordinary, the inconspicuous, that was what felt right to him.

"What is it *you* want, then?" she asked. "I've asked you that so many times. What do *you* want?"

"You have. I always told you the same thing, I want to be a good father and a good husband and at work I want to be a good fireman. Did my answers seem dull to you?"

"Dullness, no, that wasn't the problem. Simple dullness you can live with. Your dullness is deathly." She walked to the door. "I'm going to tell Jurek."

He stayed behind on his own, and a little later he heard them talking downstairs. It went on for a long time, so he went to the bathroom and brushed his teeth. He had a bad taste in his mouth. Once again, he thought about their last vacation. The last time they'd had sex, the last kiss, the last breakfast.

The one remaining boy wanted to go snorkeling there in Italy, they had driven to the lake three times, an hour and a half each time, but Jurek wasn't satisfied with that. Snorkeling in the sea was the only thing that could make him happy.

"Next year we'll go to the seaside," the Polack told him, and the boy lay in his hammock with the snorkel on his stomach and stared at the sky. He wanted to go snorkeling all day long, above all he wanted that which he could not have. Maybe he got that from his mother, she wanted mostly what couldn't be. Except for there, there above Lake Como, there she had seemed content. She had said nothing about last chances and death, about monogamy and being in love. She read and the Polack worked on his sudokus. Everything seemed in harmony. Should he have been missing something? What did Wen miss that he didn't? Did you have to fall in love fast before you died?

There had been a time when he had missed someone, it had turned out badly for him.

When he was done in the bathroom, he heard his wife still talking downstairs. She was talking more than the boy was. That didn't surprise him, she was the one who had something to explain.

The Polack lay down on the bed. He waited, without thinking much about the rest of his life. The rest would come of its own accord. He didn't worry, because he wasn't the kind of man who tends to worry.

At last his wife came upstairs. Yes, she was leaving, even though she remained his dear wife. That she would always remain. A good man will step aside when necessary. "Well?" he asked.

She shrugged. "He wants to go with me, but I told him that's not possible. Magda's house isn't big enough for that. He's going to have to stay with you for the time being, I told him. That we're not angry with each other. Just tired of being together."

"Tired of being together," the Polack echoed.

"I didn't say anything about being in love."

"Better that you didn't," the Polack said. "Does Magda have a husband and kids too?"

"No, she's not into that."

That happened sometimes, some people weren't into men and children. Although you'd expect a kindergarten teacher to like children, but maybe it was naive to think that.

"Jurek didn't say much," Wen went on. "He said 'all right' when he heard that he couldn't go along. That's not saying much when your parents are splitting up, is it? But you never say much either. You two are a lot alike. Everything's all right. Everything's always all right."

"Last summer Jurek knew what he wanted: to go snorkeling. Everything was not all right then."

"I'm going. There's some leftover soup in the kitchen. You can heat it up. And salad, a main course salad." She sounded businesslike, like a family doctor who had come on a house call and was now moving on. Everything would work out. Wait and see how it goes before calling a specialist. Other patients were waiting.

"Are you going straight to Magda?" he asked. "Or are you going to see that man first?"

She picked up her suitcase and started down the stairs.

"Let me carry that." He took the suitcase from her. Wen went into the living room for a moment, kissed Jurek on the top of the head. The Polack thought he saw a momentary flash of emotion in Jurek's eyes. Fear. Or disgust. Or both at the same time. Then he walked his dear wife to her car, he carried her suitcase as though she were going on vacation for a few days with her girlfriends. Out for a lark.

When they reached the car, he stood there hesitantly, for a moment he thought she was going to change her mind.

"No, I'm not going to that man," she said. "What kind of person do you take me for? I'm not some slut running from one man to the next. That's not the way I am. I'm going to Magda's. I'll sleep on the couch there."

He put her suitcase in the trunk. "You know," he said, "you don't have to leave on my account. Whether you're in love with someone else or not. I . . . you can stay here if you like. Even if you're in love with someone else. I won't let your infatuation bother me. I'll step aside, I'd be pleased to step aside if that would make you happy." He scratched the stubble on his cheek. And at that moment he realized why his life wasn't collapsing right now. It was because it had already collapsed. Things don't collapse twice. She was familiar with the ruins from back to front, was not insensitive to their beauty, but now she was ready to leave the ruins behind.

Except she couldn't really leave the Polack behind, even if she cut off all contact with him, even then she would not really have left. The past was draped around their necks like a noose, it was in their blood, in their DNA. In their voices and in their skin, in their tongues. That's why he was able to stay so collected, so calm, that's why he didn't scream. She would always be there, the way the dead one always was.

"I know that." She took his face in her hands. "That's what you've been doing all your life, stepping aside, and that's killing me. I'm sorry," she whispered, and she kissed him. Then she climbed into the car.

"Bye-bye, darling," he shouted, for no other words would come to him.

The Polack went into the kitchen. There was indeed a pot of soup in the fridge. He didn't touch the main-course salad. Maybe he needed to talk to his son about doing his homework. His wife had said recently: "Adolescents can do lots of things, but they can't organize their own lives. They really can't. They need help with that."

There were a few tomatoes on the counter. He cut one in half, sprinkled salt and pepper on the halves, and ate them concentratedly, with a slice of onion. The Polack picked up a little mirror that lay beside the tomatoes, it was from Wen's makeup kit, she must have left it there by accident, that morning before leaving for school. He looked at himself in the mirror and what he saw pleased him little. How could you no longer know who you were?

Going to the living room, he sat down gingerly beside Jurek. Not too close, he respected people's personal spaces. They sat beside each other for a while in silence. The boy was watching a series on TV and the Polack watched with him. When it was over, Jurek said: "You tortured her into leaving."

"Me? No," the Polack said, "what makes you think that?" He had counted on reproaches, but not right away, not so quickly.

"Well, it worked," the pre-adolescent said.

Reproaches were everywhere. You had to learn to deal with them; first listen carefully, then counter the reproach, reassure the bystander, calm them down—if not the bystander, then certainly your own son. "I didn't pester her into leaving," the Polack said. "She didn't know who she was anymore. That's something different. What do you want for dinner? There's still some soup left over from yesterday."

Jurek stood up. The look in his eye was inscrutable, you might almost call it cold. The Polack knew it wasn't coldness, it was something else, maybe you could call it self-protective. "I don't think she's coming back," he said, more to himself than to the boy. "Before long you'll spend half the month with her, the other half with me. It won't be bad. We're not mad at each other. We love each other, but she doesn't know who she is anymore."

The boy just stood there, looking at his father. "You smell like onions." He didn't walk out of the room, he stood there looking at his father. His Jurek, who had once wanted to be a fireman. His expression was a challenge. An accusation. When Jurek was little the Polack had told him about the hoses, the truck, the drills, the compressed air, the fire that had to be put out. Now the boy no longer wanted to be a fireman, he viewed the fire department only as an organization that wanted to extinguish things that shouldn't be extinguished. The disdain the boy had been showing for the last few weeks may have been a part of puberty, but in any case, it was less than pleasant. To be disdained in one's own living room is not a comfortable sensation.

"Have you got a lot of homework for tomorrow?" the Polack asked.

"Did it already."

"Which subjects?"

"Can't remember."

"You already did it, but you can't remember what it was about?"

"Yup."

"How can that be?"

"I only remember things that I need to remember."

"But homework is all about remembering things, isn't it? About learning things by heart?"

"That's how it used to be. You're behind the times. I guess because you're from Poland."

"What do you say we have some dinner?"

Jurek came and stood in front of him. From the looks of things, he was going to be taller than his father. "Why did you pester her into going away?" The son had adopted the role of inquisitor. He wanted to know the truth, and he was going to extract it from his father.

"I didn't. I . . ." He wanted to say that he had tried to be a good husband, but maybe that wasn't true. He had been more afraid of losing Jurek than of losing his wife, his wife was a sure thing, he didn't have to worry about her as much. Never had he thought that Wen was a woman who no longer knew who she was, who would say to him: "I've lost track of myself."

"I'll heat up the soup." He stood up, looked at the one remaining boy, who was still standing in the middle of the room, took a good look at him. There was no response. He stuck his hand out, to pat Jurek on the shoulder. The boy stepped back. "Keep your hands off me, cuntface."

"Don't talk to me like that." The Polack felt like smacking his son, but he didn't. Raising a child frightened him. As a fireman he knew how to keep from making mistakes, but not as a child-rearer. Modern parents accepted a great deal, and they had been modern parents, he and his wife. The child had emotions, the child needed to air those emotions. "Establishing boundaries and providing prospects, that's what childrearing is all about," was what his dear wife always said. What kind of prospect should he provide? And establishing boundaries was something he had come to detest. Whenever he thought about establishing boundaries, he saw Borys clutching at lampposts and trees because he didn't want to go to school.

He went to the kitchen, In the hope that the boy would follow. Jurek didn't follow. The Polack heated up the soup and, while the soup was heating, he went back to the living room to see what his son was doing. He was still standing ramrod straight in the middle of the room.

"We're going to have to do this together," the Polack said, and he put out his hand again. This time the boy didn't react. He moved closer, the Polack did. He held out both arms to the one remaining boy, and the boy let him, he let his father embrace him.

"We have to do this together now," the Polack repeated. "You and me. We have to do it together."

"Yeah," Jurek answered guardedly. "We have to do it together." It sounded affectionate and at the same time defiant, as though Jurek already knew that he was stronger than his father.

2

Beckers's wife finally up and died. She was now dead not only to the Polack, but to everyone, including her own husband, and to the Frenchman who never came to get her. And although the Polack had expected it to come as a relief, her being dead to everyone, her actual death came as a disappointment. There was no relief at all. He remembered quite clearly a time when his life, for however briefly, had revolved around Beckers's wife and the promise of comfort she had given. Ten years lay between the one death and the other, but it seemed like nothing. It was more like, with the real death of Beckers's wife, the love, to the extent that love was something other than a duty he was pleased to fulfill, had disappeared from his life forever.

The Polack went to the funeral, because all the men of C squad went and he wasn't sure how to act, because he was unsure of his position. In what capacity was he there? As fireman, or as a friend of the deceased? In the end, it seemed best to him to be there as a member of C squad, as one of the men. And during the speeches he did his best not to think about the Frenchman, even though he couldn't resist looking around to see whether perhaps he had snuck in anyway.

His Wen did not come back either. The love affair was lasting, apparently, although she said little about it on the rare occasions that she called, and he didn't feel like asking about it. Above all, he didn't want to give her the impression that he was jealous or hurt. If the love of God—which he had put behind him, to be sure—had taught him anything, it was this: the deeper the wound, the greater the love.

"That's not what you want either, is it?" Wen said on the phone. "That we give it another try, even though we know how that will turn out?"

He was too proud to insist, too frightened, that too. And so he said: "No, that's not what I want either." The separation was as definitive as the death had been.

Wen was extremely friendly toward him, almost sweet, but if any doubt had existed in her mind, it had left her now. All doubt had left her, and that made her happier. The Polack listened to what she said without feeling any panic, at most with the vague feeling that life could be a disappointing affair. They'd had a few disappointing years, the two of them, though there had also been happy months and years.

The next time she called, Wen asked whether they could arrange the divorce without a lawyer, just a mediator, a friendly divorce. After all: they loved each other, didn't they?

A friendly divorce, that appealed to the Polack. He didn't want a divorce, it didn't seem necessary to him, but he didn't want to resist either, because he knew it was useless. And yes, he loved her. There was pain, although he was so accustomed to pain that he barely noticed it. The pain—a 5.5 on a scale of 1 to 10—was his friend.

One week later he met his Wen—who was in fact no longer his Wen—at the café where he had once sat with Beckers's wife. He had suggested that they not merely call this time, but actually see each other, that would make things easier. Once they were seated there in that café, he asked again, because they loved each other, whether Wen now knew who she was. He could ask her things like that. She said nothing, and he pressed on. He wanted an answer, because that was why she'd left, because she no longer knew who she was. Now she needed to tell him who she was. He took her hand, he noticed that it made her uncomfortable, so he pulled his hand away again.

"It's going to take me a while," she said. "I still don't know exactly. And you, how are you doing?"

"Passable." The Polack stirred his coffee. "Passable. I miss you and it's not easy with the boy, that's going to take time."

Jurek, the one remaining boy, stayed with his father in a house that was too big for them, and he kept his talking to a minimum. Growing up was not easy, not for the one who had to do the growing and not for the people around him either. A divorce on top of that didn't help. The one remaining boy didn't want to be disturbed during the activity people referred to so deftly as "growing up." He was doing it on his own, he wanted to go on doing it on his own.

"The house feels empty . . . You finally did it, you went and left." It sounded like an accusation, and the Polack didn't want it to sound that way. A new situation had arisen, they had to get used to that. She'd always said: talk about your feelings. And he had never understood why you had to talk about feelings. You had them; wasn't that enough? And now that he had talked about them, to please her, he noticed right away the kinds of misunderstandings such talk could generate.

"I didn't finally go and leave. It has nothing to do with what happened, a long time ago. We're over that, aren't we?"

"Yeah, we're over that." The Polack wanted to say more, to take her hand again, not to declare his love for her but to show his fondness. Show his involvement, that he could be a good ex.

"I have to get going pretty quickly," she said. "I'm going to the theater. We need to take Jurek into consideration too. Does he miss me?"

"He doesn't say much," the Polack said.

"Whenever I call him, I have to drag every word out of him."

"Yeah, what do you expect. You left. He feels rejected."

"He doesn't have to miss me. That's not what I'm asking for. I left the two of you. He's allowed to be angry." Still, his wife sounded disappointed. To not be missed is a horrible thing for those who wish to believe they are loved.

Just as the Janowskis had at first tried to live as though they'd never had a son who'd ended up under a train, father and son now tried to live as though there had never been a mother, as though they had always been predestined to be stuck with each other.

"What's playing at the theater?" the Polack asked.

"Comedy. That comedian with the raw sense of humor. I'm ready for a little raw humor, let me tell you."

The Polack called for the check.

"Soon," she said, "it will all be arranged, then he'll spend two weeks with me, two weeks with you. That will make him a bit more talkative. When they get older, they start talking more. And I'm sure you'll get over it too."

"My son, Borys, was taken away from me. And you were taken from me too," the Polack said. "But I focus on what I have. Jurek. A house, a job. Feet, hands, legs, arms, eyes, I've got lots of things. That's how I see it. I'm a fortunate person."

Wen paid the bill. He tried to do it, but she was too fast for him.

"You need to get started on a new life now too," Wen said once they were outside, and he felt humiliated because she had picked up the check. Even that pleasure she wouldn't grant him, even that little gesture was one she refused to accept. "It's important that you do that."

He felt a brief urge to say that she shouldn't meddle in his life. He didn't say that, he only mumbled: "I'll see."

While walking home at a clipped pace, the Polack decided that she was right. He needed to start working on a new life. The old one was over, the new one must begin, the only other alternative was to die, and he was too young for that.

That evening at the dinner table, after he had gone to the Thai restaurant for takeout —chicken soup for the boy and a vegetarian curry for himself—he said to Jurek: "Mama's not going to come back. I know for sure now."

"Oh."

"I mean, you'll see her often enough, but not in this house."

"I already knew that."

"What do you think about it?"

"Fine by me," the one remaining boy said. "You tortured pestered her into leaving. Like I said."

"Fine by you?" The Polack raised his voice. "Your mother leaves and that's fine by you. You don't care about anything. That makes me furious."

"If you have to go furious, well then, go right ahead," Jurek said.

The Polack took a few deep breaths. Then he said: "I think I'm going to find myself a wife."

"You're going to what?" The boy was enjoying his Thai chicken soup. He liked meat, preferably nothing but. He didn't say much about the food either, growing up had made him sullen and moody, but there were certain dishes he relished with a pleasure audible and visible, and that was a kind of love too, enjoying your food.

"I'm going to find myself a wife," the Polack repeated, slowly and emphatically. Jurek had a right to frankness, to honesty.

"Good luck, man."

"Mama is okay with that, she thinks it's a good idea."

"She's okay with that?" Jurek looked at him as though he couldn't imagine such a thing. As though he absolutely couldn't imagine her saying something like that.

"She's not only okay with it," the Polack repeated, "it was her idea." She'd hadn't quite put it that way, not literally, but what else could she mean by a new life except a new wife? New children were ruled out, a new wife was the obvious move, now that the old one had gone away.

"Maybe you should ask her to go find one for you?" The boy laughed once, then went back to focusing on his Thai chicken soup.

"And what do you think of the idea?"

"Couldn't care less."

"Are you sure about that?"

The one remaining boy nodded. "Fine by me."

The fury had left the Polack now. He had come to terms with Jurek and his adolescent equanimity. Although there were times when he couldn't help feeling that Jurek's equanimity was a form of not-living, that his youngest boy too had no desire to live. Then there was the curry. The two of them shared a portion and, just to be sure, he repeated what his ex had said to him in the café. That arrangements would be made for Jurek, and that the Polack would go looking for a new love. He felt it was important to use that word, love. "She wouldn't move in here right away," he said, spooning up the remains of the curry. "But I'm going to go looking."

"You're going to go looking? Looking? Don't let me stop you, but I don't think you have much of a chance, man. Maybe you could turn homo." At that the one remaining boy put on his headphones, but the Polack didn't allow that. Not during meals. During meals there was no listening to music on headphones, even if the meal did come from a plastic container. The boy obeyed; the Polack still had a little authority. When the curry was finished too, he put the silverware and plates in the dishwasher, then started wondering about where he could best go looking for a wife. He hadn't really gone looking for the first one, he had stumbled upon her. She had presented herself, he had opened up to her. He could barely remember exactly how it went. precisely how it had gone. What he had done and said, how he had won her for himself.

Now he was old, well, old—he was still in good shape, well-groomed, bald but well-groomed, a man halfway through life, still very serviceable, in all sorts of ways. Yes, he was a very serviceable Polack, and during his search he would make no bones about that. Jurek was wrong, he would succeed on his mission. He had to go looking actively. It didn't happen by itself anymore, to the extent that it ever had. The Polack could talk to colleagues about how they had done it, after their divorce, but it embarrassed him to do so. There were two divorced men in C squad, both of them now had a girlfriend, and there were other divorced men on the other squads. He hadn't yet told them at the firehouse that his wife had left him. He kept putting it off. He would leave out the part about her no longer knowing who she was. The men of C squad had no desire for information like that. After all, they knew who they were and couldn't imagine that there were people who didn't.

3

Nine weeks and four days lay between Wen's leaving and the moment that the Polack registered with a dating site. He had kept postponing it, in doubt, had reconciled himself to loneliness (the third week), did a lot of reading in the Bible (the fourth week), and he had gone to a massage parlor and had himself massaged by a Chinese lady (the fifth week), but when she was about to start in on the happy ending, he had panicked. "So big, so incredibly big," the Chinese lady had murmured, and the Polack replied: "I'm just a tall man, this is completely normal for my length. Even a little on the small side." After that, all lust left him, he paid and drove home.

During the sixth week he tried to do lots of things with Jurek, in the seventh he had gone alone to a bar for a drink, where he got into an argument with a tipsy Frenchman, which surprised him because he wasn't the type to go looking for trouble in a bar and he spoke no French. During the eighth week he wrote a long and sensitive letter to Wen, which he then burned, and in the ninth he joined a dating site at last.

He described himself in his profile as "tall, reliable, and funny. Open to kids." The Polack didn't consider himself funny at all, but humor and reliability just went along with the search for love. He was reliable, so it was only a partial falsehood. As hobbies, he wrote: reading, movies, outdoors. That wasn't completely true either. He never read, or at least nothing but the newspaper, rarely went to a movie, twice a year at the very most, but he did enjoy the outdoors. Even more than before. Ever since he'd lived in the chicken coop, he had a special bond with nature, the trees, the plants, the moss, not that he knew the names of everything. You didn't have to know the names of the trees in order to be fond of them. He liked to walk in the hills, at every season, and he looked in amazement at the things that lived and didn't belong to the world of people. Amazement was, to him, a sign of beauty. The ugliest town in the country was surrounded by the most beautiful nature, and that made up for a lot. In the past he had occasionally taken Jurek along, but the boy didn't want to walk now. Jurek couldn't care less about the hills.

On purpose, the Polack had left his profession out of his profile; he didn't feel much like talking about his job. Fireman happened to be one of those professions about which everyone entertained ideas, opinions, and fantasies. And, for the rest, he would adapt to accommodate the demands and desires of the new partner, insofar as there was any real difference between demands and desires within a relationship. Within a short period, he had established email contact with about six women. His "open to kids" in particular seemed to catch on. He drew little enjoyment from answering the emails. One time he fell asleep while typing, The search had only just begun, and it was already making him tired and nervous. He went out for a beer with a widow his age, in the lobby of a hotel at the edge of Heerlen. She had two adolescent children. Her husband had died while playing a sport. The Polack felt it would be untoward to ask which sport. If she had wanted to talk about it, she would have mentioned the sport herself. Still, the question nagged at him. She had started in on another subject long before, but he kept thinking about her husband. Caught in an avalanche while skiing? A heart attack during a marathon? When he asked if she wanted another drink, she said: "No, I have to get to my kids, and I'm going to say this right away because when you do this it's better to be honest right off the bat: I'd expected someone with a little more verve."

The Polack didn't think she had much in the way of verve either, but was a widow supposed to have verve? He hadn't exactly been prepared for someone with verve. In fact, he wasn't sure *what* he was prepared for. Verve was something he didn't see in a lot of young people either. Looking at his youngest son, he didn't see much in the way of verve there, and on the rare occasions when he saw some of his son's friends and even girlfriends, it had been their disillusioned attitude to life that had struck him.

"What do you mean by verve?" the Polack asked.

"My husband had verve," she said enthusiastically.

But her husband was dead. He regretted not living up to her expectations, because even if he felt nothing for her, not even an aversion— that would at least have been *something*—at most a sort of dull pity, he still wanted to live up to her expectations. "I've never really been any different from the way I am now," the Polack said. "This is who I am. I'm a serviceable man."

She looked at him with a smile, almost invitingly, as though she thought he were joking, then her expression clouded over. "Well, shall we leave it at this, then?" The Polack agreed, even though he couldn't shake off a sense of failure as he drove home. His next rendezvous was with a woman twelve years his senior. Not a widow, but she had been divorced, twice in fact. She had a child who had already moved out of the house but returned after what she called a "quest," and now she wanted someone, as she'd written in her ad, with whom "to share the adventure that is life."

"I have a son who isn't nearly old enough to move out, and I've got a regular job," the Polack said. "What kind of adventure were you thinking of?" He feared that he would have to go off traveling with her all the time, and it turned out he was right. She also loved music, she told him. Concerts. Chamber music. She mentioned a few composers whose names the Polack had heard before, but that was about as much as you could say. Strangely enough, despite his evasive gestures and curt replies, she took a shine to him. "Height is important to me," she said, "I don't want a partner who's shorter than I am. I'm not particularly short myself, so that doesn't leave one with much choice."

The Polack had heard enough, although his height apparently worked to his advantage. Because he wasn't the type to say that they should leave it at this, he cast about for a diplomatic escape route. Not finding one, all that remained were little white lies.

Weeks went by this way. Beckers's wife became increasingly dead. Beckers himself was not becoming any livelier. During one of their drills, he told his colleagues that the last thing on his mind these days was finding a new wife. The Polack tried to raise his boy and care for him well, as though he had always known that his loving wife would disappear because she no longer knew who she was.

A third woman, who had responded via the dating site, cancelled their rendezvous a few times, and then the Polack had had enough. He wanted to start in on a new life, but not this way. He would steer a different course, come up with better strategies. Maybe just sit in some bar anyway, but then without getting into arguments with drunken foreigners.

The women he had met didn't seem interested in taking the plunge into a new life, not the way he did, all they wanted was to continue their old ones, albeit with a new husband.

Jurek's ridicule ("Have you found a wife yet, or are you giving up?") had made way for household announcements. "Could you take the garbage bag outside, the kitchen stinks?" for example. To which the Polack would reply: "Do it yourself." The fear of moving into the realm of childrearing did not mean he couldn't establish boundaries. He asked his son about his grades too, his exams, about school, that was the only parenting the Polack dared to do after the debacle of the past, and even so he did it with reluctance. He always had the feeling that he was expecting either too much or too little, that's why he commented as little as possible on the boy's grades.

After a time, Jurek began adopting a more civil tone on occasion, things like: "I'm eating over at a friend's. Okay with you?" To which he added: "You'll eat when I'm not here, won't you? Or are you going on a fast?" As though the boy knew that the Polack didn't cook for himself when he was home alone. The Polack was touched by that, by the solicitude, the attentiveness. It made him emotional.

On very rare occasions, Jurek allowed the Polack to get closer, allowed his father to pat his head, grab his shoulder, to tussle with him in the front yard. There was physical contact, and in that there was more love than in the conversations, which never ceased being difficult. It was those moments to which the Polack clung, from them that he drew courage.

The mediator who would arrange the divorce quickly and efficiently, as she announced on the phone, was a lady with gray hair and a French surname. The Polack suspected that she hated people, particularly her customers, and everyone with a surname that was not French, but despite the amiable disdain she radiated, she did her work as promised. She smiled a lot, which goes well with disdain. Wen and the Polack reached an agreement, the mediator noted that she had not often had clients who reached an accord so quickly. The Polack took that as a compliment, while his ex and he sat in the mediator's little office and tried to remain polite, as though life consisted of nothing but politeness.

Still, it also felt as though they were being punished for improper behavior, people who got along so well should certainly stay together. He told the mediator: "Despite everything, we love each other." His dear ex didn't respond.

Once the divorce was final—tears were shed, that went along with that kind of thing—and they were standing outside the mediator's office, Wen said: "I want you to know that I've moved in with the man I'm in love with."

The Polack looked up in the air. He remembered the dead boy, the lampposts Borys had hugged because he didn't want to go to school. "That's fast," he said.

"Yeah, I couldn't go on sleeping on Magda's couch forever. She needs some space of her own too."

"Hospitality has its limits." The Polack picked at a loose piece of skin on his cuticle.

"And you, have you already met someone?"

"Me? No, not yet."

"But you have tried, haven't you? I take it? You've done your best, right? You know that I'm not coming back?" Apparently, she was afraid that he was still hoping for her return, but that wasn't the case.

"Do my best, do my best, Christ, it's not some final exam. I'm looking around. I talk to people here and there." He said nothing about the
dating site. Things like that were no longer anything to be ashamed of,
but still.

"The longer you wait, the harder it gets. Would you like me to
introduce you to someone?"

They were walking down the street together, on their way to their
respective cars. Between the two cars, they stopped. Clumsily, as
though this were a first date.

"Are you serious?" he asked, almost angrily.

"I run into people sometime. You're the father of my child. Children. I want things to go well for you." It sounded apologetic.

"I don't need your help," he said roughly. "And I don't need your
consolation." He rummaged for his car keys. Wen stood there, looking
at him. "So is it a nice place you've got now?" he asked.

"An apartment. Nice view. Do you want to meet him?"

"That man? He does things with astrology, right?"

"Not all the time, Geniek. He's not an astrologer. It's his hobby. It
might be good for Jurek if you were to meet him." She took the Polack
by the arm, tenderly. "I'd really like you to meet him before Jurek
does. I think you two might even become friends. I think you know
him. And you're still a very attractive man, there are quite a few of my
girlfriends who say: that Polack of yours is no slouch either."

He dreaded it, but still the Polack said: "Fine, I'll come and meet
the astrologer." He wanted, after all, to be a good ex, and encounters
like that were all a part of it. In an emergency, they could always talk
about constellations. He couldn't imagine Wen's girlfriends saying that
he looked good. Wen meant well, she was just trying to cheer him up
with little white lies.

"You don't have to stay for long," she said. "Just so you know who it
is. Jurek's bound to come home with stories when he's been at our place."

"Jurek's not much of a talker, you know that as well as I do."

"Shall we meet up, the three of us, in a couple of days? At a café? A
café is neutral ground, isn't it?"

The Polack wasn't sure whether they needed neutral ground, but he
had nothing against it. Still, he was overwhelmed briefly by the feeling

that he would have liked to stay with Wen, imperfect as they were. The imperfect marriage, all things considered, had been fine with him. For a moment he was afraid that he would have a relapse, that he would start longing for the chicken coop again. He needed to concentrate on practical matters, the housekeeping, the parenting, a new love.

A few days later the Polack found himself sitting in the oh-so-familiar café, he had arrived early just to be on the safe side. After he'd had two cups of coffee, he ordered a beer. The newspaper that always lay on the bar was nowhere in sight now. Wen was running late, so the Polack had to wait for half an hour. He was more nervous than he had been during his dating site encounters, even if nothing had come of them, no love, no sex.

Meanwhile, thoughts of Beckers's wife came bubbling to the surface, how he had sat with her here, at the same table. How she had looked at him and promised him consolation. Little had changed at this café. The same guy was still working here.

When Wen finally arrived, it took him a full minute to understand that the man behind her was her new boyfriend. The Human Extension. Only when Wen said, "So, this is him," and pushed the man forward did the Polack realize that it was the extension that had made her heart beat faster.

He shook the man's hand and tried to remember what the fellow's real name was, you could hardly address him as "Extension." He had grown thin. He wasn't the same self-confident caregiver he had been a decade earlier. He had something defeated about him. Something broken.

The man slapped the Polack jovially on the shoulder, and then the Polack gave the extension a clumsy hug. He pressed his wife's boyfriend to his breast, he almost squeezed him to death in order to show his good intentions.

They sat down. Wen started talking and didn't stop, she rattled on, she said so much that the Polack could barely remember all the things she mentioned: the kindergarten, health care, her parents, the times in which they found themselves, about being a woman, he couldn't keep up with it. From her chatter he concluded that she too was very nervous. Until he interrupted her with the question: "And what would you two like to drink?"

"Coffee," she said, and the extension wanted the same. The Polack had already moved on to beer, so he stuck to that.

"I never would have figured," he said once their orders had been brought. "The Human Extension."

"Ruud," the man replied, "just call me Ruud! I always knew we would run into each other again, although not this way. Not like this." Now that he had spoken up, the human extension seemed less disheartened than he had earlier.

"How did you two meet?" That was what the Polack asked.

"Through my business," Ruud said. "I was busy with an expansion. I started with the elderly, as you know, and that was a success. There are so many old people, and there are more and more of them all the time. Who wants to die if you can receive care from a human extension? It was a success. There were human extensions making their rounds from Venlo to Maastricht, and just over the border, in Monchengladbach, Aachen too. In the course of time, I discovered that it was not only the elderly who were in need of an extension. Care is in such high demand." With these words, he stared probingly at the Polack, he let a silence fall, but the Polack said nothing.

"Once people have had the right kind of care," the extension went on, "they don't want to do without." The extension was doing the talking, so he himself could remain silent. All he had to do was listen. The Polack found that quite pleasant.

"The connection, that's what it's all about, where do you find that these days?"

"The connection?" The Polack took a big slug of his beer.

"The connection between people," the extension explained. "About a year ago, I realized that I needed to offer not only care, but also connection. Everyone who needs care also needs to be connected, there are people who don't need to be cared for, yet still they long for connection. And it was for them that I set up the second branch of my company. The branch that offered connection to people who could still dress themselves but who were missing something fundamental." The former hired-people-hand looked at Wen, and the Polack concluded that his wife had apparently been missing something fundamental.

"Aha," said the Polack, as his ex began rummaging for something in her purse.

"We grew too quickly," the extension went on. "I hired people who didn't have what it takes."

"So, but then, how did you meet my wife?" the Polack asked.

"Okay, okay." Ruud sounded annoyed. "I'll get to that in a minute. I'm just giving you the chronology, it's the same thing I always say during our intakes: stick to the chronology. You're not in any hurry, are you?"

"No," the Polack said.

The human extension sipped at his coffee. "I went back to work as an extension myself, to find out what the situation was like. To see where things had gone wrong. There were people who'd been hired who had absolutely no idea of what's involved in custom-made care and connection. They thought: working as an extension is sort of like working in a restaurant or a bar. You slap food down on the table and, if you do it with a smile, they give you a tip to boot. No, that's not the way it works." The man was becoming wound up at the thought of those unenlightened employees. He stared irritatedly into space for a moment, then resumed his story. "I'm a connector par excellence, I'm telling you straight, I started with care, but making connections is what I do best."

"Yeah. That's great." The Polack's glass was empty now. "And that's how you met my wife?" He wanted to know how the human extension had stumbled upon Wen, *how*. Not because he was jealous. He was hurt, that was normal, not exceptionally jealous. And being hurt was just a part of life.

"More or less," the man said. "She was looking for a job as a connector."

"You were looking for work?" The Polack looked at the woman who he still considered his dear wife, even though she was no longer with him and was now living together with the former hired people-hand.

"Yes," Wen said.

"But you already had a job?"

"I was looking for other work, I was trying to get oriented."

The Polack nodded.

"She came in for a preliminary interview," the connector said, "and I remembered her. I asked her: how's your husband? And then she said, yeah, then she told me how things were. She told me exactly how things were."

The empty glass of beer was resting on a coaster, and the Polack began toying with the coaster. She had told him exactly how things were. He would have liked to hear that story. Then he asked: "What does a connector do, exactly?"

"Good question," said the former hired people-hand. "That's a complicated story." The Polack immediately regretted asking.

"A connector . . ." another silence descended, "a connector connects. He connects him or herself with the other. I connect to everyone, I can't help it, it's a gift I have. Right now, for example, I'm connecting with you. Can you feel that?"

The Polack looked at him.

"Give it some time," the former hired people-hand said. "You've got to be open to it. Some people can't open themselves to it, and that's where the professional connector comes in. He's got patience. He goes looking for an opening. In every human suit of armor, there's an opening, in yours too."

The Polack didn't like the sound of that. He didn't feel like he was wearing a suit of armor, and if he was then it wasn't up to his wife's new boyfriend to go looking for an opening in it. He looked around. A woman had come into the café, she was wearing a hat, and she pulled a book of puzzles out of her handbag. He had to go to the supermarket in a bit, for tomorrow's breakfast, the yogurt and granola were finished. If he had learned anything, it was this: parenting is not connecting, parenting is setting the breakfast table in utter calm.

"So that's how you two met," said the Polack, in the hope of gradually bringing the conversation to a close. For a moment he felt the urge to say: Wen, couldn't he just have become your lover, did we really have to get a divorce right away? You could just have tried it with two men for a while.

The former hired people-hand nodded. "We wrote to each other. Letters. Real, old-fashioned letters. Because your wife, I call her your wife because in a certain way she is your wife and always will be your wife, you two have a dead child and a living child, nothing connects two people like a dead child. I respect that, but because your wife wanted to become a connector, I told her: be sure of what you're doing. Right now you're tired of the kindergarten, soon you'll start longing for the toddlers again and then it will be too late. This is no easy profession."

The Polack stared at his wife, his ex, and said: "I never knew you were fed up with it, with the kindergarten."

She shrugged. "I wasn't really fed up with it. But if I wanted to try something different, I knew I shouldn't wait too long."

"That's true," the Polack said. "If you want to try something different, you shouldn't wait too long." A silence fell, then the Polack asked his wife's new boyfriend: "You practice astrology, right?"

"Not to any major extent," the man said, "it's a hobby. When you come to our place for dinner sometime, I'll give you some information about yourself. Maybe it will be useful to you. Libra, right?"

Then they said nothing more, the former hired people-hand, the Polack and also the woman who sat between them, until at last the former hired people-hand commented: "When your son is at our place, I'll stay in the background, I need you to know that. I can't take your place. I don't want to take your place. You have to let the children come to you. You don't win their confidence by imposing on them. I'll let your son come, I'll wait calmly until he comes to me. And if he doesn't come, that's okay too."

"Yes," said the Polack, "great." Then they stood up, and the two men hugged. Then the Polack turned to his ex and hugged her, he pressed her to him. "I have to go by the supermarket," he said. "You know what I found a few days ago? The scarf you knitted for me. When you suddenly took up knitting."

"My things," she said, "my things are still at your place. Should I come by and get them? Is there any hurry? Could I leave them there for a while?"

"Your things. No, there's no hurry. The scarf turned out nice. I wear it when it's cold."

"I'm still living out of my suitcase, my things aren't in your way, are they? As soon as Ruud and I move to a bigger place, I'll come and get them."

They left the café and once they were outside the former hired-people-hand said the Polack was always welcome, but that he understood that things like this took time. The Polack should say when the time came, the time of friendship, the time of nearness and connection.

"I'll be sure to do that," the Polack called out as he turned and walked toward the supermarket. A basket would have been enough, but he took a cart and pushed it first through the produce section, even though he had all the vegetables he needed, then to the dairy section. He put two packs of yogurt in the cart and took a box of muesli off the shelf. The new life had begun. His dear ex had already started on hers. He couldn't say for sure whether she was happy or not, but maybe that wasn't the point.

He wondered how his new life would turn out. The way his father's had? Move to another town and dispense with the past? No, that wasn't how he did things.

In front of the bulletin board where people could hang up free ads, he stopped. His eye was caught by one ad in particular: "Looking for true love? Are you the romantic type? Dissatisfied with your life? Look no further." He stepped closer, the better to examine the ad. "In Russia, Ukraine, China, Peru, or Brazil, your partner is waiting impatiently for you," he read. "We'll put you in contact with true and lasting love."

He took a picture of the ad, and when he noticed someone looking at him, he left the supermarket embarrassedly.

4

One afternoon, when Jurek came back again from staying with his mother and the human extension and, when asked how it had been, answered with nothing more than a simple "okay"—just like all the times before—the Polack decided it was time to act. He couldn't go on waiting for a sign. There had been enough waiting already. Before long, Jurek would move out on his own, he would go to college or find a job, and then the Polack would be alone. He didn't even mind the prospect of that, but he was afraid of what people would say. He didn't want to end up as a lonely old man. Needy and abandoned by God and the world. The kind of man of whom you couldn't say with certainty whether he had disowned the human race or vice versa. The kind he, as a fireman, knew all too well. They often weren't even all that old, but apparently isolated, because they had lay there rotting away for quite a while, for so long that the neighbors started complaining about the stench. One time they had gone to the home of a man who had kept all kinds of birds, all of which had died in their cages. Of hunger and thirst. The dead man didn't stink all that badly, but the birds stank horribly. It was their stench that had become unbearable. No, the Polack didn't want to become that kind of person, a man surrounded by birds instead of people, and so he decided to call the agency whose ad he had seen at the supermarket.

He went upstairs, to the bedroom where his wife's things still had not been taken away. She kept putting it off. He had grown accustomed to her things, which had become all the more present in her absence. A good alternative for the person themselves: their things, their beloved things.

The agency was called Love Without Borders. He called, sitting on the bed, a bit nervous to be sure. He had never called a company like that before.

A man's voice answered: "Hello."

"Is this Love Without Borders?" the Polack asked, just to be sure. He had expected something more businesslike, now he had the feeling he had simply called someone at home, that he had called a private line.

"It sure is," the man said, and his voice sounded different right away. "This is Paul from Love Without Borders. What can I do for you?"

The Polack stared at his right hand. You could tell people's ages by looking at their hands, but his hand looked okay. He could hang up right now, then maybe a new life would never begin. "I saw your ad at the supermarket."

"Yes," Paul said. "How can I help you? What are you looking for?"

"What do you mean?"

"Something Chinese?"

"Excuse me?"

"Are you looking for a Chinese partner?"

"No, why?"

"In two weeks we'll be starting our big China trip. The pass rate in China is very high, almost every man finds something to his liking there."

The Polack looked at his fingernails.

"Hello? Are you still there?" Paul asked.

"I don't speak Chinese."

"That makes no difference whatsoever. We have excellent interpreters, and once your Chinese lady is in the Netherlands, she'll be speaking Dutch before you know it. Besides which, the language of love is international, you don't need to speak any Chinese for that.

Is this your first partner, or have you already been together with
. . . With someone?" Paul sounded more hesitant now, no longer so
assertive.

"I'm married. Was married."

"Ah, I see. Yeah. And now you're divorced?"

"Yes." The Polack shifted his weight on the bed. He looked at her
things. Even her alarm clock was still there. These days she must be
using the human extension's alarm clock. The man who knew that the
world would end up in care and connection.

"What type was your ex? Would it be useful to look for something similar, or would you like something different, something totally
different?"

"What type?"

"Blonde? Brunette?"

"Blonde."

"Blonde. So shall we go looking in that direction?" Paul asked.

"That's fine," said the Polack.

"Ukraine. You'll definitely find what you're looking for there. By
the way, what's your name?" The Polack gave the man his name.

"Ukraine," said Paul from Love Without Borders, without com-
menting on the Polack's name. "That's right up your alley. Five weeks
from now we're organizing another trip to Kiev. A high pass rate there
too. Even the most cynical of men have to admit that Ukraine gets
under your skin. What's your profession?"

"Does that matter?" The Polack really wanted to remain anony-
mous. Not everyone had to know. That he was looking for love across
the border. It made him feel embarrassed. It fell beyond the ken of
what they call normal, although there used to be a fireman in their
barracks who had a Thai wife at home, but he'd been a weird kind
of fireman. He hadn't fit very well in the group. Not a team player.
Within a couple of years he was gone. To Thailand, with his wife. He
was going to do some kind of import-export thing there. Never heard
from him again. Not even a postcard.

"You're going to have to bring your partner to the Netherlands," said
the man from Love Without Borders. "Or do you live in Belgium?"

"I live in the Netherlands."

"Right, we operate in Holland and Belgium, a bit in Germany too sometimes. It's important that you earn more than the minimum wage, otherwise it's going to be hard to get your partner into the country. Do you earn more than the minimum wage?"

"I'm a fireman," the Polack said anyway.

"Great," Paul said, "a civil servant. That should work. We don't give up. Just so you know. We never give up. The tougher a case the man is, the more we care about helping him. No one is unplaceable, every Jack must have his Jill. And I'll see to it personally that you, Jack, will find your Jill in no time. Could you repeat your name one more time?"

"Everybody calls me the Polack," he said.

"I'm afraid I need your real name."

"Geniek." He spelled it for him. And then he gave the man his email address. They would send him all the information. Paul asked if he could put his name down for the dates of the big Ukraine trip, and the Polack didn't know what to say; he wasn't entirely convinced that Ukraine was the right place. He was planning to start a new life, but now that things were getting serious, Ukraine sounded awfully far away, awfully new. Too new, perhaps.

The information arrived, the Polack filled out the forms and emailed everything back to them. Even though there were quite a few questions to which he had no good answer. He didn't know what he was looking for. Love, probably, but even that he wasn't sure of. Claims that were made on you, the melting together which, to be honest, he was dreading. Melting again. And then? How often could a person melt? Besides which, in his experience, everything he melted together with either died or took off running. For a moment he recalled his mother, there wasn't a lot he remembered about her. A void was what she was, a lack, she who wasn't there, people ended as voids in the other's memory. A plastic bag filled with peaches that she'd given him on a summer day, that he remembered. Those peaches, the way they tasted, he remembered that more clearly than he remembered his mother. And that was how his father had become a void as well, just like his eldest boy. The Polack was a man without a past, and he decided that it was precisely men like him who needed a future. Love he had come to know, long ago, with the Great Father, now he wanted to be less ambitious: having company was good enough. He did his best, he filled in all the things they wanted to know about him, his desires and wishes, he didn't skip a single question, because he needed a future. They even asked about his health and whether he wanted to have children, and when it was finished he read it all over again and emailed the form back to Love Without Borders.

Less than two days later he heard that his registration had been accepted and that he was on the list for the big Ukraine–Love Trip. Somewhere between fifteen to twenty-five men would be going, he was told, but Mr. Janowski had no reason to worry, a great deal of attention was granted to each individual participant and his specific wishes. The money was to be paid within ten days.

The Polack was still a little worried, although he wasn't sure exactly about what. The trip and Ukraine had been abstract until now, but now time was growing short and Ukraine and love were becoming grimly concrete, and expensive to boot. To start with, he had to tell Jurek about it.

"I'm going to Kiev," he said that evening. They were both in the bathroom. Jurek said nothing, so the Polack added: "Not for very long. A couple of days."

"Kiev?" the boy asked. "Why Kiev?"

The Polack was still fiddling with the towels. To be perfectly honest, he didn't know exactly why the choice had fallen on Kiev. "I looked around here, but it seemed better to me to try somewhere else. I can't seem to find a good woman here."

"Ridiculous," the boy said, holding his face under the tap. "There are plenty of women here. They don't want to have you, is that it? The chickies aren't interested. That's it, right?"

The Polack shook his head. "They're interested all right. I met a woman who wanted to have me, she wanted to go traveling with me. That wouldn't work. I have you, I have my job. I can't go off on long trips."

The one remaining boy began drying his face on a towel, then examined his nose in the mirror. It was clear to the Polack that the boy didn't much like the idea of Kiev, but then what did he know about Kiev? What was the Polack supposed to do? Sign up for the big China trip? The long flight alone was enough to kibosh that idea.

He looked at himself in the mirror too and imagined what the women of Kiev would see when they looked at him. "I want to start a new life and a woman goes along with that," he said more to himself than to the one remaining boy. "Kiev. Berlin. Maastricht. What difference does it make? Don't worry, she'll never come between us. I just want something different."

His son looked even more disapproving than he had a minute earlier. The Polack needed to explain himself better. "Kiev is a good city for love. Even the most cynical of men finds something there. And I'm not a cynical man. Ever since your mother left, something has been missing . . . I'm going to start a new life, just like your mother, who I still love very much but we couldn't . . ." He was echoing the words of the agency, echoing the words of his ex, he had no idea how to otherwise explain things to the one remaining boy. "You'll be at Mama's then anyway," he told the boy. "It won't be any bother to you. Having me in Kiev."

"Hmmm," said the boy, clipping a hair off his left eyebrow with a pair of nail scissors. "And then you're coming back?" he asked. "And you'll be standing here in the bathroom with some total stranger of a bimbo from Kiev? Okay, but then I'm moving in with friends. Or with Mama. Except I go nuts listening to all those stories from that Ruud guy."

"No," the Polack said, "there's no need to worry. That 'bimbo' won't be moving in here right away. You fall in love, then you start writing to each other and then one day she's standing here at the door with two or three suitcases, that's how I imagine it. But that day is still a long way off. And maybe nothing will happen in Kiev. And you are my number one priority."

The boy was finished examining his face in the mirror. "I don't know," he said, "I don't really see the need for it. I mean, it's fine like this. Without Mama, just you and me." The boy started to leave, but the Polack said: "I can't stay alone. It seems like a long time, I know, but one day you'll move out on your own . . ."

The boy shrugged. "It's no problem for you, being alone, you always were alone and you've got Mama. She'll come by for sure, even after I've moved out. And you know, I'm not going to start acting all of a sudden like I don't know you or something."

"No, I don't have Mama anymore. Mama has someone else. Mama didn't know who she was anymore, I think she knows now though, but you see her more often than I do."

"Yeah," the boy said, "she knows who she is again. Do you think you could get out now? I need to use the toilet."

The Polack wandered around the house for a long time. He had already taken time off for the Ukraine trip, and he'd finally told the men at the firehouse about his divorce. The men of C squad took it in stride. They didn't consider a divorce to be proof of failure, the word "failure" never crossed their lips. This new love was a pain in the neck, he had to admit. First of all because that city and that country didn't mean anything at all to him, but also because he dreaded the meeting. What are you supposed to say to the new love? Are you supposed to start talking about yourself right away?

The next day he called his ex. She asked how he was doing, and once they had run through the usual courtesies, she asked why he was calling, whether there wasn't actually something he needed to get off his chest. She sounded affectionate, even worried.

"I'm going to Kiev," he said. "At the end of the month."

"Oh."

"Get out of the rut for a couple of days. I took off from work. Jurek will be at your place, so it won't be any problem for him."

"What are you going to do there?"

The Polack toyed with a toothpick, then he said that he was going there to fall in love. It didn't feel to him like he was talking off the top of his head, that he was making it all up. He suddenly felt that he was going to fall in love in Kiev. Infatuation, that was part of a new life. First the infatuation, then the new life. If having company was all it was about, he could just as well have joined an eating club.

"Fall in love?" his ex asked. "Are you joking?" She not only sounded skeptical, she also sounded concerned.

"No. It's no joke. Sometimes you get this feeling, you know what I mean?"

She didn't reply, even though he was doing exactly what she'd expected of him, although she probably hadn't taken Kiev into account at the time. "I wanted to tell you, so you didn't have to hear it from the boy."

She sighed. Or did it only seem so? "It sounds strange to me. You haven't been taken in by some conwoman, have you? Besides, isn't there a war going on there right now?"

A war, he hadn't thought about that. Was there a war going on there?

"I think that one's already over."

"You're not jumping into something you're going to regret later on, are you?" she asked.

"Regret later on? No. I'm just following your advice."

"My advice?"

"You know, about a new life. A new love."

Again, it sounded like she was sighing. "I wasn't talking about . . . I meant . . . Yeah, Jesus, I was talking about your *joie de vivre*. I was only saying . . . I was talking about normal things. About pleasure."

About normal things? About pleasure? Not about a woman? Nice long walks? A cold beer on a hot summer night? Is that what she'd meant? But then, with whom? All alone? "Normal things," said the Polack. "That's what I'm talking about too. Normal things. I think I'll find that in Kiev. Kiev is normal." He noticed that he was getting wound up. "Why shouldn't I be able to find my *joie de vivre* in Kiev? Why do I have to go looking for it just around the corner?"

"You should do whatever you think's good for you. It's your life, Geniek. It's all yours. It always has been, even if you didn't want to acknowledge it. Do you have sex every once in a while?"

The Polack stuck the toothpick in his mouth and tried to remove something from between his front teeth. "Not particularly," he said with the toothpick in his mouth.

"I'll be honest, I'd rather have you not go to bed with anyone ever again, I'd rather have you go on longing for me forever, but that's egotistical and I'm not like that. You have to go on fucking, Geniek. Otherwise you turn into such a . . . Such a, well, you know, maybe in a pinch you could just pick someone up who you don't really find all that attractive."

"In a pinch, I'll do that," the Polack said. Then they talked a bit about Jurek and the Polack's ex said he should come by sometime for dinner after he got back from Kiev, that by then that ought to be possible, by then he'd surely feel up to it. He told her that after Kiev he would come to dinner and see the house where his ex lived with the former hired people-hand. "An apartment," she said, "we just live in a regular apartment. We're looking around for something bigger."

After they hung up he sat down at his laptop and ran through the instructions from Love Without Borders one more time. They began with the sentence: "Everyone's looking for love, but some people put a lot of work into it." The Polack had the feeling that he was one of those who put a lot of work into it, because he was going all the way to Kiev. There was no cutting corners when it came to love.

He had read the tips before, now he ran through them again for the third time, just to be sure, and took notes in a little notebook he's bought specially for the trip. He was afraid of forgetting things.

"The Ukrainian ladies go for courtesy," he read. "A flower can do wonders." And also: "Holding the door open for a lady and helping her with her coat is particularly appreciated in Ukraine."

The rest was information about how to best prepare for the love trip. "Get enough rest during the days before departure. Love Without Border's love trips are intensive, because we don't want you going home empty-handed." And that you shouldn't bring along big presents for your future belle, that the ladies did however appreciate a souvenir from the region or city where "you who are in search of love" lived.

In his notebook, he wrote: "Bring souvenirs from my own region." He hadn't the slightest idea what kind of souvenirs to buy, until he hit upon the idea of taking a few of the local open-faced pies along to Kiev. Everyone liked a piece of pie, and he was sure they didn't have open-faced pies in Kiev.

5

The day before he was to leave, he went to the bakery known as the best in all of Heerlen, and said he needed three open-faced pies to take to Kiev.

"Kiev?" said the girl behind the counter.

"It's in Ukraine."

"A long way from here," she remarked.

"Can they keep for a long time?" the Polack asked.

"When are you going to eat them?"

"In a few days." The trip would last five days, and it said in the instructions that you shouldn't fall head over heels for the first lady you met. That would not be wise. "Take a good look around," it said. "Make a carefully considered decision."

The Polack was going to take a good look around. He wanted to take three open-faced pies along with him, because he had no idea exactly when he would fall head over heels in love, whether it would happen on the very first day or only shortly before his departure. Whether the first lady would prove to be the right one. Or whether it would take him until number three to discover what the Love Without Borders website referred to as "the mystery." The Polack had read those lines at least five times over already, to be sure he completely understood what the agency was saying. Until now, he had never made the connection between love and a mystery. There was very little he would connect to that, even the months he had spent in a chicken coop were not something he would classify as mysterious.

As he waited for the girl to wrap the pies, he told himself that he had made a good choice. In case he had already passed out the first pies to ladies who, upon closer examination, proved unable to engulf him in the right kind of mystery or he them, then he wouldn't have to approach number three empty-handed.

"I'll wrap the box in aluminum foil, so no air can get to it," the girl said. "That way they'll keep longer. A fresh pie is a fresh pie, of course, but our pies can easily be eaten after a few days. If necessary, you can always heat them up a little."

The heating-up part seemed out of the question to him. The agency had given him the name and address of the (four-star) hotel, and he couldn't imagine being able to heat up something in a hotel room like that, the foil would have to do the trick. It was the thought that counted.

While he was walking home with the well-wrapped boxes in their special bag—he had gone for one cherry, one apricot, and one open-faced apple pie—he began wondering whether maybe this was a child-ish souvenir. An open-faced pie, was that masculine enough? Not that he doubted his own masculinity, but in the tips it said that masculinity was still highly valued in Ukraine, and that the participants must be sure not to confuse that with aggressiveness. "Remain a gentleman at all times," was another tip that Love Without Borders passed along emphatically to its customers.

He would remain one, he would even become one if need be, should it turn out that he wasn't already a gentleman after all. Until now he had never worried much about helping ladies with their coats, but a new life called for new customs.

Jurek had already gone to his mother and the human extension's place, and the Polack spent the evening carefully packing a small suit-case he'd bought specially for this trip. A new life, a new suitcase.

The agency had also given the travelers advice about what clothes they should bring along. "Ukraine is not a hoity-toity kind of place, although a well-tailored suit always makes a man stand out in a crowd. Bring something along for every occasion, including rain gear." The Polack owned almost no suits, the suit he was married in, of course, but it didn't seem appropriate to fall in love wearing your old wedding suit, if it actually still fit him, and so he went out and bought a sport coat at a clothing store in the center of town. The salesman said that it was smart, "but not too dressy," and that it would go well with a pair of jeans too. "Or else a pair of tight black trousers." Just to be on the safe side, the Polack also bought a shirt that went well with the sport coat. A shirt with flowers on it. Normally the Polack didn't wear shirts like that, but the salesman said: "It fits you. It makes you look younger, and fashionable." Fashionable, that's exactly the way the Polack wanted to come across in Ukraine.

That evening, when he looked at himself in the mirror wearing his new sport coat and the floral shirt, he had to admit that he looked like someone who was ready for love, prepared from head to toe for passion. This was no longer the old Polack, this was indeed the new one, even if his shoes were sort of old and worn out, but, sitting on the kitchen floor, he polished them and then you couldn't tell at all anymore. A gentleman walked around in nicely polished shoes.

He had bought himself an oatmeal bar and a thriller at a newsstand. If he happened to get bored on the plane, he would have something to read. He had also checked with the bank to see if he could use the ATMs in Kiev, and he could. A lady from the bank said his debit card had now been cleared for use in Ukraine.

He was ready to go.

The only thing the Polack was still not sure about was whether he should wear a hat. The ladies in Ukraine didn't have to see right away that he was almost bald, and if it turned out to be colder there than predicted, he would at least have something to cover his head. A cap, the Polack decided, he would enter Ukraine wearing a cap.

Then it was time for bed, but sleep wouldn't come.

Part of starting a new life was saying farewell to the old one, and lying in bed it occurred to him that he wasn't exactly sure what he was saying farewell to. He got up, turned on the light. He opened cupboards, his ex's things were lying and hanging everywhere. She had left most of her clothes here. Had she gone out and bought all new things? He fingered her wardrobe, hungrily but still hesitant, as though this were some sort of blasphemy. As though he wasn't allowed to do this anymore. The Polack sniffed at them; all he could smell was lavender. His ex liked to put little bags of lavender in the cupboards. Then he wandered on through the house, in search of remnants of the old life that was now rapidly coming to an end.

The next morning the participants would meet up in the departure hall at Düsseldorf airport. It was by his green umbrella, an email to all the participants had said, that they would be able to recognize Paul, who would himself act as their guide on this trip. It was important to start on the trip well-rested, one needed to be fit before leaving on this journey to love, but that night the Polack didn't sleep a wink. He tossed and turned, he thought he heard a mosquito, he stood outside the door of the vanished boy's bedroom, tried to jerk off, and then went back to wandering around the house as though it didn't belong to him, as though the old life was no longer his own. He needed to start living, although at the same time it seemed unfair to him to act as though he hadn't lived all those years, as though his wife and children had been stuck with a walking corpse. No, that wasn't the case. A walking corpse, that wasn't what he had been.

The Polack arrived at Düsseldorf airport forty-five minutes early, and he didn't see a man with a green umbrella anywhere. He thought about having a cup of coffee, but decided against it in the end. It would be better to stand quietly in the departure hall until the man with the green umbrella showed up. Occasionally he saw men strolling around the departure hall, and he suspected that they were going on the journey to love as well. That they were going to Kiev to let their new life begin, to find the love that they'd been cheated out of thus far.

They disappeared again, melted into the crowd, and by the time he finally saw a man with a green umbrella his thoughts were revolving more around Jurek than around the journey to love and the other participants. He hoped he would come back with a woman Jurek would like. She didn't have to be a stepmother, as long as she got along well with the boy. That was all. He had resolved to tell the ladies in Ukraine almost right away that he came with a son, and that if they didn't like children there was no use in trying.

"Geniek?" asked the man with the green umbrella.

They had all been asked to send a photo of themselves, so the man with the umbrella knew what all the participants looked like. "Everybody calls me the Polack," the Polack said, just like he'd stated already on the phone and, just be sure, he went on explain how his name should be pronounced.

The man said that he was Paul, though the Polack had figured that out, and he felt Paul's moist hand take hold of his and give it a firm shake. Was Paul nervous, or were his hands always moist? They stood face to face, not saying a word, and the Polack noticed that the travel guide was eyeing him carefully, inquisitively. Paul himself didn't look the way the Polack had expected him to, he was smaller and a bit chubby. It looked like he dyed his hair.

"You're early," Paul said, after looking around a bit. He wasn't in much of a mood for conversation, apparently; after that comment, the travel guide didn't speak a word and the Polack wondered whether it was up to him to ask a lot of questions. He was definitely curious. How exactly would they go about meeting the ladies? They had been sent some general information about that, but the Polack wanted some concrete facts. What was going to happen there in Kiev? That's what he wanted to know, but he didn't dare to ask. Finally, it was Paul who asked: "Well, are you raring to go?"

"Sure," the Polack said.

The travel guide nodded contentedly. Of course, he wasn't interested in having participants who had given up all hope beforehand, their guide wanted to be surrounded by enthusiasts. "This is my ninth trip to Ukraine," he told him. "It's one of my favorite destinations. You'll come to love the country and its women. China is great too, but definitely extreme."

"Yeah." China being extreme didn't seem illogical to the Polack. He found Ukraine extreme enough already. But he didn't want to come to love the country and its women, he wanted to love one woman, he couldn't care less about the country. Then Paul started talking about how he had met his own wife in Russia, and how he went there once a year, by car, and how adventurous that was, and all the things he had to take along from Holland for his in-laws. At first they had been reserved and nationalistic, but after a couple of years they discovered the Dutch stroopwafel, and along with the stroopwafel they had come to love the Netherlands and their son-in-law. Since then he had filled the trunk with stroopwafels each summer.

At the word "stroopwafel," the Polack pricked up his ears, because it made him realize that the three open-faced pies he had with him were not such a bad idea at all. He had chosen a good souvenir. A few minutes later, an older man with a cane came and stood with them, he turned out to be a participant too and one Paul seemed to know well. They exchanged hugs, in any case, and when the man with the cane finally turned to the Polack, he asked: "And how many times is this for you?"

"My first."

The man with the cane, who said his name was John, told him this would be his seventh trip to Kiev. He seemed proud of that. A veteran, a man who knew all there was to know about the country and its people. The Polack felt a slight wave of desperation. If this man had gone along seven times without finding what he was looking for, how often would the Polack have to go? He had counted so much on succeeding the very first time, during these five days. Maybe that was naive, but didn't the experts always say that falling in love was a choice you made, something you had to remain open to? They hadn't even taken off yet, and he was already open to it.

"Didn't you find what you were looking for in Ukraine?" the Polack asked guardedly, once Paul had gone to welcome another participant in the journey to love.

"Aw, you know," said John, who seemed like a prime candidate for an old folks' home, "you always find something, but it never lasts. Not in my case. A couple of weeks, a couple of months. I brought one of them here once. Never again. The lady in question had barely set foot in my house and she thought she could boss me around. That's not a smart move around me."

The Polack nodded sagely; he saw that a man in a gray training jacket had joined the group. A lady who came home with you only to boss you around didn't sound promising to him. On the other hand, the Polack didn't care that much whether someone at home tried to boss others around, as long as she did so out of love. At the firehouse too, he had never wanted to be the commander. During a performance interview once, they asked whether he avoided responsibility, or if he had a strong dislike of it. He said that wasn't the case, quite the contrary. He was fine with responsibility, but passing out orders, he wasn't that sort. He preferred to be the one receiving orders, to be the one who carried them out rather than the one who gave them. "So you're more like a subordinate," said the man carrying out his performance interview. The Polack nodded in agreement. A subordinate, that's what he was. Maybe that wasn't very masculine, being a subordinate. In Ukraine, in any case, he would act masculine. Hopefully his height was masculine enough.

Things were gradually getting busier around the man with the green umbrella. Most of the participants were older than the Polack had expected. There was a man in a suit and also a somewhat younger man without a sport coat, but wearing a brightly-colored floral shirt and carrying a backpack. And another man in a training suit. The Polack heard German being spoken too, by at least three of the men. It occurred to him that these were his rivals. He had thought he would be meeting kindred spirits, but when he looked at these men, he couldn't imagine them as being or even becoming kindred spirits somewhere in the course of the journey. Rivals, that was the word for it. He could barely believe that the woman he fell in love with in Kiev would give these men a second glance. They were too different, these men and he.

"Time for check-in," Paul shouted. He was shepherd, coach, and travel guide all rolled into one, and he walked out in front, as he should, as though he himself were off in search of a new life in Ukraine.

The Polack counted twelve participants, plus Paul. There was also a Chinese man among them, or at least a man who looked Chinese. He was wearing a dark-red raincoat with a hood. That looked a little ridiculous, the Polack thought, but maybe it was the newest fashion. They moved toward the check-in counter, some hesitantly, with what looked like reluctance, others with an enthusiasm that the Polack actually found repellent, as though they were planning to fall in love with the first airline attendant who crossed their path. He was standing halfway up the line; he didn't want to be seen as one of the enthusiasts making a rush for the front as though they couldn't contain themselves, nor as one of the reluctant ones who shuffled toward the counter as though being led to the slaughter. They all had a suitcase or bag that needed checking in. Only the young man without a coat announced that his backpack was carry-on baggage. He already had a boarding pass, he wasn't waiting in line with the others. He was doing something with his cell phone.

While they were waiting in line, the Polack shook hands with a few of the other participants. A little awkwardly, the way you shake hands at the birthday parties of family members so distant you can't really remember if you've ever met them before. He still hadn't actually talked to anyone. They weren't here for each other, they were here for the new life, although it would have been nice if they could have had a little sympathy for each other, if they—in spite of it all—could lend each other a little support there in Kiev. That's what he'd been hoping for, a kind of solidarity, congeniality; intuitively now, he knew that that was not the case. He was on his own in this, and maybe that was for the better. You didn't fall in love as a group, you fell in love all by your lonesome.

A man wearing a pair of new, white tennis shoes was standing behind the Polack and started up a conversation with him in German. The Polack spoke German fairly well, and he responded in friendly fashion to the questions directed at him by this man, who turned out to be from Recklinghausen and who had also never taken part in an organized journey to love.

"*Du auch nicht,*" said the man from Recklinghausen with a satisfied tone that put the Polack's mind at ease, "*dann brauchen wir uns ja nicht zu schämen. Wir sind neu hier.*" Then there's nothing for us to be ashamed of. We're new here.

"*Nein, nein,*" the Polack said, and they advanced another fifty centimeters.

The man from Recklinghausen said he was a painter, a house painter, he had worked construction jobs for a while, but he liked painting more. Especially in the winter. Working outside in the winter was the pits, inside was a lot more comfortable. He liked to paint, even though there was a lot of competition from the East these days, men who painted for next to nothing, unhindered by any skill. Poles, Czechs, Rumanians, Hungarians. They couldn't paint worth a damn. "And what kind of work do you do?" the man from Recklinghausen asked, just as the Polack was about to step up to the counter.

"Fireman," the Polack said.

"Ah, I see," said the man from Recklinghausen, and the Polack pulled out his passport, his turn was coming up.

"I bet you don't have any *Ausländer* in the fire department, now do you?"

The only person in front of the Polack now was the Chinese man in his dark red raincoat, he was discussing something with the airline attendant. It was unclear what they were talking about. The Polack explained that he was very content to be a fireman, even though a big reorganization was coming up, something no one had any use for. The on-again-off-again, twenty-four-hour shifts would be a thing of the past, the firehouse was no longer to be an island unto itself, things were not going to get any better, that much was clear. They talked about efficiency all the time now, and the Polack knew what that meant: forced personnel cuts.

The man from Recklinghausen didn't comment on this at all. "*Hey du*," he said, tapping the Polack's upper arm almost tenderly, "*ich bin Tom, und du?*"

It seemed unbecoming to the Polack to say that everyone called him the Polack, so he told the man the name he almost never used anymore. The name that had gone away.

"*Bist du Pole?*" the man from Recklinghausen asked, and the Polack told him that he was Dutch but that his father was born in Poland and his mother in Germany, in the Eifel, and that he was no longer in contact with the family on his mother's side.

"I hope you don't take it personally, what I said about the Poles," said the man from Recklinghausen. "There are decent people there in Poland, who still know how to paint a wall."

"Sure," the Polack said, even though he had to admit that he barely knew any Poles himself, and certainly no Poles who knew how to paint a wall.

He checked in, carried on a businesslike conversation with the airline attendant that was nevertheless larded with repressed lust ("May I
then wish you an extremely pleasant day," he said roguishly), a foretaste
of Ukraine, as it were, he might as well get started with lusting right
away. Then he watched a bit worriedly as his suitcase rolled away, and
took a good look at his boarding pass. They were going to change
planes at Vienna.

He followed the other men, holding the bag with the thriller and
the granola bar in one hand and the pastry bag with the open-faced
pies in the other.

The man from Recklinghausen had come after him, and he tapped
the Polack on the shoulder. "*Hey, du,*" the man said, and he asked if the
Polack was planning to buy anything at the airport. Whether he was
going to do any duty-free shopping. Booze was cheap in Ukraine, he'd
heard, but the only thing they really drank there was vodka and he,
Tom, was crazy about rum. Rum and Coke, rum with banana juice,
mango juice, orange juice, currant juice. As long as it had rum in it. So
he was planning to buy some duty-free rum. He could offer that to the
girls. Women, he added, loved rum, rum was something a girl always
appreciated.

Rum as a souvenir of Recklinghausen, the Polack found that unusual, but still he followed the man to the duty-free shop and, in order not
to be the odd man out, bought a little bottle of rum himself. Maybe it
wasn't such a bad idea after all, having a little rum with you in Ukraine,
you never knew who might appreciate it.

He put the bottle in his plastic bag. Tom had two big bottles in his
tote bag. They walked to the gate, where the men who were going in
search of love were already sitting around in a group. They talked as
though they'd known each other for years. The Chinese man was writing something in a notebook. The man from Recklinghausen plopped
down beside the Polack and started talking about Borussia Dortmund.
That he might be a painter by trade, but that he lived to watch Borussia
play, and that he had two season passes, even though they weren't easy
to get, the second one was for his girlfriend. He didn't yet have a girlfriend though, so sometimes he took other women along to matches,
sometimes a friend too, but because he had decided that the time had

come to settle down, he had already arranged a season pass for her, otherwise they'd have to wait for years. A woman who didn't want to go along to see Borussia play, he had no use for that. There was no need for the Polack to talk, all he had to do was sit and listen. That calmed him.

Then it was boarding time. As it turned out, the man from Recklinghausen was seated in the row behind him. He leaned forward and talked as though he hadn't spoken for months, but now that the opportunity had come his way, he was going to make the best of it. "When the Borussians win, that's when I fuck," he whispered in the Polack's ear, "but when they lose or when the match ends in a draw, then there's no fucking, I'm strict about that. Fucking comes only after a victory."

"*Und wo fickst du?*" the Polack asked. He couldn't come up with a better question than that.

"*Im Club,*" the man from Recklinghausen said. After that he seemed to relax, he stopped whispering in the Polack's ear. The Polack relaxed now as well; he wasn't all that fond of soccer. He took out his thriller and read half a page. The seat beside him was vacant, the seat beside that was occupied by a white-haired man who was part of their group. The man had a roll of peppermint lozenges with him. He kept popping lozenges in his mouth, and when the flight attendants were finished with their safety demonstrations he turned to the Polack. "My name's Lucas," he said. "You're part of our group too, aren't you?"

The Polack said he was, he had the feeling that they were all clandestine members of some secret society.

Lucas told him that he was retired general practitioner. His wife had died six years ago and now he had started feeling like finding a new partner. "It never worked organically," Lucas said, sounding a bit sad. "I've had girlfriends, but they always wanted either too much or too little, and one of my patients told me how he'd gone on one of these journeys to love, he was enthusiastic about it, Love Without Borders, and so I said to myself: why not? Do I think I'm too good for that? Why shouldn't a general practitioner get a little help on his quest for love?"

The Polack nodded and Lucas handed him a peppermint lozenge. Lucas had a coughing fit, and once that was over he said cheerfully that he wasn't expecting to find the love of his life there in Kiev, that in fact no one should expect something like that at his age, and certainly not in Kiev, but that he hoped to find someone to die with. The plane was taxiing down the runway now. "Someone to grow old with, that's nonsense," Lucas said, "I'm already old, I grew old all by myself. Well, officially with my late wife, but in fact I did it on my own."

Gripping his plastic bags gently between his knees, the Polack thought about his dear ex, and he heard the retired general practitioner saying that sex was good for you, even at his age. "Don't stop having it," the man said, "even if it's not easy. It's like walking. A little exercise is always better than no exercise at all. I always told my older patients: 'Not in the mood? Then get yourself in the mood!' Put a dirty magazine beside the pillow, if need be. Any port in a storm." The retired GP offered the Polack another peppermint lozenge, then went on to say: "You know, my wife was an alcoholic. I bought her liquor for her, because after a certain point you couldn't let her go out in public like that. You can think whatever you want about my doing that, but I call it loving one's fellow man."

Then the captain said they were second in line for takeoff, and the retired doctor popped the last of his peppermint lozenges in his mouth. He stopped talking, leaned back and closed his eyes, and the Polack did the same. So far no one had asked him a single question, except what his name was and whether this was his first time on a trip like this. The Polack apparently was not the kind of person you asked questions of, as though people could sense that he had nothing to say. A person who wants to give information about himself will speak up in the end, although the instructions from the agency said that the ladies in Ukraine liked it when men could talk a bit about themselves. "Don't act as though the cat's got your tongue," he'd read, "but don't be too direct either. A person who says, 'I love you' five minutes into the first conversation shouldn't count on being taken seriously." The instructions also suggested that you bring along a picture of yourself as a child. The Polack did that, a somewhat washed-out picture from his childhood. The Polack as a boy of six, back when his mother was still alive.

A few moments later they were suspended in air. The plane shuddered and shook. The Polack didn't like that, this journey to love already had him feeling exhausted.

Just before landing at Vienna, he turned to Lucas, who was staring straight ahead with a magazine open on his lap. "What did you bring along?" the Polack asked.

"What do you mean?"

"As a souvenir from your region."

The retired general practitioner shook his head. "I'm too old for that nonsense," he said. He almost sounded angry.

For a long time, the Polack had thought that the success of his mission depended on the souvenirs, now he comforted himself with the thought that he could always throw away the open-faced pies once they got to Kiev. Or eat them himself, if it turned out not to be the right present. No, love didn't depend on souvenirs.

6

At the airport in Vienna, most of the love travelers went off to do so more duty-free shopping, but the Polack didn't go with them. He stayed seated close to the gate, waiting for the plane to Kiev, the thriller in his lap. Somehow, he couldn't bring himself to open the book. When he stood up to stretch his legs a bit, he saw the Chinese man approaching. "Hi," the man said. "My name's Han, what's yours?"

The Polack told him his name, and added that everyone called him the Polack. Han said he was from Zaandam, his mother was born in Malaysia, his father had lived for a time in the former Dutch East Indies. He was, in other words, not Chinese. He asked the Polack whether he'd ever been.

"To Malaysia, Indonesia, no," the Polack said. "Never."

"I meant Zaandam," Han replied, sounding shy, "I was talking about Zaandam."

"No," the Polack said after thinking about it for a few seconds, "I've never been there either." Han stood there without a word, his red rain-coat draped over one arm, then said: "We're sort of like astronauts. Astronauts look for life on Mars, we're looking for love in Kiev."

"Yeah," the Polack said. He didn't feel like an astronaut, even though he knew what Han meant. There was something alien about it, about this trip. Still, he hoped that Kiev would be less uninhabitable than Mars. In some way or other, he felt more sympathy for this Han than for the man from Recklinghausen, who had gone in search of more rum. He could imagine Han and himself falling in love together in Kiev, not with each other, each with a different woman of course, and that then they would sit in the lobby of the hotel and tell each other stories about their budding romances. Things could go that way. He would have something in common with Han, his love, his new love. That prospect made the Polack happy.

At last, Han sat down. The Polack opened his book, read a couple of sentences, but he was restless, he couldn't concentrate. Did Han have children, the Polack asked. Han told him that he lived with his mother and wasn't so eager to have children of his own. This was his sixth journey to love. "I have a fair amount of experience. They even gave me a discount on this one. I've been to Russia twice, once to China, one time to Peru, once to Ukraine, and one time to Costa Rica, but they don't go there anymore these days."

"And how was it?" the Polack asked.

Han leaned over and spoke close to the Polack's ear. "You've probably noticed already," he whispered, "that most of the men who go on these trips aren't completely normal." Han glanced around as though to make sure no one could hear what he said. "In other words: nutty as a fruitcake. Don't tell Paul I said that, he tends to get pissed off if he thinks the participants are sabotaging the proceedings, so you didn't get it from me. Especially that trip to Peru, that was definitely not cool."

The Polack nodded and asked: "What happened there?"

"I don't really want to talk about it," Han said, "it was . . . It was excessive. The police got involved. I've never seen that anywhere else. Participants out of control. Two the guys were sent home. I don't want to say any more about it. Have you ever been on one of these before?"

"Never," the Polack said.

Han nodded. He must have noticed the look in the fireman's eyes. Anxiety, the start of disappointment. "It's bound to be okay this time," he said. "I think everything is well organized in Kiev."

Then Han stood up and walked away, leaving the Polack behind, through the big windows he could already see the plane waiting on the tarmac. He wondered why so many of the participants had been on these journeys to love so often, and why Han, who seemed less than enthusiastic about Love Without Borders, went on taking part. He also wondered what it was that made the participants lose control in Peru. That wasn't going to happen to him, falling in love was one thing, losing control over yourself was another. The Polack opened his book again, but noticed that he kept stopping to peer around, looking for participants on the journey to love, participants Han said were mostly off their rocker. He peered around to see if he could catch the men at their abnormalities. The retired general physician had seemed normal to the Polack. He had put into words precisely what the Polack was thinking: why shouldn't you get a little help on your quest for love? There were plenty of things that were normal, that was a comfort.

In the arrivals hall at Kiev airport, Paul gathered the men around him. "We have a couple of guys from Germany with us," he said, "so I'm going to switch back and forth between Dutch and German. It would be a little weird if we suddenly had to start doing everything in English. I'd like to ask our German friends to interrupt me if there's anything they don't understand, and otherwise I'll take them aside separately afterward." The Germans nodded, they seemed to be able to follow him pretty well in Dutch.

"We made it, men," Paul said solemnly. "This is Kiev. We all got through customs okay. Now we're going to take the bus to the hotel, and there you'll all have a little time to freshen up. But I want everyone to meet up with me again within an hour after arrival, to run through the program for the next few days. This is where it's going to happen, guys. Are you ready for it?"

The man from Recklinghausen shouted: "*Ja!*" Many of the others only nodded, and the Polack nodded too, at least half the men stood there looking a bit embarrassed, they looked more like a group of outcasts than gentlemen who had paid a considerable sum in order to find love. The Polack had dipped into his savings to pay for this trip, and he suspected that the savings of the other participants had taken a major broadside too.

Paul asked if they had any questions, and one of the German men said he had indicated that he had a dietary restriction, that he hadn't heard any more about it though, and that he was worried now, he was gluten intolerant and wanted to make sure that his allergy was being taken seriously. Paul replied that there was no cause for worry, that he was certainly not the first man to go on a journey to love with a gluten allergy. He and his allergy had been taken into account. There were a few others with special diets too, and it had all been duly noted. No one need worry about that, everything had been done in the service of making sure the men could focus on their most important task: finding a partner, finding true love.

When Paul was finished, a few men applauded. The Polack applauded too. Love deserved an applause. After that they were shown to the bus. No one came to sit beside the Polack, most of the men were sitting by themselves. The Polack was pleased about that; he was no exception, no black sheep. Paul was the only one who had someone sitting beside him.

The hotel was a large apartment complex that reminded him of the flats at the edge of Heerlen, of which his ex had once said that if you lived there long enough you would jump off the roof at some point. This building was even more dismal, although the Polack had good hope that the rooms would be decent.

In the lobby, where they had to wait to check in, the Polack looked around to see how things stood with fire safety here. So-so. He was a gentleman now, yet he remained a fireman.

He saw women who clearly dressed differently than women did in the Netherlands, more polished, more feminine, more provocative, but it was too soon to fall in love. The Polack wanted to hold off until the meeting, where they'd get a good explanation of what was going to happen in the next few days.

He was given a room on the eleventh floor, a double room. There were two condoms in the mini-bar. The view was not promising. Big and gray, Kiev was, and it was raining. The Polack opened his suitcase and put his clothes in the closet.

The open-faced pies didn't fit in the mini-bar, but they seemed to have survived the trip well. He found a place for them at the bottom of the closet, with the bottle of rum beside them. The room lived up to his expectations; he could, if need be, receive a new love here.

Then he wondered whether he should already put on his sport coat with the floral shirt, or wait a bit. The best thing, he decided, was to make a good impression right away at the opening meeting. He undressed, put on his shirt and sport coat, sent Jurek a WhatsApp message to say he had arrived safely in Kiev, another text message to his ex, then went to the mirror and applied his aftershave. He wondered whether or not to keep his cap on. He looked at himself with the cap on and without, and decided to take it off. He had never been vain, but a first impression could do a lot of damage. He knew that already, he needed no instructions from Love without Borders to know that. The absence of hair, with the exception of a little stubble, actually looked pretty good on him.

Once he had decided to approach the women of Kiev in a state of near-baldness, he sat down and flipped through the info package he'd been given at check-in. The meeting would take place in the Mozart Hall on the third floor. It was still a bit early, but he couldn't stand sitting around his room anymore. He went to the third floor, where he saw a Beethoven Hall and a Vivaldi Hall, but no Mozart Hall. He stopped a lady he saw pushing a food cart down the corridor. She didn't understand him at first, so then he repeated, loudly and clearly: "Mozart." And once again: "Mo-zart." At last she understood. "Around the corner," she said.

The Mozart Hall, as it turned out, was not really a hall at all, more like a big room with about twenty chairs lined up and two tables with another five chairs around them. On the one of the tables was a vase with flowers. The Polack reached out and touched them. Plastic, yet tastefully done.

He took a seat in the third row. He was excited, with a feeling he vaguely remembered from his first day of high school too. Life was about to begin, real life.

The men came trickling in. Han sat down beside the Polack. He was almost sure about it now: Han could become a friend. The boy who hadn't checked in any bags sat on the other side of the Polack and told him that he worked as a nurse in a children's hospital. "I'm expecting a lot from this trip," he said. "Love, that's what it's all about in life, right?"

It was true, love was what life was all about, even though just a few years ago the Polack would never have thought that it would come to him in Kiev. But maybe it was like they said: you found it in the most unlikely places. A chicken coop was indeed a strange place to find love.

The Polack saw that John had also put on a floral shirt, without a coat. He looked at John, compared himself to him, and concluded that he was looking good. He had transformed himself into a gentleman. The taciturn Polack he had once been hadn't disappeared, but a gentleman had arisen from within. The picture of him as a child was in his inside coat pocket, just in case of there might be encounters on the very first evening.

Paul came in, followed by a group of women and a boy. Two of the women and the boy sat down beside Paul. The others remained standing on either side of the chairs. Everyone was present, except for the man from Recklinghausen, but they didn't wait for him. Someone closed the door. Anyone coming in now would be too late, and the Polack felt pity for the man from Recklinghausen. He was going to miss so much. And he had paid for it.

Paul took the microphone. The PA system squawked. "Men," Paul said, "this is the local staff of Love without Borders, and I'd like to introduce you now. These are the people who will be your guides during your search, a search which, for many men and women, perhaps for all men and women, is the most important search of all. These ladies are your interpreters, and this young man is our coordinator. He doesn't speak Dutch, but he speaks English and a little German. He can help you men with all your questions, for example: 'I've fallen in love and I need to buy flowers. Where can I find the prettiest flowers in Kiev?'

"The first meet-ups will be tomorrow afternoon," Paul went on, "after lunch. During the morning you can do a little sightseeing. More than sixty women have signed up already, or perhaps I should say, sixty women have made it through the selection procedure, and that's a record. Our selection procedure is tough. Sixty women is a lot. Prepare yourselves well. Tomorrow you'll meet them, and maybe there are some women among them who you'll want to grow old with . . ."

Paul paused for effect, and someone shouted—the Polack couldn't see who it was: "I don't want to get old." To which the retired general practitioner shouted in reply: "I already am old, and you'll get old too, so you better get used to it."

"Guys," Paul said, "old or young, big or small, everyone wants love, and here in Kiev there are women who want the same thing you do, women who crave love. Not all the women speak English. Some of them do a bit, some of them speak it very well, others not at all. That's why we have our interpreters, our excellent and helpful interpreters who will stand by you during your quest, because although the language of love may be international, you'll occasionally need some subtitles." There was some laughter. "Okay," Paul said, "and before I go on with some general information, and before the interpreters tell us a bit about themselves, I think it would be good for us to go around the room and introduce ourselves. Who'll start? When you introduce yourself, stand up so we can get a good look at you."

Lucas was the first. He told exactly what he had already told the Polack on the plane, but he left out the part about his wife being an alcoholic and about how he had bought her liquor for her. The next one was a German who worked in advertising. Then came a physical therapist, divorced, children living independently. The next man was a veteran by the name of Richard, but everyone called him Rich. He told everyone that he done two hitches in Afghanistan and that it wasn't helping the Afghanis any, that he himself now suffered from chronic lower-back pain and that Afghanistan had wrecked his marriage too. "Thank you," Paul said, but the veteran didn't sit down. He said: "I have three kids, I'm not allowed to see them anymore. What a lot of people don't know is that the Dutch Child Welfare Council is worse than the Taliban . . ."

"Thank you, Rich," Paul said. "That's enough for now."

"I'm not finished yet," the veteran said. "A lot of people don't know that there's a fascist organization that calls itself the Child Welfare Council . . ." He spoke loudly and hurriedly. It was clear that the Child Welfare Council was an emotional thing for him. The other men stared straight ahead, no one dared to look at the veteran. Lucas sat examining his nails too.

"That is really enough for now," Paul said loudly. "Later on, you'll have all the time you want to get it off your chest." Moping, the veteran sat back down. His last comment was: "I just think it's good for these men here to know, before they get started on children, what kind of an organization the Child Welfare Council is."

And then it was the Polack's turn. He kept it brief, as brief as possible. That was probably why a fairly lengthy silence descended after he was done talking. Then came the nurse and he said what he had already told the Polack, that love was what life was all about and that's why he was so happy to be here.

Han's turn came next. He was wearing his dark red raincoat, as though it might start raining in the Mozart Hall any moment. "This is my seventh time," he said. "I'm raring to go. My mother told me not to come back without a woman, so I want to ask all of you to help me out a little. If you guys see someone and you think 'she'd be just right for Han', then please let me know."

The men laughed, all except for the Polack. He would do his best, and if he ran into anyone who was just right for Han he would let him know right away, even though he had no idea what type of woman Han was looking for. He'd have to ask him about that later on. "Thanks, Han," Paul said.

Just then the door opened, and there stood the man from Recklinghausen. He had put on a different training suit, his hair stuck out in all directions as though he had been lying on his bed for hours and then jumped up and ran to the Mozart Hall. He stood in the doorway for a moment, then mumbled something that sounded like "*Verzeihung*" and sat down behind the Polack. "The Borussians are playing, *das kan man doch nicht verpassen*. But I came anyway, I'll just have to miss the match. *Die Borussen werden das heute nicht schaffen*," he whispered in the Polack's ear. The man from Recklinghausen smelled of liquor and it was his turn right away. He told the group that he was a painter, that he had been to Zealand Province a few times with his parents and therefore spoke a few words of Dutch. Concerning rum, Borussia, and love, he said nothing. Once he was finally finished talking, he sank down in the chair beside the Polack. The man looked distraught and exhausted.

Now the interpreters introduced themselves to the group. He had no trouble at all following the English spoken by some of the interpreters, but others were harder to understand. At least two of the female interpreters he found striking. Their hair, their eyes, the way they introduced themselves to the audience.

Paul said: "I'm only going to say this once, you guys are also allowed to fall in love with the interpreters." A cheer went up in the Mozart Hall.

That evening the men had dinner with the interpreters in a typical Ukrainian restaurant—there were almost no vegetarian dishes on the menu, so the Polack ordered beet soup, which turned out to have chunks of meeting floating in it too. Out of sheer necessity, he drank the soup and avoided the meat as much as he could. He was sitting propped in between the man from Recklinghausen and the retired general practitioner, who took turns yakking at him and so kept him from addressing a single word to the female interpreter sitting across from him, who he would very much have liked to talk to. For a moment he wondered whether these men had actually come to Kiev for love, or simply for the opportunity to chatter away at will.

Only as they were leaving the restaurant did the Polack get a chance to exchange a few words with the interpreter, he even succeeded in fishing the photo of him as a child from his inside pocket and showing it to her. She gave it a hurried glance.

"Six years old," the Polack said.

"How cute," she mumbled. "So cute."

7

The first get-together with ladies in the center of Kiev was, as far as the Polack was concerned, less than a resounding success. He had spoken with five women, a major effort by his standards, and with none of them had he felt the spark. He'd either had trouble understanding what the women said or else they found him boring, and the one lady who showed interest in him he found too materialistic. She talked for at least ten minutes about exchange rates; he wasn't hard to please, but exchange rates did not interest him at all.

The second get-together with ladies from Kiev was planned to take place in a suburban neighborhood. The men traveled together by subway to the neighborhood in question, and in the subway, despite his best intentions, the Polack had grown somber. The people looked dismal to him, with their caps and winter coats, their melancholy gaze, their skin eroded by the weather, alcohol and cigarettes. For a moment he wondered whether in a city like Kiev he would ever find love that was worthy of the name. Sex you could find everywhere, even *im Club* if need be, that wasn't the problem. Those who had come along for that would definitely return home satisfied, but mere physical satisfaction seemed too cold, too pragmatic to him.

This time too, the Polack wore his new sport coat with the floral shirt. It wasn't that chilly yet, and he figured you could wear a new outfit for a few days in a row. He examined the people around him in the subway car, their dejection was deep and unfathomable. He knew of course that people in subway cars always look miserable, even in Paris, and it was for good reason that he did his best to avoid public transport. He preferred not to be confronted with the gloom of others.

At the subway station where they got off, there were lots of flowers on sale. He saw an older woman sitting on a rug with photographs of a boy arranged in front of her. There was also a text, in Russian. He suspected that this was her son and that she was panhandling, although he saw no cup for change. Hoping it would bring him luck, he placed a banknote on the rug and walked on quickly.

The Polack thought about buying flowers, just to be sure. After all, he hadn't gone to that ATM for nothing, but because none of the other men showed any interest in flowers, he decided against it. He didn't want to be the only one to show up at the get-together with roses or carnations. He didn't want to be the odd man out. If someone were to ask him now: besides love, is there anything you need, anything you wish for, he would have replied: I don't want to be the odd man out.

They crossed a park in the middle of what he found to be a hopeless-looking apartment complex. How could there be love without hope? Yesterday, one of the interpreters had told him that this was the new Kiev, full of idealists and young people who wanted to chase out the oligarchs, this place was going to be hip, the new Berlin, it was only a matter of time. But if this was the new, hopeful Kiev, what for god's sake must the old one have looked like?

The participants in the journey to love swung their arms, they walked single file like schoolchildren on a field trip or soldiers full of spit and vinegar, marching toward their fate. That was how they marched toward love.

After a little while they reached the conference center. The men who had laughed in the subway and joked with each other, the way men do when they're on a trip together, looked crestfallen now. At the same moment that these men were going in search of their true love, a meeting of handicapped athletes was being held in another conference room. There was a bit of confusion about where the men were supposed to go, and when they saw the wheelchairs and amputees they began grumbling. Lucas said: "This may sound heartless, but if we were looking for handicapped women we could just as easily have stayed at home." The other men agreed. They hadn't traveled all the way to Kiev to meet amputees, you had plenty of those to choose from in the western Dutch conurbation, in South Limburg province, and even out on the islands of the Wadden Shallows.

Fortunately, Paul shouted: "Guys, our get-together is in the next room. Don't worry. Our ladies still have all their limbs."

Just as he had the day before, Paul stopped and spoke to the men before they entered the conference room, the way a soccer trainer speaks to his team that's been on a losing streak for a few months. "Be sure of yourself," he said. "This is where it all begins. You guys deserve it. You're worth these ladies' love. All you have to do is believe in it yourselves. Do you believe you're worth these ladies' love?"

"Yeah," most of the men shouted, they believed it, although there were a few who said nothing, only stared at the floor.

Paul went on to say that this was a poor neighborhood. "This isn't the part of town with the fancy shops, the fashionable restaurants, and hip cafés. So remember, the poorer people are, the greater their desire. Don't forget that when you all go in here."

Just before the doors to the conference room were opened, the veteran started in again about the Child Welfare Council. The other men let Rich blow off steam, they were used to it by now, then they stepped into the room like victors; seated at big, round tables with candles on them were ladies drinking champagne, or what passed for champagne in the back neighborhoods of Kiev. There were also plates of cookies on the tables, and the female interpreters were walking around, ever prepared to translate a word where necessary. To convert declarations of love into Ukrainian or Russian.

The Polack walked over to the first table he saw without any other men at it; one of the women seated there was wearing a blue dress that caught his eye, it was such a lovely blue. He sat down beside her and asked her name and what kind of work she did. She said that she was a bookkeeper—he didn't catch her name—and she asked him in return: "And you?"

When he said his name was Geniek and that he was a fireman, she replied: "I love firemen."

And he asked: "Could you love this fireman? I know it's early, but could you love this fireman?" What had come over him, what emotion had taken hold of him that he dared to ask questions like this at such an early stage? But he was in Kiev and he wasn't speaking his own language, the Polack had no language of his own, silence was his language. Here he dared more than he did at home, shame had been shoved aside.

"Maybe," she replied.

Once she had said that, once she had said "maybe" and given him a look that didn't look at all like maybe but like she in fact already loved him a little on the sly, it was a done deal. Or even before that. Because of her blue dress. The look in her eye. He didn't know her name or where she was from, but he thought: this is the woman I'll grow old with. And before I grow old I'm going to live with her. I'm going to live. This is she, this is where the new life starts.

Then he took a cookie off the plate. He had spoken, now he didn't know what else to say. He sat beside her and wanted to just go on sitting there and to hold her hand. He had no more text, once again he was the same taciturn Polack as ever. Fortunately, he remembered in time that he had a picture of himself as a child in his inside pocket, and he showed it to her. She looked at it carefully, then asked: "This is your child?"

"No, this is me."

"You are handsome."

"Thank you," he said.

And then it was quiet again, she handed the photo back to him, he tucked it away and asked her if she had old pictures too, from when she was a child. From her handbag she produced a wallet, a little black wallet, and from that wallet a passport photo appeared, "Me," she said, "ten years old".

He looked at the photo and saw an angel. She had a few freckles and her teeth were all crooked, that made the angel only more angelic.

"You have not changed." He meant it. She had barely changed. She laughed and he asked himself if he should move on to another table, but he didn't want to leave the woman in blue. Then he realized that it had been boorish of him to say that she hadn't changed, and he remarked: "Your teeth have changed."

She nodded. "Yes, my teeth have changed." And she laughed with her mouth wide open, as though to show him how much her teeth had changed, that a minor miracle had taken place inside her mouth.

He remained seated, as though he was at home, and occasionally he took a cookie. That gave him something to do. He smiled at the ladies at the other tables who were nipping at their Ukrainian champagne, but he was not interested in them. Geniek wanted to take the woman in blue back to the Netherlands with him, just the way she was, with her half-crooked teeth that hadn't been straightened completely, with her dress, and the faint odor of cigarette smoke that clung to her, but he could hardly pick her up and carry her off, although she would probably have understood if he had, seeing as he'd already told her he was a fireman. Yes, he wanted to take her away without any more fuss.

Finally, he asked if she would like to have lunch with him. He repeated the question just to be sure, in case she'd misunderstood him.

"Now?" she asked.

And he replied: "Now."

She thought about it for a moment, then said she actually would like something to eat and drink.

"Do you know a nice restaurant?" he asked.

She turned to the girl seated on her left and then back to the Polack and said in his ear: "Can my friend come also?"

She had to talk loudly, because the music was getting louder all the time. The people needed stirring. That was how love began and how it usually ended too, the Polack knew from experience: with a stir.

At first the Polack was disappointed, he wanted to be alone with her, but he said it was okay. He wanted to say that her friends were his friends, and the more the merrier, but the right words in English just wouldn't come. Then she asked if they could go right now, because the two of them were actually quite hungry, and these cookies were only fattening, she wanted to eat something hearty. That, at least, was all he could make from what he heard her say, because she mixed a little Russian or Ukrainian—he couldn't tell the two languages apart—in with her English. Then he got up and left the conference room, the two ladies in his wake. He felt like a winner. All the humiliations and defeats had left him, all the humiliations had only taken place in order to make this victory possible. He glanced at the other men, but they were paying him no heed. No one seemed to see him.

Once out of the room, the women began walking quickly, they walked through the complex of conference rooms past the handicapped athletes and soon they were outside, in the merciless light of this dismal neighborhood, but he still found her beautiful, his wife-to-be, with the half-crooked teeth, less crooked than before, and her hair that smelled of cigarettes. Now she was wearing a leather jacket over her blue dress and he asked if she was sure she was warm enough. She said she was, and then he finally introduced himself to his future wife's girlfriend. Her name was Dana, and he did his best to be the gentleman that Love Without Borders had hoped to make of him, because he knew how important the girlfriends of your wife-to-be could be.

The neighborhood seemed less dismal to him now, and the Polack asked again: "Do you know a nice restaurant?" The ladies nodded and picked up the pace even further, speaking Russian or Ukrainian with each other the whole time. Every once in a while, the woman in the blue dress looked at him and then he knew once more that he hadn't been fooling himself, that his budding affection was being reciprocated. And why shouldn't his feelings be reciprocated? He was serviceable, also for those in search of love.

The restaurant looked more like a nightclub to him. The women sat down at a table in the semi-darkness, and he asked, just to be sure, whether this was really a restaurant. She said the food here was fine, so that made it a restaurant, his wife-to-be did. Then they ordered a bottle of vodka and bottle of orange juice and she asked what he wanted to drink with his vodka. "Water," he said.

The waiter placed a bottle of water on the table. Then came sour gherkins, and something else that turned out to be pickled watermelon. Once again he asked if they were really going to eat something, because pickled watermelon and gherkins seemed a bit meager to him, gentleman as he was now. He had to attend to her, he needed to take care of her. If he was in this world, then it was because he had a task to perform, namely to care for people, his one remaining boy, and now this woman from Kiev too. Right after that he confessed to his wife-to-be that he hadn't actually understood her when she told him her name and whether she would say it again, if she didn't mind too much.

She shook her head and then said her name and she laughed, and because of that laugh he missed it again. Then she took a notebook out of her handbag and wrote it down for him, she tore the page out of the notebook and handed it to the Polack. Her name, it turned out, was Yulia, but she pronounced it differently, as You-lee-ah.

Then she told him that she hadn't really caught his name either, and he wrote his name and pronounced it for her. She asked if he liked to dance.

"No, I don't like dancing."

She and Dana wouldn't take no for an answer, though. They drank more vodka and ate watermelon, they explained that he definitely needed to eat some of it too, and then they dragged him out onto the dance floor. He let them drag him, tractable he was, a tractable Polack. Had he ever wanted to be anything else?

The three of them danced, and he leaned over to his wife-to-be and said in her ear that he loved her. He said he wanted to take her along to the place where he lived, to Heerlen. "Do you know Heerlen?" he shouted in her ear, to be heard above the music.

"No," she shouted back, "I don't know."

"Do you know the Netherlands?" he shouted again.

And she shouted back: "No."

And he: "But you have heard of the Netherlands?"

"Yes," she shouted.

They went back to the table and she asked if it was pretty, where he lived. The Polack had to think about that, then he said: "Small mountains, tiny mountains. The rest of the Netherlands is flat. Below sea level."

And Yulia asked: "And you are a fireman?"

"Yes," he said with touch of pride, and he thought he saw a glimmer in their eyes. "Fireman. Are we going to eat?" He was really very hungry now. Defeats robbed you of your appetite, victories made you ravenous.

Yulia asked to see the menu. Dana looked at him with a smile and asked: "You have wife?"

"Ex-wife."

Dana nodded—there were of course men who looked for love in Ukraine while their wife and children waited for them at home—and Yulia ordered something at last. She had said that she knew what was tasty, and he had replied that everything was fine by him.

The waiter was a boy in black jeans and a white shirt, with tattoos down both arms and on his fingers too. They drank vodka and Yulia talked to her girlfriend now and then, but the Polack didn't try to get involved. It was fine like this. It felt safe and familiar, as though he had been traveling with her and with Dana for years. The food they'd ordered turned out to be a mountain of lamb; a platter with a pile of lamb chops was set on the table, and after that more lamb and bread and rice.

"You eat everything?" Yulia asked.

"Yes," the Polack said. "Everything." This wasn't the moment to say that he was a vegetarian. He would eat meat, a gentleman had to remain polite. He could explain it later, that he no longer wanted meat and fish, he would tell her everything, or at least most of it.

They ate as though they were starved, and maybe they were too, but they kept it respectable. They drank more vodka with orange juice or water, they became tipsy but they kept it respectable. The Polack barely ate—the taste of meat had become strange to him, and he feared that his stomach couldn't handle that much lamb. After chewing a bit on a lamb chop, he asked where she lived, his bride-to-be.

"Here," she said. "In the city."

"Alone?"

"No, with father," she said.

"And mother?"

"Dead."

"Ah," said the Polack. "Sorry. Long time ago?"

"Five years ago."

He took her hand. Death dispelled the last of the shame, thanks to death the beast, the lust, emerged a bit from its lair and with her hand in his he asked if he could meet her father. He said that he would very much like to see where she lived, where she had grown up, and he had brought something for her. From the part of the country he came from. A little something, a souvenir.

She didn't seem to understand. She drank what was still in her glass, took a pickle, and held it between her half-crooked teeth while she stared at him. That pickle between her teeth made him only more in love, and he said: "I have a gift for you and your father."

She kept looking at him while she crunched on the pickle. "Now?" she asked, then withdrew her hand from his in order to put another piece of watermelon in her mouth.

"No," he replied, "not now. In my hotel. Can I come to your place with the gift for you and your father?"

She looked at Dana and they discussed something in Russian or Ukrainian, and the Polack put a pickle in his mouth too while he waited for the verdict from Yulia and her girlfriend. When they were finished consulting, Yulia, after all the gherkins, lamb chops, and pickled watermelon, stuffed a piece of chewing gum in her mouth and said: "You can come tomorrow to my place."

That was all the Polack needed to know. She liked him a lot. Jurek was wrong, the chickies still cottoned to him.

"What time?" the Polack asked.

"Afternoon, late afternoon. Five. Is that okay for you?" She took a pen from her purse, she wrote down the address, handed the piece of paper to the Polack, and he examined it with the devotion of a saint. Then he borrowed her pen and wrote his phone number and the name of his hotel on a napkin, just in case. Then he said: "You must know I have a son."

"A son?"

"Yes," he said.

"One son?"

The Polack nodded. "There were two sons, but one is gone."

"Okay," Yulia said. "Let's go."

She probably hadn't understood him, he would explain it all later. Maybe he shouldn't grant it too much attention, the important thing was the son who remained. He paid the bill, for he was a gentleman—good thing he'd withdrawn a lot from the ATM, the lamb turned out to be exorbitantly expensive—and then they went outside.

It was dark and drizzly, but the Polack's new life had begun. Besides, he would be leaving here in a few days and he was going to take her with him. Not right away of course, he knew that such things take time. Together they walked to the subway, where Yulia asked if he had a token; when he said he did not, she bought one for him. He took that as a sign of love, or at least of fondness, but why distinguish between the two? Signs were everywhere. All you had to do was recognize them. And he kissed both Dana and Yulia twice, on both cheeks, and said: "I'll see you tomorrow." He watched the ladies as they walked away, he hoped they would turn to look at him again, but they didn't, they were caught up in the crowd and finally he was caught up in the crowd too. He was back in the subway amid passengers in winter coats who stared into space or stared at their telephones, but now that didn't bother him. He got off at the wrong stop and wandered for an hour through the cold city. That didn't bother him either. In the lobby he ran into the man from Recklinghausen, who said: "*Du, hey du*, have a drink with me at the bar. I'm in there with three lovely women, they still know what fun is here. The culture isn't as *versaut* as it is at home."

The Polack said he was tired and went to his room, where, sitting on his bed, he sent a WhatsApp message to his ex, telling her that his new life had begun.

Then he undressed and took a bath. In the tub he realized that he had no telephone number for his wife-to-be, although he had her address. It would work out. He jerked off successfully, but even bigger than the beast within was the infatuation.

After climbing out of the tub and putting on his bathrobe, he went to the closet to see if the open-faced pies were still there. It wasn't that he didn't trust the chambermaids, but you never knew if they hadn't accidentally been overcome by a raging hunger. Everything was precisely as he had left it, including the rum. He opened the bottle and took a few sips.

Only then did he see that his ex had written back. "How's it going in Kiev?" she wanted to know. "Ruud says this is an excellent month for Libras to fall in love. Be sure to take advantage of that, sweetheart."

The Polack wasn't all too keen about astrology, but still he appreci-ated this astrological insight. Sometimes, despite themselves, astrologists could be right. And sitting on his bed he drank the rum, one careful little sip after the other. He enjoyed himself.

8

The Polack awoke early, more or less the same way he had awakened long ago on his birthdays, impatient, full of expectation, and also with a touch of fear, that the presents would be a disappointment, that he wouldn't get what he had asked for.

He picked up his phone, secretly hoping that Yulia had sent him a message. When it turned out she hadn't, he wrote to his dear ex: "Libra has found love X." He had a slight headache, but absolutely no hangover. He was too happy for a hangover, and filled with that realization he remained lying in bed until he felt that he had done enough lazing about. He dressed, to wear the floral shirt again might be a bit too much, but he put on his new sport coat, that was no problem, no one would notice that with a normal, everyday white shirt underneath. He decided not to go to the get-together with ladies from Kiev that was scheduled for that afternoon. He had met the right lady from Kiev, why would he want to meet more?

When he left his room to go down to breakfast, he saw Han walking around in the hall in a pair of white linen trousers, as though this were the height of summer. "What are you doing?" the Polack asked.

"I'm practicing," Han said. "I've got a date in a little while, I learned a couple of sentences by heart, in Russian, but I keep forgetting them."

"What kind of sentences?"

"One of the interpreters wrote them down for me, phonetically. I will always love you. I will never hit you. Sentences like that." Han took a few steps toward the Polack and said quietly: "Last time I was here I had a date and we were just talking. At a certain point she asked me: 'Will you hit me? Because we already have enough men here who hit their wives.' I said, "Never. My mother hits people sometimes though.'"

He laughed as though It were a joke, but it didn't make the Polack laugh. He smelled Han's aftershave, not a particularly pleasant odor. "I don't know if you've got a date coming up," Han said, still talking as though he were telling secrets. "The best thing is to promise right away that you won't hit her, not even if you've had too much to drink, then you've already got a head start."

"I'll remember that." The Polack walked to the elevator. Han was going to become a friend. When Yulia came to Holland he would travel with her to Zaandam, to look up his new friend. When he looked over his shoulder, he saw that Han had gone back to pacing the hall in his flappy linen trousers.

The only other man downstairs in the breakfast room was John, the love veteran. The Polack didn't sit with him, he dished himself up some scrambled eggs, yogurt, and a slice of brown bread and found a table for himself alone. There he ate his breakfast in concentration, but still a little hurriedly, the slight headache had grown worse, but the enthusiasm that had been awakened in him, the reborn passion and a desire that he hadn't felt to this degree for a very long time, maybe never, were all so much stronger than that little headache. When he finished breakfast, he sent a message to Jurek. That everything was going well in Kiev, and that he missed him. He thought about telling him that he had found a chickie, but felt that telling his son that would be a bit premature. A message came back almost right away, something about sexting. And then, right away: "Sorry, not for you."

The Polack didn't know how to react. It would be better to start a conversation about this. He would do that when he got back, there were other things that required his attention now. Besides, he wanted to learn more about sexting before calling Jurek and asking him to explain it.

Lucas came into the breakfast room and hurried over to the Polack. "Did you get a bite?" the retired general practitioner asked. "Did the angler catch a little fish? Two little fish, I thought, by the looks of it." "I met someone," the Polack said carefully. "How about you?" "Man," the doctor said, "I met so many women. More in one day than in my whole life in Holland. Okay, I used to meet a lot of women at my office, but I never stepped out of line. Ukraine is paradise. I regret not having realized that before. Here in Kiev I've already experienced things that I never came across in all those years of marriage, and not afterward either. I don't know whether I'll die in the arms of one of these women, maybe I will and maybe I won't, but right now the last thing I'm planning to do is drop dead."

The retired general practitioner lowered his voice: "In the West, we're on our last legs. I saw that with my wife, I saw it with my patients, they didn't want to die, no, they wanted to live and stay healthy, but there was nothing like a lust for life anymore. Some of my patients recovered despite themselves. They didn't want to put any effort into it. All the effort had to come from the doctor. So what do you expect?"

The Polack didn't know what to say to that. What he said was: "And besides, you're still way too young yet," then he stood up right away as he saw Paul come in. He walked over to him, but differently than before. Like a true gentleman. "Paul," the Polack said, "I won't be coming to the get-together with the ladies this afternoon, I have a date."

"Great," said Paul. He had a plate full of cheese and sausage on the table in front of him. On a napkin beside the plate lay four slices of toast. "Are you having a good time? Are you going to need an interpreter?"

"No," the Polack said. "Her English is fine."

Paul wiped his mouth. "You can eat all you want here," he commented. "Make use of it. It's a waste not to, you paid for it."

"Yes, that would be a waste." The Polack was a bit disappointed by Paul's lack of enthusiasm, but of course the man's mind had been dulled by all these journeys to love. Back up in his room, the Polack lay on the bed and tried to pick up the thriller again, but the story still didn't interest him. He went to the window and looked out at the rain.

A woman from housekeeping came in to make his bed, moving skittishly around the room as though he were some brute. Right before she left, she placed two chocolate bonbons on his pillow. Then he had a good three hours to go. He looked at his phone. Nothing from the one remaining boy, nothing from his ex.

He took off his clothes, set the alarm on his phone, and lay down again. He wasn't tired but he fell asleep anyway, and when he woke up it had stopped raining. There was no need for it, but he shaved again. He staunched a nick with a bit of toilet paper, then hummed a song he remembered from his boyhood. He couldn't remember the lyrics, but he knew the melody by heart. Feeling aroused, not sexual arousal but the arousal of a child, he got dressed. The white shirt didn't look as good on him as the floral one did, he felt that it made him look a little grave, somber, but then a certain gravity did fit the situation, he was going to meet the father of his bride-to-be. That was no small thing, although he'd had little or almost no contact with his former in-laws, because his ex barely spoke with her parents.

Just to be sure, he put on his cap. The cap actually lent him something youthful.

Then he went to the closet and asked himself whether he should take along all three pies, or just one. He had been counting on one open-faced pie per woman, now it would feel like betrayal to hold onto two pies just in case. He had met his bride-to-be.

He grabbed the three pies from the closet and walked down to the lobby. At the desk he asked in his best English if they could call a cab for him. He showed the address to the receptionist, who passed it along to a colleague who passed it in turn to the manager and it was the manager who finally said: "We will arrange a car for you."

A man who worked at the desk led the Polack outside and helped him into a taxi. Not a normal taxi, apparently some kind of hotel taxi. The manager told him what the fare would be, a lot of money, almost as much as yesterday's lunch, but if you converted it into euros it wasn't all that bad. And when the new life was beginning, you don't worry about another ten or twenty euros here and there.

The Polack sat in the back, holding the pies on his lap as though they were his children. He saw the veteran coming out of the hotel with two women.

There were lots of traffic jams in Kiev. No matter how far to the east of the city they drove, the traffic jams followed. They drove and drove, first through the center of town, then they arrived in the outskirts and then in the outskirts of the outskirts and they still weren't there. The longer the trip took, the greater the Polack's fear became that no one would open the door, that he would find himself standing before a locked door, or that only the father would be at home and that he would say: my daughter left this morning for a six-month trip around the world, I'm sorry.

"Is this still Kiev?" the Polack asked.

"Kiev," the driver said.

Because the man didn't make another sound, the Polack kept quiet too. He had left in plenty of time, he wouldn't arrive late at his new love's house. But he wondered how he was supposed to get back, later. If she was even at home, Yulia. He couldn't spend the night there. That would be unseemly, even though he had put on his best pair of underpants, just to be sure. The new life was bound to bring surprises, he didn't doubt that.

After more than an hour's drive, they arrived at a row of high flats that made the Polack feel melancholy again. Imagine living in a place like this. Yes, he would rescue his bride-to-be from this architecture. Heerlen might be the ugliest city in the Netherlands, from the looks of this he'd say things could be worse. If she wanted to be saved, then she had found her savior.

"Our Manhattan." The driver pointed at the row of flats.

They stopped in front of one of the buildings. Children were playing with a cat, and a woman toting a pair of shopping bags had stopped to see who was getting out of the car. The Polack paid the man, which took a while because of a disagreement about the tip, a disagreement the Polack finally resolved to his own advantage. He was a gentleman, but he wasn't an idiot. Tips were given voluntarily, not taken forcibly. More than ten percent was ridiculous. The driver began ranting against Europe, America, and Africa in general, and the Polack in particular.

The Polack was adamant about it, though; ranting wasn't going to get anyone a bigger tip.

The road was muddy. He walked toward the tower block, stared after by the woman with the shopping bags. He looked at the apartment number on the piece of paper, and once he was standing at the entrance to the complex he looked for that number but saw only names, no numbers, only names he couldn't read. He felt the discouragement returning. The new life was so fragile, the passion could slip away so easily.

Fortunately, the woman with the shopping bags was coming his way. Holding the pies under one arm, he tried to look at her warmly, he knew that a foreigner always had to do his utmost, and he said in his best English: "Could you please help me? I'm looking for this family."

He handed her the piece of paper, which she took after placing her shopping bags on the ground. She looked at it for a long time, then pointed to a different tower block. "Over there?" he asked. She nodded and gave him a little push in the direction of the other building. Then she reached into one of her bags and pulled out a little Ukrainian flag, which she began waving.

He walked toward the tower block the woman had pointed out, and when he turned to look she was still waving her flag. She also shouted something he couldn't understand. Despite the three pies he was holding, he succeeded in saluting. That seemed fitting, for it seemed to him the older woman must be in the army, or married to someone who was in the army, someone who had fought for her country, at home or at the front, and who was prepared to do so again at a moment's notice. She would go on fighting, to her dying breath. That was the impression she'd given him. He was more than willing to salute those who had served, especially if they had pointed him in the right direction.

The tower block she'd indicated did have numbers at the entrance. Judging from the number Yulia had given him, he surmised that his bride-to-be lived on the eighth floor. He took the elevator up, followed the walkway to the apartment where he thought she must be living with her father. The number on the door matched the one on his piece of paper. If this was the right tower block, then this must be the right apartment. Behind this door he was sure to find his bride-to-be and her father. He waited for a moment without ringing the bell, he looked at his reflection in the little window, it was good that he'd decided to wear his cap, it really did make him look youthful. He turned and looked, the view remained dismal, although that could also have been the weather. He wondered how many people had jumped from this building, then rang the bell right away.

She opened the door herself. She was at home, it was that simple, his bride-to-be. She was wearing jeans, a pair of pink bedroom slippers and a dark-blue sweater, she was still magnificent.

"I'm so glad you are here," the Polack said.

And she answered, a bit amazed: "But I live here."

He took off his coat and she took it from him, then put it away in another room. He kept his cap on and held on tightly to the three pies. He was waiting for the right moment to hand them over to the family.

A man was sitting on a leather couch in the sparsely furnished living room. There were two black leather armchairs, and the Polack was directed to one of them. He shook the father's hand and introduced himself. Yulia asked what he would like to drink, tea, coffee, or something stronger. He chose tea, although he'd already seen that the father was working on something stronger.

"Who are you?" the father asked, once the Polack had settled down in the black armchair.

He had just finished introducing himself, but he was perfectly willing to do it again. "I'm Geniek. A fireman from the Netherlands. A fireman from Heerlen. My father was born in Poland. My mother was born in Germany. I'm born in the Netherlands. I speak a little bit Polish."

"Father doesn't see well," said Yulia, back now from the kitchen where he had heard her rattling with the pots and pans. "Accident at work. He sees half of what we see."

"Ah," said the Polack. "I'm sorry."

"Why?" the father asked.

"That you don't see well. Sorry for the accident at work."

"That's not your business." The father leaned back. He had gray hair and a firm jawline, he looked a little like a boxer, in any case like someone who had done heavy physical labor. The Polack worked with his hands too, maybe that was to his advantage. He was still sitting there with the open-faced pies on his lap, waiting until Yulia—who had disappeared into the kitchen again—would come back, because it seemed better to resume the conversation while she was around.

Once she came back and he had his tea, she drank tea as well, the father occasionally took a sip of his liquor, the Polack said: "I brought you something from my country, sir. From my region. We call it 'vlaai,' sir." Yulia was sitting beside him, he felt like putting an arm around her. He would have liked to touch her tenderly. It was too soon for that.

A silence descended. The father said something in Russian, and right afterward he said: "I don't understand. Why are you here?"

The Polack cleared his throat. "I'm a friend of your daughter. I brought you vlaai. It's something to eat. It's sweet. It comes in different tastes, apple, cherry, peach." He couldn't think of the English word for apricot. "It tastes good."

The Polack stood up to present the three pies to Yulia, but because she didn't look up he sat back down, and remained sitting there with the three open-faced pies on his lap. He found his bride-to-be so lovely, and even though this house smelled a bit stuffy, she smelled wonderful.

At that moment the father had a coughing fit that he suppressed by taking a drink, then he said: "You want to fuck my daughter, you want to fuck my family, you want to fuck my country, you are a foreigner."

The Polack nodded. From the sound of it, his future father-in-law had a lot of rage cropped up inside, but that didn't matter. The future father-in-law had had an accident at work that impaired his vision, then you were allowed to be angry. Rage was understandable, there was plenty of adversity, and rage usually followed on the heels of adversity, and then you also had people who were angry, even without adversity, more as a preventive measure. When you were half-blind, you were certainly allowed to ask the man who came wanting to marry your daughter: did you come here to fuck her, or have you got more going for you than that?

"Yes," said the Polack, "yes, I'm a foreigner, but I don't want to fuck your daughter, sir, or your country, or your family. My intentions are good. I brought you a gift." The man had something against foreigners, and the Polack understood that. He stood up, then knelt with the three open-faced pies in front of the half-blind man. The first box, a cherry pie, he opened while still kneeling there and said: "You can smell it, it comes from our region. Limburg. We call it '*vlaai*.'"

The man said: "I don't smell anything."

Upon which the Polack turned to his bride-to-be. "Do you have a knife?" There where nothing was smelled, one had to taste. She led him to the little kitchen, he laid the pies out on the counter, took the breadknife she proffered him, and cut the apple pie into six pieces, it seemed safest to start with apple. "I hope you are hungry," he said, and she replied: "Daddy is a good man. He suffered a lot. He doesn't like most people. But he is a decent man and a good father."

He looked at her with all the sympathy he had in him, he forced it out through his eyes, from way down in his soul. Although he actually had wanted not to think about suffering anymore. That had been thought about enough already. The new life would not be without suffering, it wasn't realistic to think that, but it would have less suffering. If not, then why call it new? Enough suffering, down with suffering. She took a few plates and placed pieces of pie on them. He took her right hand in his and told her that he loved her. Asked her to forgive him. "Forgive me," he said. "Forgive me." For if there was one thing he'd learned in the chicken coop, it was to be suspicious of love, if there was one thing the chicken coop had taught him, it was the teeming uncertainty about whether you could impose your love on people. Whether it wasn't better to abstain from doing that. Back then he had thought that he could go only to God with his love, his horrible love. Now he was in Kiev, and that's why he had taken this trip, to impose his love, that gruesome love of his, on people, despite everything, even if the people were in Kiev. No, not the people. One person. One Yulia. And this Yulia had had a reason to turn to Love Without Borders, she apparently wished to be imposed upon. He would hold her dear and at the same time ask forgiveness for his love, he would give love and ask forgiveness, not from God but from people, from one person.

They went back to the living room with the plates. The Polack walked behind her, he sat back down in his easy chair, and the half-blind man took a few bites of pie. Then he put the plate back on the table and said, loud and clear: "No." And then again: "No."

"No?" the Polack queried.

"No, this is not for us."

"You don't like it?"

"No," said the half-blind man, "it's dry and old and no taste whatsoever. Maybe you like this, in your country you eat this, maybe you Polish people eat this shit, but this is not what we eat here. We don't eat shit here."

"I'm not Polish. I'm from the Netherlands. My father was from Poland."

"Daddy is a very honest man," Yulia said, "he is one of the more honest men in Ukraine."

"This is for pigs," said the old man with something almost approaching high spirits.

"Ah," said the Polack, and he plowed through his pie anyway. The pie was indeed a bit dry, also a bit on the stale side, but still completely edible, and fortunately Yulia ate her pie too. When he was finished eating, the Polack rose to his feet and said: "I'm not a good speaker. I'm a fireman. My father was a humble man. Still alive. My mother came from the Rhineland, Germany. A humble woman. Dead."

"She died because of you," the old man said. "Mothers die because of their sons. Fathers die because of their daughters."

The Polack was determined not to be sidetracked by anything Yulia's father had to say. He went on: "I had two sons. Now I have only one son. I want to marry your daughter. I ask you, could you allow me to be with your daughter? Could you think of me as the husband of your daughter? Could you forgive me if I became your daughter's husband?"

The half-blind man sipped at his drink, wiped his lips, and looked at his daughter. Then he said: "The Russians fucked us. The Germans fucked us. The Americans fucked us. Now you come and you want to fuck us again. We are here where we live, where we belong, and other people fuck us, again and again and again. Leave us alone, go and fuck somebody else."

The Polack looked at Yulia and she said again that her father was such an honest man, her eyes were sad now as she said it. She said that he couldn't lie and the Polack felt like taking the half-blind man's hands in his to underscore his attempts to ask forgiveness, but he didn't, he didn't dare. He moved a couple of steps closer to the father. He knelt down, as though he wanted to ask him to marry him and he said: "Forgive me, forgive me, sir. I ask you for forgiveness, because foreigners fucked your country. I'm not here to fuck your country, sir. I'm here to marry your daughter."

"I have only one daughter," the man replied, "and one son."

The Polack thought about his own father, his ex, the one remaining boy, and then he asked the half-blind father to give permission for Yulia to go to the Netherlands. Then they could try and see if it would work out. It was a bit premature, he said. He knew that, he said. "It's early," the Polack said. But why wait, he asked. For what? In two days' time he would be leaving, then they'd be flying back to Düsseldorf.

Now he turned to Yulia, and he was overpowered by the past. The past he was leaving behind him now, here, in the outskirts of the outskirts of Kiev, he was saying goodbye to his past. To his boy who was gone, to the boy's pony, the farmer, the chicken coop, his ex, he said goodbye to it all, they filed past in his mind's eye and he had to hold on to something because the past made him dizzy.

"Come and visit me," he said. "If you don't like it, you go back. No harm in trying. If you like it, we stay together."

"I can try," she said hesitantly. "I can try."

The half-blind man started coughing again and then asked: "So you had a wife? She left you because you fucked her over, again and again and again? You gave her this shit to eat?"

"No," the Polack said, "we divorced because the love was over." He looked at the ceiling, as though the love had flown through it on its way out. He saw moisture spots. "The love was gone, but the child remains. The child will always be there. The child is stronger than love." Then he looked at Yulia, at her bedroom slippers, her sweater, and he didn't know what else to say.

The half-blind father opened his mouth, it looked like he was going to scream, then he stuck his finger in it and removed something that had stuck between his teeth. Then, resignedly, almost sadly, lovingly really: "My daughter is adult. Only one daughter. But she is adult.

Don't ask me. Ask her. I don't like foreigners. I don't trust foreigners. But what can I do? What can we do?"

Then the old man stood up and disappeared into what was probably his bedroom, and Yulia walked out too. She came back with the two remaining open-faced pies, and said quietly: "Take this with you. This is not for us."

The Polack nodded, it had simply been a little present, something from his own region, and he answered: "I'd like to take you with me."

"Yes, later," she whispered. "Maybe. If you send me ticket, I'll come."

Sending a ticket, practical things like that, the Polack hadn't thought about at all. Apparently, Yulia had. Whatever the case, he knew it was time to go back to his hotel. A little earlier than he'd expected, it had all gone quickly. The sensation of loss, of losing and being lost, descended on him, but nothing had been lost for good yet. She was willing to come to the Netherlands if he sent her a ticket. He would ultimately see to it that his future father-in-law came around. He would win his love, with patience and endurance and unflagging friendliness.

"Before I leave," he asked, "when do I see you?"

"Tomorrow," she said quietly, as though it were a secret, "tomorrow in your hotel. I bring friend. Okay? Three? Afternoon?"

"Yes," the Polack said, "yes. Tomorrow. Afternoon. I wait for you in the lobby. I wait for you. I miss you. You know my hotel?"

"Yes, I know your hotel. You always stay in the same hotel." Apparently, he was not the first man from Love Without Borders in her life, but that was no disaster, he was the real one. And then he kissed her hand. Just as he had always been a good fireman, he had now become a good gentleman. He picked up the two remaining open-faced pies and left the apartment.

Out on the walkway he stopped, she had come with him in her slippers. Wet snow was falling. "Aren't you cold?" she asked.

"No, no, I'm fine." Despite the two pies he was holding, he succeeded in taking her hand. "Because of you," he said. "Because of you I want to live."

She nodded and said: "Send me ticket. I will love you. See you tomorrow." To an outsider her words might have sounded cold. Who, after all, who wouldn't want you to send them a ticket? The Polack realized that, other people would detect coldness at the spot where he had stumbled upon something very different, he could see her eyes and when you saw her eyes you knew that her words were not spoken in coldness, that she was incapable of being cold.

He took the elevator down and from there he looked up to see if she was still standing on the walkway, but all he saw were two boys who yelled something at him, he couldn't make out what it was.

He walked back over the muddy path and turned around once more. Then he saw her, she was standing on the walkway and she waved to him. He waved back and shouted her name, clutching the two pies under his arm. There was no reason why they had to remain intact anymore. He wasn't going to give them to anyone else anyway, and so he waved to her and shouted her name with all the fervor he had in him. Until she went back in, then he stopped shouting. And he walked on, he wandered through the outskirts of the outskirts in search of a subway station, a taxi or any other form of transport. It was good that he was wearing his cap, the wet snow went on falling.

Close to a bigger road he asked a lady how to get to the hotel, she didn't understand him. He showed her the hotel's business card, she didn't know. He was lost. "City center?" he asked.

She nodded. Those words sounded familiar to the woman; those were words she seemed to understand. She led him to what looked like a bus stop, and there it occurred to him to offer her one of his pies as a sign of gratitude for her help, but she refused it.

After about five minutes the bus arrived, it was more like an over-sized van than a bus. The woman was apparently going in his direction, because she climbed on with him, helped him to pay.

They drove through the outskirts, the wet snow kept falling, and occasionally the Polack would ask: "City center?"

The lady nodded, gestured to him to remain seated, and while he sat there, he thought about love, how amazing it was that he had found love in this city. Maybe the human extension was right, this was the month of love for Libras.

When, after almost forty-five minutes, the lady hustled him off the bus with the words "city center," the Polack didn't recognize a thing.

He wasn't even sure if he was still in Kiev. But he was not only in love, he was also solution-oriented, and so he showed the hotel's business car to a number of passers-by, because his phone had no more battery. Until a man in a hat stopped and helped him. The man in the hat, in fact, spoke English very well, even better than the Polack. He told him that the hotel was a half-hour's walk from there, maybe twenty minutes if one walked quickly.

"I walk fast," the Polack said with the enthusiasm of the infatuated. And so he walked to his hotel through the wet snow. Fast as can be and deeply in love. When he got to the hotel, night had fallen completely, and only in his room did he notice how wet and cold he was. He took a bath, put on a robe that was hanging in the bathroom, and realized that now it was actually time for him to eat something. He didn't feel like going out. What was Kiev to him, now that he had found that for which he had barely dared to hope?

Fortunately, he still had the pies. The first box he opened was the apricot pie, and he ate half of it sitting at his desk, absentmindedly but nevertheless in love. He drank some bottled water, he didn't trust the water from the tap here, and although he wasn't really hungry anymore, he opened the second box. Absentmindedly again, he ate half the cherry pie. Then he took a couple of slugs of rum to celebrate life.

Afterward, he lay down in bed. There was a message from Wen on his phone: "Dear Libra," she'd written, "we wish you lots of happiness. We do miss you a bit, Jurek and I."

The Polack didn't feel like answering, he was thinking about Yulia. And he also had a stomachache, but he didn't worry about that. He had Yulia, she had him, life was every bit as desirable as his new woman. He loved her precisely because of her little imperfections (her front teeth), and he trusted that his imperfections and shortcomings would find favor in her eyes.

9

He awoke with a filthy taste in his mouth. On his way to the bathroom, he saw that a sheet of paper had been slid under his door. "To the participants in Love Without Borders' journey to love," it said. "At ten o'clock there will be an extra meeting in the Mozart Hall on the second floor of this hotel. We request that all of you be there punctually." Beneath it was the same text, this time in German.

He had to hurry up. In fact, the Polack had been meaning to have breakfast, but he took a long time showering and shaving, and besides, he had a stomachache. He would drink a cup of tea later on. Those souvenirs from his own region had, in any case, not agreed with him.

This time he left the new sport coat on its hanger. He pulled on a sweater and at the stroke of ten reported to the Mozart Hall. Paul was sitting at a table, there were one or two interpreters and the young man who represented Love Without Borders in Kiev, looking crestfallen. The men who were looking for love were there too, anxious to hear what was going on. The man from Recklinghausen nodded to him, so did Lucas. The other men ignored him. For a moment the Polack was reminded of his time in the chicken coop, the men reminded him of fallen angels, but he had been able to break his fall, thanks to Yulia. Mercy had looked upon him in Kiev. Pure mercy.

At last, Paul took the floor. "Men," he said, "we came to Kiev to find love. A few of you may have had other plans, but that's not what this is about. Some of you have already found love, because that can happen on the first day too, others have made progress, perhaps there is someone still waiting for that initial click. The most important quest in our lives can take a while, that's okay. Han has ended that quest. He has ended it all. Of course, we feel . . ." Paul took a big slug of water. The Polack looked at the other men and he had the idea that they were sitting there guiltily, but that might have been his imagination, maybe he was sitting there in exactly the same way. He hadn't even noticed that Han wasn't there. Was that the guilt he detected in himself? His having failed to notice Han's absence?

Now the retired general practitioner leaned over to him. "Didn't you hear about it?" he whispered. "An overdose of sleeping pills. Apparently, he'd attempted it before this. Housekeeping found him late last night, because he'd left the faucet running in the bathroom. No farewell note, nothing. He was lying there in the tub. With his raincoat on. Fuck this falling in love."

Lucas shook his head. The Polack thought he smelled of liquor. Kiev had its effect on men. And in his mind's eye he saw Han, in his dark red raincoat, lying in the tub, the boxes of sleeping pills beside him.

Paul coughed a few times. He wiped his mouth with the back of his hand. "Of course, we asked ourselves whether we, as organization, made a mistake somewhere," he said a bit hoarsely. "Whether we should have supervised the participants more closely, but something like this can happen anywhere. And Han was . . ." he took another sip of water, "a fantastic client. Han was . . ." Paul looked around, as though seeking the men's support, "one of our best clients. He had gone along with us so often, but he never gave up. He stayed optimistic. He saw love everywhere he looked. That's how we need to remember him too, as someone who saw love everywhere. He was convinced that this time he would succeed. Yesterday afternoon he told me: 'I think I've hit the bullseye this time.' He was so pleased." Paul bowed his head, the Polack had the feeling that their leader was sincerely touched, which surprised him because he thought this work had made Paul feelingless. An overdose of love, as it were. Too much desire coming from men on the lookout.

"It comes as a terrible blow to his mother too," Paul went on. "It comes as a blow to us."

No one was looking at Paul, and Paul himself seemed to have no idea what else to say, but apparently he didn't dare to put an end to the meeting. "We asked ourselves, of course: should we cancel this journey to love after this . . . after this accident? In consultation with the management board, it was decided that that would be wrong. Love is our mission. Han would definitely not have wanted us to stop now. We go on looking for love, we don't give up. That's what I wanted to say. Sure, I know the stories: Love Without Borders, that's the septic tank of love, those who can't go anywhere else go there. Absolute nonsense, men. Look around, look at each other."

Paul was sweating visibly, it looked like he hadn't slept all night, as though he had been up drinking all night, and a few of the men looked at each other. The Polack stared straight into the face of the man from Recklinghausen.

"Are we here, all of us, the septic tank of love?" Paul had a catch in his voice. "No, we are fortune hunters, friends of love, that's what we are, friends of love. Let us think of Han, let us . . ." Paul looked at the interpreters, maybe hoping that they would say something too.

"This morning I spoke to Han's mother. I told her that she had a fantastic son. That she could be proud of him. A true friend of love." Paul coughed. "I'd like us all to rise now and observe two minutes of silence for Han. *Steh auf, bitte, jetzt wird an Han gedacht.*"

The men stood up. But the Polack wasn't able to think about Han, he was filled with thoughts of the boy who was gone, and of Yulia.

The two minutes seemed to last forever, and he heard the men beside him shuffling their feet, he heard a woman talking in the corridor. In between, he saw Han in his dark red raincoat, lying in the bathtub. And the Polack also saw his vanished boy. His face had faded, but his clothes, his shoes, certain details, he could see them all clearly.

When the two minutes were over, Paul said: "That was all. Thank you, everyone. At two-thirty we'll be meeting in the lobby and taking the bus from there to the next get-together with ladies from Kiev and nearby. It looks like it's going to be a great one."

Then they left the Mozart Hall, without saying much. Men were whispering here and there. In the elevator, the Polack was alone with the veteran. They didn't say a word. Just as the Polack was about to get off at his floor, Rich said: "I told those bastards from the Child Welfare Council: 'If you people go on like this, I'm going to hang myself. Is that what you people want?' That's what I told them."

"Yeah," the Polack said. "I can imagine." Then he got off. He turned for a moment and looked at the veteran, as though to confirm that he wasn't going to hang himself this afternoon. Fortunately, it didn't seem so. The veteran radiated combativeness. He clenched his left fist, raised it above his head and shouted: "Sex I don't care about all that much, but I'm always up for a blowjob." Then the elevator doors slid shut.

The Polack lay down on his bed again. He wanted to send a message to his ex and to Jurek. Nothing came to mind, though, he couldn't find the right words. It seemed weird to say nothing about the incident with Han, but he didn't know how to bring it up. Although 'incident' was maybe not the right word.

He rose to his feet and pounded his fist against the wall a couple of times, he threw the remote control across the room. He hated Han. Now that the infatuation had blossomed, now that the new life had begun and mercy had been given him, Han had to go and remind him of the past, which had been so well, so hermetically sealed, Han had to go and awaken the Polack's desperation with a kiss. Han, of all people, Han, who could have become a friend. "I have no need of consolation," the Polack said quietly, "because those who need consoling are unable to give love."

He waited for the afternoon the way one waits for one's beloved, and in this case the afternoon and the beloved were all neatly wrapped up in one. He skipped lunch, took a bag of potato chips from the minibar. Even that he didn't finish completely. Then he went and put on his floral shirt, though the shirt smelled a bit sweaty, but he did it for Yulia and for Han.

He seated himself in a chair in the lobby. The way a dog waits for its master. Now, even though he barely knew her, he already felt lost without Yulia.

She showed up with her girlfriend and he suggested they have a drink at the hotel bar, but she said she'd rather go somewhere else. They walked the streets of Kiev. There was no more wet snow falling, although it was still cold. The Polack didn't really feel it, the cold didn't get through to him. Yulia was there, his Yulia. They went into a café that had pastries in the display window. Yulia and her girlfriend picked a pastry and the Polack took one too, even though he felt more like eating something hearty.

Then he said: "Han killed himself."

"Who is Han?"

"One of our group. A young man. Red raincoat? You must have seen him."

"Yes. Maybe." Yulia looked at her girlfriend. They said something to each other, then turned back to him: "I don't remember him, I'm sorry."

The Polack stirred his coffee. He looked lovingly at his wife-to-be and said: "My son killed himself."

"Your son?"

"My other son," said the Polack.

"That's awful." Yulia took his hand and massaged it. That felt good.

"Yes," the Polack said, "pretty awful." He took a bite of his pastry, but all he could concentrate on was the hand, the massage. The love.

"If you send me ticket, I come to Holland."

He looked Yulia straight in the eye and said: "I live in Heerlen. Do you know where that is?

"No," she said, "no."

"Not far from Germany. Do you want to live with me in Heerlen?"

"If you send me ticket, I come and I'll see."

For a moment the Polack found himself wondering how many tickets had been set to Yulia before. Because he couldn't contain his curiosity, he asked if she had traveled abroad very often.

"Only Russia. I speak Russian, my heart is Russian, my soul is Ukrainian."

"I see," said the Polack. "I see." Then he took her hand and, as though it were a confession of faith, stated: "I'll send you a ticket. And later I'll send one for your daddy too."

VII

YOU HAD TO HAVE BEEN THERE

1

It was hard, but the Polack finally convinced Jurek to go along with him to Schiphol. He had made a banner all by himself, during one of his weekend shifts at the firehouse, which said in big, red letters: "WELCOME HOME, YULIA."

Jurek told him: "She's not coming home at all, man. She lives in Kiev. That chickie's just coming to visit."

It had been a struggle, but the Polack won out; they were going to welcome Yulia together. And he did his best to avoid any more discussion about where home was to Yulia.

In the car, though, he had tried to explain that, to Yulia, Kiev would be no more than a detour on her way to her real home in Heerlen. The more he came up with pronouncements like that, the more he started believing in them. Along the way he had bought twenty-seven red roses, because she was twenty-seven, that's what she'd told him a couple of weeks earlier in a text message, when he had finally worked up the courage to ask her age. That is how he came walking into the arrivals hall, complete with banner, son, and roses. A happy man.

He took up position at the exit she'd be coming through, with the banner in his right hand and the roses in his left. Jurek had to hold the other end of the banner. He did it with distaste, you could tell from his face. At first he'd refused, but father had succeeded in convincing son in a none too subtle fashion. The Polack had said: "If you do this for me, I'll buy you a new phone. You can choose which one." That convinced the boy, there was lots he was willing to do for a new phone.

Father and son stood there with the big banner welcoming Yulia, the father down on one knee. "Do you really have to do that?" the son asked. The Polack replied: "I'm kneeling for her because I'm a gentleman, because I want her to know that that's what I am. This is how a gentleman welcomes his beloved."

"Please, Dad, they're going to laugh at you. All these people." The boy pointed to all the other people waiting in the arrivals hall.

The Polack took the boy by the arm. "I couldn't care less whether they laugh at me or not. Do you think I haven't noticed the way they laugh at me, all the time? You think I'm an idiot? Now move back so she can see the banner clearly when she comes out."

The boy had nothing more to say to that. And so they waited there, the one standing, the other down on one knee, as though he were a believer who wasn't sure whether to pray or not.

It took forever. They saw all kinds of passengers coming out, but Yulia was not among them. Occasionally the boy shouted: "Let's drop it for a minute, Dad. My arm hurts."

"She's not coming," Jurek shouted, "maybe she'll get here tomorrow."

"No," the Polack insisted, "she sent me a text message just before boarding. She's coming today, I'm sure of it."

He remained down on one knee, even when it looked like most of the passengers from Kiev had left, he didn't budge. He remained there like that, one knee on the floor, the banner in the right hand, the roses in his left. He didn't care about the people looking at him. He wasn't even sure they were looking at him. Other people must have stood here before with banners and roses. Maybe not down on one knee, but what difference did that make? Everything that had happened in his life had driven him to this perseverance, everything in his life had taught him that he mustn't let go, and he didn't. Not now. If he had wanted to let go, he should have done so before this.

There she came. She was wearing a beige coat and high heels, and she had a medium-sized blue suitcase in one hand. She looked, the Polack felt, like a movie star, and that strengthened his conviction that it was good that he had stayed down on one knee. He called out her name, he called again even louder. She looked straight ahead, she didn't look down, even though he'd done his best to make himself small for her, the big Polack had made himself small for his wife-to-be, because that was his idea of what a gentleman did, he made himself small for the other, especially for his own wife.

At last she saw him. She looked surprised, as though she had been expecting someone else, even though he had sent her selfies now and then to make the waiting more bearable. She came to him, and without rising to his feet he handed her the roses. "For you," he said, "for my future wife."

Only then did he rise to his feet and he hugged her, he gave her a kiss on the cheek. He had installed an app on his phone a couple of weeks ago to help him improve his English, and secretly he hoped that Yulia would notice. He had done it for her.

"You are so sweet," she said, holding the roses. She stood there looking a little shy and uneasy. She smiled, a frozen smile.

Then Jurek came and stood beside him, as though they actually didn't belong together, as though he had been waiting for someone else, and the Polack said: "This is my son, Jurek."

"I know," she said, "I know."

"Hi," Jurek said, almost inaudibly.

From her purse she took a present wrapped in Christmas paper and gave it to the boy. "It's just chocolates," she said, "but good chocolates from my country." The Polack looked at Jurek and waited for him to thank her, but the boy didn't say a thing. Not a word.

Then they walked to the parking garage, Yulia still smiling all the while and the Polack began worrying whether she had actually seen his banner at all. "It all went so hectically," he whispered to Jurek, "maybe she didn't see it?" Just to be sure, he and the boy unfolded the big banner again in the parking garage, in front of his car. The Polack told her that he had made it at the firehouse for her and that, as far as he was concerned, she had now come home.

"I saw it," Yulia said. "You are sweet. Welcome home, so sweet." The Polack was reassured, he put the banner and her suitcase in the trunk.

In the car he asked if it was warm enough for her, and what the weather was like now in Kiev. "Cold." She looked out the window and asked: "So this is Holland?" Did she sound worried? Or did it only seem that way?

"In the rain," the Polack said. "Holland in the rain. Where I live, there are hills. Little hills, but we don't need big hills." He laughed, she didn't laugh along with him.

The one remaining boy sat in the back seat with his headphones on. Now that she was here, now that she was finally here, it seemed as though they had used up all the topics for conversation in the endless messages they'd sent back and forth. Or was it that there was so much to talk about that they didn't know where to begin?

They stopped at a gas station and the Polack asked if she was hungry. "No." She had already eaten on the plane. Not tasty, but it was filling. At least that's what he figured from her words, and he said: "Tonight, we go to a restaurant, you tell me what you like. We have something to celebrate."

She said she would tell him what she liked, she would do that, and the Polack waited in anticipation but she said nothing more. She had once sent him a WhatsApp message saying: "I love sushi." Now she didn't mention it. She remained silent on the subject of sushi.

They drove on to the Polack's house. No one talked in the car. It wasn't a disagreeable silence, it was a cheerful, comfortable silence. Finally, they stood silently at the front door. The old house in the midst of the new life, that's how it felt. "My house," the Polack said after a bit, with fitting pride.

"So this is where you live," she mumbled. The Polack wondered whether she had been expecting something different, or if she was in fact pleasantly surprised.

"I'm a fireman, you know that. This is what you get with a fireman's salary. The front garden is small, but in the back it's nice. In the summertime you can sit there."

They went inside, and she stepped so lightly through the living room, stepping so light as a feather, as though she had cast off the bonds of the world. She looked at everything and here and there she put out her hand and touched something, a wall, a knickknack, a chair. "Where is my room?" she asked.

The Polack said: "You can stay in my room, but if that makes you uncomfortable, I can sleep on the couch. You tell me what you like."

"No," she said. "That's fine. Your room is fine."

They went upstairs. The boy remained downstairs on the couch with his phone, while the Polack saw to Yulia's suitcase, carrying it to the neatly cleaned-up bedroom.

Yulia opened a closet. She took out a dress. "What's this?"

"My ex-wife's dress, she still has a few clothes here. I don't want to throw them away. She will come and pick them up one day. She is, how do you say that? Busy? She is very busy."

Yulia sat down on the bed. It looked as though she was testing the mattress.

The Polack opened another closet and said this one was for her, for Yulia. "Empty, for you. Totally empty."

He showed her the bathroom, she brushed the shower curtain with her fingertips and sniffed at a bottle of aftershave. Then he showed her Jurek's room. "A teenager, you know teenagers, a mess. Always a mess." She pointed at a poster of some rapper on the wall. "Handsome guy."

Then they headed back to the stairs, but before the Polack could start down she pointed to the door leading to the room of the vanished boy. "What's that?"

The Polack stepped over to the door. He reached out and touched the handle. "The dead boy's room."

"Can I see it?"

"You want to see it?" She confirmed her desire to see the room. "Okay, but there's nothing to see. Nothing. Just a room." And he opened the door.

She went in, touched the bed, opened a cupboard, fingered a coat, picked up a shoe. "So fresh," was her reaction. "So fresh. Is he really dead?"

"I cannot throw the things away." The Polack felt ashamed of himself. A man who, after ten years, still couldn't throw away his dead child's things, that had to be a pretty weak man. "It hurts. It's better like this. It's a long time ago, but better like this."

"Beautiful room, beautiful light." She looked at a photo, taken at school, that had ended up on his desk. Yellowed, but still recognizable. It was him. The boy. "Beautiful boy. He looks like you."

"Not really," the Polack rebutted. "He looks like himself. He is totally unique."

They went out. He closed the door carefully and she followed him downstairs. He asked if she'd like something to drink, something strong, or wine or beer, or maybe coffee. Tea, she wanted tea. He made a pot of tea and poured himself a beer. They sat at the table then and he repeated that they would go out to eat in a bit, but that if she was hungry he could fix something for her right now. What kind of food did she like? he asked again. She said that she liked everything, and so he decided they would go to a French restaurant. A colleague had recommended a little French place he'd never been to. That's where he'd go, he thought, French food went well with the kind of gentleman he wanted to be, and with Yulia, elegant Yulia.

While she was drinking her tea, a little uncertainly, she hadn't been here that long after all, he recited the little speech he had prepared long before. The things he had said to himself twenty or thirty times already. That this was her house, that she should feel at home, that he wanted her in his life, that he wanted to be her husband. Sure, he'd never had a problem with being alone, but now that he'd met her, he wanted to be with her. In his thoughts, what he had to say had been much longer, and although there were all kinds of things he'd been meaning to say, he left it at that.

"I realize," he said then, "that you are much younger. You are twenty-seven. But . . ."

"No," she said, "age is not a problem. I hope this will work out. You are a sweet man. Maybe language is a problem? Maybe?"

"No. Language is never a problem. Language is just language. The people talk too much."

"Netherlands people?"

"No, people in general. Human beings. They talk all the time."

Then he showed her the back yard, and when evening came he changed his clothes. He put on the floral shirt again and the sport coat, maybe she had forgotten, and he asked if she wanted to take a shower. She wanted to freshen up. He showed her to the bathroom and left her to it. She had a lot to get used to. To the boy he said: "We're going to a French place for dinner. Put on something decent. For Yulia."

"Showboat." Jurek went upstairs and came back wearing a hoodie.

"You call that decent?"

"It's clean," Jurek said, "that's decent, isn't it? I don't stink."

"You stink of hair gel."

Yulia came downstairs, she smelled sweet, and then the Polack said they were going to dinner, he'd reserved a table at a nice French restaurant for the three of them, and he caught himself feeling that happiness again, Ukrainian happiness, that's what you'd have to call it.

They drove downtown. He showed her the square with its cafés, the shopping street that looked like all other shopping streets, which was only reassuring. Nothing was unusual here. Once you had seen Heerlen, you knew all of the Netherlands. "The city is not very nice," the Polack said, "but the nature is nice, around the city. Do you think our city is ugly?"

"Small," she said. "Small city. Not ugly."

They went into the French restaurant. It was little, tiny really, the people were packed in together and because it was so small, the Polack felt even bigger than usual. He took Yulia's coat and even though it was supposed to be a good restaurant, you had to hang up your own coat. The Polack didn't mind that at all. Still, just to be sure, he said: "This is a very good restaurant."

"Yes," Yulia said, "I know."

They sat down and the Polack ordered a bottle of red wine. "Recommend something nice," he told the waitress, who turned out to also be the owner of the restaurant. "But I don't eat meat," he added hastily.

"Let's start with your drinks," she said sternly.

The wine came, the Polack tasted. It tasted lovely, he thought. They raised their glasses in a toast. He looked deep into Yulia's eyes and said: "To our new life."

The proprietress came to tell them that, off the menu, there were also fresh snails. Escargots.

"Do you like escargots?" the Polack asked.

And Yulia said: "I don't know." Jurek said: "Snails, Dad. They're called snails." "Do you like snails?" "Snakes?" she asked. Jurek burst out laughing, he roared with laughter, but then he explained it to Yulia, because he was a sweet boy, difficult but sweet, just like his brother. "You find snails in the garden."

Yulia nodded. It was, the Polack was afraid, a nod out of courtesy. Now that the wine had been tasted, he repeated it, just to make sure: "I don't eat meat."

"And fish?" the proprietress asked.

"No, not really."

"This is a French restaurant. I'll see what the kitchen can do for you."

"But there are vegetarians in France too, aren't there?" he asked germanely.

She shook her head. "No fish, no meat, no dairy products, real French people don't do that."

The Polack ignored the prices, because he felt that paying too much attention to them did not befit a gentleman. The days of penny-pinching were over. "Order what you want," he urged Yulia. "This is the most beautiful day of my life."

Because the wine was so delicious and because love, especially new love, makes one reckless, he talked Yulia into ordering the escargots. And steak with fried potatoes as entrée. Instead of the steak, he said, he himself would have an egg. "Just a nice, normal fried egg," he told the proprietress, who replied: "This isn't a lunchroom, but if you want a fried egg perhaps the chef de cuisine can fix one for you."

"A fried egg with spinach," the Polack said.

Jurek said: "I'd like to try snails for once."

Yulia looked at the boy and said: "You look so adultlike."

"Yes," the Polack said, "he's very wise for his age. He is big." He was drinking most of the wine because, in addition to the recklessness, the remains of the awkwardness were still present too.

When the escargots arrived, Yulia said: "Oh, now I know." She ate only two snails, and Jurek on second thought was none too fond of them either, so the Polack ended up stuck with a plate of about thirteen escargots. He asked himself whether the gentleman-vegetarian was supposed to eat the leftovers too, even if the leftovers consisted of snails. He ate them anyway just to be sure, leftovers were always okay for the vegetarian. The snails tasted mostly of garlic butter.

His main course came: a plate of vegetables, an order of fried potatoes, and an egg, sunny-side up. "You don't eat meat?" Yulia asked.

"No. I told you, no?"

"But you eat those little things? And in Kiev you ate meat?"

"Sometimes. Only sometimes. With nice people. With very nice and special people."

"Special?" Yulia left half the steak on her plate too. She was a light eater, it seemed, except for the dessert, crème brûlée, which she finished in a flash.

"How is your brother?" he asked her; despite all his qualms, conversation went with the gentleman he had become, and with love.

"I don't want to talk about him."

The Polack ordered a dessert wine, but halfway through it he remembered that he was driving home. He gave it to his new lady, who knocked it back greedily. She was delighted with the dessert wine. If she was happy, then so was he.

The Polack asked for the bill, even though it was still fairly early; they could have remained seated for a while, but he longed to be alone with his new lady. The bill came. He had been prepared for a steep bill, but the price of their drinks still felt like a kick in the head. Yet he paid with the resilience of the gentleman vegetarian, and then they drove home. Jurek sat down to play a game on his phone and the Polack asked his new lady whether she was tired.

"A bit," she said.

He showed her to the bedroom. "Can I take a shower?" she asked.

"Yes, of course," the Polack said.

"Do you have a towel?" He told her there was a towel ready for her in the bathroom, he had bought new ones. The old ones had been washed far too often.

She went to the bathroom. It took a while before he heard the shower running, and he wondered what she could be doing in there. Maybe she was removing her makeup, and at that point the thought came up that she might be in there alone, crying. Sitting on the edge of the tub, distraught. Lost. She missed Kiev, her friends, her father who hated foreigners but could do nothing to stop his daughter. He saw the man again in his mind's eye, angry and yet innocent.

The Polack just sat on the bed, waiting for his new lady to come back. He pushed away the thought that she was in there all alone, weeping. She was simply getting spruced up. It was taking a long time, but after a long trip like that she of course wanted to bathe and see to herself well. Everything had to be cleaned.

At last, she came back. She was wrapped in a towel and she lay down on her side of the bed, under the blankets with the towel still wrapped around her. On the side where his ex had always lain. The Polack felt like saying something, something that had come up in him before, during all those weeks that he had waited for Yulia to arrive. No living goes on here, he wanted to say. Here, we forget to live. The new life is life itself. Now we are going to live. Because you're here, Yulia, now we're going to live. We forgot to do it, we didn't dare, we dreaded it. There was no living here, here we died slowly.

It didn't work that well in English, but he tried anyway. "We didn't live here."

"No?" she asked.

"No." He felt an unexpected rage welling up in him. It was like a wave washing over him, taking him with it. An entire lifetime of bottled-up rage rose up, strangled him, crushed him. He felt thrown against the wall.

"No," he shouted, "we forgot to live. We couldn't live." He saw that his voice, his booming voice, startled her. As though it were her fault, as though she were to be taken to account for other people's disabilities. He saw right away how unjust that was, and he corrected himself, he laid a hand on the blanket and in his usual, quiet, almost whispering voice, he said he was so glad she was here, because she represented life itself.

"Oh." She shook her head, which he took as a sign of compassion and modesty. Of course, she didn't want to represent life all on her own.

The Polack undressed, keeping his underpants on, and crawled under the blanket too. He snuggled up against her. Along with the rage, he had felt a brief moment of intense lust, the desire to rip the towel off of her, but now he was himself again, no longer in a rage, no longer aroused either, and he caressed her through the blanket and the towel. "Are you sad?" he asked.

She shook her head.

"You can tell me everything."

She said she wasn't said, and he snuggled up even closer, so that she crawled further away from him. As though she wanted to crawl out of bed, as though she wanted to crawl all the way back to Kiev. "No, I'm not sad." Then she turned to face him. "But it's our first night. By the way, I stopped smoking."

"Great." The Polack sniffed at her hair. "Yes, I can smell it. You quit smoking."

Then she was quiet again. The first night, it was their first night. Even if it didn't feel that way, it felt familiar. He had looked forward to this moment, he had experienced it so often in his thoughts that it felt like the twentieth, the thirtieth night.

"Maybe we should wait a bit," she said hesitantly, but in her lovely eyes he thought he saw desire.

"Of course. We can wait. As long as you want. No hurry." There was no rush, he said, the important thing was that she was here. That she had to settle in, he understood that, he understood everything, he wanted to understand everything. Had he been too hasty? Too impatient? And she said: "There are so many things I want to tell you, but language is a problem."

The Polack repeated that language was never a problem, that she didn't need to be afraid of that. "I remained silent much of my life. I like to remain silent." And he spoke her name. "Yulia," as though saying her name would bring her closer to him. Simply speaking that name already produced closeness, enough for now. And later, well, he would see.

She just lay there and he said nothing more, he was as good as his word, he did what he had done all his life. Then, suddenly, she started crying. The Polack didn't know how to react, especially since he didn't know why she was crying. Was he making her cry? Was his presence not what she had expected? Could it be that he made her, even her, think of death? He didn't know what to do. Could he touch her? All he knew of consolation were Beckers's wife and the chicken coop. Consolation was not always benign, not everyone could handle it.

He just wanted to be a good gentleman, but when it came to consoling, his intuition abandoned him. Should he ask her questions? Why are you crying? Was that why his boy had vanished, because he who wanted so badly to be a good father didn't know how to console? It was understandable, running away from someone else's sorrow. After some hesitation, he put one hand on the blanket and with the other reached under the blanket and took her hand. And he asked if she missed Kiev, if she missed her father and her friends. She said "yes". The crying didn't stop. He was no replacement, he couldn't replace what she was missing, and even though he knew he shouldn't take it personally, he still did.

Then he worked up the courage to ask the question he hadn't wanted to ask, that frightened him. He would almost say, the question that destroyed him, he asked it anyway because even if he got the answer that he feared he would be able to live with that, he was in fact already defeated. He could live with any answer at all. There was only one real invincibility, he had learned that in the chicken coop: to be utterly defeated. "Do you want to go back home?" he asked.

He feared the answer, but he would survive it all.

This was a home, for her too, even if it still had to grow, the home, to grow like a plant, the home would twine its way around her like woodbine. But there was also another home. He had hoped to deny it, he hadn't wanted to think about it, and before the first night had really even started, that other home forced itself upon him. They hadn't said anything about that at Love Without Borders, that those who looked for love and a better life in the West could get homesick, that they could be overtaken by a longing for their home country, even if the future there did not seem particularly rosy, even if he, thinking of her city, saw the drab, moist apartment where she lived with her half-blind and furious father, in the outskirts of the outskirts of Kiev.

She squeezed his hand, she didn't let go. She said: "I'll stay here. I'm not going back now, but can I sleep in the dead boy's room?"

He looked at her, looked right in her teary face. He dried it with the back of his hand, the other hand, the hand she wasn't holding, and he asked: "Are you sure?"

She nodded. Then he said that they could always go on vacation together to Ukraine, to visit her father, her friends. The door to Ukraine had not been thrown shut. Yulia lay quietly beside him. It was as though she hadn't heard what he had said.

"I won't touch you," he said. "I'm not that kind of man." He wanted to say more, that the rage had left him and that that was good. Lust had become a rarity in his life, but he could perform his manly duties, no need for her to worry about that: he was a gentleman. When she was ready for lust, then he would perform his duty. Waiting was no problem. He told her none of this. They lay there hand-in-hand in the conjugal bed and he could have lain there like that all night. This was enough. Nothing more was necessary. Not now, maybe never.

It was Yulia who broke the silence. "I know, you are not that kind of man. But I'd like to be alone. I'd like to be in the dead boy's room. I'm sorry."

Then he stood up. He knew what he had to do. In his underpants, he went to the vanished boy's room.

It wasn't late. The one remaining boy was still up. Sounds were coming from the living room, he was still down there gaming. Later, when Yulia was asleep, when she was asleep alone the way she wanted, he would send Jurek to bed.

Yulia followed him, still wrapped in the towel, and for a moment there was an echo of lust anyway, the memory of lust, but in the vanished boy's room, death was stronger.

He opened the door, he turned back the blanket on the bed. "It's a small bed."

"I'm not a big woman." She was standing beside him. She hesitated, with her lovely eyes and her half-crooked teeth, she hesitated and he had no trouble imagining that she was no longer sure whether she should try to sleep in this child-sized bed. Who would want to lie there? Who would want to sleep with the thought of the dead child? "I hope you don't mind," she said, and she clasped at the towel as though it was all she had left to hold on to. Only the towel still, nothing else, only that.

"No," he said. This house was her house, the vanished boy's room was her room too. He said it was no problem if she wanted to lie in there, that it was all right, that she didn't have to be afraid, he would wake her in the morning. He also said that he would long for her from his own bed, but he said that in Dutch. Then she crawled into the vanished boy's bed.

"It's strange," she said.

He nodded.

"He feels so alive."

"We keep him alive," the Polack said.

"He is a ghost."

"No, he is not a ghost. He is our son." He knelt beside the bed the way he used to kneel, tonight there was no reading aloud. We. He'd said "we," but his ex had given up the struggle. His ex wanted to live. How could one live without betraying the dead? He was going to start living again, without betraying the dead boy, he was different. Not better, different.

The Polack laid his hands on the blanket. "We belong together."

"You are a strange man," was what she said. He gulped a couple of times, surplus saliva, then he said that it was true, that he knew that, normal but still strange, in the eyes of others at least, that was one reason why he was silent, to avoid the verdict of others. That's what he wanted to say, but he didn't say it anymore.

Ever since he had moved into the chicken coop, people looked at him differently and that's why he looked differently at people too. They had become strangers to each other, he and people, but not so strange that the people had to worry about it. He belonged among them, the Polack was one of them, but still.

Kneeling beside her bed, one hand on the child's blanket, he whispered that she should go to sleep, that she would sleep well here. That he, as far as the Polack knew, the boy, Borys, had always slept well here too. Then he had nothing more to say. He was overcome by fatigue, he was exhausted, wanted to sleep too. The Polack said that Yulia could always come to him, even in the middle of the night. She could wake him. If she was scared. If she was homesick. If she was thirsty. And he also asked whether they belonged together. Whether that was really true?

It was true, she replied, and she added, squeezing his arm as she did so, that she had so much to tell him, so much, but that it was impossible because language was a problem. This time he didn't have the strength to contradict her, and straight through all the longing and the hope, through all the love he didn't doubt, that he would never doubt for a moment, he saw a strange woman lying in the dead boy's bed.

2

The Polack waited for Yulia to say that she no longer needed to sleep in the dead boy's bed. That she had grown accustomed, accustomed to the Polack, accustomed to the house, accustomed to Jurek, that the moment had come when she could lie beside him. He was patient.

She was afraid to go out on the street alone, even though she didn't talk about it. He noticed it, she just never went outside alone, on the days he had to work she stayed inside, and after he had noticed this a few times he asked Jurek if he would keep a bit of an eye on Yulia. "She's not your mother," the Polack said, "I know that. Ask her if she needs anything. Help her out a bit. Please. You're a sweet boy, you know."

"It's only because you don't understand what she says," Jurek replied. "She's not happy here, anyone would be unhappy here. I want to get away from here too, and as soon as I finish school that's what I'm going to do."

The Polack came to terms with this answer by thinking about puberty. What else could you expect from an adolescent? Straight through the armor he could see the softness inside his one remaining son.

"Just humor me, okay?" he said. "Help her out a little." The boy's remark about unhappiness was one he tried to ignore. It wasn't a good idea to react to all of an adolescent's provocations. Of course Jurek wanted to get away, adolescents always want to get away, at least healthy adolescents do.

First Jurek said that he didn't feel like it, that he had better things to do, that there was no reason for him to worry about a chickie who belonged in Kiev and who'd been lured to Heerlen under false pretenses, while no one should ever be lured into coming to Heerlen at all. "I didn't lure her," the Polack said, "love is what lured her. And now I've heard enough from you."

Finally, despite it all, Jurek went outside with Yulia once. He didn't want to talk about it much. It seemed as though they were starting to warm to each other, or at least accept each other. Maybe because they had something in common, they were both at the Polack's mercy. Had Yulia really chosen for him, the way he claimed, the way he wanted to believe? Or was it actually fate in disguise? He had seen her, he had picked her, she had let herself be picked.

He did his best to make his new lady feel at much at home as possible. The Polack went out and bought the food Yulia liked. Soup, she was crazy about soup. Chicken soup, tomato soup, beet soup, lentil soup, beef bouillon. She ate soup as though no other food existed, until Yulia stated that a bit of lamb would be fine with her too. He had found a teacher for her, a retired Dutch-language teacher who gave lessons to foreigners these days. He wasn't exactly sure whether the teacher had actually retired or if she'd had a nervous breakdown, whatever the case she had stopped teaching adolescents, only adult foreigners. And that's what Yulia was, an adult foreigner. She went to her Dutch lesson, and she thought Dutch class was fun, *leuk*. In any case, that's what she said. "*Leuk*," she'd say. "*Ja leuk*." She learned a few words with which she peppered her conversation, aptly or no, and said at least once a day that language was a problem. The Polack always objected. If anything was *not* a problem, it was language. Jurek and Yulia played games on the computer more often these days, games the Polack had never wanted to play, things for which he had no patience, that he didn't understand. No language was needed for the games, that at least was true.

And about five weeks later, Yulia said: "I can sleep in your room." They'd had lentil soup for dinner, Thai lentil soup.

She was playing games with Jurek on the computer and the Polack was sitting across from them, drinking a cup of tea. He could have watched TV, he could have read the paper, but he looked at Yulia, that was enough for him. He was, he knew now for sure, not only a silent Polack, but also a strange Polack. He saw it in the boy's eyes, in his affectionate mockery, in his not-entirely disguised embarrassment. What it was that made him strange, he didn't know, only that he was. He had resigned himself to it, to that strangeness. Which is why he sat there quietly, looking at his new lady, almost happy. "You trust me?" he asked.

All this time he had thought it was a lack of trust that kept her from coming to lie with him, that caused her to sleep in the dead boy's room where she said she slept like a baby.

"I've always trusted you, but I was not ready."

The Polack could imagine that, that she wasn't ready to take that step, the step from Kiev to his bedroom. Now she had reached that point, she had arrived definitively in Heerlen. He was ready too, ready to lie in one bed with her, ready to do with her what, according to Love Without Borders, people in love just happen to do with each other. That's what he was, after all, a Polack in love, even more than just a strange Polack. He wondered whether they should go upstairs already, or whether they should wait, she was still so involved in that computer game. She got caught up in it, just like Jurek. Until he told the boy: "And now it's time for you to go to bed. Have you actually done your homework?"

The boy mumbled something under his breath and the Polack assumed it was a "yeah." Besides, this wasn't moment to get into an argument with Jurek, this was the moment that Yulia moved from the dead boy's room to the Polack's bedroom. The big moment.

The game was shut down. "What were you two playing, anyway?" The answer to that question was inaudible too, and the Polack had no problem with that. The question was more important than the answer. This was no cross-examination, this was a conversation with one's own son.

First the boy went upstairs and then the Polack took the teacups to the kitchen, and Yulia called out after him: "It's funny, your son is closer to me age-wise than you."

The Polack came back from the kitchen. He was nervous somehow, much more nervous than when he'd picked her up at the airport and he had knelt with that banner in the arrivals hall.

"Yes," said the Polack, "funny." To which he added that it was good that she'd made contact with Jurek, at least he said something to that effect, insofar as his English allowed, and she replied: "*Ja, goed.*" Because the Dutch lessons weren't having too much effect as of yet.

They climbed the stairs, she in front, he behind, and he placed a hand lightly on her buttocks, more to give her a little push than that he was driven by lust.

Then they were standing at the door to the dead boy's room. She hesitated. "I get my T-shirt." They went inside and took her T-shirt off the bed. She closed the bedroom door carefully and a few moments later they were standing side-by-side in the bathroom, brushing their teeth.

He rinsed his mouth and she washed her face with a washcloth. She said: "You have nice teeth."

"Thanks."

"Clean."

"Yes," the Polack said. "I'm careful with my teeth, I'm careful with my body. For a fireman that's important."

She nodded, and the Polack turned first and went to his bedroom. He undressed, ran his hands over his nearly bald head, he was reminded of his ex. Ever since the new lady had come to town, she had stayed more and more in the background. He'd asked if she'd like to meet Yulia, but she said: "No, it's still too early for that."

Yulia came out of the bathroom. She hadn't wrapped herself in a towel. She was wearing a nice pair of red panties and a matching bra. She lay down beside him the way one does that with one's partner. He looked at the ceiling because he didn't dare to look at his new lady, frightened as he was of being overpowered by something more powerful than he was, by something that might hurt her. Without looking at her, he let his hand creep across the sheet and the featherbed to her arm. He took her arm and the chicken coop came to mind, where he had found out about God's love. One wasn't supposed to survive God's love. He had escaped it, but whether that was an achievement or a defeat, he wasn't sure. Maybe you weren't supposed to survive love in general—that's also why he didn't dare look at his new woman.

He felt her warm arm, further than that he didn't dare to go. He kept staring at the ceiling, he didn't know what she was looking at. It was all right like this, everything was all right. She had grown accustomed to him, that she had come to lie beside him now was a sign that she was going to stay, that she would turn her back on Kiev and her father's dismal apartment.

"You can do with me what you did with your ex-wife. I'm ready," she said.

That was love, that he would do with her what he had done with his ex, if he could only remember what he had done with his ex. The memories had faded. The feeling remained, a vague sense of lack, a feeling of incomprehension and, above all, death. When he thought about his ex he thought about the locomotive from which he had scraped his son; his ex was a locomotive that would never let him go. He let go of Yulia's arm and began kissing her, unexpectedly, unexpected even to him. He tasted her toothpaste, he smelled her facial cream, and he couldn't understand why he had waited so long, what he had been waiting for. For her, but what had she been waiting for? He didn't dare to go any further than her face, he held himself in check, he could do no other.

She pushed him away and said: "Don't be polite. I know you are not polite."

He asked what she meant and she said: "You are like other men. I know you are like other men."

Strangely enough, that sounded reassuring, he was simply like other men. Not strange, not peculiar, just like the others. He took off her bra, he kissed her breasts. Never before had he seen these breasts so clearly, he had caught the occasional glimpse in the bathroom. The breasts delighted him, just as he had been delighted by the observation that he was like other men.

Her breasts were beautiful, so unlike those of his ex, although he couldn't have explained where the difference lay. He was no expert, he was not the kind who gaped at other people's nakedness, at most he caught sight of the nakedness of the men of C squad. He was confronted with their nakedness, there was no gaping involved.

He played with Yulia's nipples for a moment, but he was afraid of hurting her, the way he was afraid of hurting people.

"Do with me what you did with your ex-wife," she said again, and she looked at him as though she knew no other desire but this, that there should be done with her that which had also been done to the Polack's ex, as though she would be denied something if she didn't receive exactly the same treatment. The ex she had never met, who now lived with a man who believed that people had no other need than to be given care.

The Polack told Yulia that he wanted to do "better things" with her, but she didn't want better things, she wanted exactly the same things. "I will be your wife?" she asked, as if that implied that she must then receive the same treatment. Good or bad, that didn't matter, it had to be the same.

"I couldn't make love to my wife anymore," he said at last. "That's the story. Not often. Not really love." That was enough said, he figured, a sufficient explanation. That the same offered no solution, that the same was a dead-end street. It had to be different, completely different.

"Oh." She looked at him, shyly but also provocatively. He thought about how she had spent all those nights in the dead boy's bed, the bed that must now smell of her.

Then she took hold of his cock and began massaging it, kneading it, as though lust lived inside her too, and he pulled off her panties, no longer fearful and polite. It had to be different. He fingered her and remembered the instructional videos his ex had shown him, that he now had to make figure eights with two or three fingers, and while he was making figure eights on her virtually clean-shaven cunt, first with two and then with three fingers, it seemed for a moment as though the lust was about to vanish. It felt as though he were running through a drill at the firehouse, but the lust returned just as God had returned, there in the chicken coop. God had forsaken him and then come back. They resembled each other, the lust and God, they came and went but almost never at the right moment. Fickle they were, capricious masters.

He entered her slowly and he said: "I like a bit of hair. You don't have to shave yourself completely."

"What do you mean?"

"Your hair. Down there. Without hair is so empty."

"Okay," she said, "language is a problem, but now you can do with me what you did with your ex-wife."

"I can fuck you?" he asked. The word excited him, unexpectedly, as though all of the commandments and prohibitions were rolled up together in that word, as though violation and remorse were confirmed in a single word.

"Yes," she said, "fuck me. Please. Fuck me. You are not a silent man. You talk all the time."

"You changed me." Then he began fucking her with all the hope and love he had in him and ultimately with the lust that resembled God and maybe even was God, and when he came he didn't dare to ask whether she had come too, but after a bit he did anyway.

"Not for now," she said.

"Shall I do something?"

"No. Just hold me a bit."

He held her tight and she asked: "Can I stay here?"

The Polack told her that of course she could stay here, that she was his woman, that she could stay here forever. In this bed that was her bed. In this house that was her house.

"You don't know me," she said.

"That's better," he replied. "Much better. We don't have to know each other; we have to love each other. The more we know, the more difficult it is."

He waited until she fell asleep. It took a long time. She tossed and turned, she held him tight, let go of him again. Only when her breathing grew calm and regular could the Polack fall asleep too.

3

That was how they became man and wife, they did what people in love do with each other, what couples usually keep on doing, even when they are no longer infatuated with the other: they made loving use of each other's sex organs. When the Polack slept at home, he went to bed with her, when he slept at the firehouse he called her in the evening, although during those telephone conversations in particular it was the silences that struck him. Silences he tried to fill by humming, and sometimes Yulia hummed back. Then he knew that he had reached her, that she was doing well.

When he slept at home Yulia only wanted to go to sleep after they had made love, as though the absence of sex, now that he was lying beside her, unleashed a deep insecurity in her. A different kind of silence, one she found intolerable. She demanded it, the lovemaking. She wouldn't let him sleep until it had happened, she grabbed his dong and played with it until the sleep left his body. She lay down on top of him and said: "I'm here. Do you understand me?" And he replied: "Yes, I understand." Then he performed his husbandly duty anyway, although it was more than just that. Duty sounded so distant, as if it were work, the lovemaking, the loving. No, it wasn't like that. There was love. He said that to himself, he said it to her, he said it to the men of C squad, he said it to the check-out lady at the supermarket and to the girl at the Japanese restaurant, because Yulia still really loved sushi. He said it to anyone who would listen to him.

And she, the new wife, went to Dutch lessons, she played computer games with the one remaining boy, she walked the streets of Heerlen, she looked at the houses, she avoided the city's dogs because she didn't like dogs at all. Sometimes they went shopping together, on rare occasions she went shopping alone, although she seemed to find that scary. They walked down the shopping street, they hiked in the hills. But she was not fond of long walks, and so they never reached the village where he'd hoped they were going. "Pretty, isn't it?" He pointed at the hills, the fields, the trees, windmills in the distance. If this wasn't pretty, what was?

He encouraged her to undertake more things on her own, to be less dependent on him. Even when he gave her a slip of paper with exactly what they needed from the supermarket and practiced pronouncing the words with her, he noticed that she had not yet conquered her fear of the unknown. It would take some time. She was frightened by people. At least, by the people in this town, people she couldn't understand. Nevertheless, she elbowed her way through the crowds. Sometimes he went looking for her, when he felt she had been gone too long, and he would find her walking down the shopping street with the groceries. "Are you lost?" he asked.

Then she would tell him that she hadn't lost her way, but that she was walking home slowly. That she was looking at things. Then she would point at a sparrow, as though there were no sparrows in Kiev.

"Okay," he said then, and took her arm, he didn't believe her. He feared that she really had been lost and that one day she wouldn't come home at all if he didn't go looking for her in time, that one day she would go walking in the hills and lose her way, would vanish, that was what he feared, and the fear was greater than the lust.

She called her father once a week, and he always had the feeling that she was arguing with the man. The way she talked to him, the way she sometimes remained silent for minutes on end, as though the father in Kiev had launched into a tirade she could only undergo, that she didn't dare to interrupt. Maybe that was how she'd always conversed with the old man in the musty apartment: he spoke, she listened. The Polack imagined that her father was leveling accusations at her, accusations actually meant for him. Why didn't you stay here, Yulia? What are you doing with that old Polack? He doesn't love you, he's just venting his lust on you. The Polack could imagine the old man saying just that, albeit in Ukrainian. Later, when she grew accustomed to this place, he fantasized, he would go to Kiev, they would go to Kiev together, as man and wife, and would win the heart of the old man as well. He would tell him that he was not some old Polack venting his lust on a young woman from Kiev. He would describe the state of being in love, of searching and finding. The life, the enlivenment. What he had seen in her when he first saw her amid all the other women: the joy. How he had picked her up at the airport. How she had come home. To him, the Polack. He would take the banner, which was packed away somewhere in the house now, to Kiev as a souvenir. He would look up the Ukrainian word for "forgiveness."

What he wanted, in fact, was to win the love of everyone, of his ex, his friends—that is to say, the men of C squad, for he didn't have many other friends—of Jurek. Only the love of his own father he was no longer interested in winning, there was nothing to win there. That was over. The love of the boy who had vanished, he didn't need that either, one can expect nothing from the dead. You had to leave them be. You had to leave them alone, however hard that might be.

Sometimes Yulia cried. One time he found her crying in the kitchen, another time sitting on the toilet, crying, and one Tuesday afternoon he found her crying in the back yard. The time she'd been crying in the back yard he'd said: "You are not happy." There was no getting around it. She cried too often. She shook her head. "You cry," he said, casting about for the English word for "homesick."

"Sometimes I'm happy."

He wanted to hold her; all he did was take her hand. "How can I make you happy?"

"It's okay, I'm okay. It's just so confusing."

"What?"

"You, the city, the language, everything."

Then they went into the house together, hand in hand, and he thought: she needs a space of her own. Where she can work, where she can learn Dutch, where she can learn and grow and above all where she can cry in private. He understood that she had a right to her tears. She, who had come all the way from Kiev had a right to that if anyone did. She who had left father, city, and girlfriends behind, who had chosen to become the wife of a man she barely knew. He needed to give her some room. She cried out on the street and on the toilet because she had no room of her own to cry. In the bedroom, her suitcase was still standing beside the bed where he had slept all those years with his ex. A new bed was expensive, a new bed was overdoing it, the old one was still fine, and next to it Yulia's suitcase remained standing, or rather, lying. A few times already he had asked her whether she didn't want him to put away the suitcase, but she didn't want that. It's true, she had taken most of the things out of the suitcase and put them in the closet he had emptied out for her, yet still he often found her lingering over the suitcase. There were certain things she hadn't taken out, a few books, lingerie that she for some reason preferred to keep in her suitcase rather than in his closet. This he also blamed on the fact that she had no space of her own, a place that was all hers and no one else's.

He needed to empty out the dead boy's room, there was nothing else that could be done, he needed to turn it into the new wife's room. All these years he had avoided it, it was one of the reasons for not getting rid of this house after the divorce, if he sold the house he would kill the dead boy all over again, but now enough was enough. The new wife was here and she needed some space. The dead need no space, they lie in their graves.

It couldn't go on forever, there was shelf life that went with keeping someone alive. There was a new wife whom the dead boy had never met. Could the Polack really expect her to live among his things and cry among his things because of a sorrow he only halfway understood himself—what did he know of homesickness?—and which, according to her, was a linguistic problem? That was asking too much. He had no right to burden her with the past.

He fretted over Yulia, about the way he wanted to live with her, while he was frying crepes, because she'd never eaten them, typical Dutch crepes. And while he was frying them the last bit of doubt disappeared, yes, it had to come to an end sometime, the fear, the denial, the avoidance. An end to honoring the dead who had no use for your honor. She was here, he should honor her, Yulia needed to be honored. He slapped the dishtowel against the counter, because he had made a decision. The photo of Jurek when he had just learned to walk was still stuck to the fridge, and the Polack realized that there should be a photo of Yulia on the fridge, that would help too.

When the crepes were done and she was telling him that they had things like this in Kiev too, he said: "I will turn the dead boy's room into your room, a room for you alone."

He saw something like delight in her eyes, but not for long, her expression went serious again right away. From the very first moment he'd seen her she had looked serious, as though she knew that love was no joke. "So I have to sleep there again?"

"No, no," he said. "You sleep with me. But you live there. When you want. It will be your room."

She nodded, and the three of them settled down to eating the crepes, sugar for him, cheese and bacon for Yulia and Jurek. After dinner she and the one remaining boy played together on the computer. She said nothing more about the dead boy's room, not that evening when they were making love and he felt the unexpected desire that always made him uneasy, and not the next morning either. Just to be sure, he asked her if everything was okay, and she replied: "Yes, yes."

Early in the morning on his day off, he called Wen. "I don't mean to bother you," you said, "but we need to talk about something. I want to empty out the boy's room. What do you think? Sorry to spring this on you."

Silence.

"Wen?"

"Yeah."

"What do you think?"

"It's time to do that, Geniek. It's time. It had to happen sometime. But it still comes as something of a shock, yeah."

"I'm sorry."

"Doesn't matter."

"Do you want me not to?"

Silence. "No, do it, yes."

"Is there anything you want to have? Shall I wait with emptying it out until you . . . Do you want me to save something for you?"

"Are you going to save something for yourself?"

Now it was his turn to be silent. "No. We have the photos."

"That's right, we've got those. I don't need anything else either. It's too long ago. It's fine this way. Believe me. It's fine. What are you going to do with the room?"

"It's going to be Yulia's room."

"Oh," she said, "Yulia's room. So she's going to replace him. Yulia's going to replace Borys."

"No, Yulia replaced you. I mean, she didn't replace you. Why do you have to start in about replacing? Now I've got that word stuck in my head. She's going to use his room as her space. Wouldn't you like to meet her now? Shall we come by sometime?"

"After the move. Oh, I didn't tell you that. We finally found something. In Eys."

"Eys. Nice surroundings. Not far from Wahlwiller. Interesting."

"No, not far from Heerlen either. Once we're over, when it's done with, I'll come and get my things, my precious things. And is everything all right with you? Have you started speaking Ukrainian yet?"

"I'm in love," the Polack said slowly. "Life has begun."

It was quiet for a moment at the other end. "That's nice."

"I just forgot to live. You have to be strong in order to live. I wasn't strong enough."

"And now you are?"

"Yes," he said, "now I am."

"What a pity, what a terrible pity that you weren't strong enough to live while you were with me."

"Yeah," said the Polack. "A pity. A terrible pity." Then they hung up.

That same day the Polack emptied out the boy's room. Everything. The desk, the bed, the sheets, the toy animals, the soccer cards, the posters, the books, the games, the shoes. The only time he hesitated was with a pair of shoes, baby shoes. He put them at the bottom of the closet in his bedroom, but otherwise he was ruthless. Yes, that's the way it felt, ruthless. Cleaning up the past was ruthless work. And then he realized: I should keep something for Jurek, I should put something aside for him. He took an empty shoebox, put the baby shoes in that, a notebook, a comic book picked at random, two soccer cards, a stuffed animal (a mouse), a T-shirt, a school picture, a toy car he found at the back of the cupboard, a school essay, a few blocks of Lego, one sock, a joystick that went with a computer game, and after a moment's hesitation he added a pair of gym shorts. Then he closed the shoebox and wrote "Borys" on the lid. When the moment came, when Jurek was ripe for it, he would give him the shoebox and say: this was your brother. You can keep it as a memento.

The rest could go. He worked like a man possessed. Whatever could be burnt was burnt in the back yard, as though it were a barbecue, a barbecue in winter. He built a small, manageable fire in the yard, but not to roast meat on, to put away the past, to say farewell to it, to announce that it had passed. What couldn't be burnt went to the garbage collectors. He chopped it to pieces and when Yulia came home from Dutch class she asked what he was doing.

"I am making space for you."

Jurek came home from school. "What are you doing?" he wanted to know too. "What the fuck is going on here?"

"I'm making space for Yulia."

The one remaining boy ran upstairs, the Polack went after him, and the boy looked at the room that was now empty, stripped, as though a renovation was underway, as though this room was about to be turned over to a new tenant. The boy said that it hadn't been necessary, that it would have been better to leave everything the way it was. "Why did you do this?"

"It was so long ago, so terribly long ago, and now Yulia's here."

"But it's my brother. Why didn't you do it before, then? Why the hell didn't you do it before? Why now?"

The Polack was determined. "Your brother doesn't need a room of his own anymore. And I saved some things for you. I'll give them to you someday."

The scrap of paper that read: "I don't have any friends. I never will have any friends. I never have had friends" was the one thing he hadn't put in the shoebox. He had put it in the drawer beside his bed. He had never looked in the rest of the notebooks and now, before burning them, he hadn't done so either. What good would it do? Knowledge wasn't going to help anymore, knowledge had never helped, and now it only arrived far too late. What they didn't know yet they would never know.

The Polack went on working for the rest of the day. He hadn't eaten a bite, he wasn't hungry. Yulia asked if she could help him, he answered: "Let me do this." She wanted to kiss him, she asked if he was doing this for her. He said: "For us." Then added: "For us. We. Both of us. You. Me."

The fire in the yard was lovely. Everything burned, the sheets and notebooks, the splinters of the desk he had destroyed. The clothes and the soccer cards. It was a beautiful fire. When everything that would burn had been burned, he stood there looking at it with Yulia. He put his arm around her, around the small young woman. Small compared to him.

He said this was it, the work was finished. At first she didn't reply, she looked at the fire and only later did she ask: "So now the dead boy's room is my room?"

"I will paint it first," he said, "and then you can work there and cry. If you need to cry you don't have to go to the toilet anymore. You go there and you cry."

"But I don't want to cry."

"No. But if you have to cry you have your own space now. What do you want to do there?"

She looked at him as though he had to help her find the right words, he, the Polack of few words. "I want to be creative."

"Okay," the Polack said, "creative, good," and they went inside.

That evening they ate at a Japanese restaurant, because Yulia felt like sushi again. She muffled the homesickness with sushi and sashimi. The Polack ordered a vegetable tempura for himself, something with beef for Jurek, and then, between the main course and dessert (green-tea ice cream) he hummed and Yulia hummed back until the other guests started looking at them, because they weren't used to hearing people hum at a Japanese restaurant. Jurek said: "Could you please stop that, Dad, we're at a restaurant." They drank sake, the Polack more than Yulia. And he went on humming for a bit, because in front of Yulia he had to show who was top dog.

They drove home and in the car he stopped humming. He went upstairs, he went to vacuum the dead boy's room so they could start with painting soon. He couldn't let go, the sooner it was over with the better. He cleaned everything, there were still a few scraps of paper lying around and he threw them away, used paper. In one of the corners he found a sock he'd overlooked before, he came across moisture spots, but this room had never been painted. They hadn't touched this room, decay had run its course here. When the room was ready to be worked on, ready for a little renovation and then to be used by the new wife, he went downstairs. They were looking at a film on the boy's phone and he had the idea that Yulia was kissing the boy. Not on the lips, not that, but in the way one beloved kisses the other. On the cheek. She ran her fingers through his hair. He stood looking at this, at Yulia and his son. He was content, maybe even happy. This was domestic bliss, this was integration. The new wife had accepted the old child. They didn't notice him, they were looking in concentration at a movie the boy was showing her on his phone.

The Polack remained standing, watching, standing in the living room doorway, almost as though he shouldn't disturb them, as though this was no business of his. Moved, but then again not. He went to the kitchen to make tea and there he began asking himself if the new wife shouldn't be caressing *him*. She made love with him. She gave herself to him, but when did she ever caress him the way she had just been caressing the boy? He couldn't shake the feeling that she liked caressing the boy more than she did him. The Polack knew that wasn't true, for she was his new wife and the boy was a child, yet the impression was stubborn. A terribly stubborn idea.

Then the three of them had a cup of tea together. That is to say, Yulia and the boy hung out on the couch and played games, and he sat in a chair and watched. The Polack didn't say a word. He was happy and content. To be sure, something was gnawing at him, but then something was always gnawing. When nothing's gnawing, you know you're dead. He looked at Yulia's hand resting on the back of his one remaining son. Had he caressed the vanished boy in the wrong way, he wondered. Could you caress people in the wrong way? Is that why his ex had shown him the DVD, because he caressed everyone in the wrong way?

Until they went upstairs, Yulia first, he followed. Yulia slipped into the bathroom and when she finally came to the bedroom, she always took so long getting ready for the night, he asked the question that had come up in him earlier that evening. The gnawing question. If he could have asked in Dutch, he would have asked differently, more sympathetically, perhaps a bit more obliquely too, but he wasn't able to do that in English: "Do you love my son?" he asked.

"Yes, I believe so."

She lay down on her side of the bed. She was wearing a nightgown that underscored her picturesque appearance. To the Polack she was picturesque, and always would be.

"Do you love him more than me?"

"No." She looked at the Polack in surprise. It was a question she apparently hadn't expected.

"Forgive me, but do you love me?"

"Why? Of course."

"You never say you love me." It sounded like an accusation, and he hadn't meant it that way.

"I say you are sweet."

"Yes," he said. "Yes, sweet, I'm sweet, I do sweet things, but that's not the same."

"I left everything for you. Everything. I'm here. I'm ashamed. I don't speak your language. I don't understand your jokes. I'm ashamed. I'm not sure if I love your son. I'm ashamed. I cry. I'm ashamed. How can you ask me this question? You don't feel it? How can you ask me this stupid question?"

"I don't make jokes. And I'm not sure what I feel, what I should feel."

She turned her back on him. She was crying, he couldn't hear it but he knew she was crying. He took her arm. Lovingly, worriedly, and yet also with a certain desire. He said there was no reason for her to be ashamed, that he couldn't help his thoughts. "I can't help it, I see what I see."

She turned back to him. Was that a good sign? In any case, the crying stopped. He had to know because it gnawed at him, he had to ask because the thoughts just kept coming. She loves the boy, not me. But why did he have to be loved, why did people have to be loved? Wasn't it enough that he loved her? That he banked the fires of love each and every day? Untiringly, sometimes with a reluctance overcome just in the nick of the time, but he did it.

"Do you want to make love to my son?" he asked.

She looked at him with those eyes he had seen in Kiev in a dark room amid all kinds of other eyes that stared at men from Holland and Germany, men looking for love across the border. He had fallen for her eyes, and for her teeth. Teeth and eyes. Eyes and teeth.

"No," she answered. "No. Of course not. He is too young."

"But maybe I'm too old?"

"No," she repeated.

He wasn't convinced. The Polack dearly wished to be convinced, but he couldn't be. He remained lying there for a few moments, hesitating about whether to say more, then he went to the bathroom, brushed his teeth, washed his face briskly, looked at himself in the mirror, and, before turning off the light, massaged his left shoulder. Something hurt, he didn't know what.

When he came back she was lying naked in bed, on top of the blankets, and she said: "I love you." The Polack couldn't help it, he thought: she's thinking about my one remaining boy right now. She's thinking about him. Who does she love?"

She gestured to him to come closer, she threw her arms around him and said again that she loved him, the Polack, and his son too. Wasn't he happy about that? "He is so shy," she said. The Polack agreed. That he was happy and that the one remaining boy was shy, although he also felt like adding: he's also very cheeky, you know. But he didn't get a chance to say that. She kissed him and he kissed back, with the keenness that overcame him only rarely, the keenness of death. He pulled off his underpants and caressed her body. Her whole body, her belly, her shoulders, her legs, her knees, her feet, as if he needed to discover it all anew, as if everything was waiting to be caressed for the first time.

"Your body is not old," she said. "You have a young body."

"Yes," he said, although he wondered at the same time what actually *was* old about him then: his face, the way he acted? "You will be his friend," he said quietly, running his fingers over her vagina the way he had seen in his ex's DVD, "You will be the best friend of my son."

"Yes."

"You will teach him to be less shy. To be a good man."

"Yes," she said. "We will be family. I will stay here. I'm not going back. I will cry but I'm not going back."

"You make me happy." He said it, but he didn't feel it, without knowing why not. Maybe saying it was enough. Feeling wasn't necessary, if you said it the feeling came by itself. At that he entered her, she had to help him a little, he noticed how her hand took hold of his penis and how she pulled her hand away once he was firmly inside her.

While he was thrusting, dazed by the arousal, by the sake, by the gnawing thoughts, he believed that she was thinking about his child now as well. He didn't know for sure, because he didn't dare to ask, even if he did ask there was no guarantee that he would get an honest answer, but he felt it. They were lying there with a third party, with the one remaining child, and while he was in her he asked if she wanted a child herself, a child of her own.

The lust became a pet again, the pet barked but didn't bite. "Maybe later," she said. "If I have my papers. If we still love each other."

He nodded. He resumed the labor of love. And while he surrendered to the labor, he couldn't help but ask the question: "Do you want to fuck my son?" He shouldn't have asked, he knew that, not this, not this question, but he saw them again in his mind's eyes, the way they sat there on the couch together, so naturally. He couldn't imagine ever sitting on the couch that way with his new wife. A bond had arisen between the boy and Yulia, one he could never get in the way of, that's how it felt, and although he should be happy, happy for his son, happy for himself, happy for Yulia, the happiness just wouldn't come. He did his best, but no happiness came, only fear and sorrow.

She pushed her groin, her lower body, against his. "No," she said, "you. I want to fuck you."

"Are you sure?" he asked.

"What am I doing? What do you think I'm doing?"

The boy was there, standing between them. They spent too little time alone together. "Tomorrow," he said, "tomorrow he is going to his mother and then we will be two weeks alone."

"You should come," she answered. "It takes so long. Come. I want you. Come in me. Don't wait."

"How can I come if you talk like this?" It was an unfair remark; she had said nothing wrong, his thoughts were wrong, his thinking was wrong.

"I told you, language is a problem," she said.

He kissed her with all the passion he found inside him. For a moment there were still images of his new wife with the one remaining boy on the couch. Then he concentrated, then he lost himself. He loved Yulia, he wouldn't allow himself other feelings from now on, when other feelings came along he would wring their necks.

4

The men of C squad had decided to organize a Christmas dinner for themselves and their partners. They were different from the other squads, after all, better and closer-knit. They wanted a party of their own. Also because throwing parties was something they were good at, because when there was something to celebrate, you had to seize the opportunity.

The Polack told Yulia about it, at first she didn't want to go, but he insisted, he said all the men or almost all of them would be bringing their partners, it wasn't right to have to go alone to a Christmas party like that.

She had been to the firehouse a few times and he had introduced her to the other men, yet he had the feeling they hadn't really come to know her. They needed to get to know her. His new wife was not a trophy bride, but he was proud of her. That she was with him, that she had left Kiev for him, that he had a new wife, with such darling eyes, with such a lovely soul, he wanted to show them that. That there was such a thing as mercy.

He wanted to stand beside her at the C squad party, he wanted to prove that everything had turned out all right in the end. "I'm proud of you," he said. "I want to show you to the world. You are not my secret."

"No," she said, "I'm not your secret." From that he assumed that she was willing to go along anyway, that she would attend his Christmas party, the C squad Christmas party.

Although it was cold on the day of the party in December, the Polack decided to wear the floral shirt he had bought in order to be a gentleman in Kiev. The sport coats that went with it as well. He left his winter coat at home. The new Polack would display himself to the men of C squad in full regalia, as the gentleman he had actually turned out to be. They took a taxi there, and with a taxi he would have himself and his new wife driven home afterward, when it was all over.

He had bought a new dress for Yulia, specially for this occasion. A new, blue dress, marine blue, because marine blue looked terrific on her. She was happy with it, she'd told him in the shop. She had thanked him a few times, otherwise he couldn't tell much, couldn't really divine what she was thinking or what she felt. Once she had asked him if he knew anything about Ukrainian politics, and he had said he didn't. Yulia tried to explain a few things to him, but all the names sounded so much alike that it only confused him. He had never talked about politics with his ex, that was something that never led to much good, talking about politics. As if she sensed that, his Yulia, she started cuddling up to him in silence more and more often after dinner. She no longer blamed language, she no longer made any attempt to try to say the unsayable. They lounged on the couch together, the way Yulia had lounged there with the boy, she caressed him, and however much the Polack enjoyed those moments, he still had the feeling that she caressed him the way you might stroke a pet.

Yulia was putting on her makeup in the bathroom. He was ready to go, Jurek was at his mother's, he was going to a party that evening too, at school. The Polack walked around the house restlessly, thinking about Jurek, anticipating the party, anticipating seeing his colleagues, his friends, the mercy he could show, the mercy that was love.

The dead boy's room had gradually become Yulia's room. She had a new desk where she could do her Dutch homework, and her suitcase was in there. He'd found a good deal on a second-hand cupboard, all it needed was a bit of painting. Sometimes he opened the door to that bedroom and was amazed to see that the dead boy's things were no longer there. It had taken a while, perhaps some would say it had taken an awfully long time, but finally he had vanished without a sound. Borys was no longer.

Yulia took an hour fixing her hair and doing her face. It made the Polack nervous. It took so long. What was she doing in there, anyway? They needed to get going. He knocked on the bathroom door and shouted: "It's just a couple of firemen. Don't overdo it."

"But they are your friends," she called back.

He went in, Yulia was standing at the mirror, braiding her hair into lots of little braids. All she had on was her underwear.

"Yes." He kissed her shoulders, she was slender. "They are my friends. But you are beautiful enough," he whispered in her ear.

She smiled, either she didn't believe him or else she felt he was sticking his nose into things that were none of his business, that much was clear. She went on braiding her hair, unflustered, and the Polack went back to pacing around the house, wandering from room to room and humming a melody.

When the taxi arrived, she was still doing her hair, now the Polack was getting really nervous, he didn't want to make the cabbie wait. "Yulia," he shouted. "Yulia. Damn it. We have to go."

When she finally came out of the bathroom, she was radiant, like she had stepped right out of the TV. It made him uncomfortable. As though he didn't deserve this, he felt little and bald beside this superabundance of youth and beauty. Little he was not, but definitely bald. Before going out the door he grabbed his cap from the rack and planted it on his head. Hand in hand they walked to the taxi and he told her in Dutch that she looked glorious, because she spoke enough to understand that these days. Little things she understood, no problem, it wouldn't be long before she spoke Dutch, then she would be a Dutch woman of Ukrainian descent with a Russian soul.

In the cab she said: "I'm so nervous. Do you think they will like me? Your friends? They will like me?"

The Polack told her that there was nothing to worry about, that the men of C squad would appreciate her, they were fine men, they had always accepted Wen too, and more, and he kept hold of her hand to take away her cares. Because he loved her, because he was living at last.

The party was in the training room. There was music, there was a smoke machine. Nelemans had brought his guitar, he sang a cheery song about the life of a lonely fireman. Loneliness could be cheerful too. A song he'd written himself, of course, that's what he did. That's what he lived for, for the singing.

The squad commander came over to the Polack. "This is my new wife, this is Yulia," the Polack said before the commander could speak. The squad commander shook her hand, smiled and said to the Polack: "The caterers forgot all about the vegetarian hors d'oeuvres. Is that going to be a problem?"

"No," the Polack said. "Not at all. I've already eaten."

"You're the only vegetarian here," the commander said. "We do our best to keep the minorities in mind."

The Polack nodded amiably and walked on, still holding tightly onto Yulia's arm. They were together. The men would see, the men would understand. They would see what he had seen in Kiev. Beckers handed the two of them a cup of mulled wine, laughing, and said: "Nelemans made it. Mulls his own wine, our Nelemans does. Not just a singer. Mulls his own wine too." Beckers burst out laughing, the Polack laughed along, and Yulia laughed a bit shyly.

Most of the men had come without their partners anyway, but they were all there. The C squad was present to a man. They drank and they ate and the Polack told his new wife that she could have as many hors d'oeuvres as she liked, that he'd had enough to eat at home. She put a mini-croquette in her mouth and took it out again, because it was too hot. "I'm making a fool of myself," she said, the croquette with a bite out of it in one hand.

The Polack reassured her and picked a few crumbs of croquette from her lips. "It's charming, everything you do is charming." So he was growing again to fit the role of the man he wanted to be, he felt less small and nondescript beside her. Nelemans sang on. This time a song that was not about a fireman, but about a mountain climber and his wife. When Nelemans was finished singing, he ducked— still holding his guitar—behind a makeshift bar, as though his life revolved not just around singing but also tending bar. "The bar is open," Nelemans shouted, the men laughed and the Polack laughed too, because this was a party, you were supposed to laugh. Yulia asked if they had vodka or a cocktail, because she thought the mulled wine was horrid. He advised her against ordering a cocktail. Better not to drink cocktails here, there was plenty of vodka. She liked vodka, didn't she? The men had all chipped in for the beverages, there was whiskey, rum, and vodka, there were all kinds of things. There was liquor in profusion, when it came to parties like this the men were anything but stingy. Holding their drinks, they walked around the training room, Yulia and he, up the stairs, and then back down again. "This is where we exercise," the Polack told her. "This is where we prepare for the fire." Yulia nodded as though this interested her, the Polack knew quite well that this was not her life, it was his life. Still, he wanted to show her something of his life, because it was thanks to her that he was alive again. "But in reality it's different," the Polack said. "It's always different." If they hadn't both been holding glasses, he would have pressed her against him. "Come on, let's go back downstairs." He told here that they sometimes climbed these stairs with bottles of compressed air on their backs, the way you had to when you entered a burning building. He wasn't sure she understood him. "A building on fire," he said. "We enter the building. We have to." She nodded. Eleven o'clock rolled around and the men from A squad stopped in for a look on their way to their shift, and right after that the squad commander of C squad gave a short speech, saying he was proud of his men, that a lot had happened, that there were changes underway in the fire department, changes they weren't all looking forward to, but that they would stick together, whatever happened, whatever decisions might be made in The Hague, these men were inseparable. They had been together so long. They would never leave each other in the lurch.

The partygoers applauded and the disco music swelled once more. Nelemans clapped his hands and people were now dancing at the bottom of the staircase where they usually did the blind trials.. The liquor had freed the men from their shame, from their caution, their shyness. They danced as though they had never done anything else, as though eternal life was theirs. The Polack and his new wife threaded their way straight through the smoke, between the drinking firemen. Drinks were being foisted on him constantly. There was liquor everywhere and everywhere were hands proffering drinks. "Cheer up, man," Nelemans said.

"I *am* cheerful," the Polack replied. "I'm extremely cheerful."

They kept on dancing, the men of C squad who never danced otherwise, at least the Polack had never seen them dance before, but this evening they danced and some of them were even good at it, as if they'd been doing it on the sly for years. Beckers danced like a whirlwind, the Polack was the only one who simply stood to one side and watched, that was enough for him, leaning against the wall with a glass in his hand and the cap on his head. Life had begun. You could also stand and observe it.

"Dance," Yulia said at last.

"No," the Polack said.

"Why not?"

"It's not for me. You dance." First he ran a finger over her earlobe, then the rest of her ear. He was relaxed.

And Yulia did just that, she went and danced. And while she was dancing she looked at him and he looked at her and the Polack realized that he was happy, that this was happiness, this was the good life, nothing except this, no more than this, and then Beckers came over to him, sweating heavily, and said: "I can't even think about having a new wife yet. It's all still too fresh. Maybe someday. Not now."

"Yeah," said the Polack.

"But you did, you decided on a new wife."

"Yeah." The Polack looked at Yulia as she danced and at his colleagues who were dancing around her. Good men, men who had once told him: we're going to pull you through this. Men who had painted his house, men with whom he'd had his picture taken in that newly painted house. In their own fashion, they had done that, they had pulled him through it.

"You had to go all the way to Kiev for that," Beckers said, "for your new wife. Kiev, is that a nice place?" Without waiting for a reply, Beckers went and fetched fresh drinks for the two of them and said: "Cheers, man. We're the new black folk. You're not supposed to say it out loud, but I've got eyes in my head. When I look in the mirror, I see a black man. We white guys, soon we're going to be a minority in our own country. They're taking everything away from us."

"Yeah," the Polack said. "That's how it goes. Minorities become majorities and the other way around too."

"Cheers," Beckers said again, and the other men danced on, even more exuberantly, as though the dancing was meant to be a parody, a parody but still serious. The Polack couldn't see his new wife anymore, the smoke machine was running hard and the disco ball kept spinning while Beckers talked, on and on, about new and old minorities. This was a party, wasn't it? Then it was no place to talk about minorities. Wasn't there anything more pleasant to talk about? "Black Peter's just a drop in the bucket," Beckers said. "We lost that battle. There's more to it than that. It's about respect. They don't respect us anymore, we built this country from the ground up, but respect? Forget it. If there was a fire in a refugee center, I'd put it out, of course I would, but I'd take it easy, I'd take it nice and slow, I'm telling you the truth, I'm not going to risk my life for those people, because they wouldn't do that for me. That's how it is, right? They wouldn't do it for us. Worse than that, they hate us."

Beckers took a big swig. "Are you happy?" he asked the Polack. "Are you happy now?"

"Yeah," the Polack replied.

"That's good," Beckers said. "That's important," and he went on talking about the future, the Europeans, the fire department, the children who deserved to have a future, and then he went back again for drink. For himself and for the Polack.

The Polack didn't know what else to say, so he said: "I'm going to take a piss."

As was his custom, he walked to the toilets in the other wing of the firehouse, where the men of A squad were sitting around, watching TV. They looked at him, they didn't say a word. He stood at the urinal, leaning against the wall with one hand. If they'd just had a few vegetarian hors d'oeuvres it wouldn't have been so bad. Frying fat always put a good lining in your stomach, a coating that let you drink a good bit of alcohol. He felt tipsy, and he could imagine the hangover he'd have tomorrow, but that was all right because here there was a party and here there was life.

He walked back slowly to the training room. The only one there was the man they called Rabbit. He had his wife with him, though, a rather pudgy lady from Liege who spoke Dutch with an accent that made everyone laugh, and who perhaps for that reason had decided to speak as little as possible.

"Rabbit," the Polack said. "Where are our friends? Is the party over?"

"No," Rabbit said, "the party isn't over yet." He placed his hand on the Polack's shoulder and asked: "How's things?"

"How's what?"

"How are you?"

"Me," the Polack said slowly. "Everything's fine with me."

"Our eldest daughter," Rabbit said, "refuses to eat meat these days."

"Oh."

"She still eats fish, though."

"Okay."

"You're the first vegetarian fireman I've ever met," said Rabbit. "You don't eat fish either, do you?"

"No," said the Polack.

Rabbit nodded. "All those meat-haters just want to make hard-working carnivores feel bad, you know what I mean? When I look at my daughter, I think: she's trying to shut the door in my face."

The Polack didn't know what to say to that, he wasn't even sure exactly what Rabbit meant. He walked through the training room to look for Yulia. He climbed the stairs, maybe she had gone up there. To the tower. You had a great view from up there, across the city, the hills beyond. With a little luck, you could see Aachen in the distance. The hills, the villages. But not tonight. It was drizzling. Still, he continued up the stairs, a route he had often taken with a bottle of compressed air on his back. Now there was no weight to lug up with him, except for his own body, but the alcohol made it harder than he'd expected. "Yulia," he called out, and he used his cell phone as a flashlight.

He ran into Beckers and Nelemans and the squad commander. They were coming down the stairs.

"Is the party over?" the Polack asked.

"Almost," Nelemans said. "We're pretty much out of booze."

"Have you guys seen Yulia?" the Polack wanted to know.

"Up there," the squad commander said.

The Polack walked on, now and then he called her name but the only thing he heard was the music from down below and he remembered how he'd had to go looking for her sometimes, soon after she'd arrived, and that he would find her in the center of town with her shopping bag. How worried he could be if he didn't find her right away. That he was afraid she would vanish, dissolve into thin air, that he would have to write to her father to say that Yulia was gone but that he was convinced that she would show up again sooner or later. That there was no reason for the father to be concerned, there in Kiev. The way Yulia could look at him so dazedly when he finally found her, as though she no longer knew who he was, as though she no longer knew what she was doing here. And that the Polack realized then that he didn't want to go on living without her, in the same way he had once not wanted to live without God. There was an absence of people and of things that seemed to him grimmer than death itself.

When he finally got to the top, all the way to the top, where on a clear day you could see Aachen in the distance, he had been here often, you could feel the wind so well here and in the summer, when it was hot as blazes down below, then it was nice and cool up here, yes, then he would sometimes stand here to catch the breeze, to forget himself, to become one with the birds and the panorama, even though you weren't actually supposed to because he had to be ready to respond to an alarm at all times. But he could be downstairs in a flash, he knew the way.

Then he didn't have to think about Yulia's absence anymore because he saw her. She was lying on the ground, as though she was sleeping, as though she had been unable to wait until they got home and thought: I'll just take a little nap right here. He bent over, shone the light from his cell phone on her face. All her makeup had run. Her carefully braided hair was no longer braided. She looked as though she had barely survived a fire. The air left his lungs, like he was standing in a cloud of smoke.

"What happened?" The Polack squatted down, brushed the hair from her face and saw the cut above Yulia's right eye. She must have hit her face against the stones. There was dried blood above her right eye.

"Yulia," the Polack said. "Yulia."

She said nothing, looked at him as though she really didn't know who he was anymore, the way she sometimes looked when he found her in town with her shopping bags. Dazed. Then she seemed to have forgotten everything. Who she was, where she came from, what she was doing here, who she loved. Then he had to say: "You are Yulia from Kiev, you are my future wife." And then he took her home with him. Sometimes he drove them up into the hills and they would stop for a drink somewhere, and he would say: "We've got a good thing going here, don't we?"

This was different, this wasn't the center of town, she was not carrying a shopping bag, she was lying on the ground at the top of the tower.

"Yulia," he said, "say something. Say something. Yulia." He thought: if I say her name, if I keep saying her name, then she'll remember it all again.

She remained silent, she looked at him with tears in her eyes, she showed no sign of recognition. "Yulia," the Polack said. "It's me." He wiped her face clean, first with the back of his hand, then with his handkerchief, but no matter how he wiped it just got dirtier.

"Talk to me. What happened? I don't know, how could I? There's no way I could know." And he saw that she had no shoes on anymore and that her pantyhose and dress were torn. She must have fallen. She had fallen. Slipped. Maybe because of the alcohol, she must have had too much to drink. He shouldn't have brought her along. He should have waited, next year would have been better. Next year they'd be sure to organize a party again. She hadn't been ready for it yet, for the party, for the men of C squad.

"Where are you shoes?" he asked. "Your shoes. And your dress. All torn. Such a lovely dress. A new dress like that." The Polack remembered how they had gone to buy the dress, and a peculiar sorrow overcame him. Sorrow about a dress, that was a peculiar sorrow.

He found her shoes but he left them lying there. Those shoes didn't matter anymore. The Polack picked her up. He picked up his new wife as though it was their wedding night and he was carrying her to the bedroom. The party was over, the night was beginning at last, the rest of the life to which bride and groom had looked forward to so much. It was a different wedding party from what he'd imagined, totally different, yet still a wedding, their wedding. There would never be another. The Polack felt it, the Polack knew it. He would take her home, the way a bridegroom was expected to. But first they had to get down the steps and that was harder for him than he'd expected, undoubtedly because of the cups of mulled wine and the other drinks they'd handed him. They were generous, the men of C squad. He went down the steps, staggering, even though he'd been trained for this. He could do it blindfolded with a bottle of compressed air on his back, and now he needed no compressed air. There was no fire, he could breathe on his own, no smoke, no fire, there was only Yulia who said nothing, Yulia and her new dress that was already all torn. He went down the stairs slowly. It was a drill, that's what he told himself, it was only a drill. A drill for love. He had been practicing for love all his life, and this was the last exam he had to complete, then he'd be ready for it.

Further down he went, step by step, careful, humming. He didn't speak a word himself now, he asked no more questions. He held her trembling body and strangely enough he thought about the apartment in Kiev and about her father. For a moment, he couldn't imagine himself ever going back there to charm Yulia's father. For a moment it seemed to him that Kiev was irrevocably a thing of the past, and he hummed, as though that was all he had to say.

The men were sitting around downstairs. The disco music had been turned off. Nelemans was playing his guitar and singing one of his own songs, another one about a lonesome fireman who remained cheerful, but when he saw the Polack with the new wife in his arms, Nelemans stopped playing. He leaned the guitar up against the wall.

They looked at him, the men of C squad, they stared at him and at the new wife in his arms and the Polack didn't know where to go. He saw it all clearly now, but he didn't know where to go or what to say. He had stopped humming too. He stood there in front of his friends, his colleagues, the men with whom he had shared a life. Finally, it was Nelemans who came over to him and said: "It was just a prank."

The Polack had the feeling that the hush was even deeper than it had been a moment before, that he could hear himself breathing.

"Come on, say so yourself," Nelemans said, "you know we were just pulling a prank."

The Polack was silent, and once again it was Nelemans who said: "She wanted it." Beckers came and stood beside Nelemans, and he said: "This is what she wanted. Believe me. She wanted it. We asked her. Is this what you want, we asked. She nodded. That's what she wanted. So who are we to say no?"

"She asked for it," Nelemans chimed in. "Apparently it had been a long time. Yeah, that's what she wanted." They sniggered furtively now, the men of C squad. They laughed the way they laughed after pulling a prank. They were a close-knit crew, they were fond of pranks.

"Don't go looking so high and mighty, and for sure don't go acting high and mighty either," Beckers said, "as if I don't know what you got up to with my wife. We don't forget a thing." Rabbit and his wife weren't around anymore. There were only a few of the men left, they looked at him in the dingy, atmospheric lighting that Nelemans had hung up around the room, they looked at him like he was an animal in a cage. The disco ball was still spinning and the Polack understood that Beckers had spoken the truth, the men of C squad never forgot a thing. Now it was the squad commander who came to him and said: "Don't make such a big thing out of it. You're a vegetarian. You're a Polack. And you lived in a chicken coop. Show that you're one of us. Fucking show us that you're one of us. It was just a prank, she thought so too."

The Polack didn't say a word. He looked at his squad commander, he had nothing to say.

"Hey listen," the squad commander said, "up there in Ukraine, they've been around the block a few times too, believe me." The Polack stared at his squad commander, and for the first time he noticed now that the man was turning gray, despite the disco light he thought he could see it. Only when the squad commander put his hand on his shoulder did the Polack's thoughts return to his new wife, whom he was still holding in his arms, whom he had to bring home. And he knew he would not be coming back here again, that they were dead, the men of C squad, his men, his friends, they were dead now too, as dead as Beckers's wife had been, even deader than Beckers's wife had been. Nelemans added: "You should have been there, up there. You should have been around. It was a riot."

The Polack looked at his squad commander as though something was still on its way. A service announcement. There was some good reason why the squad commander's hand was still resting on the Polack's shoulder, something more was coming. He felt Yulia's weight pressing on his arms, on his back, but it was a drill, he couldn't put her down.

"You're a Polack," the squad commander said quietly. "But you're not a fink, are you? You don't screw your buddies, Janowski. That's all I need to hear from you right now."

"No," said the Polack. "I'm not a fink." Then the squad commander took his hand off the Polack's shoulder.

"Back in the day, this used to happen all the time. These days people have kind of gone overboard with all the things that aren't allowed." In the squad commander's voice, the Polack heard hesitation, an attempt at conciliation. They hadn't meant it this way. That's what the squad commander was trying to say, and that's what the Polack would leave with, in the conviction that he, despite everything, was one of the men of C squad, even if the C squad was now a thing of the past.

He walked outside with Yulia in his arms, because that was part of the drill, that he would walk home with her. It was a long way, but he would complete his assignment. It was the last exam, the final trial. "We're going," he said to Yulia, once he was standing in front of the firehouse. "I don't have a coat, but I'll walk fast. As fast as I can. So you won't get cold."

The Polack walked quickly, as quickly as he could. Sometimes he had to stop beside a lamppost to shift the weight a bit. Along the way he saw people who looked at him. Some of them shouted to him, the people were tipsy, probably a party too, there were parties and get-togethers everywhere. That's what he said to Yulia: "They are drunk."

The Polack himself was no longer tipsy, he was dead sober. "We're almost there," he told Yulia, but she still didn't speak a word and he had the feeling she would never speak again. He who had always felt that speech was overrated had trouble with that, he who had so longed for silence was already missing the speaking, now that it had suddenly stopped. Something had to be said, occasionally, no matter how insignificant. She could sing too, if she wanted. Go on, hum, he felt like saying. Hum, Yulia. He was silent. And again he stopped, leaning against a tree this time, to shift the weight of his new wife from one arm to the other. She was shivering from the cold. "Yeah," he said, "I was planning to take a taxi home, but things went differently from what we were expecting, didn't they? It went differently."

He had to put her down, and he did, he had to, he couldn't hold her any longer. She stood there, staring into space. He called her name a couple of times, but though she was standing right beside him she didn't react. She wasn't there. He picked her up again. In fact, she wasn't all that heavy, she was a little woman, a slender little woman.

He walked on without thinking about the C squad or about himself and his new wife, all he thought about was the walking, about his muscles, the body he held in his arms, he knew that this was the body of his new wife but it didn't feel that way anymore. It could have been the body of anyone he had saved.

At the house he put Yulia down on the couch, he covered her with blankets he fetched from upstairs. First one blanket, then two, and finally a third from the one remaining boy's room, because the shivering didn't stop. The Polack had no idea what time it was, he made a pot of tea. "Drink," he said to Yulia. "Drink."

She took little sips of the hot tea and the shivering seemed to lessen. He sat beside her on the floor and they said nothing, the Polack and his woman. He had no idea how long they'd been sitting there when she asked: "A prink, what's that?"

"A prank," the Polack said. "Pr-a-nk. A prank. It's, how can I explain it? A joke. A little joke."

"A joke. So I am a joke?"

"No. Not to me."

"Where were you? Where were you all the time? I called you."

"I was downstairs, I was talking to Beckers, I was talking to Rabbit, I was peeing."

"You were peeing. Yes, that's important."

"I was looking for you."

"Are you going to the police?"

The Polack stood up, he began pacing around the room. "Yes, he said, "we can go to the police. Tomorrow. They will call me a fink, but that's fine."

"What's a fink?" she asked.

"Fink. Betrayer. That's a betrayer. They were my friends. They were my family. They were my men." He said: "What happened tonight is bad, I can't call it anything else, but in principle they're good men, Yulia. Believe me, I was one of them. I was always one of them. When Borys died, they said: we're going to pull you through this. I was a part of the C squad, more a part of that than of anything else. They were my family."

She was quiet for a moment and he saw how she looked at him. "What's a fink? I don't understand."

The Polack squatted down beside her. "Difficult to explain. A betrayer. That's a fink. I love you. Do you need a doctor? Do you want to take a shower? What do you want?"

"I don't know."

He stroked her leg.

"So am I a joke?" she asked again. "A prink. Are you going to take revenge for the joke, for the prink?"

"No," he said after a brief hesitation. "I don't believe in revenge. No, that's not good, revenge. My men. They like pulling pranks. Sometimes they are too . . . Too aggressive in their jokes. Just too aggressive, they don't know when to stop."

She was quiet for a moment, then said: "Language is not a problem. You are not a man, that is the problem."

He sat down beside her on the couch. He wiped his forehead, but there was no sweat. "I'm not a man. You are right. I'm not a man. But we can solve this. We can solve this. What do you want besides revenge? Tell me what you want, anything. It sounds strange, but I want to give my life for you. They were my friends, you understand?" He took her hands, her cold hands, he held them tight, he rubbed them to warm them and asked again what she wanted, what it was she wanted, what she wanted for god's sake, that she should tell him that, that her wishes were his wishes, her desires his desires, until she said: "I want to die. I want to die in my own country."

Then the Polack began pacing again, he walked around and around the living room until it became light out. He said: "That's what you think now, later you'll see things differently. Now you think that. Later you'll see it differently."

He also said: "Don't die. Don't do that. Death comes all by itself, you don't have to ask it in."

So he spoke, so he went on speaking until he noticed that he was being called again. It was time. More powerfully than the last time, he heard the voice that exhorted him, that called him, that beckoned. He saw through everything, he understood it all. Now he knew for which love it was that he had completed his final trial.

The Polack went upstairs and there he called his ex, but she didn't answer. "You have to come right away," he told her voicemail. "You need to take care of Yulia, she's lying on the couch here. Something has happened. Can you come? Would you please do that for me?"

When he went back downstairs, he saw that Yulia was asleep. He sat down beside her and when she opened her eyes he took her hands tenderly, knowing that he might never hold them again. "Everybody has secrets," he said. "You are right. There's no language for secrets. They die with you. They die with us. But that's good. You don't know my secrets, I don't know your secrets. The secrets of the boy. We don't know them. And that's good. Better. Much better."

He took a deep breath. "It's better this way. What would we do if we knew?" he said. "Nothing. We would still know nothing."

She looked at him, not even especially sad now, resigned, there was still a clot of blood above her eye. The brow was thick, swollen.

The Polack stood up.

"Where are you going?" she asked.

"I'm going, my God is calling me. I can't help it. But my ex will be here soon. Along with the human . . . Human Extension. They will take care of you. Better than I can. I cannot."

"I understand. Not a man. You are going. Now?"

He knelt beside her and said: "I'm sorry, but He is calling me. I'm not a man and you want to . . . You want to go. You want to go back. He needs me, so much more than you need me."

She nodded and said: "He needs you more and I want to die anyway."

He waited to see if the call, the lure, the voices admonishing him to leave would go away. But they didn't, they grew louder.

"I can't help it. It's stronger. Stronger than everything else." And he caressed her wherever he could, but he didn't touch her intimate parts. The Polack said again that he loved her so much, so terribly much, more than she could imagine, more than he himself could ever have imagined but that it was stronger. It. "It," he said. And she said nothing back. He stroked and stroked until he noticed that she had grown calm, that she was asleep.

Then he went. He left the house the way you leave a house on the verge of collapse. He walked toward the love that was not of this world.

Sometimes he stopped, clung to a tree or a lamppost. There were longings tugging back and forth inside him. Something inside him didn't want to go there, something dragged its feet, something in him wanted to go back to Yulia, back to the one remaining boy, to the love of this world, each time he yanked himself free, because the call of the love that was not of this world, that summons was much stronger. The unbearable love, the love that saw to it that you never had to save yourself again. That you never had to save anyone ever again.

He yanked himself away from branches, tree trunks and lampposts. Again and again he latched onto something and again he tore himself loose. He hid in bushes, under benches and in doorways, but each time it found him again and the summons went on and on. Had his eldest boy been called like this too?

He wandered through the woods until he had to lean against a tree, exhausted. He looked at the leaves on the ground. He thought he saw ants, lots of ants. The ground was teeming with them. Ants everywhere.

Then he remembered the shoebox he had put together for the one remaining boy. Jurek didn't know where it was. He had to give it to Jurek, this very day, the shoebox with what was left of Borys, the abridged life, the life that fit in a single shoebox.

First the shoebox, then the rest. Before he went back to his place in the coop, that had to happen.

The living called to him now, so loudly, so pitifully, so heartbreakingly. Yulia, his boy, his ex, even the Human Extension called out to him, they were unflagging, the living were, unflagging and inconsolable. He had to turn around, he had to go back.

Looking at the ants, he tore off his floral shirt. The Polack knelt and whispered: "Do with me what You will, Father. And I know what You will, I know exactly what You will. Because you're just as much of a dirty pig as I am. There's no getting around each other, God. We were made for each other. The chicken coop is everywhere."

Acknowledgments

Thanks to Richard Brand and Ton Keulen for their introduction to the world of firefighters.

Thanks to Brother Johannes and the abbot of Lilbosch Abbey.

Thanks to Karol Lesman.

A special word of thanks to Fedja and Janne.

ARNON GRUNBERG (1971) debuted at the age of twenty-three with the wry, humorous novel novel *Blue Mondays*, which brought him instant success. Some of his other titles are *Silent Extras, The Asylum Seeker, The Jewish Messiah, Moedervlekken* [Birthmarks], and *Tirza*. Under the pseudonym Marek van der Jagt he published the successful *The Story of My Baldness*, and *Gstaad 95-98*, as well as the essay *Monogaam* [Monogamous]. Grunberg also writes plays, essays and travel columns. His work has won him several literary awards, among which the AKO Literature Prize for *Phantom Pain* and *The Asylum Seeker*, and both the Libris Literature Prize and the Flemish Golden Owl Award for *Tirza*. His work has been translated into over twenty-five languages. He has contributed to numerous international newspapers, including the *New York Times, Times* (London), *L'Espresso*, and *Die Zeit*. Arnon Grunberg lives and works in New York.

SAM GARRETT has translated some fifty novels and works of nonfiction. He has won prizes and appeared on shortlists for some of the world's most prestigious literary awards, and is the only translator to have twice won the British Society of Authors' Vondel Prize for Dutch-English translation.

CPSIA information can be obtained
at www.ICGtesting.com
Printed in the USA
JSHW020340060423
39983JS00001B/1